Knot Your Problem

Pack Origins – Book 2

L.A. Clyne

D1620151

Cover art: L.A. Clyne

Reach me at: www.laclyne.com

Join me at: L.A. Clyne's Tribe (private Facebook group)

Follow me on:

Facebook www.facebook.com/l.a.clyne.author

Instagram www.instagram.com/laclyne_author

Pinterest www.pinterest.com.au/laclyneauthor

Dedication

My son couldn't pronounce great grandma when he was little, so my grandma became GG to us all.

GG gave me a box of her old Harlequin / Mills & Boon books for my thirteenth birthday. I've been a voracious romance reader ever since. In all its forms, from classic literature and sweet contemporary, to paranormal fantasy with an occasional side visit to erotic taboo (I mean, who hasn't taken that trip, right?).

So, this one's for you, GG. See what you did. I blame you for this book.

xxx

Content advice

This is a sweet, reverse harem, omegaverse romance written with multiple points of view. It features growly, protective alphas, a silver fox beta, and a feisty omega.

Each book in the Pack Origins series will focus on new packs, and has a happily ever after, while continuing the apocalyptic background story of the Crash. They can be read as standalones, but it is recommended to read in order to get the most out of the series. If you are reading as a standalone, check out the catch-up chapter.

The story contains MFMMM steamy scenes, with some light MM interactions, and the heroine doesn't have to choose between her men.

While this is not a dark romance, there are references to past institutional abuse and domestic violence, including historic deaths. There is no abuse within the packs or the community they have built.

If any of the above makes you uncomfortable, this may not be the book for you, and that's okay. Take care of yourself and enjoy your day. Otherwise, happy reading.

Need a catch-up?

Are you jumping into the Pack Origins series with this book, or has it been a while since you read Knot Your Princess?

If so, here's a quick explanation of how this omegaverse world works and a recap of the Crash, the Omega Palace, and what went down with Maia and her pack (they pop up a lot in this book, more than I intended, like those pushy relatives who get all up in your business but you can't turn away because you love them so much).

If not, go ahead and skip this part. You're good. I won't tell anyone.

If you're still with me, here goes. We'll start with the basics. In the Pack Origins omegaverse world, everyone has a designation as either a beta, omega or alpha. Betas are the most common designation and have no unique traits. The world considers betas to be ordinary.

The first sign someone is an alpha or omega usually presents in their early teen years, alongside puberty, when a distinctive scent forms that is unique to each alpha or omega.

Omegas are generally shorter than betas, curvy and incredibly attractive. They are usually female, male omegas being incredibly rare. Omegas crave touch and naturally give off pheromones that enthrall alphas. Even betas aren't immune to their charms.

Omegas were prized once upon a time, but are now treated as chattel to breed. They cannot own property or live independently. Traditionally, omegas were highly fertile, but fertility rates for female omegas have been dropping for decades, along with the numbers of newly presented omegas and alphas. A female omega almost always has an omega or alpha child. Betas can as well, but it is much rarer.

Alphas are incredibly strong, highly dominant and display animalistic traits. They have a tendency to growl and have a dominance bark that can make a beta, omega and even a weaker alpha submit to them. Alphas can express their bark through a growl, a word, or a sound. Beta society frowns upon alphas using their dominance bark, so an alpha will usually be stealthy or discrete about doing it. It mostly happens in dark spaces, during dark deeds.

Regardless, betas revere alphas, and they usually end up in the military or as leaders in the upper echelons of society. While omegas are taken from their families as soon as they present, sometimes forcefully, and sent to the Omega Palace, where they are trained on how to please an alpha.

The Omega Palace promotes themselves publicly as an elite finishing school, but in reality, it's more of a mandatory boot camp that brainwashes omegas into believing they are submissive. Secret, forced submission is common for any omegas who don't comply with their teachings.

After an omega turns twenty-one, the Palace presents them to society at a series of glamorous balls and parties, originally designed to let an omega find her mate. Now, it's a barbaric free for all, where alphas pick their favorite scented omega and bark their chosen into submission, usually after money has changed hands.

To the outside world, omegas appear to live like princes and princesses at the Palace, but they have no freedom or choice. Forced omega matings rarely result in pregnancy. Despite that, the Palace persists. Once forcefully mated, an omega's scent changes and they are no longer recognizable to their true mate.

Alphas and omegas who are true mates recognize each other by scent, but true mates have become little more than a legend in modern times. Once upon a time, groups of alphas also often lived together as a pack with an omega, until it became considered dangerous, as they were too powerful. Packs are now outlawed by the government, with the backing of the Palace.

Prime alphas, highly dominant alphas who could dominate more than one person at a time, and kept other lone alphas in check, also existed in the past, but they died out or were hunted into extinction, so the world has lost them to little-known history.

In Knot Your Princess, Maia is an omega who hid at her gramps' rural farm until he died when she was twenty-one and her younger brother betrayed her to the Palace. Her older brother mysteriously disappeared as a teenager and wasn't there to protect her anymore.

Maia lived at the Palace for three years, but refused to submit to any alpha's bark. The fact she had hidden for so long, by subduing her scent, and could resist an alpha's bark, made her an anomaly. The Palace studied her to learn her secrets, often torturing her with food and sleep deprivation, sometimes even beatings, to force her compliance. It never worked.

It became a challenge for alphas to take turns trying to bark Maia into submission. Until a well-connected alpha, Ronan, became fixated with her to the point of obsession. She knew she was living on borrowed time as his attempts to dominate her became unhinged and the Palace's research tests on her became more extreme. Yet she couldn't find a means to escape.

While she was in isolation, the electricity went out around the country and she emerged into a world in chaos. The government and military had all but disappeared, and anarchy descended. People called it the Crash.

As Ronan returned, accompanied by a rogue military unit, she took her opportunity to escape. Her only two friends at the Palace, Ava and Cary, urged her to flee, intending to follow when they could.

Maia stole an old rusty bike and fled blindly, with only rough directions to Ava's uncle's farm, a few snacks and an old book she had been reading just before she fled. After days on the run, exhausted and alone, she came across a gate that led to a tranquil farm. In the dawning light, she became transfixed by the sound of laughter coming from the fields and scents of home.

After being discovered, Maia reluctantly agreed to come inside the gates where she met three alphas, who all reacted to her scent instantly. When she touched one of them, her omega burst from her confines and she could no longer hide. Despite them all being true, scent matched mates, the alphas held themselves back from mating her, wanting her to accept a mate bond willingly.

The three alphas, Damon, Hunter and Leif, were ex-military who had no interest in forcefully mating an omega. They had turned their backs on society and ran the farm together with their best friend, and Leif's boyfriend, a beta named Max. They took Maia into their protection and pursued her, in their own ways, driven by an instinctive need to become a pack together. With the world gone to hell around them, they no longer felt bound by society's rules.

The farm was fully sustainable, designed that way before the Crash. The people living inside still had access to food, water, and electricity. Everyday things that were now in high demand outside their gates. It also had high fences and security, as Leif's sister Lexie ran a secret women's refuge at the farm. It was a utopia nestled discreetly into the surrounding forest, in the midst of a crumbling world.

However, trouble followed Maia. Sirena, an ex-girlfriend of Damon's, caused trouble within the farm, while Ronan stalked her from outside the gates, causing security issues. Maia decided to leave, worried for the safety of her friends still at the Palace and her new family within the farm. But Damon, Hunter, Leif and Max convinced her to stay and rescued Ava and Cary from the Palace for her.

Maia eventually stood up to Sirena and gave her an opportunity to be a better person. Maia's relationships with Hunter, Leif and Max steadily developed and strengthened into something more as she mated each of them. Damon, however, fought the pull, held back by his fears. As one of the most dominant alphas in generations, he kept himself tightly controlled.

Maia's old, very illegal book helped them discover Damon was a prime alpha. The book, and Ava's knowledge of it as well, also helped to reveal that Maia had gone into heat. A hormone fueled sexual rut that lasts for days and makes the omega and alphas highly fertile, something only an omega with a true mate will experience.

Knot Your Problem begins at the same point as Chapter 35 in Knot Your Princess, before the final climactic scenes and the end of the book. It's set just after Sam, Maia's long-lost brother, and his best friend Claudio show up outside the farm's fences to rescue Maia and end up staying to help when alphas from the Palace attack the farm.

However, Lexie isn't around for Sam and Claudio's arrival and doesn't know them when they are all thrown together a short time later with life-changing consequences. This book shows the ending from Lexie's alternate perspective and experience, then continues her story as she navigates the new world she's thrust into.

If you haven't read Knot Your Princess, you can always check it out after you finish Lexie's story, and read Maia's version of events.

Enjoy!

One

I was standing in the study of my brother's cabin as I felt a sense of danger heighten all my senses. The tension in the room was so thick I could feel it pushing on my skin like the air held weight.

The family I'd chosen surrounded me, alongside a few new friends, and I wondered, briefly, just how far I would go to protect these people from the mounting threats outside our gates.

My brother Leif and his best friends Damon, Hunter, and Max had spread out in front of the sliding glass door, scanning the edge of our farm and the forest beyond. I could see the tension in all their bodies. The dogs guarding our cattle out in the forest beyond our fences were barking like crazy and the animal handlers had just reported spotting two unknown men in the trees.

"Lexie." Damon's terse voice lightly barking my name had me tensing up and readying for action when I met his gaze. "I need you to take Cary and Ava back to their cabin and stay with them until we know more. They don't know our protocols or emergency procedures, so you're responsible for them. Got it?"

I nodded quickly, and for once, I didn't argue. Biting back my snarky retort. We had potential intruders, and our peaceful life at the farm had become precarious since the Crash. I didn't want to distract anyone from what they needed to do right now.

I took a quick, deep breath to settle myself. Then I grabbed Ava's hand and motioned Cary towards the door, but Cary turned towards Damon instead.

"I can help," Cary said, as he planted his feet firmly in place.

Damon looked him up and down. Cary was a big guy, darkly menacing and aloof, but he was a rare male omega, and we didn't know him. We had only met Cary and Ava last night when the guys rescued them from the Omega Palace.

Cary and Ava had barely gotten a night's sleep and a meal in their bellies, and now we had danger at the fence. It impressed me that Cary would offer to jump in and help when he didn't know us, either.

"I appreciate the offer, Cary," Damon said, "but I don't know your training or skills, and we don't have time to figure it out right now. Next time, I'll use you. I promise. But right now, we've got this covered, and I need you with Lexie. If things go south, she'll need your help."

I didn't need the help, but Damon's decision made sense. I figured he didn't want the distraction of an unknown male omega, who smelled tantalisingly like vanilla ice cream, hanging around when they needed to focus on the imminent threat.

Cary lowered his head slightly and swallowed hard before turning away slowly, as though the decision disappointed him, but he understood. He squared his shoulders and took a defensive position behind Ava, a spot he seemed to take instinctively.

Maia glanced at me, and I nodded again before turning for the door. I knew the guys would keep Maia safe. What she wanted, though, was written all over her face. She was silently asking me to keep her friends safe, too. It meant a lot that she had confidence in my ability to protect them after only knowing me for a short time. I wouldn't let her down.

I patted my leg for Bear to follow, out of habit, but he was already in front of me, ready to lead the way. He gave me a long look over his shoulder, the equivalent of a teenager rolling his eyes.

Bear was part of the pack that was supposed to watch the livestock. Only Bear had adopted us, mainly me, instead of our herd. Nothing I did could shake him. I didn't really mind; he was good company.

I took off behind Bear, and Ava pulled into step next to me, giving Bear a nervous glance. She was wary of him. I got it. He was a giant Anatolian Shepherd and looked intimidating. I had watched grown men shake when he growled at them, but he was a big blonde goofball when he wanted to play.

"So you read Maia's banned book about packs, huh?" I asked Ava, trying to make conversation and distract her as we hustled up the path to the guest cabins, noticing the worried frown on her face.

"Yeah, I noticed Maia was always reading it in the little nook in the library she would hide in. So I started doing the same whenever she would disappear. It made me feel like there was hope for her, and for us all."

I snuck a look behind us toward Cary, and he seemed to have stiffened up at Ava's mention of hope. Maybe he didn't hold any for himself? He watched our surroundings warily while pretending he wasn't listening to us.

I hadn't seen Ava and Cary talk directly to each other much, but they seemed to gravitate naturally to each other, and he was incredibly protective of her. Maia had told me everyone else at the Palace treated Cary like a circus freak.

"Hey, Cary," I said, wanting to put him at ease, too. "Our fences are electric, and we're one of the few people still to have electricity. People will take a poke at us, but it's only one of our defenses. The guys have got it covered. Nobody has made it through yet."

He glanced at Ava, then looked at me and gave me a quick nod before returning to watching our surroundings. I didn't think he intended to trust Ava's protection to anyone but himself.

Ava took no notice of our exchange, which seemed strange to me. Her eyes always seemed to be sliding away from him. With all that delicious dark skin, gorgeous high cheekbones, and full, pouty lips, Cary was almost too beautiful to look at. He looked like he worked out, too. Throw in his inherent omega allure, and I kind of got it. It was like looking at an exotic flower that you knew was deadly, but you felt drawn to touch it, anyway. Sometimes it was safer not to look.

Still, if a man looked at me with half the intensity Cary directed at Ava, I'd seriously have to rethink my casual sex only rule. I had never met an omega before Maia arrived at our farm, though, so I didn't know how they normally interacted. I'd heard Omegas could get jealous around each other, which was why the Palace kept them apart and isolated a lot. Yet Maia and Ava seemed tight.

I switched my focus back to Ava. Ava was an omega too, and when her dark cherry scent mixed with Cary's vanilla ice cream, it was a potent mix. She was shorter than me and seemed fragile, but had curves for days, long dark hair, a smattering of light freckles across her pale skin, and enormous green eyes. She looked like a delicate princess, making you want to pick her up and stash her somewhere safe to protect her. I was a beta and didn't swing that way, but even I wasn't immune.

I shook my head and tried to get my focus off the two intriguing omegas, and back on our surroundings. I took a deep breath again, now that I was outside. The scents of the farm that always seemed to float up the hill on the breeze, a sweet mix of fruit and fresh growing things, always centered me. The scent changed subtly with the seasons, but always fed my soul.

I caught the faint sound of people yelling hello to each other in the fields, laughter drifting down from the women in the dining hall kitchen, and animals calling in the distance. The sounds of a busy farm usually brought a quiet joy to my heart, yet right now, they seemed at odds with the tension in the room we had just left.

I increased our pace until we reached the cabin. I ushered Ava and Cary inside but left the door open, so Bear could come and go if needed. Bear's agitation as he paced between the door and the windows made me nervous. I'd learned to trust his instincts more than most people. I needed something to do to distract all of us.

Ava and Cary had arrived with nothing but the clothes on their backs, so I couldn't help them unpack or settle in. There was no food in the cabin either, as we'd been conserving food since the Crash began and eating all our meals together in the dining hall.

There were board games and books on the shelf in the living room, but both Cary and Ava shook their heads when I asked if they wanted to play something.

So there was nothing to do but sit and wait. Ava and Cary had positioned themselves awkwardly on separate couches. I didn't know what was going on with that, so I plopped myself down next to Ava.

I attempted more small talk, but we were all too tense. Now that we were no longer in motion and didn't know what was happening outside, it felt like the entire world was holding its breath. Time had slowed to a crawl. I wasn't a patient person, so the silent waiting drove me slowly mad.

"So, tell me about the Palace," I asked. Both Ava and Cary startled, as if both their minds had been elsewhere.

"Why?" Cary shot back. He was watching me closely and appeared wary of my question.

"Because Maia is my brother's mate, so I consider her a sister now. Plus, I really like her. Trouble seems to follow her and I want to know what we're up against."

Maia was a leggy blonde bombshell, utterly oblivious to her own charms. Despite everything she had endured in life, she had a quiet strength and was innately kind. Her nature drew people in, even me. She was like the yin to my loud, bratty, yang energy. I instantly knew we would be tight the moment I met her.

"Is it just the one guy from the other night stalking her, or is it more than that?" I pressed on, ignoring his reluctance. They were my only source of information right now.

"Ronan is psychotic and obsessed with Maia," Cary finally answered with a frown marring his perfect face. Yet, some of his wariness eased as he relaxed back into his chair. "If he suspects she's here, he won't stop until he has her. As bad as he is, though, it's not just him. I'm pretty sure other people at the Palace are studying her somehow. They watch her closely. I don't think they'll let her go easily, either."

Ava was staring at an old sepia photo of a barn on the wall, and fidgeting with a bracelet on her wrist. "Maia's story isn't ours to tell, but there's something going on underneath the fake glamor at the Palace.

There's a lab underneath the building. She'd never tell me what happened whenever she disappeared, but I'm pretty sure they took her down there. They seemed to single her out."

Cary looked shocked before his eyes narrowed on Ava. "How do you know that?"

Ava just shrugged as her gaze met his briefly, and skittered away again. My heart sank. I grabbed a cushion and hugged it to my chest, needing to hold on to something and not able to hug Maia right now. One psychotic guy I could handle. I'd done it before. This was much bigger.

I suspected Leif knew something about it already. He'd been cagey when I'd asked questions recently and he never usually held anything back from me. He had to know avoiding my questions wouldn't keep me out of this, though.

I wished Maia had trusted me enough to tell me about it. She'd only mentioned the attempts at forced matings the night we'd hung out and talked, but we'd only just met the day before. I hoped one day she would tell me all of her story.

"And you guys? Will the Palace come for you?" I knew it wasn't any of my business, but I had a healthy fear of the Palace and I believed in knowing your enemy.

Cary just scoffed at me. "They don't care about me. I exist purely for entertainment."

His words were flippant, but there was a thread of pain there, running underneath the surface. It was clear in the way his body tightened as he spoke, his fingers gripping the edge of the couch, as if he were bracing himself.

"You're so much more than that, Cary." Ava said with quiet conviction, as she held his gaze briefly.

Cary went still, and the existing tension in the room heightened with sparks of something raw and undefined. His scent bloomed in response to her words as he got up and walked stiffly over to the door. "I can't breed, so as far as the Palace is concerned, I'm not important."

I didn't push him, letting him have the small bit of distance he clearly needed.

"They watch Ava too much as well," he said over his tense shoulder as he scanned the trees outside, bringing the conversation back around. He attempted a casual pose, leaning against the door frame. But it fooled nobody. "They've left her alone so far, but they want something from her. I'm sure of it. If they come for Maia, they'll come for Ava, too."

Bear suddenly stilled in the middle of the living room and went on high alert. His tail dropped, his ears swiveled, and his posture stiffened. Making my response to Cary freeze in my throat.

Bear stalked to the door, head butted Cary out of the way, and looked uphill as he scented the air. Then the hackles on his back rose, and he growled deep in his chest, giving me chills, before he took off. He leaped over the porch railing and raced up the hill.

Before I could even get off the couch, I heard faint screams echo from the fields at the top of the hill. My blood turned to ice in my veins. Dave was up at the main gate.

I instinctively bolted to the door to take off after Bear, but then remembered I was responsible for two others who were in an incredibly vulnerable position. Cary and Ava didn't know the layout of the farm or friend from a foe out there, and I needed to keep them safe.

"Shit," I swore softly as I turned to Cary. "Stay here-"

"Don't even think about it," Cary warned as he cut me off abruptly. "We're coming with you."

He pushed out the door with a determined set to his shoulders and looked towards where Bear was rapidly disappearing around the bend in the path. I glanced at Ava as she moved up beside me, but she just shrugged. Well, okay then, we were all chasing the crazy dog. I'd take the heat from Damon for it later.

I grabbed Ava's hand and glared at Cary. "Stay behind me until we know what's going on."

He didn't look happy, but his gaze landed on Ava and he nodded. I pulled Ava past him, but kept her slightly behind me. There was no way I was letting her out of my reach if danger was brewing.

I led the chase up the path in pursuit of Bear. I trusted his instincts. If he was chasing something down, it was because it wasn't supposed to be here.

I heard a low keening sound as I rounded the bend near the dining hall that had me adding a burst of speed. I cried out when I saw Bear lying in the middle of the path, crumpled as if someone had felled him mid-stride. He jerked his head around with a whimper when he heard me yell his name and tried to bravely crawl towards me.

Bear was panting hard as I skidded and landed on my knees next to him. I hugged his giant head as Ava dropped to her knees next to me while he whined at me.

"He seems dazed, but he can't have run into anything," Ava said as she checked his eyes, all timidness around him suddenly gone. I got the impression she'd grown up around animals for at least part of her life.

She leaned over further and sniffed the air. "I smell carbon dioxide."

"Isn't that odorless?" I asked. "And what does that mean?"

"Omegas are highly susceptible to scent, and it's used commercially to anesthetize livestock before slaughter."

We had nothing like that on the farm. I was sure, but there was an odd odor in the air.

"Would someone from the farm have done this?" Cary asked quietly, obviously thinking the same thing I was.

I shook my head, and out of the corner of my eye, I noticed Cary whip around to scan the surrounding trees. Whoever was here had come prepared and meant business. This was no crime of opportunity or someone testing our fences like the other night.

Bear whimpered again, and the sound broke my heart, dragging at my attention.

"It's okay, boy. You're a good boy. You're going to be okay," I crooned, but I didn't know if that was true. If they'd given him enough gas, it could kill him. This damn dog I had never asked for had snuck his way into my heart, and I would not lose him now.

Bear suddenly stiffened under my hands and growled while looking over my shoulder toward the tree line at my back. He tried to get up as I struggled to hold him down when suddenly his eyes rolled back in his head, and he collapsed.

I frantically checked he was still breathing as I heard Cary yell a warning behind me, and the sound of a fight broke out.

I felt a growl build in my chest. Someone was going to die today, and it wasn't going to be my damn dog.

Two

A s soon as I was sure Bear was still breathing, I jumped to my feet.

"Stay down and watch Bear. Don't leave his side," I whispered to Ava. I knew there wasn't a lot she could do to help Bear right now, but I wanted someone with him. It would also keep her in place. It was too easy to lose track of the people you were trying to protect in a fight if they were moving around. I'd learned that the hard way.

Ava just gave me a determined nod and leaned over him protectively. For that one act alone, she was now in my inner circle. Regardless of whether or not she wanted to be.

As I spun to Cary, I counted four alphas dressed in black. I didn't recognize them, so they weren't from around here. Two alphas had him engaged, while two more were keeping watch from the treeline.

The intruders were military-trained, judging by the way they moved, and Cary was an omega. Yet, they chose to attack him rather than bark at him to make him submit. *Fuckers.*

Cary was fighting valiantly. He clearly had a lot of strength, but no training. He was swinging wildly, desperately trying to connect. The intruders were playing with him and ignoring Ava and me, for now. They had discounted us as threats.

I got it. My eyebrow ring and bright pink and red hair gave me an edge, but I still didn't look like I could handle myself. I was fit enough to be strong, but I had a lot of curves, and they were all men ever seemed to notice.

That was their mistake, and I would make them regret it.

I launched myself at the closest alpha toying with Cary, using my speed and the element of surprise to my advantage. An attack wasn't usually my style. My skills were all about defense and creating an opening to get away. I wasn't delusional; I knew I had little chance against an alpha, let alone four. But Cary needed my help.

I was significantly smaller than all of them, so it seemed like insanity to run at one, but I knew how to play to my strengths.

I kicked the alpha I'd targeted hard in the back of the knee, and he yelped as his leg buckled. I grabbed his arm firmly and dropped my weight to pull him off balance. Then I closed my stance, pushed up, and connected my knee with his head on his way down.

It wouldn't knock him out, but it would daze him and hopefully keep him out of action for a minute. I swung around quickly to check on Cary, but he seemed to hold his own now that he only had to deal with one alpha.

"Hey, you little bitch!" I spun back quickly and found one of the alphas who had stayed at the treeline, now headed my way with a snarl on his face. The last alpha kept watch.

Why was a woman defending herself always a bitch? It royally pissed me off. I mean, no one had attacked me yet, so I wasn't technically defending myself, but these guys obviously meant us harm.

The alpha swung at me, but I dodged and latched onto his arm. He wasn't expecting it from the look on his face, even though he had just watched me take down his friend. Some men can't imagine a woman will fight back, even while watching her do it. I was happy to help them figure it out.

I tried to unbalance him, but he spun to counteract me. I lost my footing on the gravel path, and I cursed myself. It was a rookie mistake, but my focus had split in too many directions. I could hear grunts and blows landing behind me, and I didn't think it was Cary delivering them.

The alpha yanked me back up and landed a savage blow to my gut that winded me, followed up with a punch to my head. I felt blood drip down my temple as the world spun wildly. My vision doubled sickeningly as I dropped to my knees. That was going to hurt later.

"That'll teach you to know your place, you pink-haired slut," he growled. Wow, he was a special little nugget. My knee had a date with his balls as soon as there were only two of them again. *And what the hell was wrong with pink hair?*

He yanked me roughly to my feet, and I saw the final alpha helping the one I dropped earlier up, too, before he headed for Ava. Cary was roughly shoved into my personal space, almost knocking me over. He was barely standing. I noticed his legs shake, but I wasn't doing much better.

"Are you okay, Lexie?" Cary rasped, sounding just as winded as I was. He wasn't watching me, though. His eyes were tracking the alpha headed towards Ava.

"Peachy," I answered breathlessly. I sensed Cary would fight to the death to get to Ava if they touched her, which wouldn't do us any good right now. He tensed beside me, and I knew I had to act quickly.

"Ava," I wheezed through gasps as I struggled to get enough air deep enough in my lungs to be heard. Ava had kept her gaze fixed on us, but she still huddled protectively over Bear with one hand on his chest.

She lifted her chin briefly to show me she'd heard. "Don't fight him. We'll pick our battle," I choked out, feeling the world tilt wildly with every gasp.

She nodded and hopped up, eyeing the alpha warily as he approached. But he just gestured for her to walk in front of him. I stumbled behind her until she turned quickly and grabbed my waist to prop me up before anyone could object.

"Bear's still breathing. He'll be okay," she whispered, and I could have kissed her.

We reached the dining hall, when the alpha who took out Cary held up his hand for us to stop. I heard voices before we were all roughly grabbed and dragged from the shadows into the daylight and pushed to our knees. I got a lungful of oranges and pineapples turned bitter with fear, and my heart dropped.

Only one person I knew had that scent, and it was Maia. The world was spinning too much for me to look up, though, and I was still gasping for air. Where the hell were Leif and the guys? I could only hope they were okay and knew what they were doing.

On the next heaved breath, I copped a cloying mix of scents from all the alphas surrounding us. But one stood out. Mushrooms. I remembered that scent from the security alert the other night, when two intruders had checked out our fences. It was Maia's stalker, Ronan. Only he seemed to have a lot more help this time.

"Is this who you were looking for?" I heard Ronan ask her. Great, so we were leverage against Maia. Which meant we were expendable. I tried to angle my head slightly without passing out and noticed Maia subtly pointing at the ground.

I hoped she was trying to tell us to stay down because I needed a minute before moving with any kind of speed, or I'd yak all over someone's shoes.

Maybe that wasn't such a bad idea, though. Who had the nicest shoes? The alpha who hit me earlier had a nice, new, sturdy pair that looked like they hadn't seen much action. I'd happily vomit on them for him and help wear them in.

Suddenly there was movement in front of me, and I heard a rough voice growl, "No, I think she was looking for you. She has a score to settle."

I relaxed slightly as I recognized Damon's voice, and he popped out of the trees in front of us. I figured the enormous boots next to him belonged to my brother, but there were two other pairs behind them I didn't recognize. Unless it was just my double vision.

Suddenly, people were everywhere; more people popped out behind Damon, and the boots behind him swiveled to have his back. Not double vision then. That was a good sign if my eyes were getting steadier.

A distant gunshot that echoed in the air made my body lock up. I desperately hoped Max and Hunter were okay and they were doing the shooting because the intruders had us outnumbered here.

At least the women in the kitchen would take shelter now, if they hadn't already, and weren't likely to wander out the back door into this fresh hell.

I was having trouble following what everyone was saying. I thought I heard Sirena yell from over near the trees, but I didn't know what the hell she would be doing here. Maybe I was hallucinating. I wanted to curl up and go to sleep, but I knew that would be a bad idea.

I almost cried in relief when I heard Hunter pipe up from the roof, and Max's voice came from the same direction as Sirena's. They were okay. We were all going to be okay now. The cavalry was here.

We were still outnumbered, but my brother and his friends were lethal. Hunter was a sniper, and he'd have Ronan in his sights. Everyone under-estimated Max because he was a beta and a tech geek, but he was just as dangerous as his mates. With the four of them working together, we had a chance of getting out of this alive.

I closed my eyes and tried to breathe deeper to focus on what was happening around me. I could scent Damon's lightning and Leif's camp-fire smoke. There was a feeling of coiled violence in the air. It was almost crackling with it as though it was running over my skin. There was a weird electricity brewing I had never felt before.

I sensed it was coming from Damon, Leif, Hunter, and Max. Meeting their true mate and the bonds they had built with Maia had strengthened them. I could feel it whenever I was around them.

I figured they were now moving their pieces into place for whatever take-down they had planned, and I wanted to be ready for it when it came. I didn't intend to sit quietly and let them have all the fun. My knee had a date with a ball sack.

I felt my head clear a little, finally. Ronan was monologuing like a classic movie villain, the idiot. *Didn't he watch movies?* It never ended well for the villain. I opened my eyes when I heard Leif call out to me a moment later.

"Are you okay, Lex? Where's Bear?" He asked in a quiet, dangerous voice.

I nodded gently and was happy when it didn't feel like my head was about to fall off, and the world stayed where it was instead of sloshing around. Although I still didn't risk looking up fully yet. No need to tempt the devil.

"I'm just pissed these morons got the jump on me. I think they knocked out Bear. He took off in a hurry when he sensed something. I found him unconscious but breathing just before they jumped us."

Technically, Bear was still awake when I found him, but I figured it was better to summarize the facts right now.

As soon as I spoke, the feet of the two men behind Damon and Leif spun in my direction, forcing Damon and Leif to turn and cover the intruders behind them. I was confused and felt the tension in the air ratchet up to a whole new level.

"Sam, I need you to focus," Damon barked in a tone that could make a beta wet themselves. But the strange feet stayed pointed firmly in my direction.

The two men had to be highly dominant alphas to stand up to Damon. *Who the fuck was Sam?*

Even though my head was clearing a little, my stomach felt bruised where I cradled it and I was having trouble taking deep breaths. I'd resorted to breathing shallowly, but it added to my dizziness, so I forced a deeper breath into my lungs now.

The moment I did, the overwhelming scents of aged leather and buttered popcorn hit me. Combined, they shot white light through my brain and pulled at me deliciously. I leaned forward without meaning to, needing to get closer. My mouth watered and my whole body roared MINE, in the most primal of ways. It was instinctive, seductive, and utterly terrifying.

I froze in place as the sweet scent of passion fruit that had haunted me most of my life teased my senses like a hidden memory. I instinctively knew it was a heartbeat away from ripping free from my body, and fear paralyzed me.

No, no, no, this was bad. I recalled what Maia had said when I asked her how she had stayed hidden as an omega for so long. She'd caused herself pain whenever her scent threatened to leak out.

I pushed against my stomach and held my breath until I saw black spots, and the pain felt crippling. I didn't want to pass out, though. When Maia met Damon, she'd fainted, and her scent had exploded, uncontrolled, into the room when he caught her.

I couldn't risk anyone touching me right now.

You're a beta. You're a beta. I chanted in my head.

Yet my heart suspected it was a lie. Betas didn't react to the scents of alphas.

Three

My senses had been on high alert since my best friend Dio and I had arrived to rescue my sister Maia. There had been something urgent and instinctive tugging at the edge of my awareness since we first approached the farm.

I'd tried to shake it off and put it down to concern for my sister and an unfamiliar environment with unknown threats.

We'd been tracking my sister since we returned shortly after the Crash. I'd headed for my family farm until I found out she wasn't there anymore. She'd been sent to the Palace years ago and nobody had told me.

I'd instantly started flipping tables and Dio had barely calmed me down before I'd been out the door, headed for a helicopter and a possible court martial. My entire team had followed, determined to go down having my back if needed.

I hadn't seen my baby sister in over a decade and dreamed of reuniting with her the whole time, so my emotions were a mess. Yet even with the joy of finding Maia, then my bone-crushing guilt at finding out she had gotten none of my letters or notes and thought I had abandoned her all those years ago, my senses had remained heightened and searching.

Something in the air around this farm had me on edge, calling to me and demanding my attention. Something more than the current threat to my sister from the gun-wielding maniac who had been stalking and abusing her. It was like the faint echo of a mermaid's siren song carried on the breeze.

Maia had found a home and her mates here. I already knew they were good guys and would do anything to protect her. As much as I wanted to be the one to charge in and save my sister, I knew her mates would beat me to it. Their reputations were well-earned. They were lethal and deadly. They were only holding back right now because it was part of their plan.

But the moment I heard that siren song crystalize into a single voice, I felt like the entire reason for my existence shifted.

That fucking voice. So sweet and sultry with a slight husky rasp that sounded like an old-school jazz singer. It was a gut punch. I spun instinctively and vaguely noticed Dio did the same as Damon and Leif spun to cover our backs while loudly cursing us.

It was all kinds of wrong. It went against all our training and put everyone in danger. I knew that logically, but my alpha demanded to know who owned that voice. I focused my entire being on the task. The logical part of my brain was no longer running the show.

I was known to be instinctive, hot-headed, and sometimes impulsive. I didn't have a great handle on my beast on my best days. But I had never felt a pull this intense and all-consuming. All my military training meant nothing in the face of it.

I scanned in front of me, and my eyes immediately pulled to a bright-haired woman on her knees, looking winded and dazed. I couldn't tear my eyes away from her.

It was like a giant spotlight had lit her up. One only I could see. She was suddenly in the forefront of my vision, and everything else retreated.

I noticed a bruise forming on her temple and blood running down her cheek. My scent spiked, a note of whiskey searing through my natural leather and oak scent. It always seemed to rise to the surface when my emotions were high. Usually, when I was angry. Or aroused.

In this case, I was definitely angry. Someone had hurt her. I scented the air but couldn't catch any scent that felt like it came from her. She had to be an omega for me to react this strongly to her. Surely.

Maybe there were just too many scents with so many alphas nearby. I could smell Dio's buttered popcorn scent. It had spiked alongside mine, with a burst of chili coming through. I could feel him vibrating with anger and sensed his intent focus aimed in the same direction as mine.

The woman looked like she had put up a fight, and the thought made me strangely proud. She looked beautiful and fierce, even on her knees.

I sensed she wasn't defeated. She had a wild energy pouring from her that lit me up inside. I was a match waiting for a spark, some friction, to burst into flame.

She was talking to Leif but looking at the ground as if she couldn't raise her head. She took a deep, jagged breath suddenly before freezing momentarily. Then she subtly moved her arm across her stomach and seemed to push on it before lightly gasping.

I don't think anyone else noticed the movement, but I did. My gaze was riveted on every ragged breath she took and the pulse beating wildly at her neck. I felt Dio stiffen beside me as though he'd caught the movement too.

Why was she still looking at the ground? She didn't look up or acknowledge us at all. I was desperate to catch her gaze. I wanted to tell her it would be alright, that I had her, but the words died in my throat.

I could vaguely hear Damon growling at me, but it flowed over me with little effect. I heard Ronan laugh menacingly before I saw him wave the gun wildly from the corner of my eye. A split second later, Maia dropped, elbowing and unbalancing him on her way down, and the world exploded into action.

Damon detonated, and his dominance exploded around us. Every enemy alpha in the vicinity dropped to their knees and froze instantly. He launched himself at Ronan faster than I could comprehend, snapping his neck and dropping him to the ground with hardly a thought. It was the quickest yet most efficient death I had ever witnessed, and I'd seen my fair share.

I was momentarily stunned. I'd heard he was powerful, but Damon's dominance was unparalleled. No alpha could dominate more than one person at a time outside of stories and legends.

Less than a heartbeat later, a shot rang out, taking out the man who had turned his gun on my sister as she dropped.

I felt torn. Leif, Max, and Hunter all leaped into action around me, moving as if they were one and completely in sync, with no audible words or orders from Damon. I knew I should check on my sister, but I still couldn't tear my focus away from the woman breathing heavily on the ground.

My body decided for me as I moved, almost involuntarily, towards her. Like I was a puppet on a string and her need pulled at me. Dio was at my side and headed in the same direction.

I held my hand out towards her to help her up, but she waved me away with barely a glance before pushing herself up with a low groan and turning her back on me. I was instantly bereft and a tearing sensation shot through me.

Did she not feel the same pull toward me? What the fuck was going on?

I was so confused. My heart was racing, and the need to touch her, claim her, was an insistent beat in my veins, demanding action. I moved towards her again, but Dio threw his arm out in front of me and held me back.

I looked at him in confusion and saw my need mirrored there, but he shook his head.

I trusted Dio with my life. I had been lost, bitter and angry when I met him. A volcano continually erupting and burning everyone and everything around me. But he had always stood steadfast at my side. He had launched himself without question, alongside me, into every stupid, impulsive mess I had gotten myself into in my late teens.

He always watched my back and pulled me back from the brink when I needed it. Plus, his cheerful, easygoing nature smoothed over every feather I ruffled, including my own.

Dio calmed me in a way few people in my life had ever been able to do, apart from my long-lost sister. I would trust him in this, as I did in all things. He'd never let me down yet.

I couldn't help the glare on my face when I raised my eyebrow at him in question, though. He just chuckled tightly in response, knowing me well.

"Wait," was all he said quietly while shaking his head. But then, something over my shoulder caught his attention before he could finish what he was going to say. He jerked his chin up, directing me to look, and I spun around.

"What the fuck?" I groaned.

My sister, Maia, was wedged between Damon and Hunter, pressed hard between them, with the dead body of Ronan lying at their feet. Leif and Max were circling them like predators. They were all breathing heavily, while Damon was growling lightly, and Maia's scent was spiking rapidly.

Maia had proudly announced all four men as her mates. Including Max, even though Max was a beta. She had refused to leave when I'd made contact less than an hour ago at the farm's lower gates, and tried to take her to safety. Just before all hell had broken loose with Ronan and his henchmen breaching the farm's defenses.

Her announcement had shocked me. Our society did not condone multiple mates, despite it being part of our natures for alphas and omegas. Packs were outlawed as dangerous, and having more than one partner was too close to being a pack.

What the hell had Maia gotten herself into?

This was going to end badly. There were too many people here, too many witnesses. I couldn't protect her if this got out.

I moved over and tried to reach for her to pull her away, calling her name, but she resisted. Damon's growl intensified, becoming aggressive before he blocked me roughly.

"Damon, snap out of it," I demanded. But his beast was firmly in control and didn't know me. He wasn't going to listen. I tried another tactic.

"Fuck, Maia. You need to try and back away from them."

I was getting desperate. Brute force would not solve this. I knew that. Dio and I were outnumbered and strangers here. Damon had been wary and confrontational when we arrived, and our truce to defend the farm was precarious.

His show of dominance just now made challenging Damon suicidal, but I'd do it for my sister. I owed her if everything Damon had alluded to was true, and she had been tortured at the Palace while I was gone. I wouldn't let anyone else harm her.

Before I could move to intervene further, a sultry voice said, "She can't and doesn't want to, anyway."

I stilled. That sultry voice coming from so close behind me had my entire body alight with need and anticipation.

"I'm pretty sure she's in heat," she clarified.

"What the hell is a heat?" Dio asked her, bouncing his gaze between everyone in front of us while he moved to my other side. He leaned in closer and took a deep breath, mesmerized.

"Oh shit, what the fuck is up with her scent? It's like a sexual napalm, and it's pulling at me," he said as he quickly stepped back again and tried to adjust his junk discreetly. I elbowed him hard, and he let out a loud grunt.

I couldn't scent anything or feel anything more than Maia's usual scent, which was stronger and sweeter. Another woman stepped forward. I think she had been kneeling next to my pink-haired beauty, but she seemed unharmed. A man jerked forward to hold her back when Maia hissed at her like an angry kitten. He was barely standing, he looked like he'd put up one hell of a fight.

I caught a whiff of dark cherries and ice cream coming from them. They were clearly omegas, and I think they were the pair Damon, Leif, and Hunter had rescued from the Palace last night.

But neither created any pull within me, unlike the woman I couldn't scent. Interesting.

I needed to find out what the hell was going on.

"Shit, even I can feel that. This is bad," the male omega grunted. He looked like he was trying not to breathe any more than he had to for basic survival.

"Damon, you need to get her out of here now. When the heat starts, it deepens her scent and draws alphas in," the female omega said. "She's definitely in heat now, and she's going to set off every alpha in the area that's unrelated to her. We don't need an alpha frenzy on our hands."

So I *wasn't reacting because I was Maia's brother?* If that was the case, and every alpha here but me was going to respond to Maia's scent, we were in some serious shit.

Leif and Max had hogtied the intruder alphas with duct tape brought by a young beta, Nick, but it would only hold as long as they were willing.

Any of them could break through if they became motivated enough. For an alpha in a frenzy, it would be like tying them up with string cheese.

"Lexie, you're in charge," Damon ground out around clenched teeth, staring at the object of my intense desire, and my hackles rose. I didn't want him looking at her right now, but at least I had a name. *Lexie.*

He must have a lot of respect for her if he trusted her with the farm and security with a bunch of strange alphas here.

"Get Dave down here and let him know Sam has backup on the way," Damon continued, not paying me any attention.

I looked at my watch quickly. My team was ten minutes away, coming in hot in a helicopter.

"Keep people away from our cabin. Feel free to smack around any alphas who get out of line. Get the other women on board if you have to. We're relying on you," Damon added.

"I'll help her," Sirena, piped up. She had been full of surprises today. I didn't know her, but we'd researched her family while undercover. I couldn't believe no-one here knew she was Ronan's sister until today. Her relationship with him, if there was one beyond blood ties, hadn't stopped her from pointing a gun at him to defend Maia.

Lexie looked at Sirena suspiciously, though, as if she didn't trust her. Which had me on edge. Before Lexie turned and nodded at Damon quickly. He grabbed Maia and swept her up in his arms. Maia immediately moaned and started kissing and sucking his neck.

I went to turn away, but Max was suddenly in front of me. He was barely in control and breathing hard, but he was doing a little better than his mates appeared to be. Not by much, though. Betas weren't as driven by scent as alphas, but he seemed to be picking up his mate's intensity. Probably something to do with the two bite marks he was sporting on his neck.

Leif looked a hair's breadth from throwing fists. At the same time, Hunter was glaring death at everyone around us, holding one hand protectively on Maia's back.

"Can you back up Lexie and help Dave secure the farm? Lexie is our sister."

Lexie was their sister? How was she all of their sister? But that was a question for another day.

"Can you promise me you won't hurt *my* sister?" I demanded. Fear and desperation for Maia were coming out in anger, making my voice growl dangerously low. I'd just found my sister and now they wanted to take her away while she was vulnerable and had just been attacked. All my instincts rebelled.

Max was in my face instantly, a ballsy move for a beta. "We would *never* hurt your sister. She's our mate," he growled, low and angry.

Leif instantly stepped up behind Max, but Dio got in the middle of us before any fists flew, pushing me back.

"We know nobody is hurting anyone here, except maybe a few sneaky kicks for the dickwad alphas behind us. Okay. We got this, Max. Go."

I was the one breathing hard now, but Dio's hand on my chest calmed me down. Somewhat.

Maia swung herself around in Damon's arms to wrap her legs around him and started grinding against him wantonly, just as her syrupy orange and pineapple scent exploded and flooded the area in a wave of pure lust. Every alpha in the area went on high alert and spun their heads toward her so quickly that I heard a few necks crack.

Fuck. We were out of time.

"Move, now," Damon yelled to his guys and took off.

I grabbed the nearest alpha and punched him hard to put him back down as he tried to rise and follow. Still, I only had two hands, and we had a dozen restrained enemy alphas.

"Grab a gun. Point and shoot if anyone moves," I yelled to anyone who would listen. No way was I letting any of these assholes hurt my sister. They would die before they got close enough to breathe near her.

I heard the male omega respond, "With pleasure."

My attention was caught by Lexie, though, as she screamed, "Take that, fuckers."

I spun to see what in the hell my firecracker was up to.

Four

Lexie

There was a moment of stillness as every head swiveled towards Maia, when her amped-up heat scent detonated and flooded the area. The instant Damon took off though, every damn hog-tied alpha in the area started struggling to free themselves.

They all groaned, almost in unison, with their pupils dilated and pained, hungry looks on their faces.

Not to mention they were all sporting huge, almost comical, hard-ons. I struggled not to giggle like a schoolgirl at the insanity of the moment. It almost looked like a scene from a raunchy comic strip.

The alphas were quickly cycling into a frenzy, though, while struggling to get to their feet. Even Cary looked pained by Maia's scent. I knew I had to think fast.

The new guy, who seemed to be Maia's long-lost brother Sam, if I'd heard right, had yelled to grab a gun, while venting his anger on the nearest alpha. Cary seemed all too happy to comply. Alphas didn't always rely on weapons. They didn't need them in close combat when they could bark someone into submission or overpower them with their strength. Cary managed to find one, though. These guys had come prepared for everything, except Damon, apparently.

A gun was an excellent backup plan because I knew Cary wouldn't be able to pin an alpha down right now. He was already injured. Yet, I didn't think threatening to shoot would be enough to calm these fuckers down.

There were too many of them. I didn't want to maim or kill a bunch of alphas just because they were horny idiots all juiced up on Maia's scent.

I turned desperately to see what else we had at hand and spotted the oak barrel by the back door of the kitchen. We set it up under a spout coming out of the wall, and all our dirty dish water emptied into it. We used organic, biodegradable detergent so we could reuse the water in the kitchen garden.

Perfect. I dashed over, grabbed a bucket, then hauled ass to the nearest alphas.

"Take that, fuckers," I yelled, venting my rage at these overbearing assholes who thought they could break in here and hurt my friends.

I hurled it at them, hoping the funky smelling water would clear their senses a little. The rank water caught the closest one smack in the face. He looked at me, stupefied, but he'd stopped struggling with his restraints. He had a piece of potato skin stuck to his nose. I almost laughed again. *Not the time, Lexie.*

Nick took one look at what I was doing and headed for the hose to follow my lead. He was young and quiet, but he was a smart guy. He turned the hose on as high as it could go and started blasting alphas in the face with water. It worked. They were sputtering and choking too much to struggle.

Ava grabbed another bucket and started hurling dirty water at alphas, too, watched over by Cary with his gun. While Sirena headed for the compost pile nearby, grabbed a bucket load and started smearing it on the faces of any alpha she could get near.

I dashed back to fill another bucket of water and turned to the next nearest alpha. He reared up onto his knees and lunged at me before I could get my bucket aimed. I recognized him.

It was the asshole alpha who had punched me. I remembered I had a date planned with his balls. So I kicked him hard. Right in the nuts.

"That's for the concussion, asshole," I yelled as I followed up with a bucket full of water in his face while his mouth was wide open on a pained gasp.

I felt a growl vibrate over my skin from behind me and I stepped to the side quickly as Sam lunged at him, grabbing him around the throat.

"You. Hit. Her," He bit out, with his menacing growl still vibrating his already deep voice. "Now you die."

Shit, I turned to his friend, the one who stopped Sam earlier when Max got up in his face. The gorgeous one with the dark, sun-kissed curls. But he was standing at Sam's side, looking deadly calm as he watched his friend choke out the tied-up alpha.

Both of their scents had spiked aggressively, trying to out-do Maia's lingering scent. Chilli and whiskey spearing through, what I figured were their natural, milder scents of buttered popcorn and leathery oak. Every other alpha in the area stilled like spooked prey.

"Stop," I yelled frantically. I wanted the alpha to hurt, but I didn't want him dead.

Sam and his friend both spun towards my voice in the same instinctive way they had earlier. But having their attention focussed solely on me while their dominance was running high and their pheromones saturated the air, intensified the impossible draw I felt towards them.

I gasped in a breath, then held it, trying not to breathe in any more of their scent. Battling my body to stay put and not fling myself at them recklessly. But fuck, I desperately wanted to lick them. Like an over excited puppy. Just get in there and slobber all over them like I had the right.

Not now. Please, not now.

I felt my head spin dizzily. I grabbed it, trying to anchor myself as waves of emotion battered me. Rampant desire with a tinge of fear, and an overwhelming urge to submit and bare my throat to them.

Sam's friend reached out toward me and I hastily stepped back out of reach, causing him to hesitate. The world tilted crazily, and I heard myself moan as I dropped the bucket and lost my balance. It was too much. I couldn't maintain my grasp on my surroundings. It felt as if gravity had shifted and every atom that made up who I was, had zeroed in on them.

Don't pass out. Don't you dare fucking pass out, girl. I cursed to myself in my head as I planted my feet and fiercely refused the siren call that grew stronger the more I resisted. I didn't know what would happen if an alpha touched me right now. Especially one of these two alphas.

Sam's friend lunged toward me suddenly as Sam dropped the alpha he was choking. I felt the ground rush toward me as the world tilted, trying to tip me forward. I heard Ava call out my name faintly, sounding far away, but a powerful pair of arms halted my fall. They scooped me up from behind and held me tight to a solid chest.

I closed my eyes momentarily and took a deep breath, finally. Trying to steady myself and control my body. I couldn't scent an alpha. Instead, I got a lungful of musky, male beta. I relaxed slightly as I tilted my head slightly to look up.

A gorgeous head of salt and pepper hair framed a set of deep brown eyes that stared down at me with worry. The crease on his brow made the laugh lines around his eyes stand out in a way that made my heart flip. Dammit, I didn't know which option was riskier, the alphas or Dave.

But his touch seemed to settle the wave of emotions and sensations, and grounded me in a way I hadn't been able to myself. I still felt the pull towards the two strange alphas, but it had calmed to an incessant, yet manageable, tug. Rather than a torrent.

"Are you okay, Lex?" Dave asked in that deep voice filled with bass that sent heat licking along every nerve in my body.

"I'm fine," I mumbled, trying to control the shake in my voice.

Dammit, Lex. Get it together.

Dave looked me over carefully, holding me gently, yet firmly, like I was precious.

"You're not fine, you're bleeding," he said gruffly.

I just stared at him, my heart beating frantically in my chest. The farm was in chaos around us and Dave was our head of security, but he took no notice of anything but me at that moment. It was heady stuff.

Until a loud growl, that I was quickly coming to recognize, broke through and Dave flicked his eyes up past my face.

"Put. Her. Down," Sam growled menacingly from behind me.

Goosebumps ran over my skin at the sound of his voice in that dominant tone, making me tense. It was close to, but not quite a bark. Despite that, Dave pulled me subtly closer into him, and I took a moment to savor the sensation.

"That's not your call," he said dismissively, as he flicked his eyes away to take in the rest of the scene. He nodded at someone out of my line of sight. I assumed it was Nick or Sirena.

Dave had some huge ass balls. Most betas would instinctively cower at a strange, highly dominant alpha growling at them like that. But Dave just dismissed him like he was of no concern.

Dave had a lot of experience with aggressive alphas from his time in the military. He was one of the few betas to reach the rank of captain, and from what my brother had told me, lower ranked alphas had challenged him a lot.

I took one final, deep breath from where Dave had me tucked into his chest. He'd always smelled like home somehow, despite not having a distinctive scent. Then I put on my big girl pants and said, "You can put me down, now."

Dave didn't bother trying to argue. He knew me well enough to know I could take care of myself, and I was stubborn. He raised one eyebrow at me, though, in a silent question. Seeming to doubt my ability to stand on my own.

"I'm fine, but can you stay close for a bit?" I whispered. It was as much as I would concede right now, despite him coming to my rescue a moment ago. Having him nearby seemed to ease the insane pull towards the alphas behind me, enough to let me get my bearings and stand on my own feet. He just nodded once and planted himself at my side without question.

I flicked a cautious glance at the newcomers as I filled Dave in on what I knew and what had happened with Maia and the guys. Sam was standing perfectly still while I talked, like a predator with its prey in his sights, while his friend relaxed beside him. He leaned on Sam's shoulder nonchalantly, looking intrigued yet amused. As if he was at a casual Sunday barbeque.

The whole time I was talking to Dave, Sam's friend's eyes were running all over the both of us, leaving trails along my skin wherever his gaze touched. When I finished talking, he immediately leaned forward and held his hand out toward us.

"Hi. Tall, blonde and growly here is Sam, Maia's brother," he said as he jerked his head towards Sam. "I'm Claudio, but everyone calls me Dio." He was all easygoing friendliness. Like he was a completely open book and there weren't any enemy alphas laying tied-up at his feet. I rolled my eyes and ignored his hand.

So Sam *was* Maia's brother. From what she had said about her family briefly, he had disappeared when she was a child and she'd never heard a word from him since. I was insanely curious about him and where he'd been. I only hoped him being here wouldn't break Maia's heart all over again.

Dave gave Dio a long look, assessing him while still ignoring Sam, before a smile tugged at the corners of his mouth and he reached out to shake.

"I'm Dave. Everyone calls me Dave."

What the hell, Dave? I needed to have a word with him about consorting with the enemy and acting professionally in hostage situations.

Dio's smile grew so big it lit up his face, before he threw back his head and laughed so brightly I felt reflected warmth surround me. Like I'd suddenly stepped into the sunshine out of the shadows on a cool day. It mesmerized me. I could see even Sam relax at the sound, as he shook his head slightly and smiled affectionately at his friend.

"So I take it you're in charge now?" Sam asked Dave when Dio finished laughing. The insinuation that someone else was in charge now that a man had shown up made me bristle.

"Nope. Lexie's in charge. That's the instruction Max relayed from Damon. I'm just here to back her up," Dave said, casually shrugging like it was no big deal. But I could tell he was still alert. He kept flicking his gaze to the alphas on the ground, making sure no-one was moving, and assessing the surrounding situation.

"Good call. Lexie seems more than capable," Dio countered, smiling as Dave glanced at me speculatively. Hearing Dio say my name made me shiver lightly. I reined it in, though, because Sam was back to watching me with an intent focus. As if he was trying to figure me out. Like I was a Rubik's cube and my colors were all in the wrong place.

I rubbed my hip lightly and tried to focus, ignoring them all. We should move away for this conversation, but I wasn't leaving two betas and two omegas alone to watch over the group of pissed-off alphas on the ground.

"What's the security status of the farm, Dave?" My body was still trying to sway towards the alphas, but we weren't out of danger yet and people were relying on us. I needed to shake off my hormonal crisis until I made sure everyone was safe.

Dave gave me a quick update. A few of the farm workers in the upper fields had secured the childcare cottage and had hunkered down there to protect the kids. The rest had headed for the upper and lower gates, as well as the breach point, to help keep them secure. They checked the boundary fence as they went.

We needed to do a sweep of the farm to check for more intruder alphas around the buildings, but we didn't have the manpower. Dave was pretty confident all of them were here, tied up, but we couldn't be sure.

I turned slightly to Sam and Dio, without making direct eye contact and trying not to breathe too deeply. "Damon mentioned you have back-up arriving. How soon and what can we expect?"

Sam answered me quickly, glancing at the alphas on the ground briefly as he did it. "We've got a small team in a black hawk helicopter. They'll drop men at the top gate."

Where the hell had they found fuel and how had they gotten it to pump with no electricity? I saw at least one alpha on the ground glance our way in surprise at that, too. Clearly wondering the same thing.

"I've got the rest of my squad on standby. I'd like to relocate them here and only leave a couple of guys watching the Palace. If you can accommodate us? I can have them here in a few hours."

"We can do that," I confirmed. It would stretch our food supplies, but our security was a more critical issue right now. Having a stash of food wouldn't do any good if we were all dead or captured. I looked at Dave and he nodded in agreement, looking relieved.

I knew he'd been worrying about our security manpower. He was under-resourced for the threats we'd been facing since the Crash. Our security had been set-up to deal with one or two angry men looking for their partners. Not groups of military trained alphas. As capable as Dave was, he only had a couple of young cadets, supplemented by farm hands when needed, for security.

"Okay, tell them the password to get access at the gate is, Lexie kicked an alpha in the balls." I smirked at the alpha on the ground, who was still curled around his junk while glaring at me. I heard Dio chuckle lightly.

"Can you let the gate team know, Dave?" He nodded and both he and Sam stepped away from each other to make calls. Dave from his two-way radio and Sam from a satellite phone.

"Could there be alpha-grade restraints in the PMV, Dave?" I asked him when he stepped back to my side. He looked thoughtful.

The guys had come back from the Palace last night with a stolen military truck, a Protected Mobility Vehicle, in addition to Ava and Cary.

"There's a good chance, unless they ransacked it at the Palace. We haven't looked through it yet."

I gestured for Nick to approach. He'd been keeping us in his sights, as well as the alphas and the two new omegas. I smiled at him to put him at ease. He seemed nervous, suddenly.

"Can you run to the PMV and see if there are any alpha-grade restraints in there? The keys are in the security office safe."

"Sure," he said, seeming more confident at the request. Nick could have run and hidden today, but he hadn't. He'd jumped into the fray with us, wielding a broomstick and rolls of duct tape against a unit of highly trained alphas. He'd been loyal and brave. We wouldn't forget that.

"Keep your eyes open and don't engage if you see anyone you don't know," I urged.

Nick nodded briefly before he turned and ran for the security office around the far side of the building. Max had been training Nick in our tech set-up, and I knew he would trust him with this task if he were here.

I sighed heavily as I turned to Sirena. "Can you duck inside the kitchen and let the girls know they can come out of hiding, but to stay inside until they hear otherwise? Also, give them a heads up about the military squad joining us. We'll need to increase the meal prep, plus they deserve time to prepare themselves for strange, armed alphas wandering around."

I tapped my lip as I thought about what else we needed, but stopped quickly when it drew the attention of Sam and Dio. "We'll also need to send food supplies to Damon's cottage for a while, and arrange a roster of women to pair up and monitor it, too. To make sure no men, especially alphas, are getting too close. They're going to be vulnerable while they're playing hide the sausage and it could last for days. We can't trust alphas to keep them safe. This one's on us."

Sirena looked startled that I was asking her for help. We didn't have the best history. But I honestly had little other option right now. Plus, I'd heard her tell Damon she would help, and I intended to hold her to that.

She nodded quickly and squared her shoulders, standing taller. "On it, will you be okay here for a few minutes?"

Her concern for me was surprising, given her past behavior, but she'd shocked and impressed the hell out of me in the last half an hour. I'd heard her pull a gun on Ronan and back up the guys, amongst all the white noise, while I'd been kneeling on the ground. I figured there was something major going on with her, but it would have to wait for another day to figure it out.

I nodded to her before I turned back to Sam, only to find his attention already fixed on me. As I opened my mouth to speak, he held up a finger in my face. I saw red instantly.

He was about to get a thorough tongue lashing, and not the good kind, when he suddenly spun and grabbed an alpha who thought he had seen an opening and tried to bolt. He'd somehow worked the duct tape off his legs without us noticing and sprang to his feet.

Sam was on him before he made it a single step, sweeping his leg out and dropping him to the ground with a thud that made me wince. Sam had him pinned in a heartbeat.

"Damon may not be here right now, but that doesn't mean you have nothing to fear. I will hold you down and let my girl kick you in the balls so hard you won't be able to piss without crying for a week. Do you hear me?"

Dominance rolled off Sam with raw aggression, and the alpha underneath him froze, as did the alphas nearest to him. Threat hung heavy in the air in a thickening wave that was spreading dangerously.

I'd frozen too, but in a totally different way. Sam had just referred to me as his girl, while I could feel his dominance brushing teasingly over my skin. Not in anger, though, not towards me. More like a caress. It offered protection and shelter.

It lit something up inside me and that memory of a passion fruit scent teased my senses again. Begging for release.

Shit. I needed to get a grip on myself. I needed this day to be over so I could curl up somewhere and process these new sensations that were hitting me relentlessly.

I pushed on my stomach again and I must have groaned, because Dio whipped around to face me and Dave stepped up close behind me. I leaned into Dave subtly and he let me, banding his arm around my chest to hold me close.

"I've got you," he whispered in my ear. But that only made things worse. The feel of his hot breath skating over my skin caused sparks to ignite. It was too much. My head got heavy and foggy with desire.

I stepped away from Dave abruptly, hugging my arms tight to my body, and yelled at Sam. "Can you please reign your dominance in?"

Sam sprung up and whirled around at the sound of my voice. He clenched his fists and his nostrils flared, but he looked like he was trying to get himself under control with extreme effort. Ava dashed over and re-bound the alpha's feet with duct tape, Cary shadowing her every move with the gun. I noticed him throwing glances my way, too. Checking on me.

"I would never hurt you," Sam ground out, eyes raking me and taking in the way I was standing protectively. He seemed to be unaware of what his dominance really did to me and thought I was afraid. That was a good thing. I needed it to stay that way. For now.

"Maybe, maybe not. I don't know you. But this isn't your average farm and I'm not just concerned for myself. I need you to listen right now, because you're going to have to handle this with your men if you plan on staying. This is important. When Damon inherited this farm, it was already a community, but it became more than that. It became a refuge."

That fact had always been a closely guarded secret, but the world had gone to shit and we had bigger threats we needed to protect these women against now.

"Most of the single women here, including many of the ones working in the kitchen behind us, have escaped abusive assholes. They've been through hell and came out survivors. They're some of the strongest women I've ever met, but a lot of them are still traumatized."

Dave spoke up from close behind me. "The refuge side of the farm is Lexie's doing. She finds and helps abused women. Many of them are hiding here, some of them with their kids. It's the reason we had fences and security in place before the crash. It's also the reason I'm here. To keep them safe and keep abusive assholes out."

I held my hand up to Dave, but gave him a small sideways smile so he'd know I wasn't angry at him. I appreciated his support, but I could speak for myself.

"I have no problem with you fucking up these alphas. I'll even help. I also appreciate you coming to our aid. But I will not tolerate you or any of your men scaring or intimidating these women."

I took an unconscious step closer to him in the sudden silence. My need to protect these women took precedence over my own fears for myself.

"Your dominance is going to terrify some of these women, and I won't hear of dominance barks being used against any of them. By you or any of your men. Or you'll deal with me and I'll do more than knee you in the balls. Are we clear?"

Sam looked like I'd just punched him, yet he took a step closer to me too, as if he was as drawn to me as I was to him. He was almost vibrating with dominant energy that he couldn't seem to tone down. I could feel it leaking all over the place. He ground his jaw so hard it surprised me when he didn't crack a tooth.

"Dio," he ground out.

Dio stepped up behind Sam before he'd even gotten his name out and wrapped an arm around his chest.

"Are you a survivor, too, Lexie?" Dio asked quietly, a tight focus settling over him that made me miss his easy going laugh from a moment ago.

The question took me aback and startled me. I suddenly noticed how close I was to these dangerous alphas and took a giant step back, but I ended up running into Dave.

"That's none of your business," I said rapidly, stepping to the side and moving away from all three men.

"Lex," Dave said, as he watched me carefully. He was always watching and always so careful. Except for that one time.

"No, Dave," I snapped, harsher than I meant to. My mouth was suddenly too dry. I felt raw and all my carefully constructed walls felt paper thin.

I gasped when a warm hand briefly touched my arm in support as someone moved in front of me, blocking me, and another comforting presence appeared at my side.

"Do we have a problem here, boys?" Sirena asked with more than a hint of sass, standing in front of me with her hands on her shapely hips. "You all need to take a step back."

I normally hated other people fighting my battles, but right now, I was grateful.

I looked to my side and noticed Isabella holding a bottle of water out to me. Her hand was shaking, but she'd followed Sirena out of the kitchen and was here, backing me up.

A helicopter interrupted our standoff as it flew low overhead. I'd heard a beating noise rising, but I'd just assumed it was my head pounding. Or maybe my heart.

Ava appeared at my other side as the helicopter whipped everyone's hair and clothes into disarray. Sam made a gesture with his hand and it veered away, heading up the hill. When it had passed and the noise and wind quietened, Ava was the first to speak.

"Lexi, if the back-up is here and you don't need us anymore, I'd like to take you and Cary back to our cabin and check you both over. I know the farm needs you right now, but I want to clean you up quickly and make sure you don't have a concussion and Cary doesn't have any broken bones."

"I'm fine, nothing broken," Cary said quickly, trying to hide his wince as he shifted feet, "but we do need to check Lexie over. She took a bad blow trying to help me. Thanks for that, by the way. You have some killer moves. Maybe you could teach me a few?"

I nodded at him, but before I could answer, Nick came barreling around the far corner with a case under his arm. "I got the restraints."

Dave looked between Nick, Cary and me, clearly torn and wanting to ask Cary questions about what had happened to me, but knowing we needed to act now.

I took charge before anyone else could say anything. "Thank you, Ava. I'll take you up on that, but we can do it in the kitchen behind us. There's a first aid box in there you can use to patch us both up." I shot a quick, reassuring grin at Cary and he rolled his eyes.

I turned back to Dave. "Can you handle getting these alphas into the storm cellar, with Nick, Sam, and Dio's help? Unless you have a better idea of where to put them?"

Dave nodded, looking resigned. "I need you to stay in the kitchen. Don't venture anywhere else until we give the all clear. We're still going to be stretched thin until the rest of Sam's unit arrives and while I sort out a sweep of the farm."

He turned slightly to look at me with a fake glare. "I'm serious, Lex. No one-woman commando shit, okay? There's a radio in the kitchen. Buzz me if you need anything."

I cocked my ringed eyebrow at him. "Who? Me? I don't know what you're talking about."

He just raised his own eyebrow in return before winking at me. Holy hotness, winking should be illegal on that man.

"Can you get Luis on the radio?" I asked, quickly. "He was working in the lower shed. See if he can come up to check on Bear. He's unconscious on the path behind the dining hall. We think they knocked him out with gas, but he was breathing. I'll meet Luis there, but I swear, it's as far as I'll go."

I sensed Dave knew what Bear meant to me, even if I'd never said it out loud. He nodded at me as he grabbed his radio. "On it."

"Sirena, Isabella, how are the girls? Will sticking to the kitchen a while longer be okay? Or do we need to escort them to a quiet cabin together until Dave can get the farm secured?"

Isabella reached over to grab my hand and gave it a shaky squeeze. "The girls are all holding up. Keeping busy helps, so we'll start the next meal prep. Sirena told us about Maia and her heat. I'll organize a roster to keep an eye on them. We owe Damon and the guys, and we like Maia. All the women will want to help. We'll make sure they're safe, and fed."

These women constantly amazed me. I nodded gratefully before I skated my glance across Sam and Dio. They were both staring at me intently, watching my every move, but keeping their distance for now.

I had a highly developed sense of danger, and I had no problem hiding when the need arose. I'd done it for years until I learned enough skills to run at it instead.

But right now, the danger I felt wasn't from a physical threat. It was from a threat so seductive it felt like it could change the very fabric of who I was. Change everything, forever.

I gave myself one heartbeat to gaze back just as intently. One heartbeat, one moment that seemed to hang in the air, caught in impossibilities, before I turned and walked away.

Five

I watched Lexie go, feeling torn about my responsibilities for the first time in a long time. My body ached to follow her. I wanted to hold her in my arms again and make sure she was okay. I could still feel the outline of her body where I'd held her to me earlier, like her body heat had burned itself into my DNA. It was like that anytime I touched her.

Yet, it wasn't my place. I wasn't her home. Even though I was pretty sure she was mine.

Lexie had secrets. She was hiding things I don't think her brother, Leif, even knew about. Even though they were tight.

I sensed at least one of those secrets had something to do with these two alphas, who were watching her walk away as closely as I was. Alphas didn't react to betas in this predatory, instinctive way, with their bodies constantly turned towards her and her every movement tracked. This was alpha and omega behavior.

I knew something was up. Lexie didn't back down from anyone. Even Damon, and he was the scariest bastard the world had seen in a long time. The way he had just dominated an entire unit of military trained alphas with a single bark was the stuff of legend.

I felt a similar coiled power coming from Sam now. Only Sam was leaking hot shards of dominance all over the place. Directionless and wild, but potent at the same time. This mysterious alpha who had appeared out of nowhere and claimed to be Maia's long-lost brother.

All I knew right now came from a rushed message from Max telling me Maia's brother was on our side and that Damon had taken down all the alphas with a bark. I'd hauled ass down here when Max finished up by telling me Maia was in heat so they were heading for their cottage, and that Lexie had been injured but was down here in charge.

My heart had stopped when I'd rounded the corner and Lexie all but dropped into my arms. I'd hardly breathed until she opened those gorgeous brown eyes and looked at me. Nothing in the world had mattered more in that moment.

Now I was left standing here with the two men she hadn't been able to make eye contact with and had flinched away from, as much as she had appeared drawn to them.

It had been like watching an invisible game of tug-of-war. I waited for jealousy to strike me, the way it did when any man looked at Lexie for too long. But it wasn't there. I was wary of their intentions, but not jealous, which confused the hell out of me.

Sam and Dio finally turned toward me as Lexie disappeared up the steps into the kitchen, shadowed protectively by the women and Cary, who gave us all one long, shrewd look before he too disappeared.

I narrowed my eyes at the newcomers. Dio grinned widely at me while Sam glowered. We were in a world of trouble if Dio and Hunter hit it off. They shared the same air of irrepressible mischief. Although Dio appeared more chill compared to Hunter's restless energy.

"Uh, can I get some help with these restraints?" Nick asked from behind me. I turned and strode toward him, and Nick's posture instantly relaxed. I couldn't imagine he'd been keen to restrain a dozen alphas by himself.

"Restrain them in pairs, ankles and wrists. It's harder to run when you're shackled to someone, and it will mean they can still eat and tend to themselves without us having to remove a dozen restraints constantly."

Sam grunted, which I assume meant he agreed. Together, we made quick work of restraining the alphas more effectively. More than a few watched Sam carefully, tracking his movements.

I didn't know what the hell we were going to do with a dozen captive, highly trained alphas. But I had more pressing problems.

"Nick, can you head back to the security office and watch the cameras? Buzz me if you see anything I need to know about. We can handle this."

He just nodded and turned away, looking suddenly weary. I think the adrenaline crash was finally catching up with him. Nick was a good man, and he'd done well today, considering he had no military training.

"Eat something sweet, it will help," I yelled after him. He just waved over his shoulder at me. I knew Max kept a go-pack with some emergency supplies in the security office, an old military habit. Nick would know where it was.

I turned cautiously as I heard a movement behind me. Four men in tactical gear swept out from behind the main building, guns raised. Sam instantly waved them down. They quickly pointed their weapons at the ground, but remained alert.

"What the hell? I thought they had you outnumbered and overrun?" One soldier asked as he took off his mask and stepped forward, surveying the scene in front of him. "You didn't leave any of these assholes for us to play with?"

"We were, and no. Damon didn't leave anyone standing, even I didn't get to play," Sam grumbled.

"Dammit, I wish I'd seen that," the soldier replied, scratching his head. Damon was well known in military circles, more than he realized, so it didn't surprise me these men knew who he was.

I knew how he felt, though. I wish I'd seen Damon in action too, but I'd been stuck up at the gate doing my job. Badly, as it turned out. These alphas tied up on the ground had gotten in on my watch, and I hadn't even been able to help put them down. It grated on me. Even more so that Lexie had gotten hurt.

Sam turned to me. "Do you want my men to sweep the farm while Lexie gets checked out?"

Before I could reply, the same soldier asked, "Hot damn, there's an actual Lexie? As in, Lexie kicked an alpha in the balls? I can't wait to meet her."

Sam and Dio both growled viciously at him, and Sam took a menacing step forward.

"Uh, Lexie's an omega and she's off limits. Reading you loud and clear," he stammered as he stepped back, holding his hands up deferentially.

"She's not an omega, she's a beta. But she's definitely off limits. She's Leif's sister," I said angrily, heat creeping into my voice. If they knew Damon, they'd know Leif. He was only slightly less scary, unless you really knew him.

Sam and Dio just looked at each other, doing the same silent communication thing Damon and his mates did, while Sam's team looked at each other in confusion. Clearly, Sam and Dio were acting out of character.

Fuck. This was a mess. I shouldn't be speaking for Lexie, or warning other men away. Sam and Dio definitely shouldn't be reacting to Lexie the way they were. Something was going on with Lexie and I needed to find out what, so I knew what was coming for her.

We didn't have time right now, though. I forced myself to ignore the giant Lexie shaped elephant in the room, and the men that were now giving all three of us curious looks, and concentrated on the issues at hand.

"No," I said, finally answering Sam's earlier question. "If your men can relieve the gates for the time being, I'll get my cadets and some farm workers to do a sweep. They know the farm and the people know them. If your men search the place, they're likely to get stuck with a pitchfork or hit with a frypan. These people are plucky and will defend their homes."

I gestured to the alphas sitting around us. "We'll need to take this lot to the storm cellar under the function center, like Lexie suggested. It's the most secure place we have. We can hold them there for the time being. Then we'll need to sort out lodgings for you all and rosters for security and watching the prisoners."

Sam was looking at the building behind us with a critical eye as I spoke. I knew it wasn't ideal, but it was the best option we had, and Lexie had been smart to think of it. It was one of the few buildings we had made out of stone, rather than timber.

"We'll have a community meeting in an hour and let the people know what's happened and introduce your men so they can move around more freely. Does that work for you?"

Sam nodded in agreement. "That all makes sense."

He looked at me with begrudging respect. Then he dipped his head at his men and one circled his hand in the air before they silently filtered out, without needing orders. They were a well-oiled team that had obviously been working together for a while.

None of this was what I really wanted to be talking about, but there were too many ears listening to every word we said.

I sighed, looked towards the kitchen briefly, then got to work issuing instructions over the radio and marching alphas into our new dungeon.

SIX

I sat in the empty dining room while Ava checked me over. Cary sat, half slumped over a table next to me, waiting his turn. He was absentmindedly running his finger over an old scratch on the wooden surface.

Ava and Cary had insisted on going with me to meet up with Luis. He'd taken Bear to the barn to give him fluids and monitor him after assuring me he thought he'd be fine. I knew Bear was in excellent hands.

Luis had tried to get Cary and me to come with him, so he could look us over too, but I'd told him to focus on Bear. We were fine with Ava and I didn't want to disappear right now, with so much going on.

Luis was our in-house vet, but our people had been quietly going to him with minor cuts and scrapes for years, rather than heading into town. He was the only medical help we had now.

I'd tried to stop and talk to the girls in the kitchen on our way back, but they'd all insisted they were okay and shooed me into the dining room. Some of the newer girls had looked a little shaken, but the others had their backs.

I closed my eyes for a moment, trying to center myself amongst the swirling emotions threatening to capsize me, but opened them quickly when I heard the door from the kitchen swing open with a creak.

"There you are," Nick's great grandma said as she pushed through the door. "I heard what happened with Maia. I wanted to let you know the elder women will take the day shifts watching over her cabin."

"GG, you don't have to do that. It's too much." Nick's great grandma was ancient. Nobody really knew how old she was, as she had no birth records. I'd heard that GG had grown up living in a remote community that held to the old ways and lived in harmony with the earth. She was the inspiration behind much of our sustainable initiatives around the farm. She'd been a good friend of Damon's grandfather and she'd always had a positive influence on Damon growing up, too.

GG often helped Isabella settle the new girls in as well. She had a calm wisdom about her and a no-nonsense approach to life that people gravitated towards. She was the adopted great grandma to most of the kids on the farm, many of the adults too. Anyone who lived on the farm and needed family found themselves mothered by GG at some point.

I didn't know what her actual name was. Nick hadn't been able to say great grandma when he was little, so he had called her GG for short and the name had stuck. She had the most beautiful long gray hair, usually woven into a braid hanging down her back. I'd once watched her great granddaughter brushing it reverently while sitting in the morning sun with her. GG's face showed her years, yet she wore every one of her wrinkles with pride. She'd earned them, she liked to tell me.

"Nonsense," she scolded me. "The younger women have too much to do all day. All we do is sit around and gossip. We can do that sitting outside Maia's cabin as well as we can sitting outside our own. And believe me, I still have some fight in me if any of those alphas come sniffing around."

I bit my lip, trying to hide my smile.

"It's already done. Nick will bring some comfortable chairs down and a cooler with some drinks. We'll be fine."

There was no use arguing with GG. She always got her way. GG ambled over to me. She didn't move fast, but it wasn't because she couldn't. GG was sprightly for her age. She'd just lived a long time and didn't see the point in hurrying anymore.

"Nick told me Damon wants to know about packs. Tell him to come find me when things calm down. No rush. I'm not going anywhere, anytime soon." GG laughed at her own joke, which made me smile.

"Now, let's see to you." Ava looked at me with wide eyes when GG started poking and prodding at me. "You've done a good job, girly, but she could do with some arnica cream. She's going to bruise badly. I've got some I made. I'll get Nick to bring it up to you later when he takes a break from the security room. That boy needs to get outside more."

"I can come down and get it from Nick, to save him from running around all over the farm on his break. I don't mind," Ava said.

"GG, this is Ava and Cary. They're friends of Maia's and they'll be staying with us for a while. Hopefully, for good." I shot them both a warm smile.

"I know that. I know all the gossip before you do, young lady."

She turned her gaze on Ava and searched her face as Ava froze. I didn't know about other people, but when GG stared at me like that, it was as if she was seeing past the image you carefully crafted of yourself and directly into your heart. "You're a dark horse, but you've also got a pure, strong heart, you're going to be just fine. You're a watcher, but you'll act when needed."

Ava blinked rapidly, looking stunned. "Um, thank you?"

I knew how she felt. The first time GG did that to me, I'd felt like a bunny rabbit in the open, nervously twitching like mad. She turned her gaze to Cary next. He'd sat up when GG had come in, out of respect, I imagined.

"You look like you put up one hell of a fight, boy." Cary tried to straighten his shoulders under her gaze, but winced as he moved. The adrenaline rush was wearing off, and I bet he was in a world of pain. "You need to speak up and fight when it really counts though, fight for what you want. Or you're going to end up a shadow."

Cary darted a glance at Ava, who was studiously fiddling with bandages and not looking at him. "Sometimes life is complicated," was his only answer.

"So uncomplicate it," GG huffed. "The only things that matter anymore are the people we love, and that's the way it should have always been. Besides, you may be a unicorn, boy, but that doesn't mean you're powerless. Don't let others dictate who you can be. You hold your own power, you just have to find it and learn how to use it."

Cary looked emotional for a moment as his eyes widened and went slightly glassy. I figured it had been a long time since anyone had really seen him. GG patted his arm affectionately.

"It's good you're here," GG pressed on, ignoring the sudden spike of emotion in the room. "You're all going to need each other. All four of you. Omegas need to stick together. Now more than ever."

"The four of us?" Ava's cute, pert nose had scrunched up in confusion.

GG stared right at me as she answered Ava. "You, Cary, Maia, and Lexie."

"But Lexie isn't an omega."

"Isn't she?" GG arched her eyebrow at me as she spoke, and damn, she had some serious eyebrow skills. She had me beat. I was an amateur compared to her.

I squirmed in my seat, staring unseeing at the table as my throat bobbed. GG's intent gaze made all my defenses feel like they were nothing but a sheer curtain fluttering in a breeze. She already knew the answer. She just wanted me to say it. To own it.

Meeting Sam and Dio this morning had left me feeling raw and exposed. I had no defenses left against GG. I could feel the weight of Ava and Cary watching me closely, too. A sudden dizziness washed over me, like my future was rushing towards me too fast.

"I don't really know what I am." I spoke so softly; I wasn't sure anyone would hear. It felt like my heart was talking for me. Taking over before I could decide what words would keep the truth at bay a little longer.

Ava gasped, but Cary leaned forward, intrigued.

I'd never said those words out loud before, but they'd haunted me for years. Now that they were out, I felt an unraveling inside me.

"Suppressing something isn't the same as not knowing something," GG scolded. "You've done what you had to in order to survive, but you know who and what you are. You are strong, Lexie, one of the strongest women I know. Your compassion is boundless and you've given so much. Now it's your time."

I looked up at GG finally, not quite meeting her eyes, though. "I'm scared."

She was right. I'd learned how to be fearless a long time ago, except for this. This one fear I'd never learned how to face. It had left me living a half life, and I didn't want that anymore.

"Of course you are, sweetie." GG caressed my face gently with papery soft fingers and kissed me lightly on the forehead before forcing me to look into her faded blue eyes.

I saw nothing but care and strength looking back at me. A strength she seemed willing to lend me if I needed it. It was humbling. "But you need to stop hiding and be true to yourself. Keeping things hidden for too long leaves a mark, and secrets always come out, eventually. Better to do it on your own terms than someone else's."

"I don't know how. It's not a switch I flipped."

Ava grabbed one of my hands and squeezed tightly as GG let me go. Ava smiled reassuringly when I looked at her nervously. "We'll figure it out."

I squeezed her hand back, needing the connection, and took a deeper breath as I felt the whirling dizziness fade. It was nice, feeling like I wasn't alone in this for the first time. The only person I'd ever been really close to was my brother, and I couldn't talk to him about this.

"It seems we've both got some stuff to figure out in this new world, Lexie," Cary said gently. "I've been suppressing my omega instincts for a long time, too. Not as completely as you from the looks of it, but I always made sure they didn't show and no-one could use them against me. I feel them though, so I know what it's like. It's why I gravitated to Maia at the Palace, knowing she'd done the same for so long. I'm here, if you need help."

Ava looked like she was about to cry. I shot him a sad smile. My heart hurt for him. Everyone on the farm had been tiptoeing around Cary since he'd arrived, not sure what to make of him. Especially the alphas. He was an omega, but he didn't act like one. I'd suspected he did it out of self-preservation, but it had to take a toll on him. He had plenty of experience being an object of curiosity. I figured he could use a friend, too.

"I might just take you up on that." His face lit up, as if my willingness meant something to him. I got the impression Cary liked to feel needed.

"I have an idea how you can stop hiding," GG said as she winked at me, pulling my attention away from Cary. "Pick one of those yummy young alphas out there and kiss him. See what happens."

There was a light in her eyes now, a shining spark that lit up her wizened face. She grinned wickedly, breaking the mood. I laughed, feeling lighter suddenly.

Ava giggled as a sweet blush spread over her cheeks. "I think you should give that a try, too."

I just might do that.

Seven

D ammit. Meeting Lexie felt like a gut punch. She was sexy as fuck and confusing as hell.

She pulled at me in a way I'd never felt before. My pheromones had gone wild the moment I'd heard her voice. My instincts were now screaming at me, demanding I claim her.

I'd never reacted this way to any woman, even omegas I'd met in the past. It was raw and instinctive, coming from deep within the beast that was my alpha nature.

I'd heard of scent matches between alphas and omegas. It was a sign of a true mate match and resulted in this kind of pull. From all accounts, it was incredibly rare.

But Lexie didn't have a scent, unless it was incredibly subtle, and I couldn't get close enough to her to find out for sure. She flinched or backed away from me every time I tried to get near her. Plus, Dave had said she was a beta.

It was impossible. Alphas didn't feel this primal pull towards a beta.

Sam had reacted to her the same way, too. And he rarely noticed women, even omegas. For the last few years, our assigned task and worrying about Maia had consumed him.

Now we were here, and we'd finally found his sister. I was the only one who knew just how much that meant to him. Yet he had been just as fixated on this woman as I was from the first moment she had spoken.

We'd spun simultaneously and instantly, like we were one. Like we were both hers.

I shook my head and took a deep breath. The last hour had been crazy, with attempting to get through the fence and reach Maia, the tense confrontation we'd had with Damon and his guys, Sam's shock over Maia insisting she stay here with her multiple mates, then the enemy breach and Maia acting as bait to flush Ronan out.

Now this. I didn't know what to make of it. None of this was remotely what I had expected when I'd cased this place a few days ago, looking for Maia.

As I turned reluctantly, forcing myself to focus on the task at hand, one of the tied-up alphas in the back gave me a discrete signal meant for a handler in an undercover situation. It meant they had information relevant to the mission at hand and needed to be pulled out.

I tried not to stumble in shock when he looked up briefly, through his long fall of dark hair, and I saw his face.

I yelled to the surrounding alphas to get up, grabbed the nearest alpha, and hauled him to his feet to cover my reaction. While Dave and Sam focussed on cutting duct tape from around ankles, I maneuvered myself towards him and gave the 'run' signal as I bent down.

As soon as I sliced the duct tape, he jumped to his feet and knocked me off balance, before he spun and kicked me in the stomach. He took off like a shot and I groaned.

I took off after him, blocking him with my body, not wanting Dave to shoot him, then tackled him to the ground. We tussled briefly, but he couldn't do much with his hands still tied. I quickly got my knee on his throat and growled at him.

"Problem?" Sam asked, as he stood watching me, seemingly unconcerned.

"No problem," I said. "This guy just wants to dance. I'm going to show him how it's done. You go on ahead, we're going to catch up." I winked in Sam's direction.

"Don't mess him up too bad. I don't want to be spoon feeding him," Sam replied casually and moved away. He gave me a discrete signal that meant 'do your thing' as he herded the alphas from behind, while Dave led the way.

"Punch me," the alpha mouthed to me. Well, alright then. I pulled him to his feet roughly, pushed him up against the nearest wall, then punched him hard in the stomach. He doubled over with a loud, "Oomph." I followed it up with a punch to the face I knew would create a large bruise but wouldn't cause any actual damage.

I noticed some of the intruder alphas eyeing us discretely before they rounded the back of the dining hall and disappeared.

"What the fuck, Pala. You could have pulled that kick."

"Sorry, Dio. Some of these guys are hardcore. I needed it to be convincing."

"Yeah, okay." I shrugged. I got it. He'd just winded me. I tried to take a deep breath without wincing embarrassingly.

"How the hell did I not see you in the group when we took everyone down?" I asked as I sliced through the duct tape on his wrists to free him. I couldn't stand talking to him while he was tied up.

Pala shook out his wrists lightly as he glanced up at me, his eyes running all over my face. "I recognized you and Sam as soon as you came out of the trees, but your attention was on the guys behind you. I blended into the background so I wouldn't distract you or have my cover blown if you recognized me."

"You were always good at blending into the background, but now you're like a ninja or some shit."

He gave me a shy smile that brought so many memories flooding back.

I reached up and hugged him. Not able to hold back from touching him and making sure he was really here. "I've missed you, bro."

"I've missed you too, brother. It's been too long," Pala said as he pulled me in harder with a tight grip while he rested his head on my shoulder.

Pala, Sam, and I had been inseparable in our teenage years. He'd lived on my family's winery estate growing up, so I'd known him since before I could walk and we'd been best friends. When Sam came to stay with my family in his later teens, we'd both naturally gravitated to him. Back then, Pala could calm Sam down almost as well as I could.

He'd joined the military too, but he'd gone into a different unit than Sam and I. We'd tried to stay in contact online while we all moved around, but mission protocols limited what we could say about where we were or what we were doing. Then he'd gone dark a year ago.

It had been tough, and at times I'd despaired of ever seeing him again. Wondering where he was, what he was doing, and who had his back now.

"What are the chances we'd all end up here?" I wondered as I pulled back and let him go reluctantly.

"Pretty good, considering Maia is here. I managed to get in with a team that turned up at the Palace a week or so ago. They were talking about a girl named Maia that Ronan was hunting. I remembered Sam talking about his sister Maia, so I volunteered for the incursion team when Ronan found her here. I didn't know it was her for sure, but if it was, I hoped I could find a way to help her."

"You jeopardized your mission to try and help Maia?"

"Of course," Pala said, looking shocked that I would even question it.

I swallowed hard. We hadn't seen Pala in years and the fact he would risk his mission on the chance Maia was Sam's sister, after everything he had sacrificed for it, had me feeling all kinds of ways.

"We tracked Maia here from the Palace, too. We heard the same thing on our surveillance and came to get her. It was one of our team, not Sam or I watching the feeds, or we might have spotted you there. How did you end up with the Palace team?"

"The Network got me into a division they'd had their eyes on, about a year ago. But it took me a while to work my way closer to the people who even remotely knew anything. There are circles within their hierarchy and you have to prove yourself before they'll even let you near the outer rings. The guys on the outer edge don't know shit about what's really going on. They only care that the pay's good if they keep their mouths shut."

He sighed and glanced at his feet before shaking his head. Like his memories disturbed him. I got it. Sam and I had needed to do shit we'd prefer to forget, too. It came with the territory when working undercover. It didn't make it easier, though.

Sometimes, in the still of a dark night, when everything felt so near and yet so far, my memories would press on me and refuse to let go until the sun rose. Mostly, it was all the times we'd had to look the other way to maintain our cover that haunted me. I'd sometimes wondered if any of it was worth the cost.

I stood by Pala, shoulder to shoulder, and let him have a moment while lending him silent comfort. I'd had Sam by my side through everything we'd gone through since we'd joined the military. We also had a team that we'd formed from guys who had become disillusioned with the military and were willing to back a change to the power structure.

They'd become a tight, loyal unit around us. Every single one had elected to come with us when we'd abandoned our posts and come home in search of Maia after the Crash. We'd been doing recon far from home when the Crash happened, and the journey back had been hell, yet we'd had each other.

Pala had been out there all alone, deep undercover, while the world fell apart. I couldn't even imagine how hard it must have been, and probably still was.

Pala was perfect for the job, though. He was like a ghost, able to almost disappear from right in front of you. He was always so calm and unassuming, people often didn't even notice him entering a room. Despite being one of the most strikingly handsome men I had ever met.

He had light caramel skin and glossy, straight black hair that fell past his shoulder blades, with a squared jaw and high cheekbones. His eyes were a dark brown, so deep they were almost black. When you really looked at him, it was easy to see the old soul staring back. He gave off an aura of calm strength, as if he was centuries old instead of decades.

His name meant 'water', and it suited him perfectly. He flowed around every obstacle effortlessly, taking everything in his stride. But I saw a darkness shadowing him that had never been there as a teenager.

"It's time you came in, Pala. You've done enough." I searched his face as I spoke, looking for my teenage friend in the harsher lines of the man before me.

He shook his head and looked up at me. I saw secrets and shadows staring back at me.

"I can't. Not yet."

"Why the hell not?"

"What are you planning on doing with these alphas?" He asked, turning to lean sideways against the wall and staring at me intensely. "You and Sam, you're not murderers, unless you've changed a hell of a lot since the last time I saw you?"

The question threw me. We were still reacting to the intruders, breaching the defenses on the farm just after we'd arrived. We hadn't had time to plan, or even assess, yet.

"I don't know. I don't think they're set up here to keep prisoners indefinitely. It's going to take a lot of manpower we don't have to keep that many alphas locked down. Not to mention feeding them. I imagine we'll let them go. I know it means we'll probably have to fight them later, but I don't see another choice."

Pala sighed again, deeper this time, and looked around him at what we could see of the farm from here. The lush fields cascading down the hill in the late morning sun, the winding river sparkling in the distance, the old water mill and the modern farm buildings, all framed by the forest beyond.

When Sam and I had staked the place out, the sound of laughter had drifted out to us regularly. It was so different from how the rest of the world looked and sounded right now. I'd felt an intense draw, a need to be inside even then.

It was a utopia, and the people who lived here seemed willing to go to great lengths to protect it. I didn't blame them. This place had a strong sense of home and community, and I didn't realize how much I had missed that. It reminded me of my family's winery growing up.

I forced myself to pay attention as I turned and gripped his shoulder. "Just tell me."

He said one word that froze the blood in my veins.

"Lexie."

"What about Lexie?" I grated out, feeling panic rising.

What didn't we know? I felt intensely protective of her and I'd barely spoken to her.

"Are you sure she's a beta? I saw both of you react to her the moment she spoke, and I was up the back. You fixated on her instantly. You all but abandoned your posts and everyone saw you both growl at your teammate when he showed an interest."

I tensed. This was going to be bad. I just knew it. The hairs on my arms rose as all my senses went on high alert. Pala was waiting for me to answer, as he watched me carefully. I owed Pala honesty. When the Network gave us two options for our military paths, he'd volunteered to take the darker, lonely path.

"I don't know. You're right. We both reacted to her as if she was an omega and we had a scent match, which would make her our true mate. What I felt was more intense than anything I've ever felt before. I can only assume it was the same for Sam." I had known Sam long enough to be confident about his reaction, but I would never presume to speak for him.

"Yet Dave said she's a beta, and she doesn't appear to have a scent. Her omega pheromones should have flooded the space with her scent after our alpha pheromones spiked. That's what the old stories say about scent matches. But it didn't. I couldn't detect a thing coming from her. Something's not adding up. I don't know what, but I intend to find out." They weren't idle words.

Pala was a pro at keeping his reactions contained. He had to be to work undercover. But I noticed his eyes tightened slightly and his jaw subtly tensed. "If she's an omega, it means she's been hiding in plain sight for a really long time. She's also managed to completely suppress her scent, not just mask it or hide it. The Palace is going to want her as soon as they find out. They'll be desperate to test her."

He paused, and looked at me earnestly, as if he didn't want to say what else was on his mind. He reached out and put a hand on my shoulder. "Dio, this is the endgame. Whoever is controlling the guys at the Palace are the men we've all been hunting for too many years to count. They *will* find out about Lexie as soon as these men report back. The way you and Sam reacted to her just outed her to the Palace. She's going to be in even more danger than Maia and Ava."

Pala opened his mouth, and it looked like he was going to say more, but he swallowed hard and stayed silent.

Fuck. I wanted to kill every one of those assholes right now. I could scent chili spiking the air as my wilder scent rose in response to my anger.

Pala's earthy sage scent had always been quite subtle, which helped him stay unnoticed and blend in. It was currently spiking alongside mine with a hint of pepper creeping through, though.

Interesting. My brain started running wild with possibilities. I watched him closer, but he wasn't giving anything away right now. He kept himself locked down tight. We'd been apart too long, and he either didn't trust me currently, or didn't trust himself. Both options pained me.

I shook out my clenched fists and waited for him to continue.

"On top of all that, Damon just took out Ronan. I get why, I really do. He had Damon's mate at gunpoint, and everyone knows he'd become unhinged. From what I can tell, though, his dad is a key player in all this. There will be repercussions."

Fucking, fuckity, fuck. Screaming obscenities out loud would be so much more satisfying right now, but I couldn't alert anyone to the conversation we were having. We were taking a big enough risk doing this here in the open, but neither of us knew the layout of the farm well enough to take it inside. Plus, I was going to have to get Pala back to the other alphas shortly if we didn't want to blow his cover.

Pala reached up and ran his hand through his long hair. It had always been a calming gesture for him when we were kids. The familiarity of it gave me a pang of longing. I needed him back in my life.

"I don't know what the hell Damon did back there. I've heard rumors of his dominance, but what he just did, it shouldn't be possible. Do you think he could force them to not say anything about Lexie?"

I thought about it, but I wasn't the person to ask. "I only met him an hour ago, so I don't know what he's capable of and I get the sense he doesn't yet either. That bark felt like raw power coming from a place of pure instinct. I don't know how the hell he controlled it the way he did. It left Sam and I alone, along with all his allies. I felt it slide right over me. I swear I almost heard it whisper as it passed."

"It felt a hell of a lot different for me. Dropped me to my knees like I no longer had control of my body," Pala said as a grimace briefly crossed his face.

I laughed and slapped him on the shoulder, but Pala remained serious.

"Put all of that together, and it means I need to go back and see what the fallout is from today. I need to figure out if I can do any damage control, especially with Lexie."

He shook his head in frustration. "Look Dio, I don't know exactly what caused the Crash, but I have my suspicions that the Palace crew were involved. The only reason I'm with them is because they bugged out quickly when the Crash happened and I delivered a package that day. I knew they'd been planning something big, but they kept information strictly need to know.

"I got the impression the Crash was supposed to happen in the future, though. I don't think they were prepared for it to happen when or how it did. They seemed panicked when they decamped to the Palace. They grabbed random shit that made no sense. Plus, they didn't help people on the way. I swear they almost knocked people down who ran out onto the road wanting help as we passed. It was sickening."

Pala was getting increasingly agitated, gesturing with his hands and his voice was rising, which was unlike him. It made me wonder what was really stirring him up.

"What I know for sure is that they have a secure military communication network that's outside of the Palace's servers and the normal military chain of command. It's how the Palace lab techs and the upper hierarchy of the military communicate. The Palace's own security is pretty lax, but they have this system locked away somewhere and keep information about it tight. I don't know where it is, but I need to find it. I think the answers we need are in there."

Holy fuck. If we could get that intel, it could change everything, but there had to be another way. Pala threw his head back and breathed hard, as if he was trying to calm himself, get his emotions under control. I had to resist the urge to pull him into me again. When he looked back at me, there was determination shining brightly in the dark depths of his eyes.

"Ronan didn't know how to lead a team, Dio. He was only in charge because of his dad's influence, which meant I've gotten away with a lot so far. But I don't know who they will send to replace him. We have a really fucking brief window to get this done."

He glared at me, knowing I was trying to figure out a way to stop him from going back. "Dio, it's the only way."

I nodded finally, knowing he was right. He breathed a sigh of relief, but there was also regret in his eyes. "I can't go into details now. We don't have time. You need to drag me back in there so we don't blow my cover. Do you have a stick? I wasn't able to bring mine with me."

A stick was our slang for a tiny device containing software developed by the Network that could copy and store information quickly, leaving no trace behind. It was an innocuous name for a powerful piece of tech that was way beyond anything else currently on the market.

I nodded. "I'll get it to you."

I wasn't happy about him going back, but I'd get him whatever he needed to get in and out quickly. I understood his dedication and his need to see this through. He'd worked hard to infiltrate this group, and he was the only one who could do this right now. Finding this intel could change everything for us, help us face whatever was coming.

The soldier in me got it. But as his friend, I didn't want to lose him again after just finding him. I sensed there was a lot he was leaving out, and I wanted to have his back.

"And when you get the intel, then what?" I asked. "The world is changing. It's not a time to be out there alone, without back-up."

"If I blow my cover and I have to leave the Palace, can I come here?"

It hurt that he even had to ask. I grabbed him by the neck and brought his forehead down to mine. I felt the trembling of his body reflected within my own.

"Pala, you're my brother. I know my family is big and I have about a million morons I'm actually related to, but that doesn't make you any less important."

I gripped him harder, needing him to hear me. "I chose you as my family a long time ago. Nothing has changed that. You always have a home wherever I am. I'm sorry if I haven't made that clear. I don't care if you disappear for a year or a decade. If you need me, I'm here. Even if you don't blow your cover, I want you to come home."

Pala let out a giant breath and nodded. I grabbed him for another hug, but twisted him into a headlock instead.

"I am going to have to punch you some more, though. I don't think I did a convincing job the first time," I chuckled.

He pushed me away and laughed. It lightened my heart. I'd missed that sound. He had the most beautiful, clear laugh. It made me feel like a kid again. Like he'd never been gone.

"Let's go," he said. "There's a dark-haired guy down there with a tattoo of a white rabbit on his middle finger. Can you rotate us somehow and get him paired up with me? He seems reluctant to do their dirty work. I think he may actually have a conscience, and I've been working at getting close to him. Also, don't bundle us all together if you can avoid it. I need time to talk discreetly to him without being overheard. He may be an ally."

"I'll make it happen."

As much as I didn't want to leave Pala down in the basement, it had to be done. He had a job to do, and it was important.

We both took a step away from each other, but a noise behind us had us both spinning instantly. Ava stood there with a basket in her hand.

"I didn't mean to overhear," she blurted. Her gaze was pinging between us and she looked like she was about to bolt, but she had stepped out into the open for a reason. If she had stayed put, we would never have known she was there.

Her gaze swung to Pala and stayed there. "I saw you on my way to the chicken coop to get eggs. You left food out for us at the Palace, didn't you? You knew we were in the library and you covered for us. I'm pretty sure you guarded the other omegas too, when the alphas were getting drunk."

Pala gave her the briefest nod. "Are you okay?" he asked her. His first concern was her welfare. I was so proud of him at that moment. Working undercover often compromised your morals, but Pala had clearly held onto his. It seems he had risked compromising his mission to help both Ava and Maia.

"Yes, thanks to you. I owe you, and I want to help."

"How?" I asked skeptically, as Pala remained quiet. Ava was a sheltered omega princess. I couldn't imagine how she could help us.

"I know where the server is and I know how to get to it."

I felt my mouth hanging open, and I was powerless to close it at that moment, but Pala remained perfectly calm. "Can you tell me, or draw me a map? Because I'm not taking you back to show me. I won't put you at risk."

"Yes. The Palace itself is ancient. It has a history that's far older than its current use. It's riddled with secret passageways that nobody seems to know about. I found one accidentally. One passageway connects to the hidden room with the server. I don't think they know the secret door is there. I marked a path so I could get back to it one day and try to figure out what they were hiding, but I never got the chance."

"Accidentally?" Pala asked.

Ava just gave him an enigmatic smile. I suddenly suspected Ava was a sheltered princess, about as much as Maia. She was like a swan. All grace and beauty that you wanted to stroke and pet, until you got close to her nest, then she'd bite without hesitation if she felt threatened.

"Tell me," Pala said and Ava did. She gave him a detailed description of how to find an entrance and the markings she had put in place.

"Thank you, Ava. I owe you a debt. But you need to go now, before someone comes looking for you and finds us."

It honestly surprised me Cary hadn't appeared yet. He shadowed her pretty closely.

"You really don't, owe me, I mean," she whispered before she turned and disappeared, moving surprisingly quietly and nimbly through the underbrush.

As soon as she was gone, I tied Pala's wrists again and we followed where Sam and Dave had disappeared. We quickly found a door and a flight of stairs down into the dank smelling darkness of the storm cellar. I threw Pala in at the bottom with a light growl, hoping I didn't cause any damage and sending him a silent apology.

Sam and Dave followed my lead and didn't react as I subtly maneuvered to get Pala tied up to the alpha with the white rabbit tattoo.

We got the sweep organized by Dave's team and when we had the all clear, Dave got the community meeting underway during lunch while everyone was in the dining room. He introduced us and our team to the farm residents, then reassured them all the situation was under control.

There was no animosity towards us, like I'd feared there might be. We were adding more mouths to feed and resources were in short supply everywhere. Yet these people welcomed us with open arms and gratitude.

It was clear everyone here had a lot of respect for Dave. He said we were good guys and here to help, and not a single person questioned it. They just got back to work and got on with their day. Even the teenagers had helped, spreading the message about the meeting and finding every-one in their hiding spots.

They were a giant family. They pulled together when times were tough.

Sam had watched me closely when I got into the storm cellar and I'd flicked him the all good signal. He'd just nodded. Sam trusted that I'd let him know what happened when I could and would deal with anything needed in the meantime. It meant we still hadn't talked about what happened with Lexie earlier, though.

I felt it as soon as Lexie walked into the dining room, like every atom in the air suddenly spun and gravitated toward her, trying to pull me with them. I tried not to watch her openly, not needing any more attention on us, but I tracked her movements discreetly. She gave us a wide berth, ignoring us completely.

Lexie was relaxed and open with the community, though, especially the women in the corner. They must be the women she was talking about earlier when she'd warned us off. Everyone gave those women plenty of room too, but with friendly smiles and a tip of the hat. Only talking to them if one of them approached. Everyone clearly cared about their welfare.

When Dave finished, Lexie had gotten up and reassured everyone that everything was fine in the absence of Damon and his mates. It seemed no-one was immune to her charms. People gravitated to her. She answered everyone's questions with a genuine smile and a casual flip of that gorgeous hair.

At one point, she tipped her head back and laughed loudly at something another woman said. I was completely and utterly mesmerized. The pull toward her hadn't lessened with distance and hours. It was like an incessant drumbeat in my veins pounding a rhythm of 'mine, mine, mine.'

I could sense Sam vibrating every time a man approached her, but he kept himself in check. He was still leaking dominance, though. He usually removed himself when he started leaking badly and worked himself to exhaustion with a punching bag until he had it at manageable levels.

Yet there'd been no time since the attack. I'd pulled Dave aside earlier and asked him about a gym while explaining the issue. He'd just nodded and given me directions to one he had set-up for his cadets in a shed, along with a key.

I lifted my arm away from Sam's shoulder, where I'd propped myself against him earlier trying to rescue him from his own social awkwardness around strangers, and I handed the key to him. "Go, I've got this."

He opened his mouth to argue, but I cut him off.

"Don't even try to tell me you've got this under control. I can feel you. You're about to explode. I'm used to you. These people aren't. You need to go work it off. Now."

I pushed him and he grumbled at me, but smiled gratefully.

"Just don't destroy the bag this time. I don't know where we'll get another one now," I called out as he walked away. He flipped me the bird over his shoulder and I chuckled. Sam had become known within our team for unintentionally destroying them with the force of his hits. The guys good naturedly grumbled about it.

I turned back to the room and sucked in a breath as I saw Lexie walking straight towards me like it was no big deal. She had a delicious sway to her hips that I'm sure was the envy of every runway model in existence. It was completely natural, with no artifice.

Glossy waves of pink and red hair slid around one shoulder as she tilted her head and arched a pierced eyebrow at me, daring me to say a word about her approach. I couldn't. I was tongue tied for the first time in my life. She was a goddess, not meant for this world.

She had the deepest, earthy brown eyes. I felt like they could see right through me. They were lighter than Pala's. Lexie's were shot through with gold and had a cheeky sparkle to them.

Her skin was pale, but it seemed to glow from within. Her heart-shaped face and full, apple cheekbones gave her an appearance of being young and naïve, but the dark plum lipstick on those luscious lips and the confident strut said otherwise.

I had leaned casually against a table holding water jugs and she grabbed one, filled up a glass and chugged it. As I watched, she pulled the glass away, and a drop fell to her lips. I almost groaned when her pink tongue flicked out and ran over her full lower lip to catch it.

I didn't know if she was teasing me or genuinely unaware of how damn sexy she was. I tried not to drop my eyes and check her out, but I failed miserably. She was lushly curvy, like an omega, with enough tits and ass to drive any man wild. She had plenty to hold on to. The dark fitted jeans and white tank top she had on hid nothing. Yet she was taller than a traditional omega, and she also seemed strong, as if she worked out.

"Thanks for your help today," she said in that husky, sex goddess voice of hers. I instantly flicked my eyes back up to hers, but she didn't make any further eye contact. I wanted her to look at me again more than I wanted my next breath. Nobody else existed in this moment, with her standing so close yet not touching me.

She discreetly dropped a piece of paper on the table behind the jug, glanced towards me, nodded her head at it, then turned and left through the kitchen door without another word.

I tried not to pounce on it. I really did. But I almost knocked the jug over in my eagerness to grab the note. I snatched up the tiny piece of folded paper and kept my back to the room as I opened it. It was a ripped corner of lined notepaper, and the words on it stole my breath away.

Meet me in the treehouse tonight after dinner - L.

Fuck me. Excitement lit through me as my entire world exploded into possibilities.

If there was one thing I knew for certain in that moment, whatever it was she needed, I would get for her. I would not mess this up.

I just hoped the thing she needed was us.

Eight

Sam

I 'd been pounding the bags for almost an hour, trying to work out the heightened dominance I could feel coursing through me. Usually, an exhausting workout helped lessen it to a more manageable level, so I didn't scare innocent people, but it just wasn't fucking working today.

I could feel the dominance swirling under my skin, agitated and demanding. It wanted the same thing my alpha did. The bright-haired vixen from this morning.

No matter what I did, I couldn't get her out of my mind. Everything in me felt pulled towards her and my senses were all attuned to her. Yet I had barely even spoken to her.

In the brief exchange we had, she'd clearly been less than impressed with me. Warning me away from the women in the kitchen. I appreciated the heads up about their situation. I would never want to make life harder for an abuse survivor. Yet, knowing she thought I was a danger to them, gutted me.

I gave the punching bag a vicious hit, shaking my head as it split down the side and sawdust poured out everywhere. I tried to hold it all in with my hands, but it was futile.

"Nothing a little duct tape won't fix."

I sighed before I chuckled lightly. Of course, Dio witnessed that. I'd never hear the end of it now.

"Come help me fix this up, asswipe."

"Asswipe? Really? You may want to be nicer to me. I have a date with our girl tonight."

My hands stilled on the bag, letting the sawdust fall everywhere heedlessly.

Dio has a date with Lexie?

I couldn't breathe. I was excited for him and jealous as all hell at the same time. If she was interested in Dio, did that mean she didn't want me? But he'd said *our* girl.

"Just breathe, Sam."

I felt Dio come up behind me and wrap his arms around my chest from behind. The move always calmed me down. I didn't know why, but I'd never wanted to examine it too closely. I just accepted the comfort.

"Tell me," I breathed, trying to calm my racing heart.

"Lexie slipped me a note, asking me to meet her at the treehouse later. I don't know where the hell the treehouse is, or what she needs, but I'm going to find out."

"What's with the 'our' girl?"

"Don't even try to pretend you didn't react to her exactly the same way I did. I saw you, I *felt* you."

"That shouldn't be possible," I growled as I shot him a dark look, but he was unfazed. Dio was used to my bullshit. He could see through it before my thoughts had even flickered into consciousness.

"Definitely possible, just illegal. But that shouldn't faze you. You just stole a helicopter and risked a court martial to come find Maia. What do you care about rules?"

I pushed him away with a rough laugh. But he sobered up fast and looked at me with that serious look he rarely used, but meant he was about to unload a heap of reality on my ass. Usually something I didn't want to hear.

"Yeah, I felt it, okay." I cut him off before he got started. I felt my body tense as hope flared in his eyes. The feelings I had for Lexie had me all twisted up, but the thought that I might mess this up for Dio had me terrified.

"I'm not denying it." I forced myself to look at him as I spoke. "It was like the entire world suddenly zeroed in on her. Nothing else existed, except I could feel you, right there with me. It felt like everything that mattered before suddenly didn't. Claiming her, protecting her, was all that remained. I can still feel it now, pushing at me, demanding I sink my teeth into her. My alpha feels almost feral in his need for her."

I grit my teeth, trying to keep myself under control.

"She feels like our mate." Saying the word mate out loud rocked me to my core. Being gifted a mate wasn't something I'd ever thought would happen to me, much less get to share one with my best friend. Or that we'd ever find her. It was like a dream. "Only she has no scent, and they said she's a beta. It makes no sense, Dio. It's messing with my head and my dominance won't simmer the fuck down."

I'd never felt so out of control. I knew I had issues keeping the fiery rage that thrummed through my veins at bay on a good day. Dio and Pala had been the only people who had ever made it cool down to a manageable level. Yet, I'm not sure even they understood how much anger and rage boiled below my surface constantly.

Now, it was ripping at pieces of me, wanting out. Raw determination was the only thing holding me together. I'd almost lost it when I noticed someone had hurt Lexie. When she'd kicked that alpha in the balls and I realized he was the one who had hurt her, I could have killed him on the spot, and probably would have if she hadn't yelled to stop.

Dio usually pulled me back from the brink, but he'd been a cold, determined accomplice at my side. I rarely saw that side of him.

Lexie wasn't weak, though. She was fierce. She shone brighter than the sun. I'd barely spoken to her and I already wanted her so badly it burned. Watching her stand up to me, her eyes blazing, had left desire sparking hotly through me. I could feel it, even now.

More than anything, though, I wanted her to be happy. If she wanted Dio, and only Dio, I would find a way to be okay with that. He deserved happiness, too, after all the shit I'd put him through over the years. He'd been my calm through every storm, and stood up for me more times than I could count. If I could give this to him, I would. If I stayed out of it, there was also less chance I'd mess it up for him.

I turned to him now. But he cut me off with a hand in the air before I could say a word. He knew me too well.

"Don't even think about pulling any of your self-sacrificing douche canoe bullshit. Not going to happen. We're going to figure this out. I'm happy to pave the way, if that's what it takes, but we're doing this together. Just like always. So, I'm not letting you get all up in your head about it. She's ours and we'll fight for her, together, if we have to. "

He gave me the look he used when he meant business; a slap upside the head usually followed it. "I don't care if she's an omega or a beta. I just need her. We need her. So tonight, I'm going to have a shower, shave, and rustle up some clean clothes to make myself look pretty. Then I'm going to go up there and give her anything she damn well wants."

He grabbed my face and smooched it up so that I was sure I looked like a fish sucking a lemon. "While I'm doing that, you're going to wipe off your resting dick face scowl, and practice putting on the charming face I know you have buried in there somewhere. So we can woo our girl. Got it?"

He let me go abruptly and slapped my face lightly, with an affectionate grin.

"Fine," I said with a light growl, rubbing my face. Trying not to smile.

"Before you get all pretty," I said as I ruffled Dio's hair, messing it all up while he tried to dodge me. "Tell me about Pala. Is he okay?"

"Yes, and no. Holy crap, it was good to see him. You know?" Dio's whole body softened and a goofy smile spread across his face.

I nodded as I stretched my arms across my body one at a time, not wanting the muscles to seize up after the punishing workout I'd just done.

It had taken everything in me not to react when I'd recognized Pala signaling. Dio had been closer and had beaten me to him, but I'd been a heartbeat behind him. Not knowing where Pala was or if he was okay had been an ache gnawing at me for far too long.

I missed his calm strength and wisdom. He was a soul far older than his years, even as a kid. I understood why the Network had wanted us separated when we joined the military. The three of us had been too close and too in tune with each other. It would have raised suspicion and made it hard to slip under the radar. They could pass two of us off as a close friendship. Three was too much like a pack.

We'd been young, and people we respected had convinced us it was the right thing to do. I had still regretted letting Pala go ever since the moment he hopped onto the bus that took him away. The Network had been trying to get more intel for years, but kept coming up short. So they had deemed our sacrifice necessary for the greater good. I don't know that I'd make the same choice now.

"Why, no?" I needed to know why Pala wasn't okay. I could feel a fist tightening over my heart just thinking about him being down there alone with those asshole alphas. Nobody having his back.

"Just a sense. He was holding a lot back and there were shadows in his eyes that were never there before. It's past the time for him to come home."

My heart sank as Dio told me how deep undercover Pala was at the Palace and what he was about to risk getting us their secrets and trying to protect Lexie. It sank even further when he told me Pala had asked if he could come back here if he blew his cover.

I felt like I had failed him if he didn't know where he belonged. My heart clenched for my friend. I needed to do better.

I wanted to go down to that storm cellar and yank him out right now. But Pala was his own man, who made his own decisions. I had to respect that. I'd make damn sure he knew where his home was and how to find his way back, though. His home was with us wherever we were.

"He does this last job, then we convince him to come home. Enough is enough. It's time."

"That's what I said," Dio agreed, nodding his head enthusiastically. He was like a giant puppy sometimes, but I loved him. Dio was more than my best friend. He almost felt like an extension of me, another part of me I wasn't whole without.

"Can we stage a breakout? Get him out of here quicker, before we send the rest of them back?" I asked him.

"That's a great idea. I'll talk to Dave this afternoon and make it happen tonight." Dio rubbed his hands together as his brain worked overtime, trying to figure out how to make Pala's escape credible. The world thought Dio was easygoing, and he was, but he was also a brilliant strategist.

"Tonight," I agreed, nudging the sawdust on the ground with my foot. "Then we contact the Network."

Dio nodded as he looked from me to the deflated punching bag. "For now, you need to work out some more. You're still leaking too much. Let me grab a focus mitt and you can punch the shit out of me."

He started rifling through equipment, hunting for what he needed to help me work off my dominance as I unhooked the punching bag from the roof and went to grab a broom.

So much was going to change tonight. I felt it coming. I could almost scent it. Like a wild animal sniffing the air when a storm was building on the horizon. I could feel the pressure mounting in the air. Whatever was going to happen would happen tonight, and I needed to be ready.

I felt my dominance rise again with an angry growl, undoing all my hard work on the punching bag and Dio's attempt to calm me down. Two words beat through my brain on repeat.

Lexie. Tonight.

Nine

I ran my hands lightly along the smooth timber railing. It was cool under my touch, having finally lost all the warmth it had stored from the sun earlier today.

The dark, yet open, space within the treehouse calmed my nervous excitement. This was my favorite place, the space in the world that most felt like me. There was a vibration, a resonance in this place that called to me.

I loved my little studio cabin down amongst my friends, but I also liked to come up here and unwind after a long day. Watch the dappled sunlight filter through the leaves as the world changed from bright sunshine into spectacular watercolors, then finally, star speckled darkness.

I loved dawn just as much, and I would sometimes steal up here while it was still dark to watch the day wake up and creep out from the shadows, as the magic happened in reverse.

That hour at dusk and dawn when the light was soft, yet the world seemed to glow, made dreams and fairytales feel possible.

We built the treehouse suspended between three huge old trees growing close together on the sloped land of the farm. So the back was closer to the ground than the front, but it backed onto a rocky outcrop that wasn't very accessible.

It had winding steps that followed the main tree trunk up to an enormous deck, with an enclosed fire pit to use in winter. The tree house itself was a simple A-frame, with a big main room that flowed in from the deck through sliding barn doors, a small kitchenette, bathroom and a loft room with a skylight.

I wasn't really sure why I didn't just move in here and tell the guys it was now off-limits. I didn't have a problem being alone. Even in the dark.

I shifted restlessly, and Bear nudged my leg, sensing my nervousness. He was back up on his feet, but he still seemed a little woozy. Bear was also hyper focused on me and was in full protective mode, as though he could still sense danger. Or maybe what had happened earlier had rattled him. I wasn't sure. Sometimes I wished I could read his doggy brain better.

I rubbed his head, and he leaned into my hip more, before he suddenly tensed and angled his head towards the stairs. I strained to hear, but I could only make out insects buzzing and the hoot of a nearby owl. A moment later, I heard footsteps approach through the leaf litter below, and I faded back into the shadows.

I was wearing a black t-shirt and a short, floaty black skirt with cabbage roses in the same shades as my hair. So I was hoping I would blend into the shadows. I wasn't really sure why I was hiding. I just felt the need to watch him for a moment, before everything changed.

The footsteps slowed and became tentative as they started up the steps in the darkness near the trunk. As Dio emerged slowly from the top, I took a moment to drink him in, as he stood bathed in pale light from the full moon.

He was a gorgeous man, with that dark olive skin that glowed with caramel undertones, and those beautiful sun kissed brown curls. His hair was short on the sides, but riotous curls dipped over his forehead where it grew longer on top. I had the strongest urge to wrap those curls around my fingers and tug gently.

He was wearing a pair of dark jeans and a white, tight fitting t-shirt, with chunky boots. The way the shirt seemed to draw all the moonlight as it hugged his chest had me wanting to check my chin for drool. He had a beautifully proportioned body, with wide shoulders that drew down to a trim waist. He had an athlete's build, strong and muscular, especially his thighs, without being too jacked.

His eyes were a piercing green that I could see blinking and darting around as he tried to adjust to the sudden light after the dark stairs. He knew I was here somewhere, and he was searching for me.

The thought made me want to run and see if he would chase me. I wanted to be such a bad girl, in the best way. But that wasn't why I'd asked him to meet me here tonight. Well, not yet anyway.

I needed to know what I was, once and for all. The way I had reacted with instant need to this man and his friend screamed omega. And I could sense that strange hint of a scent that had haunted my teenage years, almost pushing against my skin, wanting out.

Even now, just the sight of him had me feeling needy and aching. I'd had a healthy sex life before the Crash, but I'd only ever been with betas and I'd always kept it casual. No-one had ever made me feel like this, with just a look, before today.

I'd chosen Dio over Sam to meet tonight, even though they had reacted to me the same way, because I couldn't handle both of them together for this and there was too much power exploding from Sam for what I needed right now.

Dio had also seemed like he was the less intense, if not the less dangerous, of the two. Yet, right now, I had a feeling his smile, and that deep laugh that skated over my skin and begged me to come closer, would be my undoing.

I took a deep breath and emerged from the shadows of the tree branches on the other side of the deck. Dio stilled as soon as I moved, before whipping around to face me.

We watched each other quietly, stuck in a moment neither of us seemed willing to break. It felt like that moment, just before something momentous, when the air felt charged with hidden intent. I could almost see the sparks zapping between us.

I felt the pull getting stronger with every heartbeat as we stared at each other without moving. Then Dio suddenly smiled like I was the fucking sun appearing after a storm. Rather than breaking the mood, it amped up the desire I felt building in my blood.

His smile was addictive. It lit up his entire face and drew attention to his mouth and those full, pouty, kissable lips. I arched an eyebrow at him, but remained silent.

"You're so beautiful here in the moonlight, it takes my breath away," he said in a hushed tone, in answer to my silent question. He took a small step forward, that dazzling smile still lighting up his face. "I don't know why you asked me here, but I'm glad you did."

I watched him carefully. There was no hesitation, nothing held back, no artifice, no stealth or concealment that I could see. He just seemed happy to be here, sharing this space in this moment with me. His entire body was relaxed and completely open as he stood casually at the edge of the deck.

He was holding a messy bunch of flowers, tied loosely with kitchen twine, and I felt my heart skip a beat dangerously. Nobody had ever brought me flowers before. I didn't keep guys around long enough for them to get that confident.

They looked like the flowers we had grown around the kitchen garden to attract bees and help propagate the plants. He held them out to me now.

"I brought you these," he said. "Technically, I stole them, then brought them to you. I'm hoping nobody minds."

His impish grin told me he had zero care if anyone minded, and would probably charm them anyway if they hunted him down to object. I got the impression that smile helped him get away with a lot.

I went to take a step towards him, but Bear moved in front of me and blocked me. He had his head cocked to the side curiously. He ambled over to Dio, slower than his usual intimidating, long-loped stride when approaching strangers. I figured he was still a little fuzzy from being knocked out earlier.

"This must be the infamous Bear. Hi, Bear." Dio immediately lowered down to his knees to be more on Bear's level, showing no fear. Then stayed perfectly still while Bear gave him a thorough sniffing.

Dio let out a chuckle as he said, "That tickles, man," when Bear sniffed his neck and he copped a brush of whiskers over his cheek.

Bear immediately put his head on Dio's shoulder and let out a soft doggy whuff, before all but sitting in Dio's lap, almost knocking him over.

"You need a hug, don't you, buddy? You've had a rough day, from what I've heard. But you're such a good boy, aren't you, Bear? Protecting Lexie and the farm. We're going to be the best of friends, I can tell," Dio said to him quietly, as if the words were just for Bear.

Dio followed through as he wrapped his strong arms around Bear and hugged him gently, before running long strokes up and down Bear's back. He finished with a scratch around his head, which Bear loved. Bear kept nudging him for more, as Dio laughed, with joy lighting up his face. It was almost like watching two kindred spirits meet for the first time.

I was speechless. Bear was very protective of his people, which included everyone living on the farm, and gave all the new arrivals a thorough checking over. Some he warmed to, while others he seemed to reserve judgment on, watching them closely and giving them warning growls. Others he straight out disliked, and we were always wary of those people. Bear was an exceptional judge of character.

But I'd never seen him react to anyone, other than me, this way before. He liked Leif and his friends, and mostly followed their directions when it came to farm protection. But this was different. It was almost like he considered Dio his own pack.

Dio pulled back a little, grabbed Bear by the face, stroked it and said, "Hey Bear, why don't you get some rest while I take over watching Lexie for a while?"

I swear Bear nodded, as he whuffed gently again and nudged Dio's face. Then he slipped off Dio's lap, with amazing grace for a dog of his size. He gently picked up the flowers that Dio had rested on the ground in his enormous jaw before he turned quickly and padded over to present them to me. Dio laughed.

"Hey, you cheated. They were from me."

Bear whuffed over his shoulder at Dio, and I swear he was saying, "Too slow, loser," before he ambled over to his bed, circled twice and collapsed in a big heap. He was lights out in seconds.

I'd never seen Bear fall asleep so fast. He always seemed to have one eye open, watching for danger. But right now, he was completely relaxed, almost as if he trusted Dio to have his back.

I looked over at the man in question, one eyebrow raised again. Dio just shrugged as he got to his feet. "I like him. He's got big balls. Literally," he said as he wiped his pants where Bear had been sitting on him with a fake grimace. "He can have this bunch. It just means I'll have to bring you more."

I lifted the now slightly crumpled flowers to my face and sniffed them, trying to hide my smile. "Can we talk for a moment?" I asked him, a little breathlessly. "I have some questions."

Screw asking questions, just screw him. My instincts were screaming at me. Making my breath come out in little pants and he hadn't even touched me.

"Sure, anything you want to know, I'll tell you," Dio said as he prowled over to me. He moved with a casual, relaxed grace that belied the strength in his body. Yet his attention was wholly on me now, and he raked his gaze over me as he came closer, paying particular attention to my bare legs.

I felt goosebumps raise over my arms at the way his eyes never left me. He licked his lips as though he was imagining how I tasted.

Dio stopped close to me, but kept some distance. He pointed to a bucket of water I'd brought out, intending to water some plants on the deck, but hadn't gotten around to actually doing so.

"Is that clean water? Can I wash my hands?" I nodded, and he turned then bent forward, giving me a delicious view of his ass in his form fitting jeans.

He had the most gorgeous bubble butt I'd ever seen. It was all lush curves and my hands itched to run over it. He washed his hands quickly before shaking them out and I forced myself to look away before I got caught ogling him like a hussy.

Being a hussy wasn't something I was actually worried about. I was all for women exploring their sexuality the same way society encouraged men to do.

I just wanted to focus for a second and eyeing his butt was giving me all kinds of ideas. There was enough sexual chemistry already pulsing between us. I didn't need to add to it.

He straightened up and leaned against the railing, all casual curly haired gorgeousness, and gave me an encouraging smile as he waited for me to start my questions with a glint in his eye, like he knew I'd been checking him out.

I shook my head slightly, trying to get my horny thoughts off his ass and back on track as I laid the flowers on the railing gently. "Did you tell Sam you were coming to meet me?"

I was curious to know. I didn't want what I was about to do to come between Dio and Sam. They appeared to be close.

Dio seemed surprised by the question, but he nodded quickly as he settled in to lean against the railing. "I have no secrets from Sam. I trust him with my life."

My body relaxed a little at his words and his honesty. I'd developed an acute sense of danger from having been around it constantly as a child. I knew what it felt like, the shapes it liked to take, and what it tasted like in the air. I got no sense of danger from Dio, or Sam, despite his leaking dominance. Only that incessant pull.

Right now, I couldn't think past Dio's buttered popcorn scent hitting me on the faint breeze. It almost made my eyes roll back in my head.

"Why are you and Sam here?" I needed to know what had brought them to the farm, especially now.

"We've been tracking the people we think caused the Crash and also looking for Maia. Sam needed to know she was okay," he replied.

"How did you and Sam meet?" I knew it was an inane question, given the intense energy that was building between us with every breath, but I needed a sense of who they were. Or maybe I was just being a chickenshit and delaying the inevitable.

Dio took another small step towards me. "Is that what you really want to know? I'm happy to tell you. But what do you really need right now, Lexie? I get the sense you need more than to ask a few questions. Whatever it is, I'll make it happen."

Dio had his eyes fixed on my hands as I tapped nervously on the railing. This was an enormous leap for me, even if Dio didn't know that. I didn't let people in easily and I held my secrets close. I took a deep, steadying breath and plunged into the unknown.

"I need to know what I am. I've lived my life as a beta, but a faint scent haunted me on and off in my teenage years. Nobody else ever scented it. That they told me about, anyway."

I crossed my arms as I searched Dio's face for any sign of disbelief or derision as I was talking. I would shut this down so fast if he showed any signs of freaking out or not taking me seriously. His body was relaxed, and his scent hadn't changed. Yet his head tilted to one side, as if he was curious and wanted to know more. He nodded at me as I paused, so I kept going.

"I've never mentioned it to anyone, even my brother. I worried it was just in my head. Presenting as an omega would have been dangerous for me in the house I grew up in as well. So I ignored it and shoved down the idea every time I even thought about it. Eventually, it seemed to go away."

Dio stiffened and clenched his jaw when I mentioned my house being dangerous. "Dangerous in what way?"

I eyed Dio warily, but he was being open and honest with me and I'd only just decided to open up and ask for his help. Holding back now, as soon as things got uncomfortable, felt wrong. I needed Dio to help me figure this out, and he deserved to know what he was getting into.

"My father never hid the fact he hated my very existence. But when I hit puberty and developed what seemed to be the classic, exaggerated omega curves, he started watching me. A shady guy I'd never seen before came to the house when Leif wasn't home and checked me over. I later overheard him talking to my father about what kind of price I might fetch if it turned out I was an omega. He said he knew people who would pay well for an omega that the Palace didn't know about."

I remembered my horror at hearing the conversation. It hadn't sounded like a fate I wanted to endure. My life had already been hard enough.

"So when I started getting faint whiffs of a passion fruit scent, I panicked. My gut turned to lead every time. I started starving myself and visiting my brother's gym when he wasn't around to run for hours on the treadmill."

It hadn't been healthy, and I'd come damn close to passing out a few times, but I hadn't known what else to do. I'd been determined not to become even more of a problem for Leif.

"When an omega scent didn't present after a year or two, my father assumed I was just an unusually curvy beta and went back to being bitterly disappointed in me. The workouts became an escape, so I kept them up.

"I was never really sure if what I had scented was real, or just my imagination, but the thought of becoming an omega while living in my father's house was terrifying. Eventually, it all came to seem like some horrifying dream I'd once had. Until now."

Dio just watched me closely, his jaw ticking and a dark look in his eyes. I forced myself to uncross my arms and relax my shoulders a little. Saying this out loud for the first time was daunting, I could feel my hands trembling lightly, but it was time I dealt with it.

"Today, when I first saw you and Sam, though, the scent came back and not just a vague hint. It felt like a barrier was about to break and a torrent was going to unleash. It was the worst place and time, so I fought it, but it was a bare knuckle fight with you both so close and your scents flooding the area."

Heat flared in Dio's eyes, overriding the anger. He swayed towards me slightly before he caught himself.

"I've never reacted to anyone the way I did to you and Sam earlier. I need your help to figure out once and for all what it means."

Dio seemed pensive for a moment, as he searched my face and my posture, but then he shot me a grin so sexy it made my toes curl, and held out his hand towards me.

"I think we need to get closer if we're going to figure this out."

I needed answers, and I wouldn't get them by talking. I wanted nothing more than to take his hand and let him pull me towards him. But I needed to do this at my pace. I took another deep breath.

"I need you to stay perfectly still. Can you do that for me, Dio?"

Dio shivered lightly as he dropped his arm and shoved both his hands into his pockets to keep them still. His long eyelashes fluttered against his cheekbones as he closed his eyes briefly.

"I'll do anything you ask if you say my name again in that sexy as fuck voice of yours." Dio gave me a devastatingly potent smile that caused a dimple to pop out in his smooth cheek, and I almost melted into a giant puddle of need at his feet.

I took a small step forward and his smile grew even bigger. I mentally added that dimple to the list of things that should be illegal on men.

My legs felt like jelly as I got close enough to him to feel his body heat. His scent deepened in response, with a hint of caramel rising to the surface. I watched his face the whole time, mesmerized by that smile lit with moonlight. Half his face was in shadow, but that smile rivaled the stars floating above us.

"Hold still," I reminded him in a whisper as I stopped only inches away from him.

He nodded gently, as he watched me with wide eyes, a look of wonder stealing over his face. I leaned forward slightly, as I dipped my head into the hollow of his neck and breathed him in deeply without touching him anywhere. His breathing turned ragged and the caramel popcorn scent became more potent, making my mouth water.

"Fuck," he whispered on a long exhale. "You're killing me, Lexie."

A strand of my hair fell forward and grazed his neck. I felt his groan reverberate in my blood as it heated rapidly, taking up a pounding beat.

I felt drunk on his scent, as a tease of passionfruit entered the intoxicating mix. I wasn't sure if it was actually there, though, or just a phantom memory.

He breathed deeply as well, without moving. "I can scent your sweetness," he whispered. "It's like a hint of something just out of reach, and it smells so damn good."

So it wasn't a memory, or a figment of my imagination. I needed something more definitive, though. I pulled back slightly, catching my breath for a moment.

He stiffened when I shifted back, as if he was bracing himself from moving closer. His pockets bulged, like his hands had formed fists as he tried to hold himself back from touching me.

This sweet alpha could dominate me with barely a thought, but he was here, holding himself still, letting me do anything I wanted to him. Watching him battle to rein in his need, just to put me at ease, made my heart flutter in my chest.

"Can I kiss you? For research purposes?"

Dio's breathing sped up rapidly. "Kissing is the very least of what you can do to me, Lexie."

God, the sound of my name in that deep voice did all kinds of things to my lady bits. I had to clench my thighs together. What he made me feel without ever having touched me was primal and raw.

I moved so slowly it felt like time had become suspended in starlight, as I brushed my lips over his with the barest caress. He tasted so goddam sweet. I was suddenly ravenous.

"More, please," he groaned in a voice that had gone gravelly, sounding almost like he was in pain.

I swayed toward him just enough for our lips to brush more firmly before I opened mine and ran my tongue lightly over his full lower lip.

Dio gasped before we both exploded into action, connecting with a frantic, messy and wild kiss that was full of heat and intense need. We devoured each other with lips, tongues, and teeth as we collided.

My body erupted in a passionfruit and meringue wildfire that had the air around us sizzling with syrupy heat and Dio growling possessively.

I was an omega. There was no longer any doubt in my mind. I'd answered the question, and now I felt suddenly starved for his touch. For everything denied to me for so many long, lonely years.

I'd opened a floodgate I couldn't close, and now I had to deal with the fallout.

Ten

Lexie

Dio yanked his hands out of his pockets and anchored me to him so fast I barely even saw the movement. One hand went around my neck possessively and the other wound around my lower back as he kissed me like he needed me more than he needed to breathe.

My arms went around his neck as my entire body melted and lit up at the same time. I barely even felt it as Dio spun me and pushed me up against the railing, his mouth never leaving my skin.

My whole body was lit up as though a hundred fireworks had set off all at once. Every color of the rainbow invaded my senses as wild, unrestrained need blasted my body wide open.

I felt a seismic shift, as if the world spun off its axis and settled into a new one. Sensations, scents, sounds, all rushed me at once, as though I'd only been experiencing half the world until now. Behind it all was an overwhelming need to touch and be touched.

I tried to breathe through it, but his scent and touch branded me like he was re-writing every molecule in my body and making me his.

He drove me mindless with need as I ground shamelessly against the leg he had thrust between mine. I could feel his hard length against my upper thigh and I whimpered, needing more. So much more.

"Fucking hell, Lex," Dio moaned against my mouth before he pulled away and licked a line of hot, wet, open-mouthed kisses along my neck. He pulled my head to the side and latched onto the soft skin where my shoulder and neck met, biting firmly but not yet hard enough to break the skin, while he growled darkly.

His alpha was in control and there was only one thing he wanted at that moment. Me.

I knew this because I could feel it through a faint, shadowy bond that had sprung up inside me, connecting us. It took my breath away. My whole life I had wanted desperately to feel connected to somebody, on a level as deep as this. To belong to someone as much as they belonged to me.

I bared my neck to him willingly, mindless with need, as I felt his awe alongside his desire for me. The bond gave me a faint sense of who he was, and it matched everything I had witnessed today. His loyalty, rock-solid dependability, open friendliness, and his joy for life. Driving it all was a deep love of family.

He was a genuinely good guy, and I wanted him as my own with a ferocious need that outstripped anything I had ever felt for anyone in my life. It was pure, raw, primal possessiveness.

He startled me as he jerked his head back suddenly with a shouted curse and shook his head, fighting his need to claim me as he kept his body hard against mine. He swore incomprehensibly when I climbed him like a stripper pole and started thrusting against his hard cock.

"Dio," I moaned, doing my best impression of a porn star. I was completely gone as need shot through every nerve in my body and turned me into a wanton creature.

"Lex, tell me to stop. You have to tell me to stop now." He ground out through gritted teeth.

"Can't. Fuck me, Dio, or I'm going to die. Please." I felt so freaking dramatic right now, but I wasn't exaggerating. I felt like I would die if he didn't get inside me. My suppressed instincts were demanding immediate action as they leaked out everywhere.

"Lex," he all but begged. "If I fuck you right now, I'm going to claim you. I'm barely holding back, baby. I need you to back away, because my alpha is running the show and he wants to knot and claim his mate more than he wants to live right now."

"Okay," was all I said, all I felt capable of saying right now. He had just called me his mate and my omega was here for it. The word washed over me and settled into my bones. It felt so right, like he had always been, and always would be, a part of me.

He swore again as I ground against him harder.

I was so goddamn wet and hot and my body ached for his touch. I felt like every cell in my body was alive and alight for the first time. Every stroke, every lick, set sparks spiraling within me. I was going to burn into nothing if he didn't take care of me now.

"I need to get you inside," Dio groaned. "Your scent is going to set off every alpha on the farm. It's mouthwatering."

"Barn door. Behind you," I moaned, sounding almost desperate, which I was.

He turned and got the heavy door open while still kissing me and holding me up with one arm. It probably helped that I'd wrapped myself tight around him like one of those soft toy monkeys with the velcro hands.

We had too many clothes on. I needed to feel his skin so badly I could already taste him. My hands ran down the hard planes of his back, then up under his shirt, pulling it up and exposing acres of glorious skin just begging for my tongue. I yanked at his shirt and tried to pull it over his head while he was still trying to close the door behind us.

He helped me by pulling it over his head from the back while he had my pelvis pressed against the door. I leaned forward slightly and ripped my own shirt up and over my head, desperate to feel his skin against mine.

I started running my hands and tongue over every inch of him I could. I was so hungry for his skin right now. A kind of hunger that had me tipping towards a frenzy.

"Lex-" he started, like he was going to deny me, but I cut him off.

"Stop fighting this, Dio. I want you and I'm not so pheromone crazed right now that I don't know what I'm doing."

I grabbed his face and forced him to look me in the eye. "I've been hiding for too long, Dio. I want to be free. I want to feel everything and I want to do it with you. I choose you to be my partner in this, whatever it is. Can you do this for me, with me? The only way this is stopping is if you say no."

I barely knew the man, yet the words rang true in a way I'd never felt before. Vibrating on a level beyond my understanding, with a touch of the arcane. The sentiment felt new and ancient at the same time. Like we'd never met, yet something too potent for our minds to grasp had always connected us.

He groaned roughly, thrusting against me as he kissed me almost violently. I could faintly feel his raging need to be inside me, to meld with me and claim me. It was hammering at him the same way it was me. It felt like a tsunami was being held back by fractured glass.

"Lex," he growled. "I feel like I've been waiting my whole life for you. If you're all in, I am too."

I liked that he didn't make me beg, or doubt my clearly spoken words by asking if I was sure. He heard me and I sensed he trusted me to know my own wants and needs. "Stairs. Loft. Now," I demanded between desperate kisses.

He turned and bolted for the stairwell, sliding his hands under my skirt before grabbing handfuls of my ass and thrusting me against him as he went. I unclasped my bra and dropped it, not caring where it landed. I just needed to feel all of him against all of me.

I grabbed at his jeans and popped the button, slipping my hand inside to grab his firm length just as he reached the bottom step. It jerked in my hand and he stumbled as he felt my hand wrap around him, laughing as he caught himself on the railing before he went down.

"You are trying to kill me, aren't you, you little vixen?"

"Nuh, uh. You're no good to me dead right now," I chuckled as I clumsily stroked him while still trying to grind against him and cling on for dear life.

"I may kill you later though, so don't fall asleep," I whispered in his ear, while tracing my tongue up the edge.

He laughed against my neck, before biting and sucking on me as he toed off his boots and socks, before he adjusted his stride and took the stairs two at a time. I liked that he could laugh with me in the middle of this heated, lust soaked frenzy. It made this moment feel real, as a connection formed between us that went beyond our bodies.

Although, I could also feel the sheer power of his body as he held me effortlessly while powering up the stairs. His muscles rippled as they flexed. It amped up my need to an insane level. I was desperate to feel him thrusting into me using all of that power.

I felt weightless for a moment as he turned himself at the top of the stairs and fell backwards onto the closest mattress, bringing me down on top of him so he wouldn't crush me.

I looked down at him, startled, as he looked up at me with a mix of need and awe. I'd never had sex with an alpha, but I'd imagined their dominance would come out even more during sex and they would take what they wanted.

Dio seemed to read my thoughts as he reached up to stroke my face for a moment while he said, "Lex, I told you. I'll give you anything you need."

The tenderness in that statement and in his voice almost undid me. He'd only known me for hours, but he was looking at me like I was the only thing that mattered.

Dio wasn't just physically strong, he was also incredibly dominant. But he carried his dominance with a confident subtlety, like he didn't need to wield it all the time to know it was there.

He seemed to almost switch it on and off. I'd seen it turn on with the intruder alphas earlier, staring death at the alpha who had hit me. Yet, right now, with me, he was happily letting me take control like it was no big deal.

I'd been keeping the world at arm's length for years. Yet this alpha had crept underneath my armor with just a gorgeous smile, a delicious scent, and a hug for my giant dog. Who knew I was really so easy?

He stroked the bruises forming along my ribs, and a frown marred his gorgeous face. He looked angry for a moment before he shook it off.

"Is your head okay? No concussion?" He asked instead.

"I'm good. The dizziness and headache only lasted a little while." I had a nasty bruise forming under my hairline along my scalp as well, but I didn't want to tell him that right now.

"You say stop, and this all stops, okay? I don't care how far we've gone. I'll make it happen," he said.

I leaned down and kissed him, slower this time, savoring the taste of him as he wrapped me up tightly in his arms. I could feel his skin slide against mine and the sensation was driving me mad. Yet, I also felt how much he meant those words through that tiny, fragile bond that was growing stronger every moment we maintained skin contact with each other.

"Right now, I just need you," I said, my voice coming out a little rough, not used to showing so much emotion while being so physically exposed. My bare breasts were currently smooched against his rock, hard chest.

I sat up on a whim and straddled him, needing him to see me. Feeling wild, proud, and a little brazen. I shifted back slightly as I pulled his zipper down and pulled his hard cock out of his jeans. I raised my eyebrow at the lack of underwear.

He shrugged with an easy laugh. "I didn't have any clean underwear to change into after I had a shower. I've been living in the bush on rations for days."

"Rations, huh? Maybe I need to feed you then," I said, surprised at my own audacity. I was confident in bed, but not usually this forward. Dio made me feel as though I could ask for anything I needed, and he'd be more than happy to give it to me.

I crawled up his body slowly, noticing he became transfixed with my breasts as they passed. He started panting lightly with his mouth open as his tongue peeked out to swipe over his lip. As if he was desperate for a taste, but was holding back.

I straightened as I settled with my knees just past his face. I ruched my skirt up my thighs slowly, teasing the moment out until I exposed my black lace g-string to him.

"Eat me," I said, with a deeper, husky rasp to my already naturally smoky voice.

"Fuck, yes," he growled with a sudden intensity blazing from his eyes.

He pulled the lace aside roughly, leaning up to inhale deeply as his eyes almost rolled back into his head. "You smell like passion fruit drizzled on meringue, like the best kind of sugar high."

"How do I taste?"

He pulled me apart slowly, exposing my pussy completely to his hungry gaze. I was so wet I was practically dripping as he flicked his tongue out and tasted me.

I groaned at the sensation of his hot tongue licking gently over my core. A moment later, I felt heat bloom inside me and a sticky slickness flow down onto my thighs, shocking me.

"Oh fuck. Your slick. I've never tasted anything so good. So goddamn sweet," Dio groaned as he licked my thigh.

A slick was unique to an omega. It only happened when an omega was receptive and incredibly turned on. Given the way most alphas treated omegas, it had become a rarity, almost an urban myth.

He licked my pussy again, lapping at me in earnest, but my underwear kept getting in his way. He growled in frustration before he ripped it off my body and I gasped as the burning in my blood intensified.

I knew rationally I should probably object. New underwear was going to be hard to find now. But I didn't have the brain capacity. The feel of the lace ripping off my skin had fried it.

Dio slid his hands around to my ass and spread me from behind before he all but attacked me with his mouth, licking and sucking furiously. He alternated nips to my clit that had me seeing stars, with deep thrusts into my core with his tongue that made me moan and shift restlessly against him.

I tried to keep my skirt out of the way and hold myself up slightly so I didn't suffocate him. But he wasn't having it. He pulled me against him harder and ground me against his face as his eyes slid closed in pleasure. I could feel his rapture coming through the bond and it amped up my need until it was almost painful.

"Oh god, Dio. Yes, right there. Oh, fuck."

I could feel heat pooling in my belly and shivers wracking my whole body as the sensation overwhelmed me. My nipples were hard and aching, begging for attention.

His whole body was jerking underneath me, like he was thrusting into the air behind me. As if he was so turned on by what he was doing, he couldn't hold still. I leaned back slightly to get a better angle to thrust against his mouth and looked over my shoulder.

His cock was hard and jutting with every thrust, straining upwards from between the fly of his jeans and leaking pre-cum. It looked angry and delicious at the same time. He was thick and long, and the thought of him shoving all of that inside me made me clench on his tongue.

I felt him slide a hand around to my front and slip a finger inside me on a quick thrust, before adding a second and scissoring slightly to open me up. I moaned and ran a hand up my body to grab my breast, still staring in fascination at the size of his thick cock. Until Dio growled against my pussy, and reached up with his other hand to swat mine away from my breast.

"Mine," I heard him growl, and I looked back down to see him watching me from between my thighs with blazing eyes, all humor gone.

He chose that moment to shove inside my pussy roughly with two fingers, that he bent slightly to stroke against my inner walls. The second he stroked over my g-spot, I almost exploded. My whole body shook. I was so close.

Since the moment I'd scented them both this morning, I'd been simmering with lust. I wouldn't last long enough. I didn't want to come so quickly, and I didn't want to come without him.

I jerked backwards and slid down his body. He let me go, but he tracked every movement with predatory intent. His abs clenched as he rolled upwards to follow me, while he wiped across his glistening face with his arm. I almost growled possessively at the thought of my scent and my slick all over him. The need to mark and claim him was riding me hard.

Dio's alpha was back in control, and he wasn't letting me create any distance between us. He leaned up and flicked a wet tongue over my nipple, still keeping eye contact with me, making me shake with need.

"Need you, Dio. Now."

He leaned up further and kissed me roughly. I could taste myself on his tongue, and the depravity of it made me wild.

I shoved at his jeans roughly, but I was too far gone to pull them all the way off.

"Hang on a sec, Lex," Claudio said, trying to help me.

"Shut the fuck up and get your dick in me like a good boy," I all but growled. This was taking too long. I was losing my mind.

"Fucking hell. You're perfect," Claudio moaned as his dick jumped in response to my words.

"Hold your cock and guide it into me," I demanded, and he obeyed instantly.

I sat and lowered myself onto him. He was so thick I felt it stretching me open with a delicious burn, but my slick helped ease the way without any real pain.

I moaned and panted, bouncing on his dick while he continued to lathe his tongue over my nipples before his hands joined in, massaging and pinching in a maddening rhythm. I arched my back and thrust my chest onto his tongue, needing more friction, needing more everything, now. Needing him in every way I could have him.

I rested my hands on his shoulders, pushing myself down onto his thrusts as he struggled not to impale me too fast. I moaned loud enough for the entire farm to hear as the edge of his knot bumped against my overly sensitized clit.

Dio grabbed my hips and impatiently began lifting me and impaling me onto his dick while he thrust up from below.

I spread my legs wider and angled forward so I could rub my clit against him and he kissed me with raw need. Suddenly, he flipped us and pushed me into the mattress as his delicious weight settled over me.

"Lex," he moaned my name against my mouth. "What are you doing to me?"

He sounded wild and almost agonized. He ripped my skirt down and off, along with my ripped thong, before he lifted my legs roughly. I locked my ankles behind his back as he started pounding into me with a frenzy that pushed me further back into the soft mattress.

"Making you mine," I replied. His hard knot was rubbing against me, teasing me, and I wanted it so badly. I knew he was holding back with the last of his control, but I wanted everything he had to give.

"More. Knot me, Dio," I demanded. He growled low, deep in his chest, as if my words had sparked a primal possessiveness within him. He was almost mindless with need as he thrust roughly until his knot slipped inside with a spike of pleasure so intense I almost blacked out.

I heard him roar, and my whole body sparked with tiny fires that lit a bonfire inside me. One I couldn't hope to curb or control. His scent intensified, the caramel taking over and my meringue scent answered as pheromones flooded us both and syrupy sweetness filled the air.

I felt a wild part of my soul burst forth and I latched onto his neck with my teeth, sinking them into him and biting hard. The moment he did the same to me, I exploded with wave after wave of a pleasure so fierce it altered my very existence.

The world exploded into light as the mate bond snapped fully into place between us, connecting us on a level beyond just the physical. I felt tears run down my face at the sheer beauty of the moment, as I felt his own amazement reflected in the bond.

He was still grinding into me lightly while he had me locked onto his knot, and it caused tiny aftershocks to fire along my body.

It was almost too much, and not enough at the same time. I opened my eyes, not realizing I had closed them, to find him watching me. His open expression mirrored the awe I felt from him in the bond.

"You're mine now, no take-backs," I whispered.

"Always," he murmured back, before kissing me so gently it brought fresh tears of joy to my eyes.

He wrapped his arms around me and smiled at me, with a smile so joyous and devastating it imprinted itself onto my heart.

I didn't know what the future held for us, but I would fight to keep this with everything I had. I felt like I'd truly come home for the first time in my life.

It was scary and exhilarating, and I felt it all reflected in Dio. I knew trouble would brew from this, but at this moment, I couldn't find it in me to care.

"We'll figure it out together, okay?" He said as he brushed the tears from my face. I didn't have to tell him they were happy tears. He could feel it.

I was an omega, and my true mate had claimed me. Lying here, locked to his knot, was the only place I wanted to be.

That was, until I suddenly heard Bear barking angrily outside, followed by a ferocious roar and the sounds of a fight breaking out.

Eleven

Lexie

"Fuck." Dio cursed as he whipped his head around. "That's Sam, but I don't know who the hell he's roaring at."

We needed to get out there, but Dio had me impaled and locked on his knot. It didn't seem to bother him, though. He wrapped his arms around me and hauled me up as he rose onto his knees and then his feet. He had incredible strength in his legs.

I instinctively wrapped my legs around his waist, but he had a tight grip on me. He'd grabbed a blanket off the bed on his way up and wrapped it around me now to cover me up. Then he shuffled his feet out of the jeans that were still pooled around his ankles.

"This won't be pretty, or fast. Don't judge me, okay," Dio said with a wink as he made his way over to the stairs and hustled down them awkwardly. His knot was pulling on me deliciously and I tried hard not to moan at every step.

I could still hear the fight going on outside and Bear growling threateningly. So grinding on Dio was not a great idea right now. Plus, I didn't want him to drop me on the stairs. We got down to the main floor and out the door before his knot softened enough that I could slip off.

He gave me a quick kiss, followed by a piercing look. "Stay here, okay?"

No way was I agreeing to that, but before I could say anything, he turned and vaulted over the railing, butt-ass naked.

I gasped and rushed over, my heart hammering, convinced I'd see his broken body lying at the bottom. We were two-stories high up here. But he'd grabbed onto one of the knotted ropes my brother and his friends had installed so they could challenge each other to rope climb races. Instead of using the stairs like everyone else.

Dio was rappelling down like a damn ninja. I hoped he didn't get any rope burn on his dick, though. I had plans for it later. My gaze darted over to the clearing as I spotted movement at the bottom of the stairs, but it was too dark in the shadows to make out who it was from here.

I cursed to myself as I tried to slow my heart rate and run down the stairs while trailing the blanket I was clutching around myself. When I reached the bottom, I recognized Dave's outline in front of me, as if he was guarding the entrance. I'd spent a lot of time secretly watching him. I knew his shape, even in the darkness. Bear was growling lightly at his side.

Beyond them, illuminated in a shaft of moonlight, Dio was standing with his hand on Sam's chest. The picture they made in the moonlight took my breath away.

Dio looked like a fae creature come to taunt the devil, with his curly hair all mussed up and all that gorgeous olive skin gleaming over his sculpted back. And fuck me, that view of his perfectly rounded ass needed to have songs written about it.

While Sam behind him looked like a fallen angel. His golden blonde hair was glowing in the moonlight, and his dark blue eyes were wild as he scented the air. His tight fitting black clothes hugged him to perfection. He had incredibly broad shoulders, tapering down to a narrow waist, and his biceps were straining the stitching on his t-shirt as he clenched his fists. I half expected to see black wings sprout behind him.

Together, they looked like sin.

"Didn't Dio ask you to stay put?" Sam growled through clenched teeth, without even looking at me.

Oh no, he didn't. I straightened my spine, readying to push back.

"No. Dio told me to stay put. But I'm a big girl who can take care of herself and doesn't like to be told what to do, so here I am." I may have just mated Dio, but I wouldn't let that change me. I'd spent far too long learning how to stand on my own, to sit in a corner now.

"It wasn't for your protection, Lex. It was for Sam's," Dio said, sounding exasperated. "He caught your scent and his beast is riding him hard. He's trying to hold back, but he's not in complete control right now."

Oh. Oh shit. Dio was protecting Sam. From me.

Sam suddenly scented the air and growled low in his chest, as he swiveled his head to stare straight at me in the shadows. It wasn't an aggressive growl, though, more a darkly possessive one. Don't ask me how I knew the difference, I just did.

It was probably because of the goosebumps that growl gave me, and the way it made me ache to be claimed. I stepped towards Sam, but Bear blocked me once again. I huffed at him. "Stand down, Bear."

Bear completely ignored me. Instead, he took a step closer to Sam and Dio, intensifying his own growl in response to Sam's. Dave was a silent shadow at his side, watching the scene in front of him carefully.

Damn males, none of them paid attention when I needed them to the most. I knew from experience working with dominant alphas that I couldn't back away now that I was here. Or I'd never get Sam's respect.

I growled my frustration and took another step forward. This time, Dave shifted to let me pass and Bear moved with me instead of blocking me. Dave pulled into my side, slightly behind me. His solid presence there was reassuring. I had an urge to reach out and grab his hand, but I didn't think that would help the situation.

I looked at him over my shoulder. He had a rip in his shirt and his salt and pepper hair was all mussed up too.

"You're bleeding," I gasped as I spun to face him. I disentangled one arm from my blanket and cradled his face as I gently wiped away the blood from his split lip.

He brought his hands up to grip my waist before he stilled underneath my touch. He watched me intently. I was his sole focus at that moment.

There had always been something about Dave that drew me to him, as much as we both fought it. Not in the epic, rock my universe way that Sam and Dio did. This was a subtle, but a no less powerful draw. Dave fulfilled something in me I couldn't define.

Our eyes caught on each other, something we rarely allowed ourselves.

Bear whined, and it broke the spell we'd woven over the moment. Dave shifted back slightly as we both dropped our hands. He brushed mine lightly with his own as we moved away, though, as if he couldn't help himself.

"I'm fine," he said gruffly, still watching me.

I nodded and forced myself to turn back around and step toward Sam and Dio. Dio was eyeing Dave and I with curiosity, but Sam's gaze was hungrily devouring me. I adjusted my blanket, so it was more securely wrapped around me. Like a chunky sarong.

My step forward had put me into the moonlight, and Sam's eyes widened as he saw me fully. Standing in all my blanket covered nudity. His eyes locked onto my neck and I realized I had uncovered Dio's bite mark. Sam went as still as a statue, and his possessive growl cut off.

"You claimed Lexie," He ground out. It wasn't a question or an accusation. The statement had an echo of inevitability, almost finality. As if he'd seen this coming.

The way he said my name, though, each syllable was soaked in raw need. Achingly hungry and darkly possessive in a way that had me biting my lip and halting in place.

His eyes flicked back up to my face at the slight whimper that escaped me and a barrage of need hit me that was so intense I could almost taste it. His natural leather and woodsy oak scent had turned molten with a shot of whiskey laced through it.

It was the same scent he'd given off earlier when he was angry, and I didn't know what that meant.

Heat flooded my body at the intensity of his eyes on me, and I was instantly aching for him even though I'd had the most mind-blowing orgasm of my life mere moments ago. I had to fight the desire to drop my blanket and stand proudly naked under his scorching gaze.

"Yeah." Dio sounded almost apologetic. "I wasn't intending to tonight, but when she kissed me and her scent exploded, it was intense and my alpha went wild." He paused for a minute as he glanced back at me.

"I think we answered the question of whether she's an omega or not." Dio tried his usual deflection method, humor, but he sounded strained. He hadn't taken his hand off Sam.

Sam was still staring at me with enough heat to melt lava. Dio tried to step further between us and block Sam's view of me. But Sam moved him aside roughly with a snarl and Dio stiffened like he was preparing to fight back.

Crap on a cracker. I hadn't wanted to come between them when I chose Dio to meet me at the treehouse, but now they looked ready to throw down. I needed to fix this.

"It's my fault," I said. "I kissed him and I claimed him first."

Dave stiffened beside me, but said nothing and didn't turn in my direction. I couldn't look at him right now, either.

Sam suddenly scented the air again and swung his head back to Dio. Raking his gaze over Dio until his eyes landed on his shoulder and the fresh bite mark that seemed to be almost glowing.

"You claimed him too?" Sam growled, not looking at me, the pitch changing from angry to almost agonized.

"Yes," I said with pride. I stood tall, but spoke so softly I barely heard it myself. Sam flinched at my words. I would not apologize for my actions, though. What had happened with Dio was driven by pure instinct and I would stand by it.

I felt Sam's intense desire swirl into rage as the sharp bite of aged whiskey intensified so swiftly it stung my nose. Bear growled again, low and aggressive. Not at all afraid of the big, bad alpha.

"Shit, Sam. You've got this. Just breathe for me, man. Then we'll take a walk and go punch some more shit together." Dio all but begged as he wrapped Sam up in a giant hug, trying desperately to calm him. But we were way past breathing exercises, or hugs.

"I. Can't," Sam growled with darkness underlying each bitten out word. "Get her clear, Dio."

I naturally bristled at Sam's demand, but stayed quiet, trying not to make this worse.

"Sam-" Claudio argued.

"NOW. Dio." Sam's growl turned fractured, as if his control had splintered, as he disentangled himself from Dio with jerky movements. Dominance roiled around him, yet his desperate gaze remained locked on Dio, a silent plea in the storm.

"FUCK NO, Sam. You're about to lose it. I am not leaving you alone. I never have and I never will. Do you hear me?"

Shit. This was escalating fast. Sam was shaking, clearly at the limit of his control, and I did not want to be the reason anyone tipped over the edge. I spent my life trying to put people back together, not destroy them. I knew with sudden clarity, their truths sinking in, that I wasn't helping either of them by being here right now. My stubbornness and pride needed to be cast aside for a moment.

"It's okay, Sam. I'll go. Dio, stay with him." I raised my hands in a futile attempt to placate Sam, but it only seemed to rile him up further.

"No." Sam growled. His one word bled dark, potent fury around the clearing that made my nipples ache and my body want to sway towards him. He still refused to look at me, though. "She's your mate. Go with her. Protect her, Dio."

My heart fractured. Sam was fighting his own alpha nature in a desire to protect me. From him. Pulling away from his only support, risking losing himself in a frenzy to make sure I was safe.

"She's our mate," Dio yelled, not budging an inch in the face of Sam's rage, as if it was an old friend. "I can look after you both. I swear." Dio's voice cracked as he put one hand back on Sam's chest, over his heart, but glanced back at me. His eyes were wild, and he looked a heartbeat away from spilling his own blood if he thought it would help Sam right now. Or me.

"Dio," it was a broken whisper that ripped out of me. I could feel his fear that this was all spinning out of control, and his need for both of us. I don't even know what I was asking him for. I just didn't want him to hurt.

I'd only met them today, but I already knew I'd tear myself apart rather than hurt either of them. I took a step back, trying to make the decision for him, but it felt like moving through quicksand. Dave shifted behind me, and his hand lightly grazed over my back, lending me his strength.

"Go, Dio. I've got this," Dave said. His voice was firm and calm.

"No. You don't-"

"I've pulled dominant alphas back from the edge plenty of times. I led Damon for years. You don't know me, I get that. But I need you to trust that I've got this, Dio." Dave sounded steady and sure, as if mountains could break over him and he'd still be standing strong.

I glanced at Dio as Dave stepped forward and stood close by Dio's side, as if offering him his strength now. Dio was glancing between Dave and Sam, clearly torn.

"Sam can't calm down while he can scent and see you and Lexie, and as much as you want to, you can't take care of them both right now. So let me do what I do best while you take care of Lexie. You're not choosing between them, we're just playing to everyone's strengths right now. Okay."

"Please. Dio," Sam ground out.

Dave gently tugged the younger man back, causing Dio to drop his hand, as he looked at Dave with a strange expression. Something intense and unspoken passed between the two that I couldn't discern before Dio took a deep breath and nodded shakily. I let the breath I had been holding out in a whoosh.

"I'm trusting you with my family," Dio told Dave, transferring his hand to Dave's shoulder and squeezing hard.

"I'm trusting you with mine, too," Dave said, as he put his hand over Dio's and gripped it for a moment that felt laden with hidden words. "I won't let you down. Now go."

Dave didn't seem at all bothered about having an intense moment with Dio while Dio was naked. I assumed men got very comfortable seeing each other's bodies when they were in the military. What with group showers, dorm rooms, and such.

Dio sent one last, piercing glance toward Sam, who was standing alone with his entire body clenched. "I'm only going for now, only because you asked and Dave's here. I'll find you later. Nothing has changed. Okay. You've got this, Sam."

Dio swore quietly under his breath as he turned and moved stiffly towards me, as if that quicksand was pulling at him too. He grabbed my hand and tugged gently as he reached me, but I felt torn, too. My gaze locked on Sam in his anguish and rage.

Sam's pain pulled at my newly awakened omega instincts. They were running rampant and stampeding all over my heart. I wanted to comfort him almost as much as I wanted to punch him for demanding Dio take me away. I ached in a way I'd never felt before. His rage riled me up almost as much as his clear desire for me, just in different ways.

The barrage of emotions was confusing and overwhelming.

Dio put his hand on my face and gently diverted my attention to him. "Lex, now is not the time." He watched me with sudden, sharp concern, as if he could sense my messy emotions now that he had some distance from the barrage of Sam's. "Let Sam calm down and we'll figure it out, okay?"

I wanted to fix this. There were so many heightened emotions running through us all, I could almost taste them on the air. I could suddenly feel fear and worry coming from Dio, and I gasped.

"I can feel you." The sensation was shocking, yet the connection became stronger the longer he had his hand on me.

Dio nodded gently at me. "I can feel you too, Lex. It's fucking amazing, but right now, we need to take this inside or we're going to hurt him more. Will you come with me?"

I nodded at him, appreciating that he had asked instead of demanded. Before we left, I turned to Dave, seeking him out. I needed to know he was okay.

Dave had his back to Sam for the moment, already angled towards me. He was gazing at me with his arms crossed over his chest, making his biceps bulge.

"Good girl."

Oh god. I felt myself grow wet at his words as heat flooded me. I'd never gotten the whole praise kink thing until this very moment. Whenever anyone tried to praise me in the past, especially during sex, I'd felt like kicking them in the balls.

Yet, coming from Dave, with that look in his eye, I felt desire and need overwhelm me. I felt my nakedness underneath my blanket intensely as my nipples hardened and my slick dampened my thighs.

I'd had the urge to run and be a bad girl with Dio earlier, but now I wanted to sit at Dave's feet while he guided me to suck his dick just the way he liked it until he praised me again.

I wanted to earn another 'good girl' so badly it took my breath away. Passionfruit flooded my senses as my pheromones responded to him.

I felt, as much as I heard, Dio's strained chuckle. A split second later, though, a growl filled the air with menace once again, as Sam pushed up against Dave with his pupils blown wide.

Bollocks. It was time for me to go.

Twelve

"Bear, stay with Dave." I pointed at Dave and Bear dipped his head, almost in acknowledgement, without taking his eyes off Sam. Bear had stopped growling now that I had taken a step back, but he was still on high alert.

I yanked on Dio, who was still holding my hand, but was now looking over his shoulder at Sam worriedly. Dio followed me though, and as soon as we were back into the shadows of the stairwell, I pulled him into a hug. I wrapped my scent and my body around him and tried to soothe him.

We waited as we listened to Dave give an order to Sam. Firm, direct and to the point as he always was with his cadets.

"Cut the crap, pup. We're bugging out. Now. Move."

Dave didn't have any power behind his voice or his words, the way an alpha did with their bark. There was no dominance or compulsion for Sam to comply. Yet I didn't hear any angry response or pushback from Sam, just paws and feet shuffling through the leaf litter until they faded.

"Holy crap," Dio whispered. "How does Dave do that when he's a beta? Is there something I need to know?"

I shrugged at Dio and pulled him further into the stairwell. Not knowing how to articulate everything that Dave encompassed.

"I just trusted Dave with my best friend, who was in the middle of an epic meltdown, Lex. I need to know I didn't just make a mistake in leaving that could hurt Sam."

Dio was tugging at my hand, as if part of him still wanted to turn back.

"There's nothing specific, Dio. There's just always been something about Dave that's hard to define," I said. I tried to corral my thoughts as we took the steps slowly, the quicksand feeling easing. "All I know is that he was Leif's commanding officer, and he and his friends respected Dave. Still do. Even Damon. Enough that they trust him with the security here and listen to his advice. It means a lot because they don't trust easily. Sam's in capable hands."

I felt Dio relax slightly at my words, although he was still tense. We reached the top and stepped back out into the moonlight on the deck. Dio was gazing back the way Sam and Dave had gone, but a shooting star on the horizon caught my eye.

One thing to be thankful for with all the electricity gone. The sky was spectacular at night, especially high in the tree canopy. The night sky exploded with stars overhead, with no light pollution to dim its beauty. I would never get accustomed to it, marveling at it every time I stepped outside at night now. It always made me feel humble. Looking up into the endless expanse always seemed to make my problems seem small.

I leaned against the railing to appreciate the view for a moment and center myself amongst the vortex of emotions whirling through me. Sam's pull had lessened as he moved away, but I could still feel it gently tugging.

"What about you? What's the story with you and Dave?" Dio asked after a moment's hesitation.

I blushed as I peeked at him. He was watching me now, as if I outshone the sky. I didn't sense any jealousy from him, which was odd to me, just curiosity.

Dio reached up and brushed a stray hair behind my ear as he leaned against the railing next to me. I'm sure my hair was a sexed up mess. Dio and I had just shared an intense claiming, and I wasn't sure what tomorrow was going to bring. Yet, I knew I didn't want to start out with lies or secrets.

Plus, as weird as it was to talk about another man to him right now, Dio had just trusted Dave with Sam. His question was valid, and he deserved my honesty about him.

"Leif used to write to me about Dave when he was in the military, about how much he respected him. He wasn't in any of the photos Leif sent me, though, so I didn't know he rocked that hot dad vibe before I met him." Dio's lips twitched at my description of Dave and it lightened my heart. Seeing him so torn up about Sam hurt me.

"When they all retired, and the guys invited him to come and work here, I felt drawn to him from the first moment. Nothing happened between us, though. I'd catch him watching me a lot, but we both always held back and I was never even really sure why. I think, for me, I was unconsciously scared that letting any man I cared about too close could trigger a reaction in me and make that mysterious scent come back."

I paused, not wanting to be flippant right now or misrepresent what was between Dave and I. Dio just watched me intently while holding my hand. Hand holding had never really been my thing, but it was nice to have some skin contact at the moment, after everything we had just shared. I wasn't ready to let him go.

"Well, we held back until we kissed a few days ago. We had a community meeting that turned into a kind of party. I needed some air, so I headed outside and stepped under a tree. Suddenly Dave was there. He'd blended into the darkness and I hadn't noticed him. We kind of fell into each other and kissed without saying a word. It was hot, and intense, yet surreal. It felt like someone had suspended reality for just a moment. Just for us.

"I heard Leif call my name, and Dave quickly stepped back. I yelled at Leif that I was fine, but when I spun back to Dave, he was gone. We've never talked about it. Both of us have been pretending it never happened."

"He's an idiot, if he's had you right in front of him and never made a move," Dio said with an affectionate smile breaking through and a glint stealing into his eye. I wasn't sure if the smile was for me or Dave, though.

"Did you know him in the military?" I asked.

Dio shook his head as he brought my hand up to kiss it lightly, causing goosebumps to spread down my arm. "Not personally, but I knew of him and his reputation as being tough but fair. There was a lot of respect for him amongst the units he worked with."

It was Dio's turn to pause and take a breath, as he glanced out at the darkness surrounding us again.

"I know we only met today and we've already mated with each other. It's a lot, and it's going to take some time to adjust to that and figure out what it means for us. But I want you to know that I don't want our bond to limit you."

Dio turned his earnest gaze back to me and watched me closely to see how I would react to his words. I searched our bond and felt nothing but reassurance coming from him. I'd known monsters and Dio definitely wasn't one. There wasn't a single regret in my heart about what we'd just done. I wasn't sure what he was alluding to about limiting me, though.

I leaned into Dio and kissed him with a sweet, chaste kiss, befitting the moment, and sent back reassurance through our bond. Yet Dio pressed on. It appeared he had more to say on the subject.

"Sam is reacting to you just as strongly as I did, and there's clearly something between you and Dave. Watching Maia with your brother and his friends earlier today, proudly claiming them all as her mates blew my mind. The way they all gravitated to each other and seemed to be completely in sync was a beautiful thing. It went beyond family. Sam and I have always felt more than family to each other as well."

"I noticed you said 'our mate,' not 'my mate,' to Sam just before." When Dio had said those words, a thrill had run through me and a yearning had flared to life inside of me. Sam felt just as much mine as Dio did, but there was a vulnerability hidden within Sam's messy dominance that cautioned me to tread carefully.

"You heard that, huh?" Dio chuckled. "It kind of slipped out. I don't want to scare you or push anything on you. Whatever happens next is up to you. But I wanted you to know I'm okay if what we have extends to other people. As long as we're honest with each other."

Shit. Did Dio want to be with other people? I growled lightly at him, feeling suddenly territorial and jealous. The thought of Dio with another woman made me feel murderous. I knew that was irrational and unfair considering three men currently had me transfixed, but my hormones were out of control after being repressed for so long.

"I'm not okay with you being with other women." My words sounded choked and angry, even to my own ears, and I felt my whole body tense.

Dio instantly stepped into me and wrapped his arms around me tightly, while kissing the side of my face and nuzzling me. He was rubbing his scent all over me.

"I didn't mean like that. You're it for me, Lex. I knew it the first moment I saw you. I just meant that I'm not afraid of the word pack. If we bring other people into this, it's with you in the middle, as our omega. It's your choice. I just want you to be comfortable exploring this new part of yourself."

I didn't know what to say to that. I wasn't used to being so open about my feelings with people, and my feelings right now were all a confused mix of new instincts and wildly swinging emotions. My intense need to claim him had been pure instinct, and I hadn't thought in the moment about what that would mean for us, or for Sam and Dave.

When I didn't answer, Dio picked me up and took me through the open door into the lounge area. He fell backward onto the couch with me straddling him. I had to throw an arm out to keep myself from face planting into his chest. The blanket I had clutched in my hand moved with it, exposing my breast to his gaze.

Dio licked his lips and chuckled lightly as his eyes dipped before his gaze shifted right back to my face.

"Nice distraction, but it won't work."

"Your naked ass is on my couch," I said, trying to change the subject.

"You like my ass. I saw you ogling it earlier." He winked at me and gave me a cheeky grin, his naturally easy going personality coming back online. I knew it didn't mean he wasn't still worried about Sam, but this was his love language. Teasing.

I raised one eyebrow in question, but he just smiled at me wider, his dimple showing. *Dammit.* My stern eyebrow move usually worked to get people talking. It seemed Dio was immune to its powers. I was definitely not immune to that dimple, though.

"Talk to me, Lex. I'm not going anywhere."

"Packs are illegal. The government thinks they're dangerous," I said, needing to start somewhere simple.

"Uh, huh? I've barely known you a day, but I've seen enough to know that you're not afraid to break a few rules and bust a few balls. You live your life your own way, without apology. So why change now?"

He looked out the window for a moment, his eyes unfocused, as if he was seeing something else rather than the dark outline of trees in the moonlight. "Plus, the world outside these fences has gone to shit. It's not like anyone is going to care. The government and the military are completely missing in action."

I sighed, knowing both those points were valid. *What are you even arguing about, Lex?*

He was right. I wasn't a rule follower, especially if it was a stupid rule that didn't benefit anyone except the people making them.

"Are you telling me you wouldn't back up your brother if he and his mates call themselves a pack? The way they act, they're all but a pack, just without the title."

He had me there.

"I would back my brother up with anything he needed. Anything," I said with fierce determination.

Dio ran his hands smoothly up my legs and onto my back, calming me with long, comforting strokes up and down my spine. It didn't really have the effect he intended, though. It made me want to arch into him and stick my funbags in his face.

"I have no doubt," was all he replied, briefly flashing me with that dimple again.

I wasn't sure why this was so important to him, and why we had to discuss it now. He watched me for a moment longer, before something seemed to shift in his eyes. He pulled me into his chest and I snuggled into his neck, breathing in his comforting buttered popcorn scent.

"I grew up on a winery estate that felt very similar to this place. My whole family lived there, aunts, uncles, cousins. Some special uncles, too, that weren't related to us but lived in their own cottage right next to ours. They spent a lot of time in our home. They were often already there when I woke up in the morning. All the adults seemed to communicate without talking at times, just sharing a look. They were all very affectionate with each other too, and they all treated me like I was their son.

Dio's voice lightened as he talked about his family. I could hear the smile in it as I felt the vibrations against my cheek. There was clearly a lot of love there.

"Nobody talked about it openly," he continued. "It felt normal. It was all I'd ever known. The winery wasn't open to the public, so we had very few visitors. Our large extended family and the worker's families were our entire social circle, and we were enough. We had a small school on the estate for all the kids. It was basically an online distance school, overseen by the mums, like a lot of rural kids do.

"I never questioned it until I got older and started going out into the world. My dad sat down and had a talk with me. Told me seriously to never mention my uncles and how close they were to us. That it could cause trouble for all of them if people found out and called them a pack.

"I was confused, and I didn't get it, but I agreed. It wasn't until later that I realized they *were* a pack. But they had to hide their entire lives. Living in fear of being found out. Not even able to be open with their kids about it."

Dio tensed a little, as if he was nervous about my reaction. He was trusting me with his family's secret. I reached out and grabbed his hand where he had rested it over his heart while he was talking about his family. Gently encouraging him to keep talking. He relaxed again and pressed a kiss to my head.

"What I'm trying to say, in a long roundabout way, Lex, is I'm not afraid of being a pack, having that connection. What my family shared was beautiful, and it pains me they couldn't live openly. They weren't hurting anyone, and they definitely weren't dangerous.

"Sam knows because he lived with my grandpa on the estate for a few years. So does our friend Pala. He's been my best friend since childhood. His family worked on the estate. We all got the same talk before we left. We never really discussed why we were all so close and what it implied. Words are dangerous, even when you think you're alone, especially in the military.

"But what you and I just shared, to me, it feels like Sam, at least, should be part of it. I know you don't know him like I do and I know he can be hard to get to know. He's so full of rage, but he has his reasons. He'd never hurt anyone, though, unless he was protecting someone else.

"I just, I need you to be open to getting to know him, and open to possibilities. The thought of watching one of my closest friends share your body and your heart brings me joy. Don't write him off just yet, please."

I'd been quiet while Dio talked, respecting what he was telling me and enjoying the feeling of being snuggled into him. Feeling how our bond grew as my feelings for him deepened.

"Thank you for trusting me with your secret," I said, simply. That he would trust me with words he'd never uttered out of fear of betraying the people he loved meant the world to me.

I shrugged out of my blanket and let it fall to my side, needing to be open to him in every way right now. I slowly caressed his gorgeous, earnest face with both of my hands, stroking him gently.

"Your family sounds like a dream, Dio. Leif was the only shining light in my childhood. To have that shared connection with people I trust, a connection even stronger than family. Watching the way he and his mates are with Maia. I want that too. I never knew it was something I could even wish for.

"I'm not scared of Sam, even his rage, Dio. I kind of want to lick him when he gets all growly. Or maybe push a few of his buttons and watch him explode. I think angry sex with Sam would be hot as hell."

Dio groaned and thrust up against me subtly, shifting me slightly so that my wet heat pushed up against his hard cock.

"I've been around a lot of angry guys. To be honest, I was worried when Sam first let his dominance slip this morning. But I can feel now that he isn't the type to take it out on other people. He'd hurt himself before he would hurt anyone else. I can see that."

I sighed, trying to figure out how to articulate what I really felt. "I don't want to hurt Sam any more than you do, but he and I are both complicated people. With you, it felt like kismet the moment you stepped on that deck earlier. With Sam, our energies together are explosive. We're going to have to figure each other out before we jump into anything, despite the pull. Does that make sense?"

"And Dave?" Dio asked.

I smiled at him, and the mischievous twinkle in his eye. I got the impression he liked to push people, but he did it so charmingly you didn't even mind.

"Dave has my trust already," I said, keeping it mysterious and vague for now.

"What about your other friend, Pala? Are you planning on inviting him into my harem, too?" I asked as I ran my hand down Dio's shoulder to his chest and tweaked his nipple, hard.

"Ow," he yelped, laughing. "Pala is definitely in, too."

I tried to move my hand to his other nipple, but he caught my wrists and moved them over his shoulders to trap them between his head and the couch cushion. Before he ran his hands back down my arms and over my breasts slowly, circling my nipples so gently, I thrust my chest into his hands, needing more.

"Anyone else?" I asked as I started a slow grind on his hard cock. "Do you have any other open spots you're looking to fill in this mythical pack you're building?"

"You want more?" He asked, licking his lips.

I shook my head. "Right now, I just want you."

"What my mate wants, she gets," he said, as he flipped me onto my back on the couch and lifted my legs over his shoulder in a move so smooth I didn't even have time to protest, not that I really wanted to, before he rammed into me.

I moaned loudly, clenching my toes and grabbing onto the couch cushions to stop myself from sliding up the couch. Dio set a furious pace while maintaining intense eye contact with me, seeming to grow more frenzied with every shudder and whimper I made. The ferocity of his need, contrasted with his usual gentle nature, had me mesmerized.

"Is this what you want?" He asked, panting and grunting with effort. "If not. I can stop, anytime."

"Don't you dare fucking stop, Dio. I, oh-"

Words failed me as he lifted my hips and found an angle that made his cock hit my g-spot on every single thrust. I saw stars as an intense, brutal orgasm exploded through me, making my legs shake and my eyes roll back in my head.

Dio followed straight after, coming on a deep groan as his eyes blazed. He thrust a few more times through the aftershocks of my orgasm, sending delicious tingles spiraling through me, until he dropped my hips and collapsed on top of me.

His weight pushed me into the couch cushions, squashing me slightly, yet making me feel strangely comforted. I could feel his heart thrumming quickly in his chest as he struggled to even out his breathing.

"Happy now?" He asked, still panting lightly.

"Well, it was a little quick, but it will do for now," I gasped, trying to catch my breath.

He laughed and shot me that sexy grin as he shifted to my side. Before leaning over and kissing me thoroughly.

"In my defense, that was the hottest foreplay of my life. Watching you seducing Dave with a single touch and getting ready to throw down with Sam in nothing but a blanket with my cum and your slick still running down your legs."

I moaned. "Jesus, Dio. Give me a minute to recover before you get me all worked up again."

My pheromones were out of control, and all it took was his dirty words to have me ready to go again. The room already smelled like passionfruit meringue had a party with caramel popcorn.

"Too much? It's okay. We have plenty of time for me to practice so I can get it right," he chuckled. "But for now, wifey, we need to get you cleaned up."

"Wifey? That's not going to be a thing. Is it?" I'd never had a nickname before, apart from Lex. It was nice, but I wasn't sure about wifey.

I suddenly realized that getting married, becoming husband and wife, was what betas did and what I'd always expected to do one day. But alphas and omegas didn't get married. They mated instead, and it was for life.

I'd just had the alpha equivalent of a quickie wedding with Dio.

Dio watched the changing expressions on my face. He just chuckled as he slid off the couch and stood in one long, lean movement before he picked me up in a bridal hold.

"I have a few more fun nicknames I can try until we find the right one. We have plenty of time for that, too. Now where's the shower?"

I pointed towards the door past the kitchenette. "I can walk, you know." It was a lie. I really couldn't. My legs were like jelly, but I figured I should protest being carried around.

"I know, but, um, where's the shower again?" Dio asked after he shoved through the door and looked around at the toilet and vanity.

I giggled as I pointed to the external door. His brow furrowed adorably as I fumbled with the handle and we slipped through the door, but his eyes widened when he got a look at what was on the other side.

"Holy shit, this is gorgeous."

It really was. The door led to an enclosed rear deck that was open to the sky with four giant rainfall shower heads facing each other on either side. It also had a built-in timber bench running along the far wall with a step up to a built-in bath. It was rustic and beautiful, with the foliage from the tree canopy peeking over the edges and the stars wheeling overhead.

Leif's boyfriend Max had configured the treehouse with a combination of filtered rainwater and river water, along with solar power. He was a freaking genius when it came to technology and sustainable living. We wouldn't be functioning at all without all his expertise.

"It's official. I'm moving in with you. This treehouse is fucking incredible."

"I don't actually live up here."

"Why the hell not?" Dio looked down at me as his eyebrows almost hit his hairline.

I shrugged. "I have a little cabin near the workers on the hill, but I spend a lot of time up here. The guys and I built this treehouse as a kind of clubhouse, but they hardly ever come up now. It's mostly just me."

"Did you help design it?" He asked.

"Yeah. I did most of the design and helped the guys build it using recycled materials from around the farm. Why?"

"Lex, you designed the perfect pack house, complete with a nest upstairs, somewhere you felt safe. My mum had a nest she would go into for comfort when she needed it, or when the world was overwhelming her senses. Her pack would often stay in there with her. It wasn't until I left the estate that I realized nesting wasn't something most omegas openly did anymore."

"No. No way." I shook my head, but the truth settled into my soul as I remembered the way Maia had instinctively created herself a nest in the sunken lounge room of Leif's house after she'd met them. She'd filled the area between the u-shaped couch with mattresses, cushions and soft blankets. She'd gotten territorial when Ava, Cary, and I had approached.

I didn't like anyone going upstairs to the loft. It always made me grouchy. Even Leif and his mates didn't go up there. Dio was the first person I had felt comfortable taking up.

Dio just laughed at me again, as my mouth fell open and realization set in.

Holy freaking cow balls. I'd built myself a nest.

Thirteen

We reached the slight bend in the river where the rushing waters ebbed, the spot I had directed Sam towards. I had signaled to the workers watching the gate that we were going through and unlocked the lower gate when we reached the fence line.

It broke all our protocols, going outside the fence at night, but this was necessary. I could have taken Sam to the millpond, but it was too close to Damon's cabin where Maia was going through her heat. The women keeping watch for lurking alphas outside didn't need to hear or see Sam right now.

One of the new alphas from Sam's team had gotten turned around and came down the wrong path near the cabin earlier. GG had whacked him with a broom and chased him off. The poor guy had been so rattled, he refused to go anywhere remotely near the cabin again.

I could also have taken Sam to the hot spring, but it wouldn't have had the same effect. Sam didn't need a relaxing bath. He needed a shock to his system. The river came straight down from the nearby mountains, and the water was cold now that the weather had turned and the nights were cooler.

Sam had stalked the entire way here like the devil was riding him hard. Fists clenched and growling to himself. Or maybe he was growling at me. I didn't give a shit, though.

"Strip and get in the river," I demanded, standing steadfast with my arms crossed and giving him my best steely glare. I'd perfected it over the years, so it worked with both angry alphas and cocky cadets who thought they knew everything.

"What? You've got to be fucking kidding me," Sam snarled while glowering right back at me.

I just smiled, like I had all the time and patience in the world. I'd learned a long time ago never to react to an alpha's tantrum with anger or fear. Both riled up an out-of-control alpha even further. Ignoring their growling, like it had no effect on you, worked much better.

Many people whispered about my ability to bring a raging alpha to heel, particularly Damon. Most betas took one glance at him when he was angry and fled. I had no flashy tricks or secret superpowers, despite the rumors. Although, that would be cool. The truth was incredibly boring. I just earned their trust and respect before I tried to intervene in a situation with them.

I hadn't had time to do that with Sam yet, but I was banking on his need to win over Lexie and my close connection to her. Pissing me off was not in his best interests right now. He knew it, too, despite the pheromone fuelled swing he took at me earlier when he first scented her.

"You heard me, pup. Now."

"Stop calling me pup, for fuck's sake."

"I'll stop calling you pup when you stop acting like one. Now get in the water."

Sam muttered angrily to himself as he stripped, but he did as I asked. He needed help, and he knew it. Holding on to his riled up beast while his dominance leaked everywhere was like trying to grab water.

I could feel his dominance pushing at me, but I stood firm. I sensed he didn't want to be this angry, raging beast, the same way Damon hadn't wanted to be a cold, controlled beast that locked his emotions away.

Neither of them had any idea how to channel their overpowering dominance in a more positive way. I didn't really either, but I knew how to snap them out of a tailspin and get them to focus on their coping mechanisms.

"Fuck. It's freezing. I'm not sticking my balls in there. They'll fall off," Sam growled as he splashed into knee deep water, but stayed close to the edge.

"Do you want to be out of control, in a rage spiral every time you talk to Lex or catch her scent?"

Sam just glared at me, but he shut up.

"Not that you'll get anywhere near her in this state, because Bear and I will stand between you until you get your shit together." Bear whuffed, as if he agreed, from where he was standing at my side.

Bear was still on high alert and hadn't taken his eyes off the alpha bristling with rage in front of us. It didn't bode well for Sam. I knew Lex placed a lot of faith in Bear's instincts about people.

"I don't know if you realize this, but I'm not the one you need to convince. If Bear doesn't like you, Lex will never give you a chance. She trusts Bear more than she trusts most people. And right now, he's sending you serious fuck off vibes."

I saw Sam's eyes flicker to the dog with concern and Bear let out a well-timed growl. It wasn't the 'I'm going to bite your face off if you take one step closer,' growl from earlier. He'd relaxed slightly since Sam had moved away from Lexie. It was now more of a 'just try me, asshole,' growl.

"You'll get in up to your waist, plant your feet, then dunk your entire body. Hold it for five seconds, then surface. You can do that five times and we'll see if we need to go for ten seconds.

Sam turned and waded into the water while clenching his whole body so hard I could even see his ass cheeks pinched in. I almost laughed, but I didn't want to set him off right now.

I'd give him credit. Sam stopped when he was waist deep, then dunked himself for five seconds, following the routine I had set precisely. A beta would risk hypothermia right now, but alphas ran hotter and had more stamina. Sam could handle it.

He surfaced after the fifth dunk and I asked, "Well?"

"Again," was all he said, before he dunked again, this time for ten seconds.

When he had reached ten dunks, he turned and waded out of the water. His limbs were shaking, but he seemed calmer.

When he reached his clothes lying on the bank, he grabbed his t-shirt and started patting himself dry. I tried hard not to stare. I didn't swing that way, but he was a beautiful specimen of a man, especially in the moonlight. His pale skin seemed almost carved from stone by a master sculptor. Each muscle outlined and highlighted to perfection.

The way he submitted begrudgingly to my demands while leaking dominance had a weird reaction in my body. I wasn't interested in him, but the thought of directing him while he was fucking Lexie had me aroused.

I shook my head, trying to get the image out of my head before my hard-on became obvious and made things awkward. If I kept going, I'd need a dunk in the river.

"Feel better?" I asked gruffly, having to clear my throat to get my voice working properly, while Sam put his pants and shoes back on and slung his damp t-shirt over his shoulder.

He nodded as he looked up at the sky and took a deep breath. "Yeah. I couldn't stay away. Her scent blindsided me, though, and I was already riding the edge."

Sam turned and finally looked me in the eye. "Thank you."

I nodded, acknowledging it simply. Thanks weren't something I needed or sought. I would do anything for Lexie, including getting her potential mate to calm his farm. But I could respect a man who would give it willingly.

"Why are you helping me?" Sam asked. The question saddened me.

"Because you needed help, and I was there."

"Yeah, but you could have kicked me off the farm, sent me away. Instead, you're here helping me. That's the closest I've ever come to losing control over my beast as my rage spiraled. Aren't you afraid I'm going to hurt her as soon as you turn your back?"

I thought Sam was taunting me at first, but he was watching me with a confused expression.

"No," I said, and realized I meant it. I felt a strange kinship with this wild beast of an alpha. "I knew you weren't angry at her. You were angry at yourself."

Sam's head reared back in shock, and my sadness for him increased tenfold. Had none of his mentors or guardians trusted him to handle himself, or realized where his anger originated? I didn't know what his life had been like since he disappeared from Maia's, but I got the impression there hadn't been a lot of understanding or support. Or even help.

I wanted to kick someone's ass, but it wasn't his. He suddenly seemed very young and unsure. As if I'd shaken his world.

"Is that what you've been told all your life? That you're dangerous?"

He didn't answer, but his silence was enough. It told me everything I needed to know.

"How did you know that would work?" Sam asked, changing the subject. I let him. I needed to earn his trust before I'd get his story.

I gave him a casual shrug as I looked out to the forest, checking for movement and making sure we were alone out here.

"I used to make Damon get into ice baths when we were on tour and he was about to rip the head off one of our commanding officers. It was enough to shock his system into calming down, so he could process things and make better decisions."

Sam frowned at that. "Why do you keep comparing me to Damon?"

If he didn't know, I didn't want to be the one to tell him.

"I'll let you figure that one out," I said, as I turned and walked away. Damon's secrets weren't mine to give away. It wasn't my place, but I had my suspicions about Sam.

He and Damon were a lot alike. They just had different coping mechanisms to deal with the insane levels of dominance pouring off them. Damon trapped his inside with iron control, while Sam let his stream out, then burned it off until it was manageable.

"Can I ask you a question?"

I sighed as I turned around to find Sam standing in the same spot, not moving.

"You just did," I replied with a wink, trying to lighten the moment.

He rolled his eyes. "Who are you to Lexie?"

I stiffened slightly. There was so much I wanted to say, but couldn't. I dug the toe of my boot around in the river pebbles while I figured out how to answer that question for him when I couldn't even answer it to myself.

"Her friend and her brother's employee." It wasn't a lie, but it wasn't the whole truth.

"Is that all?" Sam asked, pushing, as if he could sense I was holding back.

"That's all you need to know." It was all I was going to give him right now. He hadn't earned my full trust yet, either.

Sam looked frustrated, but he took a deep breath and tried to settle himself.

"Did you know she was an omega?"

"I don't think anyone knew she was an omega, not even Lexie. Not for sure, anyway. Unless she was a brilliant liar, and that's one thing Lexie's not. She'll tell you plainly what she thinks, especially if you're being an idiot."

Talking about her being an omega reminded me of the moment Lexie walked out earlier with that goddamn mouth watering scent pouring off her. It had almost made me lose my mind. I'd had to fight to stay still. Scent didn't affect betas in the same maddening way it did to alphas, but it still packed a punch. At least hers did for me.

Focus, dammit.

"She started acting strange as soon as Maia showed up, and it got worse when you arrived this morning. Which makes me wonder if she suspected but told no one. Her house wasn't somewhere you wanted to grow up as an omega. It would have been dangerous for her."

"Dangerous? How so?" Sam asked with a growl. His dominance rose instantly and whiskey spiked the air.

"That's a question you'll have to ask her," I replied.

"Just tell me, does it have anything to do with Leif or anyone currently in her life?" I could almost feel him vibrating as his rage threatened to burst free again.

I shook my head and Sam narrowed his eyes at me, but nodded and the pressure against my skin eased.

"There's a more important question about Lexie you should ask me." I said.

"And that is?" Sam demanded. He was watching me so intently I felt an irrational urge to check my forehead and make sure there wasn't a hole burned through it.

I looked around at the dark forest again, feeling uneasy. No-one from the farm should be out here beyond the gates at night, but the number of fence alarms we'd had since Maia arrived worried me. Anyone else could be out there. The sound of the river should cover our voices from any betas overhearing, but I wasn't sure about alphas.

Sam shifted impatiently, and I turned back to him.

"Can you scent any alphas nearby?"

He spun his head to look at the forest, then scented the air in all directions, knowing instantly where my thoughts had gone.

"The only things I can scent are dogs and cows. The herd is nearby. I'm assuming if anyone was out there, the dogs would alert us, the same way they did for Dio and I this morning."

I relaxed slightly, but Sam was too impatient to wait for me to gather my thoughts.

"The question?" He bit out, trying not to bark at me.

"How are we going to protect Lexie from the Palace?" Sam just watched me carefully as his gaze turned speculative and his mind worked over-time. I could almost see the gears turning inside his brain.

"They're hunting Maia because she hid on a remote farm, masking and subduing her scent until she was twenty-one and betrayed by your brother," I said. Sam flinched at that, but stayed silent once again.

"What do you think they'll do when they find out Lexie suppressed her scent completely until she was twenty-four, living openly in society as a beta?"

I kicked at the rocks uselessly in my frustration, feeling like I was the one out of control now while Sam watched me carefully. I rarely let my temper get the better of me, but the attack this morning and seeing Lexie hurt had rattled me.

I didn't have the resources I needed to keep her safe, and all my connections were in the military. So I couldn't trust any of them right now, even if we could reach them.

"She'll be an even bigger target now than Maia or Ava. They'll want to run tests on her and figure out how she did it and why she's unique." The thought alone made me want to punch things.

"I'll die before I let the Palace grab any of them, but I can't protect them alone. I don't even know if Damon, Leif, Hunter and Max will be enough."

I shot a look at Sam. "Having your team here will help, but we need more. We don't know what resources the Palace can call up. We need allies."

Sam and I watched each other as I waited to see what he would say. It was my turn to narrow my eyes at him. He was far too calm, standing casually with his hands in his pockets.

My brain started trying to puzzle him out. Sam had a whole military unit with him, but they clearly weren't answering to the military right now. He had ordered eyes on the military's movements at the Palace and had backed us up against the soldiers we had trussed up in the cellar without question.

"Spill it. You have an ace up your sleeve, and I want to know what it is. We're going to need it."

I could see his lip twitch in response to either my deduction or my demand. But instead of answering me, he lifted his chin and countered with his own question.

"Why did you retire from the military? You had a decorated career as a highly respected commander. Even if you're in your early forties, I'm guessing at that, you're fit and strong. You could have worked operationally for a decade yet. Or demanded a cushy desk job higher up the chain of command. You'd earned it."

Damn. He wasn't pulling any punches with his questions tonight. I decided to be brutally honest, without giving too many details. It was the only way we were going to figure out if we could trust each other.

"I had to choose between my career and my morals. They were demanding I order my men to do things I couldn't stomach asking them to do."

"Does Damon know?"

I shook my head as I watched the river rushing past. I remembered standing on a different river bank with Damon, just before I retired, holding all my secrets inside. It felt good to let some out. "Some of it, but not all. It was my decision. That man takes on enough of the world's problems. This one was on me."

"So he's a man and I'm a pup? Good to know," Sam said with a sly grin.

"Yep, for now. Unless you prove otherwise."

"Fair enough," Sam said as he chuckled and I relaxed. If Sam was laughing right now, he had to be confident in his ability to call in reinforcements.

"Last question. Why did you trust Dio with Lexie?"

"It wasn't my call. Bear trusted Dio with Lexie. I just backed him up." I smirked at Sam. Bear whuffed gently at hearing his name and sat up. He had relaxed since Sam had gotten out of the water, and had been laying at my feet. He was still keeping an eye on Sam, though. I reached down and stroked his giant head, and he turned to look up at me.

We were in sight of the gate and I had left it open slightly in case Bear had felt the need to go back to Lexie. With Sam now calm, I wanted another set of eyes on her. I figured Dio was probably too distracted right now to keep eyes on the perimeter of the treehouse.

"Go keep watch over Lexie, Bear."

Bear looked at Sam and gave him a light warning growl before he affectionately nudged my hip with his head and took off towards the gate.

Sam sighed heavily, and his shoulders slumped. "I've got my work cut out for me with him, don't I?"

"Yep." There was no use sugarcoating it. "But it will be worth it when he accepts you into his pack."

Sam raised his eyebrow at the use of the word pack, but I ignored it.

"So, did I pass your test?" I asked.

Sam tilted his head and looked me up and down speculatively. I kept my posture open and casual, standing with my hands behind my back. It was a habit from my military days.

"What I'm about to tell you could endanger people if word got out. There are protocols and a strict vetting process for bringing new people in, but the Crash has changed everything."

I nodded at him. "Understood. You don't know me yet, but I will do almost anything to protect the people on this farm. The only line I draw is hurting other innocent people. If whatever you're involved in doesn't cross that line, your secret will be safe with me."

"I know more about you than you think, Dave. Have you ever heard of the Network?"

I sucked in a breath. "It's real?"

It was Sam's turn to give me a curt nod. "What do you know?"

"Nothing. I came across a young soldier who wasn't part of my team. He was dying from a gunshot wound while on patrol, but we weren't in an active war zone area. The kid kept mumbling, telling me to find the Network. He tried to pass me a note, but it had his blood all over it and I couldn't work out the code that was written on it. He died in my arms."

Sam tensed up at that and took a half step towards me. "When was that? Do you still have the note?"

"It was a month before I retired. I burnt the note. There were too many eyes on me at that point. I couldn't risk it being found. Somebody covered his death up and I never saw it in any official reports. I don't know what happened to his body. Not being able to bury that young man honorably is one of my biggest regrets."

"Dammit, that must have been Kenny. He was deep undercover when he made contact because he thought they'd made him. We lost contact with him before we could get him out." Sam rubbed at his face and closed his eyes for a moment, as he half turned away from me. I stood quietly and gave him space to grieve his friend.

Sam shook himself after a moment. "Thanks for telling me."

"I'm sorry I couldn't do more for him."

"Don't be. He knew what he was getting into. It's good to know he wasn't alone when he died though, he was a good man."

"Who was he working undercover for, and what is the Network?"

"People like you, mostly ex-servicemen who saw too much and got out before they lost their lives. Most of them knew something was wrong within the military, but they didn't know what. They formed a clandestine network to share information.

"It started decades ago with a few men, but it's grown to hundreds. Some recruits shared vague yet terrifying information about shady things the military was getting involved in. Including some kind of planned coup or shake-up of the current regime that involved the government as well."

I grit my teeth as he talked. What he was talking about felt all too familiar.

"There were lots of rumors, but we didn't know how or when, or even exactly what was being planned. There were too many stories that correlated, though, and a lot of disappearances. So now it includes active servicemen who are working undercover for the Network to find out more, get proof and hopefully stop whatever was being planned. It seems we were too late."

"Are you telling me the military and the government are involved with the Crash?" I asked.

"You honestly think they aren't?"

"No, I'm sure they are. I'd heard whispers and rumors as well. I've been trying to find the Network since I retired, with no luck."

"You've been on our radar for years. You were on our list of potential allies, which is the only reason Kenny would have risked trying to pass you a note as he died. Damon, Leif, Hunter and Max were on the list, too. They've been watching you all since you retired. I don't know why they hadn't made contact."

"How did you get recruited?"

"My gramps was a member. He sent me to the Network when I presented as a highly dominant alpha."

"Fucking hell, you must have been just a kid."

Sam just nodded matter-of-factly.

"That's where you've been all these years?"

"I got moved around a lot, living with original members. Mostly old men and all betas. There aren't a lot of alphas who are members, especially in the original old guard. I didn't have any stability until I went to live with Dio's grandfather. He saw how Dio, Dio's best friend Pala, and I all bonded. We were inseparable. He kept us together until we were old enough to enlist."

He seemed intensely sad just talking about it and I got the impression there was a lot unresolved there. I wanted to ask more about why his gramps had sent him away, and why it went down the way it did, with Maia in the dark. I got the feeling, though, that it was intensely personal and something he needed to talk with Maia about first.

He shook his head a little and got back to the point. "Dio, Pala and I, we were never working for the military. We were always undercover for the Network."

I needed a minute to take it all in. I'd never heard of the Network until Kenny. If the military knew about them, they were keeping it within the higher ranks. Or at least a group they didn't invite me to join. I knew there were shady units within the military, but I'd always steered clear.

"Can you still contact them? Or is the Network down, like everything else since the Crash?"

"The Network is a bunch of batshit crazy, paranoid old military men who have been prepping for the end of the world since before I was born. It would take more than the Crash to take them down. They're still out there."

I smiled at that. They sounded like my people. "Damon and his mates need to know. So does Maia."

"I know. We didn't have long to talk this morning before the attack on the farm. I plan on telling them, though, as soon as they resurface. With Max's help, making contact will be easier."

Max could definitely help with that. He was a tech genius and had stayed online during the Crash.

"I still have one more question. Who is the alpha who signaled while we were tying them up this morning? The one Dio was pretending to rough up."

Sam stepped over to me and clapped me on the shoulder, as he looked at me with a new respect. Then he grinned, and the transformation was almost shocking. His eyes sparkled and his entire face lightened. I could suddenly see the resemblance to Maia. They had the same smile.

"I'd like to introduce you to Pala, but we might not have time. He's about to escape from the storm cellar and head back to the Palace so he can sneak into their secret server connected to the military, download everything they have and get it to us before his cover gets blown."

Hot damn. I breathed deeply for what felt like the first time in weeks. We had allies, and we were back in the game.

Fourteen

I woke up slowly, curled in blankets and a hot body. A hand ran up my thigh as I stretched, but I wasn't getting distracted today.

I jumped out of bed before Dio could grab a hold of me and pull me back. We'd spent two nights and an entire day mostly naked in bed together. It had been heaven. I'd never spent so much time intimately with a man. I'd thought I would feel uncomfortable, but everything with Dio was so easy. It had been a honeymoon, of sorts.

I had shit to do though, and a farm to run.

"Hey, no fair. I was about to grope you. Get back here." Dio pretended to sulk while rubbing the sleep out of his eyes until a giant yawn broke through. He looked sleepy, rumpled, and adorable.

I turned my back on him as I tried to figure out where my clothes were. I couldn't look at him or I'd fall back into bed. The sexual high of the last thirty-six hours had been intense, but I felt like it had helped to settle the explosion of omega pheromones and instincts that had almost overwhelmed me the first night.

"You know that view is no less of a turn-on," he said to my back as I bent over to search through the bedding. I smirked to myself, silently preening under his praise. What a guy thought about my body had never been something I'd really cared about before. I'd only ever cared that I was fit and strong.

Yet the obvious pleasure Dio showed whenever he got his hands on me, or even looked at me, fulfilled something in me I didn't even know was missing.

"Did I tell you I love your tattoo?" He asked.

I halted my search through the blankets and turned sideways to him, looking down at the tattoo on my hip that read *I am the storm*, in a cursive script.

"I noticed when we first met you that you rubbed your hip a lot. I thought it was an injury at first. But then I got you naked and noticed the tattoo. It's from a quote, isn't it? *The devil whispered in my ear, you cannot survive the storm, today I whispered back I am the storm.* Is that right?"

"Something like that. There are a few variations around," I said as I stroked it, feeling the power the words held over me. "I don't always notice, but I rub it when I need to remind myself I'm strong."

"When did you get it?"

"When my dad forced Leif to join the military, Leif moved me out of home and got me set up on my own. We'd both worked part-time and saved our money, so we had enough to pay my bond and the first few months of rent. He sent me most of his military pay after that to help keep me afloat. I got the tattoo the day he left. It was my sixteenth birthday."

"Fuck, Lex." Dio jumped up and pulled me into his arms. He looked angry and as if he had a million questions he wanted to ask, but he was pursing his lips, holding them in.

"It's okay, it wasn't a bad thing, Dio. It was an escape and a celebration. I felt free for the first time in my life. I was determined to never need someone else to protect me again, and I could finally figure out how to do that.

"Leif spent his entire childhood protecting me, putting himself between me and our father. I missed Leif terribly at first, and I worried about him in the military because he has such a gentle nature. But he found his family there, and they had his back."

Dio stroked my hair gently. He'd become fixated with it. He often ran his hands through it and watched the pink, purple, and red shades fall through his fingers with a smile.

"Just because you learned to protect yourself doesn't mean you don't deserve people in your corner, Lex. You shine so brightly, and you're so strong. At the very least, you need someone around to worship you, and I'm the perfect man for the job."

I slapped him on the chest lightly, jokingly, to deflect how emotional those words made me feel. But any contact with Dio's skin just made me want to purr and rub all over him. He'd just spent thirty-six hours worshiping my body, proving he meant what he said, but those words and the feeling behind them in the bond felt incredibly intimate. I wasn't used to hearing such loving words, even humorous ones.

I briefly considered telling him to get on his knees if he wanted to worship me, but then we'd never leave the treehouse. So I gently pushed him away instead, with a feather soft kiss and a smile. "I'll keep that in mind, big boy."

"Big boy, huh? I'm okay with that nickname. We can keep that one."

I laughed. We'd been teasing each other with atrocious nicknames in between bouts of sexy times.

I appreciated him not asking more about my dad right now. We hadn't really talked in depth about our childhoods. We'd been too busy knocking boots. It was a conversation that would come; I knew that, but we had time. The thought filled me with joy.

I finally remembered the antique chest in the corner and headed over to it. There were clothes in there for me, Leif, and his mates, that I'd put there in the past. I liked to stash things for emergencies. I knew it was a habit I should have long since given up, but it comforted me and made me feel prepared.

I squealed like an excited toddler when I found my old favorite pair of denim overalls. They were baggy and soft, yet perfectly worn in. I'd been wondering where they went. I grabbed a white cropped t-shirt out as well, along with some new underwear still in its packaging. Like I said, I liked to stash for emergencies.

I threw a pair of jeans and a tee, along with some new underwear, at Dio. He looked at me strangely.

"Uh, whose are these? Did you have sleepovers up here with someone?"

I could see his mind working, trying to figure out who I may have had up here. I got a flare of jealousy and possessiveness through the bond that wasn't there when he mentioned Sam or Dave. Or even the mysterious Pala.

"Calm down. The clothes are clean old ones of the guys, but the underwear was new, just in case anyone needed them."

Dio was still watching me closely and looked confused. I sighed inwardly. I wasn't used to explaining my oddities to people. I usually kept my home space pretty private.

"My dad was a dick, and I had to hide a lot as a kid. I learned early to stash snacks and toys in the hidey holes my brother created for me around the house. Eventually, I started leaving clothes in them too. Sometimes I'd fall asleep in there. I know it's odd. I've just always kept up the habit. If you poke around, you'll find weird shit stashed all over the place. Fair warning."

"Fair enough," was all Dio said. He seemed relaxed, although I could see questions blazing in his eyes as they swept over me.

I walked over and kissed him, feeling tenderness bubbling up inside me like fizzy champagne with a strawberry dropped in it. "Thank you."

"What for?" He asked as he pulled back from where he'd been about to kiss my neck, and his eyes widened.

"Not making a big deal about it and not pushing for answers right now. I just want to enjoy you for a while without dragging up a lot of crap that I've left far behind me."

"Lex, we've got time to get to know each other. Yes, I'm curious about how you grew up, but I don't have to know about it all today.

"My childhood with Pala was pretty idyllic, if a little secluded. Sam didn't have the same luxury. It took a while for him to open up to us about what he went through. He did it when he was ready, though. I could never imagine forcing him to tell us stuff that was still painful. All I cared about at the time was that he was with us and safe.

"I feel the same about you. If there's stuff you want to tell me one day, I'll listen. I may get angry, but never at you. I know all I need to know about you for now. You're fierce, loyal, and you care about people. I also suspect you're a little bit wild and you'll kick my ass if I get out of line. I'm good with all of that."

Before I could say anything in response, he swatted my ass, and my mouth fell open in surprise.

"Now get this gorgeous ass in the shower, and get dressed, before I get ideas and we end up in bed for another day."

"Last one there has to give a piggyback ride down to the dining room," I yelled as I pushed him back down onto the mattress and took off down the stairs. I could hear him laughing as he jumped up and took off after me.

"If you wanted a ride, all you had to do was ask," he declared, panting, after he fell through the door only just behind me. I'm pretty sure he jumped some stairs, and maybe even the landing, given the thuds behind me and the way everything rattled as I ran.

"I'll happily ride you later, after our chores are done," I said as I winked at him.

He groaned and watched me as I turned on the shower and got under it, letting the water run over my body.

"I thought this shower was heaven, but it's actually hell. You're never going to get clean because I'm just going to keep dirtying you up out here."

I shook my head at him. "Chores first, then playtime, stud muffin."

He smirked at me, as he started slowly lathering soap all over his delectable body and it was my turn to groan. The hunger I had for him was all-encompassing.

"You can eat my muffin anytime, baby cakes."

"Aaaannnnd, we're done." I said, as I rolled my eyes and shut the water off.

"We're never going to be done, hot stuff," he chuckled as he grabbed me and threw me over his shoulder while I squealed for the second time this morning. He was careful not to jostle me too much or put pressure on my stomach, though, where I still had healing bruises. He'd growled when he'd finally gotten a good look at the one on my head yesterday.

He took me inside to where we'd dropped our clothes and we got dressed quickly. I wanted to head to the dining room and help with the breakfast shift. Someone had been dropping food at the treehouse throughout the day yesterday. I suspected Ava as GG's arnica cream had appeared, as well. Dio had studiously and gently applied it for me, leaving a tingling sensation all over me, both from the cream and his touch.

A radio had also appeared for Dio so he could check in with Sam. The radio had helped him relax. There had been an underlying tension, even with all his easy going teasing, until he'd known Sam was okay.

Dave had also slipped a note under the door for me, saying he'd told everyone I had a concussion and would be out for a couple of days, and that he was taking care of things. It was sweet of him to cover for me, but there was really nothing wrong with me and I didn't like to be waited on by people who had enough work to do.

Being an omega wasn't an illness, and I had to come out sometime. Plus, I was starving. I'd worked up an appetite. I headed for the door, but Dio beat me to it.

"Are you sure about this? People are going to scent you straight away. Are you ready for everyone to know you're an omega?"

"I'm not staying inside forever, Dio." I tensed and crossed my arms, preparing for our first fight. But Dio put his hands up in reassurance.

"I'm not asking you to. I'm just asking if you're ready for what you're about to walk into."

I thought about it for a moment. I didn't want to cause a scene, but I equally didn't want to stay away from people forever, either. There was life to be lived.

I turned back and began rummaging through the drawers in the small kitchenette.

"Aha, this should do the trick." I shoved a bottle of perfume into Dio's face.

"Perfume? Your scent will be stronger than that."

"Oh, you underestimate the terrible, potent power of this perfume," I cackled like a deranged witch, and Dio grinned.

"A woman I helped gave it to me as a thank you. She had so little, but it would have offended her if I refused. So I accepted it. It's a drugstore perfume, so it's cheap and strong. Trust me, it's up for the challenge. It's also fruity, so it should help at least confuse my scent."

I sprayed a liberal amount all over me but started coughing immediately, and my eyes started watering. Dio bent to take a whiff, but ripped his head away before he even got close to my neck.

"Nope. Hard pass. That's not fruity, it's toxic. What the hell is that? Scrub it off." He was holding his nose and waving his other hand around in front of him.

"Ugh, I swear, it never used to smell quite this bad," I said, trying to wipe some of it off with a wet hand towel.

"It's designed to make betas smell like an omega. But it's very artificial. So your sensitive little alpha nose won't like it, but it should have the same effect on other alphas too. I don't know why betas think an alpha would like it. I used to chase Hunter with it and threaten to spray him when he was being an ass."

Dio grinned. "You have a sensitive little nose too, now that your omega is free. You're going to notice smells a lot more." He went to hug me but caught another whiff of the perfume that seemed to cling to me and started to sputter and cough instead. He held up his hands in defeat.

"Okay, we'll give it a go. I don't think we have much choice now, anyway. You'd need industrial cleaner to get that shit off. You're going to need to stay downwind of me, though," he said when he could breathe again.

"That won't be possible. You lost, so you need to give me a piggyback ride to the kitchen."

He groaned playfully, but he took my hand and we headed out the door and down the stairs. I stopped short at the sight that greeted me when we reached the bottom, accidentally yanking Dio's hand as I pulled him to a halt. He looked back over his shoulder at me questioningly.

There were two hammocks stretched out between the closest trees and the support beams for the treehouse. They were military hammocks, designed for soldiers to sleep outdoors, with fine mosquito nets strung up over them like a little tent.

Dave was reclining sideways in one with the netting flipped off. He was watching the forest, with Bear at his feet. Sam was fast asleep in the other hammock. I couldn't take my eyes off him. He looked so peaceful, like the angel before he fell.

"Is that the perfume you like to spray all over Hunter? Dave asked as he turned to me. I forced my eyes away from Sam's sleeping face as Dio leaned over to wake him up. He must be exhausted to still be asleep. Or he'd been up late.

"Sure is. Think it will do the job enough to let me help in the kitchen this morning without having to make any big announcements?" I felt suddenly awkward around Dave. There was so much unsaid between us, especially after the other night.

"Maybe. It won't work for long if it does, though," he said. Something subtle seemed to have shifted with Dave as he glanced at Dio and Sam, but I couldn't tell what.

I just nodded at him and fiddled with the pocket on my overalls. I caught myself as I reached up to rub at my hip and forced my hand down as I looked towards Dio, too. Both he and Sam were watching Dave and I intently, like we were their favorite TV show to binge watch.

"Do you guys need some popcorn?" I asked. Dio just grinned, but Sam was back to looking angry. Or maybe he was hangry? Maybe he really could use some popcorn.

"So, uh, what's going on out here?" I asked Dave and Sam, my gaze swinging between the two of them. I was dying to know what had gone down the other night that ended up with them sleeping out here. "Did you two feel the sudden need for a camp-out? A bit of male bonding? Did you run naked in the moonlight and howl at the moon?"

Dave's lip twitched. "No. Security detail on the treehouse."

"Why does the treehouse need security?"

"Because you're in it," he replied calmly, looking completely unruffled, as usual.

"Why do I need security?" His words had me completely taken aback.

Dave finally stood up from the hammock, doing it so smoothly, it boggled my brain. Nobody got out of a hammock without rolling out or falling on their ass. Or maybe that was just me.

He took two giant steps towards me and settled that unflinching gaze on me. It held me completely immobilized. "Because you're important."

My breath caught in my throat, unsure of his meaning.

"If the Palace finds out that you've been an omega all along, they'll attempt to snatch you," he said with a furrowed brow, probably at my sudden silence. I wasn't known for it.

I swallowed hard. Of course. He was talking about my importance to the Palace and not himself. Hope had flared hard for a moment, that maybe he was ending this dance we'd been doing around each other.

Was that what I wanted? Did I want Dave to make a move? I wasn't sure. He knew my secret now, but the man was a vault. In many ways, I knew him so well. We'd spent a lot of time around each other on the farm. He'd more than proven he was kind, steadfast, and loyal. Yet, he was also a mystery to me. I had no idea about his life before he came here. I couldn't deny our attraction, but maybe we were too alike? We both surrounded ourselves with people, yet also kept them all at arm's length. I didn't know what it would take to get one of us to breach our own defenses.

"The Palace doesn't know about me and we have all the alphas who do know secured," I answered, swallowing my confusion and keeping my response practical.

"Tied up in a function center cellar does not mean they're secured, Lex. If even one escapes and scents you, they may try to grab you on the way out. They're already suspicious after the performance of these two during the fight. Your secret won't be a secret for long."

"I-," but he didn't let me finish.

"I know, Lex. You can look after yourself. It doesn't mean you have to."

Dave flexed his hand out subtly at his side, like he wanted to reach for me, but was holding himself back.

"Fine. If you want to sleep in a hammock every night, I'm not stopping you," I ground out. I knew Dave, and there was no arguing with him about security on this farm. I knew how to pick my battles and I figured I was going to have bigger ones than this coming up.

I turned away from him and faced Dio, reminding myself we didn't have all day to stand around arguing. We all had shit to do. I crooked my finger at him. "You owe me a ride."

"Yes, ma'am," he replied, as he bent over in front of me and let me hop up onto his back.

"Is that a good idea? She's still injured," Sam said to Dio.

"I'm right here, you know. If you want to ask about my body, you can talk to me," I said, as I glared at Sam. "Besides, this is nothing compared to what I did with him last night."

My snarky words just made him narrow his eyes and growl in a way that made my nipples perk up.

Before he could reply, I slapped Dio on the ass and yelled, "Giddy up."

Fifteen

Dio took off at a run, sensing my need to get out of there, before he slowed when we were around a few bends. Bear had followed us and was ambling along beside Dio. I didn't bother to make sure Sam and Dave were following, too. I hadn't had a coffee yet and I couldn't deal with either of their issues without one this morning, so they were both currently in my bad books. They were also both in my spank bank, but that was a whole different issue.

Dio dropped me just outside the kitchen garden, where the trees hid us from prying eyes.

"Are you okay?" he asked. I'd basically just reverse hugged him the entire walk, feeling confused and leaning my head on his shoulder, and he'd let me.

"Sure." I gave a halfhearted shrug.

"You forget, I can sense you in our bond now. There's no point bullshitting me."

"I'm not. Honestly, I have enough to worry about this morning just walking into that kitchen. I don't see the point in talking about other shit I can't do anything about right now."

Dio sighed. "A lot has happened quickly Lex, just give them both a chance to adjust."

I blushed, not wanting to point out that Dio hadn't needed time to adjust. He'd been all in from the moment he spotted me during the fight.

"Look. I may not have this omega shit figured out yet either, but neither Sam nor Dave are rushing to declare their undying love for me. Or even their desire to bone me. You're projecting."

Dio laughed at that. "Didn't I just tell you to stop bullshitting me? They may talk crap about security protocols, but nobody else has men posted outside their door, even Maia and Ava. Both guys just spent two nights sleeping rough outside your house, when they have comfortable beds to go to, because they couldn't bring themselves to leave."

"I, that's not...they were there both nights?"

Dio nodded. "They took turns keeping watch and sleeping."

"Huh."

"You work with abused women, Lex. You know to look behind people's carefully crafted facades. Just do me a favor and really look at them both, at their actions, not their words. I know why Sam is holding back, and we're probably going to have to push him a little. I don't know about Dave yet. We're going to have to figure him out. Because I'm telling you now, both of those men need you, but they're going to have trouble getting out of their own way to come get you."

"We?" It was all I could focus on. Leif and I had always been a 'we' growing up, but he had his own family now. They always tried to include me, but it was different. Now I had Dio, and he made me feel connected to something bigger than myself.

"Yeah, we, Lex. We're in this together."

Dio chuckled at the stunned look on my face as he grabbed me, pulling me in tight to his body, before kissing me thoroughly. He slid his hands down through the low sides of my overalls and under my boy leg underwear to grab my bare ass, touching a lot of skin on the way because of the cropped t-shirt I was wearing.

"I really like these overalls," he mumbled against my lips. "I never knew baggy denim could be so damn sexy."

I pulled away from him when my scent started spiking, passionfruit bleeding through the horrible perfume.

"Look what you did." I said, waving my hands around, trying to waft clean air onto me and dissipate our mingled scents.

"I have zero regrets. I want the entire world to know you're mine, Lex."

He kissed me again lightly, then pulled the neck of my shirt to the side and licked over his mate mark as I gasped. It felt like he was tonguing my clit. I was about to grab him and make him follow through, but he spun away and disappeared into the bushes with a groan. Leaving me feeling achy and needy. *Damn sexy ass alpha scrambling my brain.*

I took three quick breaths in, then one long breath out. It was a technique Leif taught me when I was young called the bunny breath. He encouraged me to do it whenever he needed me to calm down and focus. I still did it sometimes, and it always gave me an instant sense of calm.

I was pretty sure Leif learned it from a parenting website. I used to catch him scrolling them sometimes, instead of looking up fart jokes like a normal kid. He was four years older than me, and I was grateful for him every day. He was the only real parent I'd ever known. Yet sometimes I worried I'd stolen his childhood.

I smiled when I thought of him and Maia. He'd been smitten at first sight and he deserved all the love in the world. Everything had changed for him when Maia stumbled onto our farm, and I was so glad she did. I hoped her heat was over soon. I couldn't wait to spend more time with her. She was a cool chick, and way more badass than she realized.

There was so much I wanted to talk to her about right now. I didn't regret mating Dio, but heading back into reality this morning I was starting to worry I didn't know how to be a good omega for him. I didn't want to let him down.

I was running on pure instinct at the moment while getting bombarded with new emotions and needs now that my omega was out. I was craving Dio's touch, and I'd never felt that way about anyone before. Maybe there were things he needed from me, too, that I didn't know about.

Enough Lexie, get your ass in the kitchen and stop mooning over alphas.

Pep talk over, I turned my butt around and got moving.

Everyone looked up as I appeared at the door. A chorus of greetings and women asking if I was okay followed me as I walked through. I grabbed an apron and fussed over putting it on, before anyone could get too close and hug me. I waved my hand in a shooing motion at them all.

"A tiny knock won't keep me down for long. I'm fine, ladies." I felt myself wince slightly as I reassured them. It felt like I was lying to them right now, letting them believe I'd had a concussion the last day or so. But I wasn't ready to answer questions just yet.

These women meant the world to me, but I'd also helped most of them escape situations far worse than mine. I had become their safe space to land, so I had always kept my issues separate.

I looked around to see what needed doing. I spied Ava standing awkwardly behind a long stainless steel kitchen bench. It felt weird seeing Ava without Cary hovering. I hadn't seen him leave her side since they'd arrived. Her face lit up when I noticed her and I gave her a grin as I headed her way.

"Is Cary healing okay? Where is he?" He'd been in a lot of pain the last time I'd seen him.

"Cary was with Nick earlier. He's still limping a bit, but he won't sit still." Ava sighed and shook her head. "Nick's been showing us around the farm. Cary wants to figure out where he can help."

"Oh, okay. That's good." Cary didn't seem like the type to sit around and let people wait on him, either. Lucky for him, there was always plenty to do on a farm. I looked around again to see what we could do to help.

"Do you want me to start the next batch of eggs, babe?" I called over my shoulder.

"Yes, please. Thank you." Isabella sing-songed from across the kitchen. Isabella had worked in hospitality before she arrived here. She had been invaluable in helping us set up the function center that we were now using as the communal dining hall.

In a commercial kitchen, most kitchen hands addressed the head cook as chef, but that had felt weird here right from the start. It wasn't our vibe. We were much more casual, but we still needed some kind of order to get things done. So we'd all taken to calling her babe when we were working. In this kitchen, she was the boss.

Without her, we'd all be lost. She'd become the unofficial mother hen of the group, which had taken some of the pressure off me when I kept bringing more and more broken, abused women home to the farm.

"Do you know how to cook scrambled eggs, Ava?"

Ava shook her head, seeming a little shy and flustered suddenly as she looked around at all the kitchen equipment. "They didn't teach us cooking at the Palace. I'd love to learn, though, I've always wanted to."

"I can teach you. Scrambled eggs are a simple place to start." I gestured her around to my side of the bench and she came eagerly. Yet there seemed to be a hint of sadness about her, too. I wasn't sure what was causing it.

"Are you okay? For real?" she asked quietly.

I looked at her and remembered her sweetly offering her help the other morning when we were talking with GG. "Could we maybe hang out for a bit after the breakfast is done? I could use your advice with, um, stuff."

"Of course." Ava said as she smiled warmly. She shifted closer to me and her nose wrinkled briefly, but she didn't mention anything about the cheap perfume. She had perfect manners, like a well-turned out omega princess. Which is exactly what the Palace had trained her from a young age to be.

She surprised me, though, when she looked sideways at me with a grin and said, "I can't wait to hear how GG's suggestion went. From the intense scents around the treehouse when I dropped off the food, I'm guessing it went well?"

I'd confided my plan to ask Dio to meet me at the treehouse with Ava and Cary. I tried not to be the one blushing this time, as I remembered just how well that had gone. "Uh huh," was all I gave her.

I grabbed the tray of eggs and showed her how to crack them without getting shells everywhere and gave her a few to practice on in a fresh bowl. When she'd gotten the hang of it, I showed her how to whisk them with some milk and season them.

I looked up from watching her whisk and noticed Maia standing by herself, patting Bear by the back door, watching us all. Her heat must finally be over. I yelled her name as I dashed over to her and threw myself at her, forgetting to keep my distance. She wrinkled her nose, like Ava had, but hugged me back.

I teased her with a half a dozen rapid-fire questions about what she'd been up to and where the guys were, but I froze when I heard footsteps approach the door to the dining room. I knew instinctively who it was.

Dave walked through, followed by Dio and Sam. They were all dressed nearly identically, with black tight fitting t-shirts, black military pants that hugged their thighs and black boots. They all moved as if they were in sync too, the same way Leif did with his mates. It took my breath away. Damn, they looked fine.

I only barely noticed Cary slink in behind them. His eyes were sliding away from Ava when I spotted him.

"Maia, I thought I heard Lexie yell your name. Where's your pack? Are they here?" Dave asked.

It surprised me he was using the term pack so openly, but we were all family here. He was moving toward the door to look past Maia as he spoke, but she put her hand out to stop him and shook her head.

"No. I let them sleep."

"Damn, I'm going to have to wake them. We need them if your heat's broken. We've still got trouble."

Maia seemed to blush at Dave's mention of her heat, and I snickered at her.

"What's going on?" She tried to raise her eyebrows at Dave, the way I always did with the guys to get them talking, but she looked more startled than demanding. Dave just looked confused. We were going to have to work on her eyebrow skills.

Before Dave could answer, Dio piped in while casually leaning on a bench and munching on a stolen piece of bacon.

"The trouble with the Palace isn't over. Ronan said they've been studying you, and they think you and Ava are both important. We're worried they'll try and grab you both again. It sounds like they had been waiting to start their tests on Ava and they won't be happy she's gone. Plus, we need to figure out what to do with the men we captured during the attack."

Dave glared at Dio, who shrugged with fake innocence. Maia had a far-away look in her eyes. She glanced over at Ava, who had followed me over. Ava leaned towards Maia and whispered, "We can't leave them in there. We need to get them out."

Get who out? Were they talking about the other omegas at the Palace? Before I could ask, Sam distracted me when he approached his sister. Their interaction had me transfixed.

Sam ruffled her hair like she was a kid again. "Are you okay, Mai?"

She nodded, seeming to take a deep breath. "Of course."

He eyed the bite marks on her neck. Two were fully visible, while another two were partially visible on her cleavage. She shrugged and answered the question he hadn't asked.

"My pack claimed me," she said, as she sat up proudly.

Sam just nodded and Maia seemed almost confused for a moment, like she'd been expecting an argument.

"Have you been helping Lexie and Dave secure the farm?" Maia asked him as she reached out subtly and stroked his arm lightly, as if she was afraid he would disappear at any moment. The way she looked at him with light shining in her eyes, but hesitancy in her movements, it was clear she had idolized her brother, but was a little unsure about where they stood now.

Sam turned to me at the mention of my name, and I blushed before turning away quickly. I felt a lot of eyes on me suddenly and tried to busy myself drying some cups that were already dry on the rack.

Maia rescued me when she mumbled, "Uh, incoming."

A heartbeat later, thumping footsteps came barreling through the dining room, and the swinging door was flung open. Leif, Damon, Hunter and Max came bursting in, attempting to get through all at once, looking panicked and only half dressed. I burst out laughing.

"Sunshine," Leif growled as he manhandled the others out of the way and stomped over to Maia, wearing only one shoe and no shirt. He picked her up, wrapping her in his giant teddy bear embrace. "We felt your anxiety. It woke us up, but you were gone."

"Who upset you?" Damon growled from behind Maia, where he had his arms wrapped around both Leif and her, but was glaring at everyone in the room.

"Dio did," Sam piped up with a smirk. Dio choked, spluttering out protests along with half his stolen bacon, while Damon glared at him. Oh, so Sam had a cheeky side. I wanted more of that.

Max and Hunter distracted my ogling of Dio and Sam, as they knocked everyone else out of the way and crowded into the group hug with their pack.

"Who the hell are all the military guys in the dining room?" Hunter growled.

"Uh, they're with me," Sam said. "It's the rest of my team."

I noticed Max was wearing a hot pink unicorn tee, but no pants, only his underwear, which made me laugh harder.

"I'm fine, guys," Maia squeaked out from inside four sets of muscled arms, all trying to get skin contact with her. "I was just getting some breakfast, and Dio was bringing me up to speed on some things we needed to talk about."

Maia winked at Dio, and he grinned. I had to hold down a sudden growl from bursting out of my chest. *Shit, settle petal.*

"You might want to put on some more clothes before you meet Sam's team." Maia suggested, as she turned her attention back to her mates, and I took a deep breath. She eyed off Max's toned legs as he blushed. I heard a woman behind me catcall, and Maia laughed brightly.

She seemed much more settled in her bonds now that her pack was complete and they had all claimed her.

"We need to add Nick's family to the list of things to talk about," Damon said. "They know about packs and prime alphas. We need all the information we can get about our new dynamics. We also need to know if there are more people like us out there."

He smiled softly at Maia as he talked, even though he was addressing the others.

"Uh, I spoke with GG quickly just after Maia went into heat. She said for you to come find her when things calm down. No rush." Damon nodded at me and shot a grateful smile my way.

Dio cleared his throat and looked uncomfortable for a second. "I have some people you can add to your list who know about packs, if we can get in contact. I don't know what a prime alpha is though, so I can't help you there."

"A prime alpha historically was an incredibly dominant alpha that draws other alphas in," Maia said quietly. "They could dominate multiple alphas at once and kept rogue alphas in line. I have an old banned book about packs that talks about them. They appeared to have died out in recent history, though. I think groups of lone alphas hunted them out of existence or they went underground

"The book says they usually struggled to handle their extreme levels of dominance on their own, often becoming aggressive or losing their minds, which is where packs came in. They provided an emotional base for the prime alpha and helped balance them out.

"Nick's family has kept a lot of old histories alive, and knows about packs, too. They knew Damon was a prime alpha. It's how he dominated so many alphas at once the other day when we were under attack. He could only do it because we had all started our bonds, we were channeling the power he was drawing, evening out the load. It was heady and felt freaking amazing."

Holy crap. Dave, Dio and I all spun towards Sam and stared at him. I had heard the guys and Maia talking about Damon being a prime alpha, but I hadn't asked what it meant. What Maia was saying seemed to describe Sam perfectly too, though.

"Holy shit." Dio said, a look of awe passing across his face as he looked at Sam.

"What?" Sam growled at us. "Why are you all staring at me?"

Everyone was staring at Sam now, except for Leif, who was looking at me.

"Lexie, are you okay?" he asked, startling me. He had a frown on his face and a curious tilt to his head as he walked over to me, before he leaned over and sniffed me. "Why are you wearing that awful perfume, and what is that other scent?"

I tried to lean away from him, but he suddenly had a wild look in his eyes. He grabbed my arm to hold me still so he could sniff me better. He wasn't rough, but it was enough to pull the arm of my t-shirt as I panicked and jerked away, exposing the bite mark on my shoulder.

He stilled as soon as he saw it, and his beast instantly rose to the surface. I saw the transformation in his eyes as the warmth bled away and all traces of my gentle, giant brother disappeared in cold fury.

"Who the fuck bit you, Lexie?" he growled, dark and menacing as his gaze swung around the room, trying to find the culprit.

A warm, growling body appeared out of nowhere and inserted itself between Leif and me, pushing me back a step. Dark curls obscured my view as Leif growled back before bodies collided and fists started flying.

A roar suddenly shattered the air in the kitchen, followed by another competing roar that left my ears ringing. The two together sounded like a sonic boom detonating in the room, and competing waves of dominance hit me almost at the same time.

A rush of men suddenly burst through the swinging door, with guns pointing wildly as Sam's team tried to figure out the threat.

Holy hell, that escalated fast. I looked desperately behind me to see Cary shielding Ava and as many of the frightened women from the kitchen as he could, directing the rest down behind fridges and cupboards. He made a move towards me, but I waved him back. I wanted him exactly where he was, to watch the other women.

No way was this going down on my watch.

My omega protective instincts snapped and fury ran through my veins as I turned and launched myself into the melee.

Sixteen

Dio

One minute we were all talking calmly, and I was happily munching on stolen bacon. The best kind, in my opinion. The next Leif growled while holding Lexie by the arm and my beast erupted.

I flew across the room to push my way between them and shoved at Leif, barely restrained violence pounding a demand through my veins, forcing Leif to drop his loose hold on Lexie. I could feel a growl vibrating my entire body, raising the hairs on my arms.

Leif's answering growl was pure fury as he swung at me and I dodged in front of his fist instead of away from it. Taking the blow to make sure Lexie didn't accidentally get hit behind me. I barely felt it in my rage. I threw a wild punch of my own, my knuckles splitting as I connected with Leif's jaw, leaving a red, bloody line across his face.

I had no time to think. This wasn't a calculated fight, with opponents circling each other. This was going to be raw and brutal. Nobody manhandled my omega, not even her brother.

A roar pounded the air and my body swayed with the need to drop to my knees, but a competing roar released me. The clash of the two roars vibrated the entire room, but I only had a moment to assess the next swing coming at me before a surge of anger filled my new bond and a bright head of hair popped into view between Leif and I.

Cold terror filled my veins at seeing my omega in the middle of two alphas fighting. I desperately tried to lunge for her, but she was moving too fast.

Lexie was strong, but she wouldn't survive a punch to the head with her brother's full weight behind it. I saw terror flash in his eyes the same moment it hit me, before a yank had my head turning sideways and pain tore through my earlobe. I saw Leif's head yanked at the same angle, making the world seem tilted.

"Cut it out now." Lexie's outraged voice and pure strength of will cut through the melee and froze everyone more effectively than the roaring had a moment ago.

"Don't make me come over there and kick your asses," she yelled at Damon and Sam where they were facing off a few feet away, with Dave trying to intervene between them. They all turned to stare at her, speechless. Maia was desperately trying to push past Hunter and Max, who had her pinned against the wall behind their broad backs.

"All of you, out of the kitchen right now. You're scaring the women, you giant, flea-bitten, nerf herders."

Pain overtook my shock as a yank on my earlobe precipitated each word. My head was then jerked sideways as Lexie manhandled Leif and me out the door.

Leif's groan matched my whimpered, "Ow," as we were almost bent in half while being yanked through the doorway into the bright sunlight of the kitchen garden outside.

Lexie dropped her hands and let go of us with a final yank, followed by a noise of frustration as she whirled on us, taking in Sam, Dave, and the rest of Leif's pack as they followed us out the door.

"Stand down," Sam yelled over his shoulder to his men who had followed us to the door, guns still raised. They complied with giant grins on their faces.

"Make yourselves useful and help Cary check on the women," Lexie yelled, and they turned tail and fled willingly. I kinda wished I could go with them, as I rubbed my ear. I could see Leif discretely doing the same to his bright red earlobe.

Maia stepped up to Lexie's side in silent solidarity. She glared at Damon when he opened his mouth to say something. He snapped it shut. Smart man.

"That will NOT happen again. I know you're all big scary ass alphas, and instinctively protective of omegas. But those women are here because this is a SAFE space and that kind of alpha macho shit can set them back, months, maybe even years, in their progress. Do you hear me?"

We all nodded sheepishly. That had gotten out of control fast, and none of us had been thinking about our surroundings.

"You will all apologize to them when we're done. Quietly and calmly. Then you will take over the breakfast shift and let those women put their feet up and breathe for a minute. Are we clear?"

We all nodded again. Even Leif, although he was still staring at his sister intently with a clenched jaw. He was studiously avoiding looking at me for the moment.

"I'll apologize for scaring the women, Lex. It wasn't my intention and I feel shit for doing it. But I won't apologize for defending you. I need to know you're okay before we go back in there." Leif's giant hulking body was shaking slightly as he talked, as powerful emotions pummeled him.

Lexie sighed before she turned to her brother and wrapped her arms around him. I wasn't jealous. He was her brother, after all, but I felt rattled and I wanted those arms around me right now. I had a feeling I was in the doghouse, though. I could still feel Lexie's anger through the bond.

"I'm fine. More than fine, big guy. I'm actually better than I've been in a long time. Just ask me next time. *Me*, not the rest of the room, okay?"

Leif nodded, eyes downcast, looking chastened. "I'm asking now Lex, who bit you?" His eyes flicked in my direction for the briefest glance before returning to his sister.

"Leif, meet my mate Dio. He bit and claimed me right after I bit and claimed him." She waved her hand in my direction and I stepped up beside her as I let out a giant breath.

She still wasn't looking at me, but she had just claimed me as her mate in front of her brother and his pack. For half a second, I hadn't been sure she would do it or if I'd broken something between us. Our bond was still so new.

I was trying really hard not to beat my chest and roar "mine" right now, though, because I didn't think it would help my cause. So I just pulled the shoulder of my shirt down and jutted my chin out while standing strong and proud at her side.

There were shocked breaths and open mouths all around. I stepped in closer to her, subtly, giving her my support. Sam and Dave were watching everyone warily, but didn't make a move towards us.

"But you're a beta. Aren't you?" Maia asked Lexie quietly. She looked hurt, as if Lexie had been keeping something from her. Leif wasn't doing much better. He looked gutted.

"It's a long story," Lexie said with a sigh. "I'll tell you everything, but can we do it inside while we cook, please? We need to fix the mess we just made."

I got the feeling Lexie was a pro at shouldering through the tough stuff and wasn't really used to explaining herself. Keeping busy, rather than standing here talking while everyone stared at her, would probably make her feel more comfortable.

"That sounds like a great plan. Let's move it inside people." I jerked my head at Sam and Dave, and they made the first move to turn back to the kitchen. We'd only really made it a few steps outside, so they were back through the door in seconds. I saw Damon looking at Dave in confusion.

I grabbed Lexie's hand, and she didn't pull away from me, but she still wasn't looking at me. Leif narrowed his eyes at me, though. Until Maia took his hand and led him inside gently. The rest of her guys followed her, still in their various states of undress.

"Lex, baby. I'm sorry if I scared the women inside, but I won't apologize for defending you, either. This is all really new for me and I didn't know I was going to react so quickly or so strongly until after I'd done it. It was just, seeing someone grab you the first time we're around people after we claimed each other. My beast hasn't fully settled and was out before I even thought to let him."

I needed to touch more than her hand right now. I needed to reassure myself she was okay. But I had to tread carefully if I was going to fix this. "I'll work on trying to chill, but-"

Before I could finish, Lexie whirled, and all but climbed me, throwing her arms and legs around me. I took a half step back to steady myself before she was kissing me wildly.

It took me half a second to catch-up; I was so surprised. She groaned deeply as she abruptly pulled her mouth away, much too soon. My breath was coming out in hard pants as I nuzzled into her neck, her scent calming me. "I thought you were mad at me?"

"I am," she said, "but I'm more mad at myself for putting the women in that position. It was always going to go badly if Leif figured it out before I told him. I should have known that, made an excuse and left as soon as Maia showed up." She shook her head against my neck and I pulled her tighter in to me, soothing her.

"As inappropriate as it was, though," she continued, "watching you defend me from my man mountain of a brother was hot as hell. So badly timed and unnecessary, but so fucking hot. I'm such a contradictory mess of emotions right now."

I kissed her forehead as I let her legs drop to the ground. "I was terrified when you jumped between us. Please never do that again."

"No promises," she chuckled.

"At least find a more manly way to pull us apart next time?" I asked as I brushed my thumbs across her waist. I couldn't seem to keep my hands off her. "My grandmother used to drag us around by the ear when we were kids. It hurt like hell then, too."

"Nope. If you act like a child fighting over your favorite toy, you get treated like one."

I laughed, feeling lighter now that I knew she wasn't mad at me. "Fair enough." I seemed to say that a lot around Lexie, but I found myself wanting to please her. There was very little she could say that I wouldn't be okay about.

"Are you ready to go back in there, or should we run away?" I queried, looking down at her slightly and trying to fix her hair for her where I'd mussed it up. I sounded like I was joking, but I was serious. If she couldn't handle this right now, I'd get her out. No questions asked.

Lexie groaned, and not in a sexy way this time. "This is going to suck. Let's get it over with."

We headed up the stairs. As soon as we walked through the door, we got one grumpy glare, followed by a round of applause and catcalls. Lexie's friends were still in the kitchen, hovering around the far door.

"Sorry, Lex. We didn't want to leave until we were sure you were okay," one woman called out, "but judging by that kiss, you're fine as hell."

Lexie blushed furiously, which was cute as fuck. I grabbed her hand, bringing it to my lips and kissing it.

"Where do you want me, Lex?" I asked.

"On the bench, it's the perfect height. Just make sure you clean it after," another woman called out as they finally left and the rest cackled. Yeah, the women were fine, too. Most of them were tough and had all seen worse, as sudden and shocking as our fight may have been. There were a couple of fragile-looking ones, but they all had another woman's sturdy arm around them.

I walked over to the sink and washed my hands, getting a grin and a fist bump from Hunter as I passed. Lexie headed the same way, punching Hunter in the arm when he tried to fist bump her, too. She was trying not to make eye contact with anyone else.

"Wait for Max, then I want that long story, Lex," Leif growled as Maia wrapped her arms around him. He slid his hands up Maia's arms and pulled her in tighter. Neither of them seemed to care that she had dirty hands from grating potatoes.

I looked around, wondering where Max had gone, but I didn't ask. There was enough tension directed towards me right now. He re-appeared a few minutes later with clothes and shoes for the guys so they could finish getting dressed and weren't cooking half naked. Probably a wise move.

"Do you want Cary and I to go?" Ava asked from where she was whisking eggs beside Maia, with Cary hovering, holding pepper and pretending to help while watching all the alphas in the room nervously.

Lexie shook her head, sending Ava and Cary a small smile. Neither omega seemed all that surprised about Lexie's revelation, which had me suspicious. *Did she confide in them?*

I felt a growl rise in my chest to see her smile at Cary, but I stuffed it down. I was fighting my need to keep every unknown male away from her right now. It was instinctive with our mate bond so new, but I didn't want to get my ear pulled again so quickly.

Lexie started talking as she worked to finish cooking homemade hash browns. She gave the cliff notes version as she got everyone up to speed on what had happened between her and me, leaving Sam and Dave out of it for now. There wasn't much to tell there yet, anyway. I was planning on changing that, though.

Damon, Hunter, and Max looked shocked. They had all known Lexie for a long time. Leif looked half destroyed.

"Why didn't you tell me when you first noticed the scent years ago?" Leif asked quietly.

"I wasn't sure. I honestly thought I was just imagining it. It kept coming and going, and it was only the faintest hint. More like a memory of a scent teasing me. When Dad brought that creepy guy home to stay and check me over, it terrified me. I shoved the possibility down so hard and refused to even consider it."

Lexie had been focusing on flipping hash browns, and not making eye contact with anyone, so she missed the way Leif's face crumpled.

"What creepy guy?" Leif asked, with so much raspy pain lacing his voice I couldn't bear it, and I barely knew the guy.

Lexie swore as she looked up and her face drained of color. She'd told me this story the first night, but it was clear this was something she'd never told Leif. The answer was all over her face without her saying a word.

"When did this happen?" he ground out.

Lexie seemed hesitant to answer, but his eyes were pleading with her.

"When you went away to that school camp."

The broken, guttural groan that escaped Leif was heartbreaking, made worse by the tears that tracked down over his cheeks while he shook.

Lexie leaped onto the counter in front of him, knocking utensils off the table recklessly, and wrapped her whole body around him.

"I failed you," Leif all but whimpered.

"No. No, you didn't, Leif," Lexie seemed frantic to convince him. She was squeezing him hard, but he was rigid with his arms hanging down his sides. I could almost see the self recriminations flashing through his brain like an old slide show.

"You were the best big brother. You were a kid yourself and you did more than any kid should have had to do to keep me safe, then you got me out. He doesn't get to take that away from you. Or me. He doesn't. Don't let him. Please." Lexie had pulled back from him slightly, with tears running down her own face, and was banging on his chest.

"You should have told me," he said in a voice that had gone flat and seemed deadened somehow.

"No. You took enough burdens on yourself. That one was mine," Lexie whispered.

He moved suddenly and wrapped her up in a giant bear hug as she hiccuped out a long, shaky breath against his chest. His movement seemed to break everyone else's stasis, as Damon, Hunter, Max and Maia all surrounded Leif from behind. Hugging them both and comforting them.

Feeling her pain through our bond tore me open. I approached behind where she was sitting on the narrow, steel kitchen bench and wrapped her up in my arms, leaning my head on her back and joining the tangle. I felt arms come around me too, as Dave, Sam and even Ava and Cary joined in.

Their pain united us. Bonded all of us in something bigger than ourselves. I didn't know what it meant at that moment, or what would come of it, but I felt nothing but love surrounding and flowing through us all. Love in all its pain and its beauty.

I knew I would do anything to keep this family for Lexie. For all of us.

Seventeen

I 'd never felt as close to a group of people in my life as I did at that moment. As much as Leif and I had been there for each other growing up, we also protected each other, and sometimes that meant secrets. I was used to keeping things to myself, shouldering burdens I didn't think he needed to bear, and he did the same.

It was nice to just let it all out and have other people catch us. I looked up at Leif and he smiled down at me gently as I wiped his tears away with my hand.

"Are we good?" I asked him.

He nodded slowly. All the fight had left him and my gentle big brother was back. His eyes roved all over me, looking for signs of injury or pain, the way he'd always done. "Always, Lex. Just don't shut me out of this, okay? I want to be here for you."

I nodded as I felt a moment of pure relief and joy. I didn't deserve Leif, but I loved him fiercely. My joy lasted all of three seconds until Hunter piped up.

"Is it wrong that I have a boner right now?" He asked from behind Maia.

"Ew, gross." I laughed while reaching over and trying to pinch him as he ducked away. Maia just rolled her eyes at Hunter with a loving smile.

"Is that what you wanted to talk about after breakfast?" Ava asked, a little hesitantly, as she stepped away and I unwound myself from Leif before swiveling back around and hopping down from the bench. Knocking another spoon off as I went, before picking it up and adding it to the others in the sink.

"Yeah. I was hoping you could give me some omega advice. Before I met Maia, I'd never even been around an omega before, let alone had the Palace training. I was hoping you could help and answer some questions?"

"Absolutely. The rush of conflicting emotions can be intense for new omegas. It must feel like a lot with everything you've suppressed. I'd love to help," Ava answered sweetly. Just her telling me the wildly swinging emotions were normal had my hunched shoulders relaxing.

"You seem to be doing just fine," Maia piped in with a wink as she brushed my messy hair off my face. "Plus, the omega training isn't all it's cracked up to be. Some omega chat time sounds like a great idea, though."

"Why don't you grab a few plates from what's already cooked and head up to the treehouse now," Dio said, watching me closely. "We can handle breakfast."

"Hell yes, to breakfast in the treehouse. I've been dying to see it since Hunter told me you guys built one. I bet it's cute as buttons," Maia said.

I just looked at all the guys skeptically. I knew Leif and his friends were all badass alpha warriors, but I'd never seen them do more than reheat food. With the other women given the morning off, too, I wasn't sure what would come out to be served for the rest of the farm workers and our new guests. Although most of the prep was already done.

"You know that means cleaning up afterward, too?" I didn't want the other women to walk back into a destroyed kitchen.

"We can keep everyone fed and alive for one morning without your help, Little Mouse." Leif said with an affectionate smile, using the nickname he'd had for me when I was little. "And yes, we'll do the dishes, too. Go, we've got this."

"Just don't go too far and stay in contact if anything happens. And I mean anything. If you feel uncomfortable for any reason, we'll be right there," Damon growled lightly as he passed a radio to Maia.

"Okay, if you're sure," I answered for Maia, as she seemed a little busy grabbing Damon's face and sucking his tonsils out. The thought of leaving Leif and Dio together right now made me a little hesitant, but they both had back-up. I wanted them to get along, but they needed to figure out how that would work for themselves.

"Cary, you're welcome to come. You're an omega. You qualify for omega chat time." I said as I glanced at him. He was an anomaly, like Maia and I. I was interested in any insights he'd have. He glanced around the room and we both noticed the sudden tension coming from Dio, as well as most of the other alphas in the room.

"I'm happy to chat, but maybe right now isn't best. Emotions are running pretty high. Another time, when everyone's calmed down a little more," he said and smiled gently at me.

I nodded at him. I was disappointed, but I understood now wasn't the time. Cary being a rare male omega living on a farm full of alphas, was tough enough. I didn't want to make life harder for him.

I'd be having a word with Dio later, though. I wasn't going to keep my distance from someone who was in need, and could help me in turn, just because of stupid pheromones.

I grabbed some muffins someone had baked earlier, along with some bacon, toast and the hash browns I had just cooked, stuffing it all on a big plate.

We could do without eggs for one morning. I didn't want to hang around for them to be cooked and risk the guys changing their minds when they realized what they had just taken on. I noticed Ava grab a small jug of milk as Dio moved towards me and kissed me lightly, before stealing a piece of bacon from my plate.

I shook my head at him and snuck a look at Dave and Sam. They were both watching me. Dave just nodded his head and smiled. I had a feeling he would be discreetly following us to the treehouse before long, to keep watch. Sam was looking between Maia and me with a torn expression. He clearly wanted to spend some time with his sister, but she kept getting pulled away by drama and the other people who now filled her life.

We would need to make sure they got some time together soon, but not now. I felt kind of mean, but he'd been waiting a decade, he could wait a few more hours. I needed my friend right now. So, I forced myself to turn away from him and headed out the door, assuming Maia and Ava would follow.

"See ya later, boys," I called over my shoulder.

The last thing I heard was Hunter asking, "So who knows how NOT to burn toast?"

Maia and Ava burst out laughing right behind me. I shot them one look, and we all took off running until we were out of sight, Bear loping along beside us. I led Maia and Ava up the curving path towards the rocky outcrop that was surrounded by tall trees and high shrubs. The early morning light filtering through the trees made the air seem soft and golden, like something out of a fairytale. The scent of oak trees and earth, interspersed with wild flowers filled my senses and made me smile.

When we strolled into the small clearing in front of the treehouse, Maia gasped and pulled up short. She whacked me on the arm as I turned to her in confusion, almost making me spill our breakfast.

"What the hell is that?" She asked, as she pointed at the treehouse.

"Uh, a treehouse. What were you expecting?"

"Oh, I don't know. Maybe a few planks of wood and some crooked railings cobbled together. Some old kids' toys stuck in branches and maybe a ripped curtain. You know, a treehouse."

She waved her hands around wildly in the treehouse's direction. "That is a gorgeous, house in a tree. That's a completely different thing."

She stood with her hands on her hips, glaring at me accusingly.

"You're seriously underestimating your mates if you thought it was going to be a shoddy little kiddy thing," I said. "They do nothing by halves."

"I can't wait to see inside. Meet you at the top," Maia yelled as she bolted up the stairs.

"I'm going to carry this tray up the stairs like a regular person, but have at it." I yelled back at her. I watched Maia disappear with a smile.

"It's nice seeing her so happy and carefree," Ava said, echoing exactly what I was thinking. She had been so shut down, yet determined to survive her fate with her head held high when I met her. Seeing this relaxed, fun side of her made my heart happy. Finding her pack had clearly been good for her.

When we reached the top, Maia had only made it as far as the deck. She was standing at the railing, taking in the expansive view.

"This is gorgeous. I bet it's stunning at night, too." She let out a soft sigh as she turned back to us. "I love the old barn door as well."

I passed her the plate to hold and slid it open for her. She wandered inside, exclaiming over the timber interior and all the natural light. She ran her hand over the kitchen cabinets, loving the duck-egg blue color. Ava followed behind her, taking it all in with a quieter appreciation.

"You've got a kitchen and everything you could need in here. Why the hell are you living down in that tiny cabin, cute as it is, when you could be up here?" Maia asked.

I just shrugged, but Maia didn't notice. She'd already spun away, trying to take everything in. I grabbed the plate back from her before she dropped it.

"What's up there?" Ava asked, pointing to the stairs.

"A loft bedroom. There's an A-frame ceiling with a skylight and an enormous picture window at the end. It's beautiful. It has mattresses and blankets all over the floor, so it's comfy too."

"It sounds heavenly," Ava said sweetly.

I was suddenly uncomfortable, feeling like I should offer to show it to them, but I really didn't want anyone up there. Especially other omegas.

"It's okay," Maia said as she touched my arm gently, suddenly serious. "I get it. We can stay down here."

"Thank you," I mumbled, feeling grateful for these two women. "Dio thinks I unconsciously designed this place as a pack house, complete with a nest for myself."

"Did you?" Ava asked quietly, like she was trying not to spook me. For a good little omega princess, she seemed to be endlessly curious about packs, heats, and nests. Everything the Palace said was illegal or had forced into extinction. I didn't know if it was her natural instincts coming through or something else.

I shrugged, trying to sort through the barrage of feelings that were bombarding me right now. "We intended it as a hangout pad when we built it, but the guys have never spent much time here. It never occurred to me that I could live up here. It didn't feel right somehow, or didn't feel right yet? I don't know," I said as I sighed in frustration, staring at the plate in my hand as if it had all the answers. It was a lot of pressure to put on bacon.

Everything had felt so easy, like it fell naturally into place with Dio. But I'd been away from him for five minutes and now I was getting antsy. I suddenly wanted a hug from him in the worst way. It was disconcerting. I'd been so independent and self contained for years. Keeping everyone at arm's length for fear of triggering something in me. Now, suddenly, I felt like I needed him near or I couldn't breathe right.

Maia slid her hand down my arm to grab my other hand. "Here, let's sit and we can talk it out."

I followed her and put the plate on the timber coffee table before I plonked down on one of the comfy couches in the living area.

"Is this the same couch as in the guys' cabin?" Maia asked, running her hands over the soft sage colored leather.

"Yeah, they had their u-shape couch custom made to fit the sunken living room in their cabin, and their size. I liked it too. So they got a few three seaters to put up here at the same time."

With the green couch and the blue kitchen bringing all the colors from outside, inside, it made the tree house feel even more open.

I grabbed a hash brown for comfort as Maia snuggled into my side while munching on some bacon. Ava sat on my other side on the floor at my feet and helped herself too. She froze when Bear plonked himself down almost on her feet, but he just looked from her to the bacon and back again.

Ava grabbed some off the plate and held it out to him hesitantly. He grabbed it with his teeth so gently and delicately, avoiding her fingers, that she relaxed. He bumped her leg with his giant head in thanks and promptly fell asleep snuggled against her, making her smile.

Being here with these two women felt nice. It felt right. I'd spent a lot of time around women but I'd never really hung out with any outside my work. I had a feeling both of these women were going to become important to me. There was a kinship there that was instinctive and would only grow with time. I really needed to stop repressing everything and closing myself off if I was going to get their help.

I took a deep breath as Maia prompted, "Talk to us." She seemed concerned at my silence, which was funny considering she mostly just shrugged at us when she first arrived here.

"It's just, I honestly had myself convinced I was a beta. I had the rest of the world convinced too, so I must have done a good job. Yet the moment I met Sam and Dio, everything changed. It felt like this tsunami of need and want threatened to spill out of me. I felt a pull to both of them instantly, but we were in the middle of a fight with you at gunpoint.

"Then I smelled that scent that had haunted me, and it was so much stronger. I panicked, and I tried to shut it down, but for the first time, I couldn't. It was too potent. I had to use your trick of hurting myself so I didn't start a frenzy."

"Sam and Dio?" Ava asked. "I remember they both spun towards you during the fight the second you spoke. Does Sam feel the same way as Dio?"

I froze. "Shit, I need to shut up today."

I couldn't look directly at Maia, but she sat forward slightly to search my face.

"Why would you try to hide that?" She asked, tilting her head, seeming to be genuinely confused.

"Well, he's your brother, for starters," I shrugged.

"Yeah, and Leif is yours. It doesn't mean I'm going to hold back and not talk to you about him. I distinctly remember grilling you about all my guys when we had movie night, and they all consider themselves your brother."

I smiled at the memory. She'd not long arrived at the farm. I'd been sussing her out, feeling protective, knowing how my brother had instantly reacted to her. She'd been so sweet and open, yet so obviously lonely. Her quiet inner strength had called to something within me. I'd ended up all but adopting her as my sister before the night was out.

My smile fell a little as I thought back to Sam and my conflicted feelings for him. Dio had felt like a warm hug from the first moment, but something about Sam had me on alert. Bear felt it too. I wasn't afraid of Sam, but I could sense he was on the precipice of something explosive. He felt unpredictable, like a wild card.

Sam and I were both complicated and hot-blooded, plus I was impulsive. I worried if we started something and unknowingly pushed each other's buttons, I'd push him over whatever edge he was balancing on.

"Sam is so full of rage, yet despite how much dominance he leaks, he's so contained. Was he like that as a kid?" I asked Maia.

Maia's smile fell, too. "No. Sam was fiercely loyal, protective, and generous with himself. He looked after me even before my mom disappeared, when he was little more than a kid himself. He was a lot like Leif like that. Sam always put Ben and I first, making sure we were fed and tucked in safely at night. He even went without, giving us his own food when there wasn't enough. He was our shield against the world."

Maia was staring blankly out the window, lost in her memories for a moment.

"Yet he disappeared without a word when you were still a kid. Did he explain why?" I wasn't there when Sam arrived and I hadn't found out what he said to Maia when he showed up. The intruders had struck just after he arrived, then Maia had gone into heat.

Maia didn't answer immediately, as she slumped back down onto the couch next to me. Her fingers fidgeted restlessly with the buttons on the long cardigan she was wearing over a cute floral mini dress, as if she was considering her words.

"I'm sorry to push." Maia's conflicted emotions were clear on her face. "I just sense there's trauma there now. That guarded look he wears, that says he's trying desperately not to unleash his damage on other people. I've seen that before. I don't want to hurt him, but I'm worried I will without meaning to if I don't know what I'm dealing with."

Maia flicked her gaze at me and nodded. "He seemed shocked that I thought he disappeared without a trace. He said he wrote letters and sent money, and Dio backed him up, but I never saw any. We didn't get time to talk about the details, about why he left and where he was that left all that darkness. He just said he had no choice."

She blew out a long breath and scoffed lightly. "To be honest, I'm being a coward. I'm so relieved he's here. Part of me always believed he'd be back one day, but I'm avoiding talking to him about why he left. I'm scared that his answer won't be enough and I don't want to be disappointed or angry. I just want my brother back."

Maia stared straight at me now and I could see that core of steel she hid so well. "That damage. I can see it too and I want it gone from his eyes. If you're his mate, I'm hoping you can help me with that."

Our gazes stayed locked for a moment until I gave her a small nod. I didn't know how I could help, but I'd face his monsters if I had to. For Maia, and for Sam.

Maia sat up again and seemed to shake herself mentally, giving a rueful smile as she reached for some more bacon. Bear perked his head up and she threw him a piece.

"As for omega training, Lex, you don't need it," she said. "The Palace tries to break omegas and train them to be submissive, because when left alone to develop naturally, we're not really submissive at all. Except maybe in the bedroom." She gave me a quick, cheeky wink.

My smile bloomed in response to hers. She had that effect on people. "I hear you, but how am I supposed to know if I'm doing things wrong with Dio? How do I know what he needs? I don't know how any of this works and instincts will only get me so far. Part of me is a little worried I'm going to break this perfect thing we've just thrown ourselves into blindly."

She reached out and touched my arm gently. "There's really no right or wrong way to do this. All alphas and omegas are instinctive creatures. Your instincts have kept you alive, Lex. You may have repressed the obvious signs you were an omega, but I think your omega instincts have always been there. The same as mine. It's what makes you so empathetic to people and helps you recognize when someone's in trouble. So listen to your instincts. It's your time. You've got this."

I sat for a moment quietly, just taking in what she said. It made sense.

"She's right," Ava said, breaking the silence in a way I was coming to realize was typical of Ava. She said little, but when she did, she'd thought it out and said it with utter conviction.

"The Palace wasn't the safe space for omegas they made people believe. They've twisted the natural instincts of alphas and omegas. To the point where we're dying out. Yet still they persist for their own power."

"Wow," Maia said, with her mouth hanging open slightly, "and here I thought you were a Palace princess, that you'd bought the fake fairytale. I was honestly worried about you coming up to your debut," Maia said, looking a little surprised.

Ava just grinned, and it was like a curtain lifted and we got to peek at the magic that flourished in the shadows. It was illuminating.

"No, I just rebelled in my own way. I made them think I was the perfect princess, so they mostly left me alone. I never intended to make my debut, though."

"Wow, you had me fooled. Do I even know you at all?" Maia asked, looking at Ava as if she'd never seen her before.

Ava looked upset at the question, a frown marring her gorgeous features. "Of course you do. I was only ever myself around you in the brief moments we got together in the library. You were my lifeline in there, and I didn't want to ruin it by talking about things we couldn't do anything about at that point.

"Besides, I didn't want to risk saying anything because I couldn't be sure no-one was listening, even in the library. There was too much at stake for both of us."

Maia's eyes raked over Ava, looking for signs of deception. All I got from Ava, though, was sincerity, and a little distress at upsetting her friend. I held my breath, the moment feeling fraught, but Maia relaxed finally on a deep sigh and nodded at Ava.

"I believe you. That place twisted us all, but you were my lifeline, too. We're circling back to this whole 'rebelling in my own way' thing later, though." Maia made a circling motion with her finger and narrowed her eyes at Ava. Ava looked relieved and bent her head to pat Bear, the dark curtain of her hair falling over her face, as if she needed a moment.

Maia and I glanced at each other. There was a lot there we needed to dig up. Ava, it seemed, was a dark horse in the perfect sweet disguise. Before we could bombard her with a million questions, she carried on, as if we'd never deviated down an intriguing path.

"Anyway, you don't need omega training. You've built something amazing here, helped so many women. Maia's right. You've been following your instincts for a long time. You just need to trust yourself, and us, now. We've got you," Ava said with a quiet dignity.

I was deeply humbled by the strength and grace of these two women who had been through so much, yet were here taking care of me. Instead of resenting the way I avoided being sent to the Palace, the way they were. They were championing me. Making sure they had my crown fixed firmly on my head.

I leaned forward and grabbed both of their hands, feeling lighter. "Thank you."

"No thanks needed, Lexie. I'm in total awe of you. I'd love to count you as a friend," Ava said, making me blush a little.

"Already done," I said.

Maia shrugged. "I'm not that easy. Payment will be required in cookies. I heard you make the world's best chocolate chip cookie, Lex. I'm going to need a taste test to see if the guy's claim stands up."

I sighed. "I would love to make you some cookies, but I don't know if we have any chocolate chips left, or vanilla extract. These are the things that we're going to run out of, if we haven't already. Things that we don't grow on the farm."

The thought of how much we still needed to figure out in order to survive if the electricity never came back was sobering. Not that chocolate chips would help us survive, but there were plenty of things that we would need long term that we didn't have here and couldn't grow. The problem had been gnawing at me and was taking up increasing space in my brain.

Plus, what about the people out there who didn't have as much as we did as a starting point? How the hell were they surviving? I'd been part of the wider community before the Crash. I hadn't isolated myself on the farm as much as the guys had. There were people I was worried about out there, particularly in the small town down the road.

"No! I refuse to live in a world without chocolate chip cookies." Maia's outburst jolted me out of my short reverie. She was looking at me in growing horror, as if she'd been waiting on me to solve the problem while my mind wandered.

"We're going to have to figure that one out. Apocalypse be damned. I can do without a lot of things, but chocolate is not one of them," Maia said passionately.

Ava and I burst out laughing. "I'm serious," she said indignantly.

"She is," Ava piped in. "We didn't get a lot of sweet stuff at the palace. They were pretty strict about our diets. Maia used to squirrel chocolate away whenever she discovered it, and hide it in the library behind dusty old books."

Maia moaned as if she was remembering the taste. "I'm an idiot. It's an apocalypse, and I left all that delicious chocolate behind. We're going to have to go back and rescue the chocolate... I mean omegas. We're absolutely going back to rescue the omegas."

Ava laughed lightly at Maia, the sound clear and sweet.

"We'll figure it out," I said, as I patted Maia on the shoulder. The omegas were a whole other problem to solve. There was no way I was leaving them there at the Palace at the mercy of the assholes running it.

"What about Dave? Where does he fit in?" Maia looked pointedly at me as she said his name, but I ignored it, pretending to look at my fingernails innocently. As if I was checking out my non-existent manicure. They weren't having a bar of that, though.

"Yeah, I'd like to know about Dave too. If a man as hot as Dave looked at me like he does you, I'd melt," Ava said.

Maia and I both gaped at Ava incredulously. Maia spluttered something unintelligible and Ava looked at us with her eyebrows raised in surprise.

"Uh, Cary?" was all I could get out.

Ava blushed furiously. "He's not interested in me like that. He's my friend. Besides, he's an omega. Omegas don't mate with other omegas."

"Girl, you cannot be that naïve. He watches you like he'd die if you so much as got a split end in your hair. That man is gone for you," I said.

Maia finally found her voice again. "Besides all that, who decided two omegas can't be together? Not us. Lex and I are breaking all kinds of rules. What's one more?"

Ava looked sad for a moment as she played with the bracelet on her wrist. I noticed she did that a lot whenever we talked about Cary. "It's complicated. I can't go there, but I don't want to get into why right now.

Besides, he's protective and a little intense, but he's never made any kind of move on me. Sure, he stays close, up to a point, but he's never even touched my hand. He keeps a certain distance as if there's a force field around me."

"Yeah, same," I said with a sigh. "Well, except for that one time, when Dave kissed me."

Maia squeaked like a startled mouse as she leaned forward on the couch, grabbing my arm and shaking it. "I knew it. When did this happen?"

I looked sideways at her, pursing my lips and trying not to laugh as she jostled me. "At the community meeting, the night you got together with Hunter."

"Yes." She pumped her arm like she'd just bested us in an epic board game battle. "I knew something was up the next day. He couldn't keep his eyes off your ass and you were all like, 'who are you again?'"

I laughed and threw a muffin at her. Which she caught and started demolishing. She totally had me pegged right. "Leif unknowingly interrupted us and Dave disappeared while I had my back to him, then he pretended like it never happened."

"Oh, he is going down. You're my sister now. I will not let this go unavenged." Maia had dropped her muffin into her lap and had her hands steepled together and was tapping her fingers in a classic evil plotting pose. All she needed was a maniacal laugh to complete the picture. Ava was grinning along with her and I didn't want to know what those two could get up to together.

"To be fair," I held up my hands, trying to hide my smile and calm them down before they unleashed hell on Dave, "we both kissed each other and both acted as if it never happened."

"Doesn't matter. We're going to have so much fun with him," Maia said emphatically, as if it was a done deal.

"I'm in," Ava said, looking surprised at herself for speaking up and jumping in. Maia just cackled and gave her a high five.

My smile finally broke free. Everyone needed girlfriends who would take down a douche for you.

Not that I thought Dave was one, but there was definitely something holding him back and I was interested in seeing how he would react to Maia's evil plans.

Maia and Dave sparked up an instant friendship from the minute he found her half starved and alone outside our fence. I knew he was almost as protective of her as he was of me, but more in a concerned, fatherly kind of way. Not the good girl, kind of daddy dom vibes I got from him.

I would intervene if it got too bad, though. Maybe.

Eighteen

The next hour was utter chaos as eight grown ass men tried to make and serve breakfast for a few dozen people. I eventually roped my team in. I figured if they were going to laugh at us, they could damn well help us. They just added to the chaos, though. Too many alphas in too small a space. Cary had looked like he was going to bolt. I eventually kicked them back out.

Despite the frustrated growling going on in the kitchen, whispered questions like "why is my batter so lumpy," and Hunter and Dio getting into a light-hearted tea towel whipping fight that nearly ended up with Hunter's ass in a bowl of eggs, we managed to serve up edible food. Every resource was valuable now, so there was no way we were going to ruin any food by being careless.

All the women thanked us when they came back in, for the morning off and the laughs at our expense. They'd completely forgiven us for our earlier fracas. They seemed happy with the sparkling state of the kitchen when we were done, too.

I looked around and realized the kitchen was clean, but we were all looking a little worse for wear. Dio had bits of pancake batter in his hair, but the giant smile on his face reflected on the faces around us in a way that lightened my heart.

These people were making the best of an awful situation and rallying together in a way that was rare. There was so much life happening within these gates, while so much destruction was happening outside.

Life here was still precarious, though. People outside were going to covet what they had. People who wouldn't care about spilling a little blood to get it. I decided I was more than happy to spill a lot of blood to preserve it, though. This place spoke to me in a way I'd been missing for a really long time.

It hit me that this farm was Maia and Lexie's home. I hoped that meant it would become my home, too. It had been too long since I'd had one. I wanted a home and family with a deep yearning, but I was equally terrified of fucking it up and getting myself banished again.

While everyone had focused on their tasks this morning, there was still a lot of tension towards Dio and me, particularly from Damon and Leif.

That meant I needed to resolve all the unanswered questions between us and Maia's mates. I turned to Dave. "Can we arrange a sit-down with Damon and his mates now? There are a few things we need to discuss, and they can't wait any longer."

"On it," was all Dave said before he spun away and started rounding up the guys. Dave was quickly growing on me. There was no pretense or bullshit. He was straight to the point. A guy you could count on to have your back. Despite the fact he was a good fifteen years older than me, he felt like a friend. To my beast, he already felt like coming home, the same way Pala and Dio did.

It scared me almost as much as Lexie did. I was tired of disappointing people I respected. Every father figure or mentor I'd had in my life had been wary of me and sent me away, eventually.

"Sam." I shook my head and focused on the voice calling my name. Dave was standing in the doorway to the dining room, with Dio standing next to him, looking highly amused.

Dave was looking at me expectantly, like it wasn't the first time he'd called my name. I looked around and all the other guys had left. I was standing in the kitchen by myself.

"You okay? You kinda zoned out there for a minute," Dio asked. I could hear the laughter in his voice.

"Shut up," I groused at him. He ruffled my hair affectionately as I passed him at the doorway. I pulled up short when I found everyone watching and waiting for me. I really needed to get my head in the game.

"I'll go drop some breakfast to Nick, then go watch the treehouse from a distance, if you're all going to be here," Cary said as he hovered on the outer edges of our group. He seemed antsy and I don't think it was just because Ava was gone.

"Cary," I called out, halting him as he turned to leave. I'd been watching him and seen how uncomfortable he was around us when he wasn't focused on protecting Ava. As if he was just waiting for one of us to pounce on him instead. He was Maia and Lexie's friend and I wanted to reassure him that someone had his back.

"I just wanted to thank you for defending Lexie and Ava the other day, when the Palace alphas attacked." I knew it wasn't my place to thank him, given Lexie's mate and brother were in the room, but I felt it had to be said.

"I think it was more Lexie defending me in the end," he said with a self-deprecating shrug.

"Regardless, you could have taken Ava and fled when the farm was attacked, but you didn't. You stayed and fought."

"So did you. Maia was here, and knowing Ronan was after her, there was no way I was leaving."

I nodded, remembering the panic of the moment I realized Maia wasn't leaving. That I couldn't get her to safety before the attack came. It still made me feel ill. "Yeah, I get that."

"You defended Lexie and Ava during the attack?" Leif asked quietly. He'd only just resurfaced from Maia's heat, and he and his mates weren't up to speed on everything yet. Cary looked uncomfortable with us all watching him and just shrugged.

"Thank you," Leif said. He moved towards Cary but hesitated, then pulled back when Cary tensed. I got it. Cary looked like any of our guy friends. He could be one of our team, just a highly attractive one. Yet I wouldn't hug or approach an unmated female omega. Especially one that smelled as delicious as Cary did. It was confusing our alphas.

Cary nodded and turned away again, but that wasn't all I had to say. "Before you go, Cary." He looked at me over his shoulder and watched me a little warily.

Shit. I wasn't the best person for this. Talking to people was not my strength. I had a point. I just needed to figure out what it was and get to it.

"I imagine it can't be easy for you, being around this many alphas. But you have my promise that nobody here will hurt you while I'm around. If anyone is making you uncomfortable, even if it's one of my team, you let me know and I'll handle it." My words weren't just for Cary, they were for every alpha here. I glanced at Dio as I spoke.

Cary looked startled. I got the impression this was the first time in his life anyone had offered to defend him. He was usually very closed off and a little snarky, but he looked incredibly vulnerable suddenly, as if he'd been putting on a tough front that had melted away at my words. Like ice cream left in the sun.

"I figured that went without saying," Damon said, "but if it needs to be said, I'll second that, Cary. You are safe from anyone inside this farm. I know Maia convinced you to stay for now, but I hope you will consider staying permanently. We'll do anything we can to make you comfortable here."

"Yeah, what he said," Hunter added.

Cary's vanilla ice cream scent spiked, and I had to take shallow breaths, trying not to breathe it in. I wasn't worried that his scent would draw me to him. My every thought centered on Lexie now, but his scent still pulled at my alpha. It made me want to protect him and I didn't want to get all growly and make him uncomfortable. I noticed Hunter, who was closest to Cary, took a subtle step back.

"Shit, sorry," Cary mumbled as he clenched and unclenched his hands. He seemed rattled as he took a step away, too. "I usually have a better lock on my scent. It doesn't mean I'm attracted to any of you. It just spikes when I get emotional, and that doesn't happen a lot anymore."

"Fuck," Dio swore softly. "You don't have to apologize, Cary. I'm sorry if I tensed and made you uncomfortable before, when Lexie asked you to go with them. I feel like shit. That wasn't fair. And it wasn't because you're an omega. It was because you're a guy. This is all new for me and my alpha is feeling very territorial over Lexie while the bond is so new.

But that's my problem. I'll try to tone it down. You're welcome to spend any time with Lexie she wants."

Cary just nodded at him while shifting uncomfortably. He seemed lost for words.

"Okay, everyone can tone it down," Dave said with calm authority. "Are you okay, Cary?"

"Yeah, just embarrassed," he muttered as he ran his hand over his short hair.

"Don't be. You don't need to control or suppress your omega here. All these guys toss their scents around like candy on Halloween. It's fine. There's a plate of breakfast for Nick in the fridge. Max was going to take it down when we were done. Grab it and if you want to watch the treehouse after, head on up. You don't need to hang around outside."

"Okay. Uh. Thanks." He glanced at everyone in the room to make sure we knew he was thanking all of us. He gave us an awkward wave as he turned and disappeared through the doors to the kitchen.

I could see Dave eyeing the door and I figured he wanted to head for the treehouse himself, but knew he needed to be here.

Damon, Leif, Hunter and Max all settled around one of the dining tables. They each fit ten people, so there was plenty of room for all of us. The guys appeared to be lounging casually, but they didn't fool me. They were on alert and watchful, and I knew any of them could turn deadly in an instant if provoked. The tension in the room spiked quickly now that Cary was gone and Maia wasn't here. We had no distraction from what was about to go down.

I was suddenly nervous. This was Maia and Lexie's family. I knew of these guys, but they didn't know me, Dio, or my team. From the cool looks they were currently giving us, they were reserving judgment. The camaraderie from the kitchen earlier had dissipated.

I needed this meeting to go well, but I also couldn't be a pushover. These guys would never respect me if I was. I wouldn't respect myself either. They needed to know if they could trust us around their mate and sister, and they were about to push us to find out. I didn't blame them. I'd do the same in their position.

I noticed Damon's eyes narrow further when Dave sat down next to me. I didn't know if it was a strategic move by Dave, designed to show his trust in us, or if he just wanted to be near at hand if I lost my shit. Either way, I felt comfortable having him at my side.

Dio bumped my arm gently from my other side and fake coughed as Hunter smirked. *Shit, I called this meeting. Now everyone was watching me again.*

"Where do you want to start?" I asked, spreading my hands wide as if I was gesturing at an open buffet. "With Lexie and Dio, farm security, the Palace, or my team and why we're here?"

"Lex," was the unanimous response, almost in unison. It was eerie. Yet, their instinctive choice was one more example of the powerful sense of family between them and where their priorities lay.

"Over to you, Dio," I turned and smirked at him. He looked momentarily startled. Clearly, he hadn't expected me to throw him to the wolves. He recovered quickly, though.

"Uh. Hi," Dio grinned easily. "So Lex is my true mate and I've claimed her, which makes us brothers now. So go easy on me, okay?"

Hunter chuckled dryly, shaking his head. "No way in hell. If we're brothers now, we're not pulling our punches. You get the full brother experience."

"Awww, hell," Dio grumbled, but he was still grinning until he sobered up abruptly and leaned forward, instantly matching the tone of the room. He placed both his arms firmly on the table and stared them down. "Seriously though, Lex just became one of the most important people in my world. I will not hesitate to fuck any of you up if you piss her off. I will take her side unconditionally."

He paused for a beat, and they all just watched him. Like an impenetrable wall of testosterone. Dio didn't flinch, though, and he didn't appear daunted, at least on the outside. I could sense he just wanted his next words to sink in.

"Also, I know she's independent and a total badass. I wouldn't dream of changing that. But if you think she needs something she's not getting from me, or I've been an idiot and upset her without meaning to, which lets face it, is entirely possible, you come to me. I will fix it. All I care about is that she's safe and happy. I'll take any hits I need to in order to make sure she doesn't have to. The same applies to Sam, too."

"Dio-," I interjected.

"No, Sam. Let me say my piece." Dio shot me that determined look that said he would fight me if he had to, in order to protect me. "What I mean is, if Sam is being a grumpy asshole and has pissed someone off, or you can tell he's riding too close to the edge of his control, you don't push his buttons, you come to me."

My heart clenched as I tensed and braced myself for their reaction, ready to back Dio up if needed. Even if it came down to me and him against the world. As nervous as I felt sitting down and formally meeting these guys, I wouldn't let them walk all over us. Weirdly, though, they all relaxed at Dio's words, as if they could respect where he was coming from.

Most people didn't understand when Dio got protective over me, but as the guys all shot protective glances at Damon, I sensed they did.

"I can accept that for now, but I'm going to be watching," Leif said, speaking plainly.

"We'll all be watching," Damon countered.

"I wouldn't have it any other way," Dio said, still being serious for once. "The more people who have her back, the better. I have no problem with any of you looking out for our girl. Family goes both ways, so know that you now have more eyes on Maia, too."

Leif got up, circled the table and held his hand out to Dio. "Welcome to the family, Dio."

Dio ignored his hand and got up to hug him. "I grew up in a big family, and we didn't shake hands," he said, sounding relieved and a little emotional.

Leif hugged him back and let out a huge breath. Max and Hunter followed closely with a lot of heavy back slapping from Hunter before they all sat down again.

I couldn't have been more thankful for Dio at that moment, and I shot him a grateful smile. He had an easy, open way with people, even when he was laying down the law, that I could never hope to emulate.

People responded to his manner instinctively, becoming more open themselves. Everyone loved him. I wouldn't have gotten as far as I had in life without him to pave the way for my grumpy ass, and I knew it.

I could feel Damon was still sitting watching us, though. Like a predator waiting to pounce. This wasn't over. He was just getting started.

Nineteen

 Sam

"I appreciate your help with the attack and your team helping to watch over the farm since then, but I have questions," Damon said, his gaze and his words delivered bluntly. He was going to be a much harder sell than the rest of his mates.

I forced down an instinctive growl at his high-handed attitude. This was Damon's turf, and I had to respect that. I had a few questions for him, too.

"Shoot," I said roughly and felt more than heard Dave sigh next to me. I wasn't deliberately trying to provoke Damon with my curt attitude, but the tension had my beast riled protectively. Plus, when I was nervous, what came out wasn't always what I meant to say, or how I meant to say it.

"You reacted exactly the same as Dio to Lexie the other morning."

"That's not a question," I replied, trying to keep things light. I would not get into this with them before I'd even discussed it with Lexie.

"Don't be an asshole. Tell me what's going on with you and Lexie," Damon growled as tension spiked further around us.

Dio opened his mouth to say something, always willing to jump in and defend me, but I put my hand on his shoulder to stop him and reassure him at the same time.

"If anything develops between Lexie and I, you won't hear it from me. If she wants you to know, she'll tell you," I growled back at Damon. "I can assure you, though, I have no intention of messing with her, or hurting her."

Everyone tensed, waiting to see if this would escalate. But Damon just switched his attention to Dave. I felt guilty for feeling relieved Damon's attention wasn't on me anymore.

"And you?" He asked Dave, with less growl but just as seriously. Hunter looked between Damon and Dave incredulously.

"Um, what the hell?" Hunter stuttered, his head pinging between Damon and Dave.

"What about me?" Dave asked Damon in a flat voice that had shut down all emotion, ignoring Hunter.

Damon just watched Dave with an unwavering stare that gave nothing away about what he was thinking.

"She needs you, Dave. We need you, too. It's time," Dio said in a sure, calm voice, surprising the hell out of me and everyone else at the table. Everyone except Damon.

Dave flicked his gaze to Dio briefly before something seemed to settle in him and he straightened in his chair. "I will continue to work security for this farm, but I'm resigning from my role as Lexie's surveillance operative and undercover bodyguard. Effective immediately."

I took a shocked breath that was mimicked by Dio. I glanced at Leif. He seemed uncomfortable, while none of his mates looked surprised.

I instantly saw red and my rage erupted, whiskey spilling into the air. "You've been surveilling Lexie? Does she know?" I asked Dave in a voice as cold as the river I'd dunked myself in the other night.

Dave sighed and turned reluctantly to Dio and I. "Yes. And no, she doesn't know. Not that I'm aware of, anyway."

"Why would you betray her trust like that?" I ground out, fury riding me hard. My fists clenched and my dominance leaked everywhere as I stood up and crowded Dave. I saw Dave shift back slightly as the strength of my dominance pummeled him, but he stood up and braced himself with his legs apart.

Everyone else at the table stood up abruptly, too, chairs screeching and crashing to the floor, as if they were getting ready to intervene. The tension in the room was so thick now, it was stifling, making it hard to breathe.

"I accepted the job before I met Lexie. Max found out Lexie was taking some extreme risks to help the women she was rescuing. There were also threats towards Lexie from abusive exes looking for their ex-girlfriends and wives. Some of them were alphas," Dave said evenly and slowly, not making any sudden movements.

I tried to hear what he was saying, but rage was pounding me raw. Thinking about anyone following Lexie without her knowledge made me want to punch someone, but the thought of assholes threatening her had me twitching to spill blood.

Leif took a slow step closer from where he was standing part-way around the table. "Lexie refused to stop her work, and we didn't want to hold her back. She also wouldn't let us help in case we scared the women. We couldn't intervene stealthily without her noticing. We tried. She caught our scent every time. She kicked our asses for it."

Damon moved himself slowly but purposefully into my line of vision behind Dave. While Dio put his hand on my shoulder, squeezing hard as he pushed in close behind me.

"We asked Dave to move here and help with security, because we needed it. We also asked him to watch Lex, redirect any assholes coming for her, and be invisible back-up if she ever needed it when she did something reckless," Damon said.

"Don't judge them too harshly," Dave sighed. "They felt it was the only option they had to keep her safe. Tracking and surveillance are two of my specialties and given my own history," Dave visibly swallowed and took a breath before he continued, shaking his head slightly. "I was more than happy to help keep her safe, knowing how important she was to the guys."

"Your own history?" Dio asked quietly from beside me.

"That's not up for discussion right now," Dave said firmly as he shut Dio down, completely unapologetically, without breaking eye contact with me.

"What about after you fell in love with her? How many lines did you cross while watching her? Or have you been messing around with other women while you have feelings for Lexie? Because it's clear that she has feelings for you," I asked Dave, fearing the worst as I pushed my chest against him and got into his space. His eyes flared in response and his hackles rose. If he was an alpha, he'd be growling at me right now.

"I've kept my distance until recently. I tried to stay away and let her find someone her own age who could be there for her in ways I can't. For fuck's sake, I'm almost two decades older than her. I could be her goddamned father," he said in a low, menacing voice.

"And I didn't want to betray the guys' trust in me. They're important to me too," he added, as his eyes flared even hotter and he stepped into me, not giving an inch.

"But since the day I met Lex, she's the only woman I've thought about. The only woman I've wanted. I'm going to say this to you once and it's the only time I'm going to say it. She's everything to me, and I would die rather than do anything to endanger her or take advantage of her. If you insist on talking shit about me and Lex, we're going to have a problem. Do we have a problem, Sam?"

"Holy shit. You're a vault, man. I did not see that coming," I heard Hunter gasp. From the ensuing silence, Leif, Damon and Max were not as blindsided. "Did you guys know? If you did, you all suck."

"Max and I suspected," Leif said calmly. "We didn't realize Damon did, too. But we trusted Dave to handle his shit."

I could feel the authenticity of every word Dave said. He was practically vibrating with his truth. But my frustration that I couldn't be as honest or as open with myself had my rage spiraling. Dio squeezed my shoulder in warning.

"Dio, I think we need ice. Damon, can you grab some?" Dave said with forced calmness.

"It works on him, too?" Damon asked Dave quickly, before Dio could reply. At Dave's subtle nod, Damon made to step away, but I growled low in my throat.

"The first person who dumps a bucket of ice over my head is going to die," I growled. I flicked my gaze to Damon for the briefest moment before returning it to Dave.

"I'm not so far gone that I can't pull back. I just need to know. Are you going to tell her about it before you make a move?" I growled at Dave, almost daring him to lie to me. It didn't matter if they had their reasons for keeping her in the dark initially. As soon as Dave developed feelings for her, he should have ended it.

"Yes," Dave replied without hesitation. "I'm not saying I will make a move, but I will tell her about everything and let her decide my fate."

"Oh, she's going to be pissed!" I heard Hunter say in the background. He sounded almost amused about it. I suspected the guys felt a lot of pride in Lexie's strength.

"My money's on Lex," Max said. I could hear palms slapping like there was a round of high-fiving going on.

"For the record," Leif said, "I have no problem with you and Lexie, Dave. I already consider you a friend. It would be an honor to call you brother."

The other guys all voiced their agreement, but I was the only one who saw the relief flood Dave's eyes; from where I still had us locked in an intense stare-down. It was followed by a flash of deep vulnerability that had my alpha momentarily wanting to wrap him up and protect him from whatever had put it there. It didn't abate my anger towards him, though, not if he was hurting Lexie.

Dave nodded once in acknowledgement of Leif's words, but didn't take his eyes off me yet.

I forced myself to take a step back, using every inch of willpower I had to make my limbs move. Dio shifted with me, but stayed close. I shook out my clenched hands before I put my hand over his on my shoulder and squeezed it tightly.

"Dio's right. She needs you," I bit out, flinging my words at Dave. "You're an asshole if you don't step up now, and that's only about you. Don't think for a minute your age has a single fucking thing to do with it," I said.

My breath came out on a long exhale, as I forced the worst of my rage to simmer down to a low boil. I relaxed a moment too soon, though, because it was Dave's turn to step into me. "I know why I'm holding back. What's your excuse?"

With that one question, my poisonous rage turned back on me. I had no answer I was willing to give right now. I leaned into Dio and dropped my gaze, something I wouldn't do to anyone else except Dio and Pala.

Dave seemed to sense I was at my limit as he searched my face. "I won't push you today, but we're not done. We're circling back to this." He glanced at Dio over my shoulder briefly before he turned to the other guys. "Everyone, sit the fuck down. Damon, if you have more questions, now is the time to ask them."

Damon smirked and spread his hands, as if to insinuate he wasn't the one causing trouble. Dave just shook his head and stretched his shoulders out to force them to relax.

"Fine," Damon said as he turned and sat down again. He jerked his head toward their chairs, and his mates followed his lead. "Next question. You knew us on sight outside the fence the day you arrived. How?" Damon asked. He had his arms crossed, and a finger was tapping against his arm impatiently, as if he'd been waiting to ask this question for a while.

Fucking hell. I had no time to relax. We were jumping straight into the next fire. Damon wasn't pulling any punches as he watched Dio and I closely, noting the way we were still standing together. I took another breath to center myself, drawing strength from Dio's touch, before I patted his hand on my shoulder. He let me go reluctantly before we both sat and pulled our chairs into the table.

I waited until the guys had all picked up their chairs and sat down as well. Max ducked into the kitchen quickly and came back with a large bottle of cold water and glasses. He passed me a glass, and I drank it gratefully. I shot him a small smile of thanks.

The pressure in the air dissipated slightly, but things were still tense.

"I don't know any of you, but I know of you. Your exploits are legendary. You're even more famous in military circles than the twins," I answered, as I slouched down in my chair, attempting to look casual.

Damon just raised his eyebrows. It wasn't a query, though. He knew who I was talking about. Most people just didn't talk about the twins so openly. They were death incarnate, appearing out of nowhere with lethal efficiency and disappearing just as quickly when their job was done. Nobody knew who they reported to or where they came from, but rumors of their exploits were rampant.

"You knew me on sight," Damon argued. "You knew Leif, Hunter and Max as well, and we never worked a mission together."

I just shrugged while he glared at me. I'd answer him eventually, but I needed my own answers first. People's lives were riding on who I trusted with this information. "My turn. Why did you leave the military?"

Damon looked incredulously at me, his eyebrows raised so high they were almost hitting his hairline. "You're dodging my question, but you expect me to answer yours?"

I growled lightly at him. Dio put his hand on my arm again, but it only calmed me slightly. Damon was completely unruffled, and his mates just watched me with amusement, as if I was a stray puppy barking at the devil.

"He's asking for a reason, Damon," Dave said, intervening before the situation escalated. Again.

"Do you know the reason?" Damon asked Dave, flicking his eyes towards him.

Dave nodded. "I do, and I answered the same question he's asking you."

Damon grunted in annoyance, swinging his dark gaze back at me. He obviously trusted Dave implicitly, though, which increased my respect for them both. It was rare for an alpha and a beta to have such a rapport. Most dominant alphas treated betas like a necessary evil, or as little more than servants.

"We left," Damon said begrudgingly, looking like he wanted to punch the smirk off my face, "because we suspected Dave was about to take on a world of hurt to protect us and we couldn't allow that to happen."

Dave stiffened at my side, and I heard his surprised inhale.

"Plus, we'd lost trust in his superiors. We signed up for our own reasons, some of us against our will. Regardless, we only wanted to protect people and when it became clear the military didn't hold the same values, we figured out an exit strategy. What happened with Dave just meant we got out faster than we planned."

Silence reigned for a moment until Damon's eyes flicked to Dave again.

"You knew about the shit that was going down?" Dave asked.

"Yeah," they all answered in unison again. "And we weren't going to let it happen," Damon finished.

Dave looked conflicted for just a moment, before he sat forward in his chair and rapped his knuckles on the table.

"I should have known. Nothing gets past you guys." He looked over all four of them with a mixture of pride and affection.

Dave turned to me next, and I fought the urge to sit up straighter. I wanted to earn that same look of pride, maybe even the affection too. "Tell them," he urged. "It's the only way we can keep Lexie, Maia, and Ava safe."

I looked around the empty dining room, making sure we were alone. "Have you ever heard of the Network?" I asked, keeping my voice quiet.

Damon, Hunter and Leif all looked blankly at me, but something sparked in Max's eyes. I swiveled my gaze and narrowed my eyes at him. His mates did the same.

"When we were trying to figure out how deep the military corruption went and what our exit strategy would be, I came across some vague references that mentioned the Network. I dug further, but I couldn't find anything else. I kept coming across scrubbed files and closed systems. There was so much else going on, I let it go. I couldn't risk triggering anything. We didn't need more heat at that point."

"Why didn't you tell us?" Damon asked.

"I was looking for evidence of crimes. When I'm hacking, I have to skim information quickly and decide what trails to follow. I assumed at the time it was talking about some kind of new, top secret software or digital system they wanted to implement. It wasn't what I was hunting for. I figured I could come back to it later, but then we got out and I never did. It was more than that, though, wasn't it?" He asked, as he looked at me curiously. He'd leaned closer towards me as he talked. His interest sparked.

My smirk grew into a smile. "It's so much more than that."

Max's eyes lit up, his thirst for knowledge clear. Dio laughed beside me as he spread his arms theatrically. "Prepare for your little minds to be blown."

I huffed and rolled my eyes at him. "Not the time, Dio."

"Just spill it already," Damon snapped, getting impatient. "We're gaining enemies as quickly as we're running out of resources. We don't have any time to waste right now."

"Gaining allies, too," I asserted. "The Network has had its eyes on you for a while. All of you." I explained everything I had already told Dave as quickly as I could. Damon had much the same reaction as Dave did the other night. He grinned. It wasn't a peaceful smile, though. This one promised mayhem and chaos.

"So you've been part of the Network and working undercover all along?" Damon asked, and I nodded.

"Can you contact them with everything that's down?" It was the same question Dave had immediately asked, but this time, it came from Max.

"With your help, I'm pretty sure I can." Max was a tech genius. If he couldn't get me back online, no-one could.

"What do you need? Tell us and if we don't have it, we'll get it," Damon growled.

"It's called the Network because that's what it is. Each person has contact with one other person, who can contact someone else. It keeps them hidden and ensures if someone's cover gets blown, the whole web doesn't go down. There's a failsafe if someone goes dark, which my primary has, but my failsafe is my gramps' farm.

"He had a hidden system, and I don't think my little brother knows about it. Gramps had no plans to bring him in. It should still be there as my failsafe instructions stayed the same even after gramps died.

"It will take a couple of days to travel there by road, which is risky right now but doable. It'll be much quicker if we can get fuel for the Blackhawk, though. We used most of ours to get here. We've got enough fuel left for maybe one short flight, but not enough to return. Is there anywhere nearby that may have helicopter fuel?"

"Dude, you have a helicopter? I thought I heard a helicopter fly over not long after we got back to the house when Maia went into heat. You guys said I was crazy," Hunter gloated, and Max whacked him on the back of the head. "Not the time, Hunt."

"There's actually a small helicopter sightseeing company that takes people up to the mountains near here. I looked them up one day as a date idea for Max," Leif said.

Max turned to him with his mouth open. "We never went on a heli-copter date."

Leif looked embarrassed. "Yeah, I chickened out. I was worried you would think it was weird. We've never gone on a date before. We were in the military when we met."

Max grabbed his hand. "I would love to go on a date with you."

"If we can get the fuel, Sam and Max will need to fly to his gramps' farm. You can tag along, Leif, and call it a date. Sam will pilot the helicopter so you guys can make out as much as you want in the back," Dio piped in.

"No date," Damon growled, "if we're going to your gramps' farm I'm coming. I want to chat with Ben, your little brother. Is that going to be a problem?" he asked, giving me a hard stare.

Leif, Hunter and Max all tensed at the mention of my brother Ben. The anger rolling off them was intense and had my senses on high alert. Damon had hinted at trouble with Maia and Ben when I arrived, implying he had betrayed her somehow, but I hadn't had time to hear the entire story from Maia.

From Damon's tone, and the amount of dominance I could feel pummeling me, I didn't think the chat was going to involve a lot of talking. "If Ben needs a chat, I'll be doing it. You're welcome to come along and watch. I need to hear Maia's story from her, though."

Damon clearly didn't agree, but didn't waste time arguing either. "You need to talk to Maia, then. I want to try for the fuel this afternoon. Max, Hunter and I will go, and if we get it, I want to head to the farm tomorrow."

I nodded in agreement. "That works for me. I'm expecting intel from the Palace and I'll need your help with that, too, Max. I'm hoping it will be here in the next day or two."

"What intel?" Max asked, sitting up from where he had slumped slightly in his chair, with his arm around the back of Leif's.

I looked at Dio, and he looked at Dave, raising an eyebrow. "You can trust them with your friend. Nobody here is going to betray him," Dave said.

I swept my eyes over the group of men in front of me, trying to convey how serious this was for me to divulge. "We have a friend, Pala. He's undercover at the Palace. He's risking his life right now to download information from their secure, encrypted, military server. The one the Palace uses to communicate with the highest levels of the military."

I shifted slightly to look directly at Max. "Those secure fire walls and scrubbed files, Pala's about to get you past them."

Max's eyes lit up. "Hot damn, I knew there was more. What I found out about Maia was bad enough, but there were holes. I knew there had to be more systems there. I just couldn't find them."

I ground my teeth. There was only so much I could take today without losing my shit, and I'd already come close. "What you found out about Maia?"

Max suddenly paled and looked at Damon, who nodded at him.

"Uh, the Palace documented the abuse of your sister pretty extensively while they were studying her. They tried to dominate her for years, and she refused to submit. They were using torture methods on her. There's video and blood test results. They think she's some kind of evolved omega. They were studying all the omegas, but she bore the worst of it by far. It went on for years."

My rage spiked with every word out of Max's mouth. Dio cursed and tipped his chair precariously to hug me sideways, while Dave reached out and grabbed my shoulder. Fuck, I needed more than cold water for this. I gripped the glass so hard I heard a crack before Dave grabbed it out of my hand.

"That's what Ronan was talking about when he tried to kidnap her the other day?" I asked, feeling like my soul was being ripped from my body in tiny strips, leaving me raw and bloody.

Max just nodded. I wanted to bring Ronan back to life so I could kill him all over again. The rest of the scientists at the Palace were dead men walking.

Damon's voice snapped me out of my murderous reverie. "I know it's a shock, but we have to deal with the problems we have in front of us now. The Palace is on everyone's hit list, okay? We need you to focus."

I nodded at him jerkily, not really capable of words right now. Dio jumped in, always knowing when I needed him to step in and deflect everyone's attention without me having to say anything.

"Which is why we have to talk about the Palace men tied up in the storage cellar underneath us right now. We need to figure out how we're going to let them go," Dio said.

"Let them go?" Leif growled. "They've tried to abduct Maia repeatedly. Why would we let them go?"

Max put a hand on Leif's shoulder, reassuring him, while Damon eyed Dio speculatively.

"We can't kill them after they've surrendered," Dio said, "and we don't have the manpower or the facilities to keep them safely secure. The storm cellar is only a temporary solution. I'm surprised it's held them this long. They outnumber the guards we have on them four to one. I suspect they're only still here because they want to be, probably to get intel on our movements and resources. If they change their mind, people could get hurt."

"You're right. We don't have a choice," Damon agreed with a fierce scowl, clearly not liking the situation.

Leif sighed. "I know you're both right, but it still doesn't feel right to let them go."

"We need to at least wait until tonight, though," Dio amended. "Pala has been undercover with these guys for a while and he thinks some of the alphas in our cellar can be turned. We need to separate them today and make contact. It's a risk, but I think it's worth it. If we can infiltrate the Palace from the inside, it will make taking them on so much easier."

"Do you trust your friend enough to justify the risk? We need more allies, but turning people can be tricky," Damon said, although he looked unhappy about our lack of good options.

"We'd both trust Pala with not just our lives, but with Lexie's," I ground out. Damon looked surprised, but Dio shot me a cheeky grin. He was up to something, but I didn't have the focus to figure it out right now.

"Okay, then." Damon rubbed his neck as he sat up straighter and was suddenly all business. "If we release them early this evening, it will give us more manpower and free us up to do the supply run tonight. That gives us only today to get ourselves sorted.

"Max, can you jump onto the satellite and see if you can get a view of the helipad facility and where they were storing fuel? Also see if it's manned. Look at the route, too, see what kind of inhabited areas we'll need to move through to get there and back.

"Leif and I will start figuring out what we have that we can trade for fuel if needed. I'd rather trade for it than take it by force-"

The radio loudly interrupted Damon, blaring to life with a strange voice. "Captives escaping. Headed for lower gate. Two cellar guards down. Need backup now."

"Fuck," Damon yelled as we all pushed to our feet.

We were out of time.

Twenty

Fucking hell, what a day. I thought to myself as I trudged up the hill to the guest cabins in the darkness, a full fourteen hours after we'd gotten that radio call about the alphas escaping. I was escorting Ava and Cary back to their cabin before heading up to the treehouse to check in on Lexie. Nobody had seen her in a while. Or Bear.

Every one of my years was weighing on me heavily. I was fit and healthy; I made sure of that. Yet, today had been full of emotional and physical chaos that had left me feeling like I needed a hot bath and a hug. Not necessarily in that order. I was pretty sure another night in a hammock was all that awaited me, though.

"How many alphas escaped this morning, and how many stayed?" Cary asked me suddenly as we walked, startling a warning hoot from a nearby owl.

"Six of the Palace alphas escaped and the other six asked to stay," I told him. Winston, the asshole who had punched Lexie, had led the escaping alphas. My blood had boiled when they told me Winston had wanted to grab Maia, Ava, and Lexie on the way out. Maia and Ava because they were valuable omegas, and he thought it would get him a promotion if he brought them back, and Lexie because he had sore balls and a grudge.

I wouldn't tell Ava and Cary that, though. I wondered that the Palace didn't seem all that interested in getting Cary back. If they knew about his attachment to Ava at all, and if it would change things if they found out. Nobody really knew that much about male omegas, they were so rare.

He had me curious, but he'd been so closed off until this morning, it had been hard to get to know him.

"Do you trust the ones who stayed?" I didn't respond right away, not wanting to blow Cary off with a flippant response. The new alphas were in a guest cabin nearby, with Sam's team between them and Ava and Cary's cabin, to monitor them. It was a valid question.

"I trust Dio and Sam, and they're trusting the alphas. Damon has vetted them too, and he has pretty good instincts about people." I was pretty good at spotting an asshole, but alphas had another layer of instincts I would never have.

"If those six alphas hadn't intervened this morning to help the guards when the others escaped, and then alerted us on the radio," I said, choosing my words carefully, so as not to say too much, "the guards would be dead and the escaping alphas would have caused a lot more trouble on their way out."

"You mean they would have grabbed Ava and Maia." Cary said, not holding back. He was far too perceptive. I sighed and nodded.

"They would have tried," I acknowledged, shooting a quick look at Ava.

"How are the two injured guards doing? One was quite young, wasn't he?" Ava asked. She had a serious frown on her face and looked really concerned.

"Yeah, he was one of my cadets." The guilt was eating at me. I never should have let him into the storm cellar, but he'd wanted to prove himself and assist the guards, and we were badly under-resourced. "It could have been so much worse. Luis said they'd be fine, but Damon is trying to grab some more antibiotics and medical supplies if they can find any while they're on the supply run to the airfield tonight."

Dio had been right about the Palace alphas. We didn't even need to turn them. It turned out more than a few no longer wanted to follow orders they couldn't stomach for people they didn't believe in. If there was a resistance brewing, they said they wanted to be a part of it. All of us could relate.

"I heard the alphas that stayed behind asked for help to free the rest of the omegas at the Palace. Will you help them?" Cary asked. He was walking casually with his hands in the pockets of his dark jeans, but his body was tense and he watched me carefully. This question was important to him.

"You mean, will *we* help them?" I gestured between us. I wanted Cary to know he had a home here if he wanted it, not just a place to stay. "You get a say in that. For us, we've always intended to try and free the omegas, ever since Maia turned up and told us what was really happening up there at the Palace. We just needed to figure out how when we've been way outnumbered. So yeah, we'll help them. Or they'll help us. Either way, we'll be freeing those omegas."

"I want to help when we go," Cary insisted, his tone firm.

"Me too," Ava added.

"We're going to need all the help we can get," I reassured them. Ava was a sweet kid. I didn't know what the hell she could do to help. She looked so fragile, almost ethereal, in the moonlight. But I'd been around enough to know people had a way of surprising you when you least expected it.

I was damn tired of these Palace alphas getting the jump on us. We needed to get on the offensive, but we didn't have the resources yet. Thinking of Lexie and the increased danger she was in now had my chest tightening and my fingers twitching for my gun.

I desperately needed to see her. I hadn't laid eyes on her since this morning and it was making me vibrate with an itchy sensation, like there were bees under my skin. We'd both been so busy we'd been missing each other all day, even at lunch and dinner.

Lexie had spent the day helping to settle all the new alphas in and finding supplies for them. They had nothing but the shirts on their backs. She also sorted out all the minor crises that popped up on the farm. People naturally came to her with problems and she always jumped right in to sort them out. Meanwhile, I'd been busy helping organize the supply run and security at the farm for tonight.

The urge to find her and just touch her, breathe her in and make sure she was alright, was overwhelming. I sighed at the memory of watching her emerge from the treehouse in the dawn light this morning looking adorably sexy and well-fucked, with a giant smile on her face. Even that god-awful perfume hadn't been able to tamp down my insane need for her.

She always liked to wear baggy overalls around the farm, thinking they hid her natural curves. Yet today she had paired them with a snug fitting cropped t-shirt that turned the entire ensemble into a peep show. If she charged money to let men sit and watch her work all day in it, I'd buy the whole damn front row.

Watching her stand there holding Dio's hand, I'd wanted to go to her and grab her other hand so badly it had almost hurt to keep still. Her revealing as an omega hadn't changed the way I felt about her at all. Neither had her claiming a mate. Her new scent and the glow surrounding her just enhanced her natural beauty, and made her even more unattainable.

I'd forced myself to stare at the trees instead of her as I'd asked myself, not for the first time, if I dared risk everything and make her mine. *Could I live with myself if I didn't, while watching her build a pack without me?*

I didn't know if she knew that was what she was doing, but I could see it clearly.

Given what we now knew from Maia and her ancient book on packs, a healthy pack needed a beta to balance them out. Despite what I had said this morning about not making a move, I didn't know if I could sit back and watch another guy take the place that felt like mine. *Did I deserve her, though, with all the secrets I carried?*

I shook my head at myself. The guys all calling me out this morning had settled me somewhat and that feeling of rightness thinking about Lexie and I hadn't left all day, even with the chaos that followed.

Knowing Leif and his mates were okay with the idea had made me feel like I could breathe properly for the first time in years. Yet, Sam had been staring me down with enough aggression to inflate a hot-air balloon. Jesus, that guy desperately needed a pack.

I was pretty sure the only reason Sam wasn't completely wild and gone rogue years ago was down to Dio, filling the role of the pack as best he could. He wasn't even really all that subtle about it, not with the way he touched Sam constantly to settle him, at least in front of us. It reminded me so much of Damon and Hunter when we first met.

Dio needed help, though. The level of dominance Sam displayed was on par with Damon, and it was too much for one person to manage alone. Leif and Max had helped Hunter and when Maia came along, the whole pack had clicked into place almost effortlessly. At least once Damon stopped fighting it.

I could already see the effect Lexie had on Sam and Dio. The three of them forming a pack felt inevitable, despite the way Lexie and Sam were circling each other warily.

The satellite phone clipped on my hip rang suddenly, startling me out of the reverie I'd fallen into as we'd walked the last stretch of path in silence. It could only be Damon. He was with Max, Sam, Dio and half of Sam's team on the supply run.

I stopped where I was on the path as I grabbed it. Cary and Ava paused alongside me. I'd been waiting for this call. They were overdue to check in. "Talk to me."

"We reached the airfield and found it locked up. There was only one old guy here, a maintenance guy, all alone. He said we can take anything we want if we bring him back with us to the farm."

"Holy shit, that's good news. Make sure the maintenance guy brings his toolbox as well. Having him around will come in handy when things break down." Our workers were good at patching things up, but we relied on a mechanic in town for bigger issues. Hopefully, this guy could help us keep our machinery going.

"On it. He said they ran a flying doctor service into the mountains from here too, so there's a medical office we're going to raid. It means we don't have to find an unlooted pharmacy on the way back. Can you find Luis and get him to call me back with a list of what I need to prioritize? I'll try to grab as much as I can, but we're exposed out here and I don't want to hang around and draw people to us. If there's something he really needs, I don't want to leave it behind because we didn't know and left in a hurry."

"Got it. He's in the new infirmary. Give me five minutes." I hung up and groaned quietly.

Luis was the only medical help we had now, and he was handling it like a champ, but he had no medical supplies for people. We'd set him up in an unused cabin as a makeshift infirmary this afternoon. Some elders and women were helping stock him with natural remedies and showing him how to use them.

I understood Damon's reluctance to hang around the airfield for too long, though. Nick was watching them on the satellite feeds, but they were in unfamiliar territory and we didn't know if other groups were in the area. He could only give them minutes' warning.

I looked up in the treehouse's direction, feeling intensely agitated. Knowing Lexie was alone right now, and no one had eyes on her with both Sam and Dio gone, made me uneasy. My need to see her, with my own eyes, even briefly, felt like it outweighed everything else right now.

Cary reached out his hand toward me and gestured for the phone. "We've got this, Dave. Go check on Lexie."

I hesitated. It was my job to get Luis. I should let Ava and Cary go check on Lexie, but I felt torn and he could see it. He gave me a rare, soft smile in understanding and solidarity.

"A wise woman told me recently that the only things that matter anymore are the people we love, and that's the way it should have always been," Cary said. "This is just a task. One of hundreds you've already done today. Go, we've got this. We'll find you if there's a problem."

I noticed Ava shoot him a look I couldn't discern in the dark. It was always the looks with these two. They never seemed to touch each other at all, keeping a careful distance that seemed fraught with longing. I could relate.

Instead of handing Cary the phone, I grasped his hand and pulled him into me for a one-armed hug. He stiffened slightly, then relaxed into me with a small sigh and squeezed a handful of my shirt, as if it had been a long time since anyone had hugged him.

If he was going to find his place here, we needed to trust that he knew his limits and let him step up. I knew the alphas felt a need to protect him, being an omega, but he was clearly a capable guy.

"Thanks," I said, simply.

He just pulled back with a nod as I handed him the phone. "Do you think I could join in on the training with your cadets sometime? I'd like to learn some self defense moves. They let me work out at the Palace to look fit, but nothing more. I recently discovered I can't land a punch on a moving target to save myself."

I slapped him on the shoulder. "Absolutely. Our training schedule is out the window at the moment, but I'll let you know when I get them all together next. If it doesn't happen soon, I'll make time to give you a few one-on-one lessons. But don't sell yourself short. You held your own against an alpha, at least for a while, the way I heard it."

"He was just toying with me for kicks, but thank you," Cary said, as he let out a big breath and more of the tension left his body. He turned to go and Ava fell into step next to him.

"You're a good guy, Dave. Go get her," Ava said softly over her shoulder with a small smile, before they both strode away into the darkness, back down the path.

I hoped that meant there was no more salt in my coffee in the future. I watched them for a moment, feeling protective of them. They both felt lost, and there was an underlying sadness that wove through both of their energies. Tying them together, yet also holding them apart.

Once they'd disappeared around the bend, I turned and headed up the hill. I felt a renewed energy now that I knew I was finally heading to Lexie. My feet sped up as I hustled up the path, used to moving around in the dark now. I couldn't see any movement on the deck, but it didn't mean Lexie wasn't up there.

Maia and Ava had last seen her down at the dining hall, but they'd told me Lexie had been planning to head back up here after dropping some food to Nick in the security office earlier.

"Lex, you up there?" I called up, like a coward, as I eyed the stairs. I so rarely invaded her personal space. It felt wrong to just waltz up. There was no response, though. Only the sound of leaves whispering in the light breeze and a nocturnal animal rustling through the underbrush that I had startled nearby.

I warred with myself for another minute, but I knew I couldn't rest until I saw her with my own eyes. So I turned and walked up the stairs, not trying to mask my approach. I didn't want to take her by surprise. I reached the top and searched the deck as my eyes adjusted to the moonlight after the darkness of the curved stairs. No Lexie, curled up asleep in her favorite swinging chair, like I was hoping.

"Lex," I called out as I knocked on the old barn doors. I tried the doors, and they slid open easily. *Why was there no lock on this fucking door, and why was I only realizing it now?*

"I'm coming in," I called out loudly. She would know my voice, so I didn't bother announcing myself.

The inside was in shadow, with the downstairs curtains drawn and the only light coming from the skylight in the loft. I opened the door wider to let in more light before moving further into the room. I couldn't see her lying on the couches, and I couldn't hear the shower running, which meant if she was here, she was asleep in the loft.

The thought had my dick perking up like I was a horny teenager. I'd left my teenage years far behind, but just the thought of Lexie lying in bed, maybe just wearing one of Dio's t-shirts with nothing underneath, had me hard as a rock.

"Get it together," I muttered to myself. I tried to think unsexy thoughts, but the vision of Lexie splayed out with a t-shirt riding up her thighs was burned into my brain.

"Don't be a fucking creep," I muttered as I headed up the stairs. I'll just make sure she's there.

"Lex, are you awake?" I called out softly as I neared the top. Forcing myself to stop when I saw the edge of the bedding.

"Lex," I called again, louder this time. Still no reply. Dread spread icy fingers up my spine.

She had to be here, right? Unless Maia was mistaken and Lexie had gone back to her cottage? But Maia had said Lexie was definitely headed here, to wait for Dio, as he didn't know which cabin was hers and she 'didn't want him getting confused and walking in on some other girl when he got back late.' Maia had laughed as she'd used her fingers to air quote Lexie's words.

I gave myself a mental slap and took the last three steps, bringing the entire loft into view. No t-shirt riding up. No bare legs. No Lexie at all.

Fuck. I raced back down the stairs again.

Why the hell hadn't I kept my eyes on her all day? What if Max had been wrong and Winston had circled back?

Nothing was more important to me than Lexie. Yet I'd gotten up in my head after coming clean to the guys about her this morning, and let myself get distracted with a thousand useless tasks. I should have stuck to her like glue, instead. She would have hated feeling like I was babysitting her, but at least I'd know where the hell she was right now.

I flicked on a light switch, not giving a fuck about letting the light escape with the door open right now. I was five seconds away from waking the whole damn farm up.

I spun around the room. The denim overalls and white t-shirt she had been wearing earlier had been flung over a chair, and her white sneakers were lying on the floor nearby. But there were no signs of a struggle and if anyone had taken Lexie, my girl would have put up one hell of a fight.

She had clearly come back here and gotten changed at some point. I turned again, trying to think. I went to check the outdoor shower before I completely lost my shit. *Maybe she was just drying off? Maybe she has headphones on?*

I was grasping at straws and I knew it. When I spied a note on the kitchen bench as I passed, I snapped it up.

Dio, I got an emergency alert from my safe room in town. One of my girls is in trouble. I've gone to get her. Be back in a few hours. Lexie xx

My body turned to ice and my heart kicked into overdrive as I read the note and realized Lexie was on her own, outside the gates, while a psycho alpha was on the loose and gunning for her.

Oh fuck, no. I was running before I'd even finished reading.

Twenty-One

I eased onto the brakes on my dirt bike as the trees thinned out and I saw the outline of buildings rising out of the gloom in the distance. I angled the bike off the road and into one of the last stands of trees.

I was lucky the moon was so bright tonight. Riding the fire trails through the forest into town at night was normally a thrill. Without using headlights, it was a crazy, wild ride that had my stomach sitting up in my throat.

It wasn't the only risk I was taking tonight. My bike had modifications to make it as quiet as possible, but it was still a gas powered dirt bike so I couldn't avoid noise completely. In the new stillness of our dark world, sound carried even further.

I'd looked into electric dirt bikes when they came out a while ago. They were sleek and silent, but I kept mine in a lean-to shelter in the woods, with no power. I only used it when I needed to sneak out without my brother and his mates tracking my every movement. So an electric one wouldn't work.

I cursed that now. Before the Crash, hearing a dirt bike in the distance hadn't been unusual. Even at night. We were a semi-rural community surrounded by forest. Most of our neighbors had at least one.

But post-Crash, you couldn't pump fuel without some kind of alternate power and the sound of cars and bikes had all but disappeared. I had briefly considered taking one of our electric carts. I would have had to take it out one of our main gates, though. Which would have led to a lot of questions and probably a call to my brother or Damon.

I understood their need to protect me. It was their instinct and sweet, but annoying as fuck at times. I was a grown woman and had been doing this for a long time. I took risks, yes, but that was my decision and my choice.

With half the team out on the supply run right now, and the rest on high-alert back at the farm, I wasn't pulling anyone away from their duties to come with me.

All of that meant I'd had to use the secret tunnel out of the farm, making Bear wait at the entrance when he'd wanted to come with me, then park and leave my bike an annoying distance outside of town, to walk the rest of the way in.

Being alone, on foot, was a whole other risk these days. I kinda wished I'd let Bear come. I glanced around, trying to note any landmarks in the dark. I wanted to make sure I could find my bike again in a hurry if I needed to.

The walk into town at least gave me time to plan my next movements. I hadn't had time to plan since I'd walked into the security office to take Nick some dinner and noticed a code on one screen. It was one Max had set up for me and came from the safe house I had created in an apartment in town.

I had an informal network of contacts that I trusted, that worked in places like local gyms, coffee shops and in schools. They each had a card with a code on it that would unlock the door. The safe house was for any woman they had vetted that was fleeing a domestic violence situation.

Lucky for me, Max had set the safe house up with an independent solar battery system for power. So no-one could cut the power supply from the outside. It was off-grid, the same as the farm.

I wasn't affiliated with any official groups or the government and I funded the safe house setup myself. There were many support groups in place for women that were doing amazing work and I donated to them too, but my safe house was for women who fell through the cracks.

The women who needed urgent help and couldn't go elsewhere, for reasons usually out of their control. Women who needed to disappear and do it quickly. The ones no-one else could help and too often ended up dead. If someone had entered the safe house, it meant their situation was desperate. It wasn't a weekend retreat.

The code on the door not only let them in, it also sent an alert to my phone. If I didn't acknowledge within two hours, it then went to Max's security system as a fail-safe. The women were told to lie low inside and someone would come to get them within twenty-four hours.

That someone was me. Leif and his mates knew about the setup and had made me promise I would ask for their back-up if I ever needed it, no questions asked. I started this work while they were away in the military, though, and I knew what I was doing. They tried to respect that.

I asked for their help occasionally. I wasn't stupid, and I didn't have a death wish. But only when necessary. A big, scary military looking dude walking through the door rarely helped the situation.

The guys always pitched in, regardless, when I brought the women back to the farm. The traumatized women often took some time to feel safe around strange men. Max and Hunter usually eased the way and the other women I'd rescued always closed ranks around the new women, too.

Nick hadn't seemed to know what the alarm meant and had asked me if I knew. I'd just told him, "Yeah, it's not about the farm. I'll take care of it. When did the code appear?"

"A few hours ago. It popped up just after Max left, but I didn't want to bother him while on the supply run," Nick said.

I hadn't given Nick a chance to ask questions after that. I'd just put in the received code at our end, to stop it flashing, checked the feeds inside the apartment, then left abruptly. Cursing myself.

I continued to curse myself as I'd dashed to my storage facility, grabbed what I needed, then ran the entire way back to the treehouse. I'd stopped carrying my phone with me the last few days. It had seemed like a waste of electricity to keep charging it when no-one was calling me. I hadn't thought about Max not manning the security office, though, and no-one else knowing what the innocuous code on the screen meant.

I usually staked the safe house out discreetly before I entered, but the world had changed and time was not on either of our sides. I had seen a woman curled up on the bed on the feed. She was wearing a giant hoodie and I couldn't see her face. It looked like she was sleeping, but she may have been crying. She was in the fetal position and had likely been there for hours, terrified and alone.

I increased my pace through the last of the forest, wanting to get into town as quickly as possible. It was full dark now, but my eyes had adjusted and the moon was lighting a silvery path for me through the short, grassy fire break at the rear of the town. I had no cover from this angle, but the main road was an even worse bet.

I forced myself to walk at a sedate pace through the open fire break. I'd learnt a long time ago that crouching and running looked way more suspicious than sauntering in as if you owned the place. The eye picked out movements that were out of the ordinary, but often glossed over something that fit into a normal pattern of behavior.

When I reached the dilapidated buildings at the rear of town, the moonlight became a patchwork quilt, leaving half the world in shadows. I'd long since made my peace with them, though. Shadows were my old friends. I stuck to them closely now, while keeping my eye on the light. I wore head to toe black clothes, with a dark hoodie firmly settled over my bright hair.

My safe house was in an old sandstone building that someone had converted into stylish apartments. It was next to a historic pub that I had expected to be empty, but appeared to be full of people, with lights blazing. I could hear a gas-powered generator running out the back and smell the noxious fumes. I hadn't realized how quickly I had adjusted to natural scents taking back over our landscape.

Shit. My options, from where I stood in a shadowy junction, had become limited. I peeked around the corner, but the breeze here had turned into a wind tunnel that blew my loose hoodie off my head. I yanked my head back, desperately hoping my bright hair in the moonlight hadn't drawn attention.

I debated my path, and was just about to make my move, when a hand clamped over my mouth and pulled me further back into the shadows. I instantly felt like I was being electrified as a tingling current zipped over my skin.

A dark, masculine voice whispered, "Don't fight me."

Like hell I wouldn't fight. Balls were about to be kicked.

I got myself into position to twist away but froze when the hand over my face softened into a caress that ran down to my throat, as an earthy scent of sage hit my senses and lips touched my ear in the lightest of caresses.

One tortured, whispered word teased my ear as white light shimmered through me.

"Mine."

Twenty-Two

 Pala

Since the first moment I'd spotted this woman, I'd had one thought drowning out everything else. Claim her. Yet I'd needed to complete my mission to keep her safe.

I'd been sure she was an omega. My body had known it, even though the world believed she wasn't. That I hadn't scented her the first time I had seen her was the only reason I'd been able to leave her behind.

Her scent saturating my senses right now had every cell in my body alight. It drenched me with need and a dark possessiveness that took any thought not completely centered on her and cast it adrift. The word, 'Mine,' was pounding a heavy beat through my soul as the word slipped out on a groan, needing to be given life.

My beast was raging to spin her around, push her up against this dark wall and claim her so fiercely there would never be a question about who she belonged to. Her body had gone limp in my arms and her fresh passion fruit scent had deepened into a syrupy meringue that had my blood heating in my veins.

She had been readying to fight. I'd felt her tense and begin to twist in my arms in a practiced move I knew would break my hold. Until my scent, sweetened with cinnamon from the feel of her lush curves pressed up against me, surrounded her just as possessively as my hand on her throat.

Her instant submission had my beast roaring in my head. But the beast also sensed danger near and the threat had the world sharpening into focus again.

Our combined scents were spilling into the air, saturating my senses. If anyone caught a whiff on the breeze, we would be in real trouble. There was a pub full of alphas barely a hundred meters away.

"We have to move," I breathed quietly into her ear. "You're not safe here."

I had to force my fingers to release her throat, but I kept my other arm in place around her waist until it felt like she was standing steadier.

She spun in my arms and I fought for control as her gaze landed on me for the first time, branding me to my core. Her eyes widened, and in the darkness I couldn't make out the color clearly. Yet I could see every other feature of her heart-shaped face in the shimmery moonlight. She had me completely captivated.

Her skin was pale and silvery as my eyes caressed every curve of her cheekbones, before they dropped to her perfect bow-shaped lips as they parted slightly on a breath. The urge to kiss her was like a wild frenzy inside me, but I knew if I did we'd both be lost to a battering of sensation that would leave us vulnerable.

I forced my attention to covering her hair, but that was hardly better. The bright pink strands glowed in the moonlight. I pulled her hood back over her head and tucked a stray strand behind her ear. It felt like silk on my fingertips.

I jerked my head over my shoulder to tell her we needed to move, not trusting any more sound right now. But she shook her head and opened her mouth to speak. I quickly slid the hand that was still clinging to the nape of her neck, back over her mouth.

I held up two fingers in front of her, then bent them and pointed them over her shoulder, indicating two hidden guards around the corner. I felt sick at the thought of what would have happened if she'd stepped out.

Her eyes widened even further, and she nodded slightly under my hand to show she understood. I shifted my hand back to her neck, not able to resist the lightest swipe with my thumb over her lower lip that had me swallowing another groan.

I stepped back, attempting to get some clear air and control, before I grabbed her hand and turned to go back the way she had arrived. She followed me patiently until we reached the furthest building, before she tugged on my hand and dug her heels in, forcing me to halt.

When I looked over my shoulder at her, raising one eyebrow in question, she pointed in the direction we were going and shook her head. Then pointed back the way we had come.

What in the hell could be so important back there that she refused to leave? Her eyes were begging me to stop, and I couldn't deny her. I swiveled us into a dark recess, but it barely fit the two of us, and forced our bodies up against each other again.

My nostrils flared as her scent spiked and invaded the small space. I replaced the chant of *mine* pounding in my head with, *not here.*

I lowered my head so she could whisper in my ear. "I can't leave," she whispered, as she reached up to shift my long hair away from my ear.

The sound of the voice that had been haunting me since I had first heard it days ago, accompanied by her breath feathering across my cheek and her fingers in my hair, almost had me losing all control. I locked my limbs in place to stop myself from touching her more than I had to right now.

No woman had ever affected me this way, and left me with so little control and a raging need that felt like a wild fire surrounded by kindling. My family was native to our area and clung to the old ways. I was no stranger to mysticism and fables, which is what I had believed stories of true mates to be.

This was no fable, though. Without a doubt, this strong, defiant, beautiful woman was my true mate. I felt the mystics of old laughing at me from a great distance. I almost heard them on the breeze, as if they had sent me her way right when she needed me.

I'd been about to cross the firebreak on my way out of town, heading towards the forest, where I felt more at home. I had sensed her a moment before I saw her step out of the trees and into the moonlight.

I knew it was her instantly. It made no sense, though. I'd left her safely at the farm, to go do what I had to do and finish the job I had started. I'd believed her to be in the safe care of Sam and Dio, or I never would have left. Yet here she was. Alone.

It seemed our mate was going to keep us on our toes. The thought brought a smile to my face. I hoped she would shake up Sam's world and soothe him at the same time. He needed both, or he had before I had made the hardest decision of my life. To leave my brothers, my mates.

The last few years had been dark and lonely. I wasn't the same man anymore, and the darkness had whispered that I wouldn't be welcomed back. It made me hesitate even more now. I knew I would do anything for this woman, but the thought that I may have to do it from a distance filled me with a sudden sadness and longing.

Dio had said my home was with them, but did he mean it in the same way I wanted it?

Lexie pulled back slightly and searched my face as if she was trying to see my soul through my eyes, and I was lost. Her fingers were still twined in my hair and I suddenly felt like anything was possible, if she just let me be near her.

"What do you need?" I breathed into the quiet darkness.

She closed her eyes for a moment and I got the feeling it was a question she hadn't heard a lot. Or at least, not that simply. When she opened them again, she looked determined and spoke rapidly.

"I have a safe house nearby. A woman has taken refuge there and I need to get her out." The emotion in her hushed voice told me how much this meant to her.

"How far away?" I asked.

"At the back of the apartment conversion, in the old sandstone building next to the pub."

I cursed inwardly. It was the worst location possible in this town right now.

"How did you get here?" I asked.

"I have a dirt bike stashed just outside of town, in the trees about half a mile past the firebreak," she whispered.

I could work with that. "I'll get her and bring her to you. Meet me there. Don't wait for me, though. If you're discovered, head straight to the farm. I'll follow you there."

"No. No way am I sitting out there waiting like a good little girl, while you go and -"

I pushed into her space and kissed her. Branding her the way she had me. Her lips parted in shock and I couldn't resist the opportunity to taste her fully. She tasted like sin and sweetness mixed in a way that exploded like candy on my tongue. I pulled back as suddenly as I'd started, leaving us both breathless.

"What the hell was that?" She asked quietly, looking dazed.

"You were mad and your voice was getting loud. You were going to give us away. I quietened you the quickest way I know how," I whispered into her ear.

"Oh," was all she said, looking a little crestfallen as her mouth turned down slightly in an adorable pout. I wanted to kiss it off her, but I only had so much willpower.

"Plus, I've been wanting to do that since I first laid eyes on you," I added.

I saw her mouth twitch slightly in the darkness, like she was fighting a smile.

"You've barely known me for a minute," she sassed, while trying to keep her voice hushed.

"Have I?" I whispered in her ear, causing her to shiver, before I pulled back to look at her with my eyebrow raised in question.

She suddenly looked adorably confused. "Do I know you?" Lexie asked. "I feel like I've always known you, yet also never seen you before."

"Wait," she said, as she tried to step back, but the wall at her back blocked her. She looked suddenly mistrustful, as if her brain was trying to fight past the omega pheromones pumping through her body. "Are you one of the alphas who escaped the farm today?"

"No," I said, "I'm the alpha who escaped the first night."

She looked confused again. I could almost see her brain working, trying to make connections. "What's your name?" She whispered suddenly.

"Pala," I answered honestly. I would hide nothing from this woman.

She gasped loudly, and I ran my mouth over her open lips again. "Are you begging for another kiss?" I asked hoarsely. She chased my lips and forced me to pull back before I forgot myself.

"Are you Dio's Pala?" She whispered against my mouth, torturing me.

I brushed my hand down from where it had found its home around her nape, again, and pulled the neck of her black t-shirt to the side on instinct. I traced my finger over the bite mark there and she shivered again.

"More like he's our Dio," I whispered back.

Awareness and understanding flashed across her face as I watched her emotions play out, followed by desire and guilt.

"I would never do a thing to hurt either you, Dio, or Sam," I said, as I looked her in the eye and spoke my truth. "Ever."

"Dio was pitching you as a potential mate from the first night we were together. Now, I know why. You feel right. Like you're a part of them."

I swallowed hard at her words. The intense way she was looking at me made me want to do significantly more than kiss her, but this wasn't the time or the place. We had already dallied too long, too close to danger. We were on borrowed time.

"He's a good man, and cares deeply about people, despite his easygoing nature. Family and bonds are important to him. To Sam and I, too."

"Yet, you left them? They've been hurting at your silence." Her tone wasn't accusing, but curious and only slightly remonstrating. I could tell she cared deeply already, too.

"It hurt me too, but it was necessary. I don't plan on staying away anymore, though."

She was silent for a moment, taking me in, tracing my features with her gaze. Learning my shadows. But a sudden noise nearby had me stiffening and whipping my head around to the entrance of our little recess. No more sounds followed, but I focused again as I remembered where we were.

We would have time for this discussion soon. I would make sure of it.

"Back to the plan," I whispered, "if we want to get your friend and make it back to the farm. We're running out of time. I don't doubt your ability to get this woman out ordinarily, but there is a pub full of escaped alphas next door who know you by sight, and your omega scent is currently in overdrive. If even one alpha comes across it with this breeze, it will lead a path directly to you and your secret will be out."

I paused. "And not just you. Even if you get her out without being discovered, your scent is going to linger and will leave a path right to the safe house. It's not a risk you need to take right now, when I can go for you. My scent is already all over this town. I've been staking it out for hours."

Lexie wanted to argue. I could see it in her eyes, but she couldn't fault my logic. "Fine," she huffed.

I hadn't been around women a lot, having been in the military most of my adult life, but I knew enough about them to know when they said, 'Fine,' things were rarely actually fine.

I leaned in towards her and whispered in her ear again. "I won't let you down. I'll get her out, I promise. Then you can take it from there. I have no problem letting you do your thing."

I shifted down further to breathe her scent deeply from the curve of her neck, the spot I had been dreaming about claiming. I licked her lightly over the sensitive spot before blowing on her skin gently as I worked my way back up to her ear. Loving her shivers at my slightest touch and the tiny moan that slipped out.

"The way you handled those alphas after the fight at the farm was intoxicating," I whispered again, my lips gliding down towards the corner of her mouth. "I could hardly take my eyes off you. I've had to force myself to focus on finishing my mission, because I knew it would help keep you safe. But all I've been able to think about since the moment I left was getting back to you, Dio, and Sam."

Lexie was panting hard. The close quarters in the darkness, the sense of danger and the true mate bond I could feel drawing us together made this moment feel too much and not nearly enough at the same time. I wanted all of her and I didn't want to wait. I'd been waiting my whole life already.

Not the place, Pala. Don't start something you can't finish here without putting her in danger. I cautioned myself. Keeping my body away from hers right now, or my mind focused on the task at hand, was proving hard. I used all of my willpower to force myself backwards in the little space we had.

Her eyes looked glazed, almost drugged in the tiny amount of moonlight that was filtering into our recess. That would not help her run if she needed to escape. I put my hands on her shoulders, to stop her swaying towards me as her body tried to follow mine instinctively.

"Now," I growled lightly, "tell me what I need to know to get your friend out safely."

Lexie nodded, and I removed my hands from her reluctantly. I put them behind my back and leaned against the recess wall behind me to stop myself from touching her again.

Get her out. Get her safe. Was my new mantra.

She quickly told me the passcodes, the security measures on the safe house, and how to get out through the secret passage if I needed to. It could only be accessed from the inside. I focused all my attention on her words, not wanting to make her repeat herself.

My skin prickled with a sense of imminence, as if something was coming. It got steadily stronger, as Lexie whispered her last words and raised an eyebrow at my silence. I placed a finger over her mouth to warn her to be quiet now. As I opened all my senses up to the darkness surrounding us.

There, another noise, this time much closer. The slightest scrape of a shoe and a rustle of clothing as someone shifted position. Someone was hunting us. We were out of time.

I slowed my breathing and focused all my senses on the alleyway beyond us, knowing the only way out now was through whoever was out there.

I gave Lexie the stay signal, hoping she understood after being around her brother and his mates so much. Then shifted silently, so I was better poised to move. Knowing the moon was at the opposite end of the alley as whoever approached, I was confident I would see them before they saw us.

My entire being focused on this one threat, one rectangle of filtered, silvery light. No one was hurting Lexie on my watch.

The moment I saw a shadow move, I launched myself through the recess, grabbed the intruder, and slammed him up against the wall with a chokehold against his throat. The alpha had the nerve to laugh.

"I thought I had scented you earlier. I heard you're MIA from the Palace. Did you escape with a tasty omega, because something smells delicious down here? Should have headed anywhere else, because now you're going to have to share her with all of us. Those fuckers at the Palace are stingy with the omegas, but if one is MIA with you, she's fair game and you're nowhere near dominant enough to stop me."

The intruder alpha groaned before cackling like a deranged maniac. "Fuck, she's a potent one." He sounded high.

Suddenly, a door opened in the alcove behind Lexi. A dark figure shot out and pushed her into the moonlight. She stumbled, trying to maintain her balance on the uneven surface in the alleyway. The alpha followed too closely behind her, though. He grabbed her arm, before I could intervene, and pulled her around in front of him, keeping her unbalanced until he pulled her against his body.

My blood boiled in my veins at the sight of another alpha touching my omega. Lexi's face wrinkled at his proximity and his noxious, weedy scent. Her omega didn't like it either.

"Well, well, what do we have here? It seems someone has been holding out on the Palace. Lexie, isn't it? Who could mistake that hair?" he asked as he took a long sniff of it. "Winston is going to be thrilled to see you."

"No," the first alpha groaned as he pushed against me. "I found her. Let me have a turn first. Winston will never share."

I growled low in my throat and I could see the other alpha's eyes glinting dangerously in the moonlight as he continued to hold Lexie in place.

"Roger, Alfonso, I should have known if anyone was doing shady deals in back alleyways, it would be you two. At least now I can end you with a clean conscience."

I looked over at Lexie and saw the determined gleam in my girl's eyes. She was about to throw down and I was here for it. "Make him pay, my heart."

She smiled at me, and honestly, at that moment, she was a little terrifying. Her gorgeous bright pink hair was flowing lightly in the breeze and she was standing strong, with her feet firmly planted now and her body relaxed, ready to move.

People often said her brother, Leif, looked like a Norse god, which was fitting. Because right now, I swore I could see Freyja, Norse goddess of love, fertility, war and death, staring back at me in the moonlight. Her spirit was fierce and wild, and the thought of battle woke something up inside her.

I'd never gotten the connection between love and war before, or even death, always thinking it an odd combination. I saw it now though. Love shone through Lexie in everything she did, but she was also a force to be reckoned with. I knew instinctively she would start a war to save the people she loved.

Lexie pulled a move so swiftly, I barely even saw it. One moment she was standing, being held in front of an alpha who towered over her. The next, he was on his knees and she was behind him, his own pocket knife stolen from his belt, held to his throat.

"How do you like it, watching a knife get held to your friend's throat?" she asked the alpha I still had pinned. "Doesn't feel great, does it?"

"Holy fuck, that was hot," the alpha I held sputtered, and I grabbed his throat so hard I heard a crack.

Lexie just sighed. Completely done with these two. She looked almost disappointed, like that had been too easy.

"You need to go, now, Lexie," I said. "We're out of time."

"I'm not leaving you here with two alphas," she hissed at me.

I barked a command at the alpha in her hands and he froze instantly, a look of agony passing over his features briefly. She stepped away from him in shock.

Many people underestimated my dominance because my scent was subtle and mild, and I appeared to be quiet. But I was just at peace with my beast. We co-existed naturally without competing, unlike most alphas who fought their own beasts for dominance and tried to suppress them when they didn't need them. Mine was always with me.

I let my true beast shine through my eyes and Lexie gasped. "Go now, my heart. I've got this. These alphas aren't hurting anyone ever again."

The alpha in my hold stiffened in fear and I willed her to go. I could see she wanted to argue again. She looked between the two alphas I had immobilized. One with my body and the other with my will. I knew instinctively she would argue to spare their lives, but they had seen her and scented her. There was no way they could live. She'd never be safe.

I saw the moment she realized the same thing. This was a moment for death and war, in the name of love.

I let my beast recede a little. "I swear I'm going to make that detour and be right behind. But we have to go now, and I need you out of this alleyway first. Please."

She nodded, pocketed the knife with a grimace, and stepped away from the frozen alpha at her feet. I had a feeling she rarely used knives and wasn't a fan of them. Before I could say anything more, she stepped into me. Not caring at all about the alpha I had pinned against the wall, completely dismissing him.

She rested her hand on my face, caressing it gently. "Promise you'll meet me. I'm not losing you on the same night I found you. If you die on me, I will resurrect you and kill you again, slowly."

I stared at her intently, feeling this woman settling deep into the core of my existence and marking me as hers with her words. "I will deny you nothing, in this life or the next."

Lexie searched my face again, before she nodded, turned and disappeared into the darkness like she'd never existed. I knew she was real though, because I could feel a tentative bond connecting us, like a new flame struggling to grow.

I turned to the alpha in front of me. He whimpered as I let my beast back out and my inner darkness crept into my voice.

"It's time for war and death."

Twenty-Three

I waited, hidden in the darkness, my eyes focused on the entry to the alleyway. I knew Pala had asked me to go, and I knew why. So I went, but I wasn't heading back to my bike until I knew he was okay.

I scanned my surroundings and noticed movement heading towards us. *Christ on a cracker. What now?*

I'd made sure I had an alternate exit, but it involved running through the exposed fire break. So it was a back-up plan. Plus, if I ran, they could take Pala by surprise when he exited the alley. I needed to find out what was heading for us first. I pushed myself further into the shadows and tracked the movement.

Whoever it was, they were moving stealthily, staying in the dark spaces like me. Either they were tracking us, or not where they were supposed to be. From the outline, it was a teenage boy or a small woman. I could handle myself easily with either, if I needed to.

As they crept closer, I relaxed my body, preparing to strike. I took a slow breath in just before they cut across near me and I got a brief look at them in the moonlight. I knew that face. He was the son of one of my contacts and a good kid.

"Ziggy," I hissed into the darkness. He spun towards my voice, but couldn't see me. I stepped out slightly, so he could see my face, before I reached out and grabbed him. I didn't want him to yell and give us all away.

He took one look at me and lunged at me, hugging me fiercely. As well as being a contact, his mum was also one of my self-defense class students. Ziggy sometimes hung out at our lessons while he waited for her, so he knew me. I'd even taught him a few simple moves one afternoon.

I could feel him silently sobbing against my shoulder. He was clearly terrified right now. I pressed him into my shoulder and stroked his hair and his back gently until he stopped shaking. Poor kid was barely thirteen years old, and skinnier than I remember the last time I saw him.

"What are you doing out here alone at night? Where's your mom?" I whispered, as my stomach sank, realizing she could be dead.

"She's in the storage area behind the old museum with some of her friends. Nobody has tried to ransack it yet, because there's nothing useful in there. But we've run out of food and water."

I breathed a sigh of relief. My friend was safe, but something was off. "Why isn't she at home, and why are you out here by yourself?"

Why isn't she in the safe house? I added to myself.

"We were at home, but when the alphas came and set up at the pub, they tried to get people to trade their wives for food. When nobody took them up on it, they started ransacking nearby houses, looking for single women. They were drunk and shouting. Mum got us and some of her friends out and we've been hiding since."

I had to force my rage down. This kid didn't need to see me wigging out right now.

"When was this?" I asked, trying to keep my voice even.

"About four days ago. Most of the alphas disappeared after the first night. Only a few stayed, but the rest came back earlier today. I've been trying to find food, but the alphas spotted me one day. When they asked where my parents were, I told them both my parents took off and left me. They've been making me run errands and scavenge for them since then, but I sneak away to take things to my mom."

His body trembled as he paused, and he looked over his shoulder. "Water, I can get from the river, but I know one alpha has been secretly stashing food in a storage room in the alleyway over there. I watched him. I was going to steal it for mom and her friends."

My heart shattered for this brave, terrified kid. Nobody should have to suffer what he was going through. Life had clearly forced him to grow up really fast and make some tough calls to protect his mom.

"We can help with that," came a dark voice from behind me. I whipped around to find Pala leaning on the wall, barely a meter away from us. I glared at him.

"You scared the crap out of me. I think a little pee actually came out," I whispered, a little harsher than I intended, while my heart was racing.

He just arched an eyebrow at me. Shit, that confession was definitely not sexy talk. *Damn ninja alphas. How long had he been standing there?*

Pala pointedly looked at the boy I had shoved between me and the wall. "So we're ransacking the supply closet for his mom, or are we taking them with us?" He asked calmly, yet resolutely. Like it was a given, we were going to help the kid.

I narrowed my eyes at Pala before I turned back to Ziggy. "How many women are hiding in the museum?"

"Three, including my mom."

My heart dropped. I couldn't transport that many back right now and it was a long walk to the farm for people who hadn't had regular meals in days, or longer. Plus, I knew his mom was a fighter. She was a teacher at the local high school and she loved this town. She raised all kinds of hell at local council meetings to get resources for the kids. I knew she'd want us to save the town, not just her.

"Can you hold on for a few days if we get you the food and into a safer place? You're going to have to lie low too, because we just took out two of their men," I asked.

"Plus, you now have her omega scent all over you," Pala added. "You can't go near an alpha for a day or two or they'll scent her. They won't be nice about asking where she is."

My head filled with curses for not even thinking of that. I'd just put an, 'I know an omega' neon sign above this kid's head. It sickened me that I had put him in even more danger. I was used to being able to hug whoever I wanted without branding them.

I was grateful that Pala had thought of it. I was going to have to show him just how thankful I was later.

Ziggy nodded at Pala, but looked at me strangely. "You weren't an omega before."

I sighed as I ruffled his hair affectionately. "Yeah. Long story, kid."

He groaned quietly and dodged my hand, flattening his hair back down. I tried not to laugh. Even in an apocalypse, teenagers were all the same.

"You need to head back to the bike. We'll grab some food, head to the museum, then get everyone to the safe house."

I wanted to argue, but I knew his original argument still stood. If I attempted to go near the museum, I'd lead a scent path straight to it. I'd just started to reconcile myself to the idea of being an omega, because the sex was fan-fucking-tastic, but my new scent was quickly becoming a pain in the ass.

How the hell was I supposed to sneak around and help people if everyone could smell me coming, or smell where I'd been. My anger made my passionfruit scent spike even higher, with a slight, yet sharp, tang of lime entering the mix. I groaned in frustration.

"Fine," I ground out.

Pala leant down and straightened out one of my fists to hold my hand, brushing his thumb gently across the back. "I know this isn't fair, but thank you for trusting me to do this for you."

Cue swooning. I swear I could hear cheesy music playing somewhere. My anger dissipated like smoke on a breeze. I had to stop myself from melting into him as the draw between us intensified and my scent swung back to syrupy sweet passion fruit meringue. Who the hell was this guy? I really wanted to climb him like a tree right now.

I shook myself instead and stepped away. His eyes tracked my every movement.

"Ask his mom why she isn't in the safe house instead of the museum. She has a passcode. See if there's anything going on there we should know before you head there. I don't want you walking into a trap."

His eyes lit up in the darkness at the smallest evidence I cared about his welfare, and his earthy sage scent sweetened with cinnamon. At the first hit, I covered my mouth and nose with my hand, and tried not to breathe. The pull between us didn't need to flare any hotter right now.

"Keep him safe," I begged.

"Goes without saying," Pala replied calmly.

I turned to the kid. "Listen to Pala. He'll show you the stop and move signals. Watch him and follow closely. I know you've probably gotten good at keeping to shadows and sneaking around the past few days, but he's a master at it."

I gave one last glance to Pala, desperately hoping I'd see him again and that he wouldn't disappear into the night. I refused to be a needy omega and beg him, though. He seemed to sense my unease, regardless.

"I'll make it back to you, or I'll die trying." He declared simply, but the effect it had on my omega was like a firework set off in a soda can. It split me open. It didn't make it easier to leave or even think coherently. I grabbed him and kissed him hard and fierce, running my hands up into his long dark hair and pulling hard, wanting him to feel as much pain and desire twined together as I did right now.

I groaned as I wrenched myself away and turned my back on him to walk away for the second time tonight. I felt a physical ache settle into my bones and I chanted in my head with every step, *it's not goodbye, it's not goodbye.*

I was going to figure out how to walk towards, instead of away from, this intriguing, beautiful man before the night was out.

"You're clear. Go." He urged. So I went without looking back. For now.

I forced myself to keep to an even pace once again, trusting Pala to give an alert if I needed to run. When I hit the treeline, I disappeared into the shadows and hustled the half mile back to my bike.

I found it, with one wrong turn in the dark and only a few muttered curses.

My bike wasn't alone, though.

Twenty-Four

Someone had propped another bike next to mine, this one electric. It wasn't a bike I'd seen before. Any type of electric vehicle was rare in these parts. The only ones I'd seen around here before were on our farm.

I stood in the shadows, trying to decide whether to retreat or show myself when I felt the heat of a solid presence warm my back. I really needed to work on my peripheral senses.

"Lex," Dave whispered, his voice dark and raspy. "Do you know how many years you just took off my life?"

I felt him grab my hips from behind, roughly, as if he was trying not to touch me but also couldn't go another minute without it. It felt like he was at war with himself as his hands squeezed my sides, anchoring me in place.

His hold reminded me of our secret kiss in the darkness of a different tree, and I briefly wondered why Dave only dared to touch me in the shadows. *Was it guilt? Denial? Or maybe just the allure of the forbidden?*

He tugged me back against his tense body, before he relaxed slightly at the contact, and slowly slid his arms around my waist to hug me from behind. He rested his head on my shoulder and breathed out heavily.

I had so many questions right now. *How did he find me? What did I mean to him? Why did he smell so freaking good?* Dave had started to smell like both Sam and Dio, as if their scents clung to him, but with his own musky undertone.

I tentatively reached up and wrapped my arms over his around my waist. His touch felt strangely familiar. It was as if he'd been touching me my whole life rather than the strict hands off policy we usually observed: like it was some kind of secret agreement that we'd never voiced.

I leaned into him and rested my head back onto his shoulder while looking up into the darkened branches above us, silently offering him the comfort he so clearly needed. Sparks usually flew between us, hot and intense, whenever we were near each other. Yet, this moment felt peaceful.

We stayed that way for a few minutes, listening to the sounds of the forest slowly coming back to life around us, now that we were no longer trampling around and disturbing the inhabitants. An owl hooted over-head, making me jump slightly, and Dave chuckled, his breath ghosting over my neck.

My skin instantly heated and I let out the smallest moan as I finally noticed his hard body pressed behind me. He tensed up again, as if only just now realizing how many places we were touching, too. He eased back up and away from me, and I felt the loss of his touch keenly.

I swallowed, hard, as I forced my desire for him back down into the box I kept it in. I stepped away too, but kept my face averted as I partially turned. How could a man destroy me without me even laying eyes on him? It was torture.

"Lex...," he whispered with a groan. He left the one word hanging as if there was more he wanted to say, but knew now was not the time.

"Pala will be back soon, with the woman from my safe house. I assume that's why you're here?" I said, an edge of frustration in my voice that I couldn't mask, no matter how hard I tried to swallow it down.

"Pala? How does he know about your safe house and why is he going instead of you? Did you run into trouble?"

I could feel Dave's eyes running all over me in the darkness, looking for signs of injury or distress. I glanced at him and he had one hand reached out as if he wanted to grab me again and pull me closer. He clenched his hand into a fist and dropped it as I watched.

This dance we were still doing felt like it belonged to another time. I needed his solid presence to anchor me in the maelstrom of emotions my life had become since my omega had burst free. I didn't know how to tell him that, though. We'd been keeping each other at a distance for so long, it had become a habit I didn't know how to break.

I sighed and brought him up to speed with everything that had just happened, wrapping my arms around myself to cover the suddenly empty feeling stealing over me. It had been a long, intense day, and I needed comfort in a way I'd never felt before. I wanted to rub myself all over something soft and familiar.

I'd always been so self sufficient, but it no longer felt like enough. My omega needed touch, and I realized denying touch from the people around me had been one way of denying my omega all these years.

Yet Dio wasn't here right now, and Dave seemed unwilling. The thought made me feel unbearably sad. Dave watched me closely, seeing way too much as always, before he stepped into me and hooked a finger under my chin as he forced me to look up at him.

"What do you need, Lex?"

I tried to shake my head, but he swept his thumb up along my jaw in a way that made me shiver, before he used it to grip my chin firmly. I wouldn't accept a hold like that from any other man, but Dave owned me in a way I didn't yet understand.

"You and I need to talk, Lex. There are things that need to be said, but now is not the time."

His pale blue eyes bored into me, flecked silver in the moonlight, and they kept me trapped even more than his grip.

"That doesn't mean you can't lean on me. Whatever you need that is in my power to give, I will give you," he said, like he was the rock the world would break upon if I needed it.

I felt pinned beneath that gaze, split open and raw. I wanted to submit to him and let him take everything, all the weight, all the loneliness and the burdens. Even all the secrets. Take them and shoulder them for me, even if just for a moment. So I could breathe.

But more than that, I just needed him.

My silence frustrated him and he all but growled at me.

"Lex," he rasped, looking like he wanted to shake the answer out of me.

Or maybe spank it out of me, I thought, as his other hand stole around behind me and gripped my ass almost aggressively while pulling me closer to him.

I gasped at his firm hold on me, and he stared at my open mouth in a way that lit me on fire.

"I need you to kiss me," I moaned, sounding unlike myself. And yet I felt more myself in this moment than I could remember being in a long time. I was completely at his mercy right now and unable to hide a single thing from him.

He groaned, long and low as the hand on my ass spread out possessively and the one on my chin slipped around to grip my neck. His eyes, though, never left my lips.

"Fuck, Lex. Do you have any idea what you do to me?"

"Please," I begged, feeling empty and almost desperate. The sensation was so overwhelming and the need to beg was so foreign, yet persistent. If he didn't kiss me right now, I would never forgive him.

He seemed to sense that, as whatever internal barrier had been holding him back disappeared and his gaze turned molten.

"Forgive me," he murmured so low I only barely heard him, as he brushed his lips tantalizingly over mine. Before I could do more than register the words, he was kissing me as if he was staking his claim.

The kiss was possessive, firm, and delivered with intent. Dave was in control and I was completely at his mercy. It was nothing like our first kiss, which had been all frenzied heat and pure abandonment. This kiss was purposeful and designed to make me his. He kissed me like he owned me.

My body was a riot of sensation as he held me immobile while he ravaged my lips. I completely submitted to the feelings he stirred up in me and let him take the lead, knowing this man would never hurt me. It was liberating and heady.

I had no idea how long we kissed. It could have been five minutes or five hours. I lost track of all time until a pointed cough had us both freezing. Dave released me with one final, dark, possessive look that made me want to push his boundaries and see what kind of punishment he would deliver.

Dave tucked me in behind him as he turned to face our intruder. I peeked past him and noticed Pala standing between two trees on the opposite edge of our little glade, with Ziggy on his back.

"What happened?" I cried out, probably way too loud, as I pushed past Dave and stepped toward them. Ziggy slid off Pala's back, looking embarrassed. Either at the piggyback or busting us kissing, I wasn't sure. He was standing like a typical slouchy teenager who didn't want to draw attention to himself. He didn't look injured.

"He's fine, as promised," Pala said to me quickly. "I just wanted to move quickly and stealthily through the forest in case anyone else was out here."

"Oh," I said. It was my turn to look embarrassed. Dave and I had definitely not been on the lookout for people wandering through the forest. I suddenly realized I had kissed both men within an hour and now they were standing, watching each other carefully.

I refused to be embarrassed about that, though. My omega was firmly in control right now, and it seemed she was a thirsty creature.

"What happened with Ziggy's mom and the woman in the safe house?" I asked Pala, moving things right along.

"You don't know who was in the safe house?" Pala asked, confused.

I shook my head. "No, I get an alert when a code is used to enter, but I didn't stop to look up whose code it was and I couldn't see her clearly on the video feed."

"Her name was Romaine. Ziggy's mom seemed to know her. She refused to go with me and leave Ziggy behind when I told her I could only take one person right now. She insisted he come with us to the farm and she'd stay with the other women instead."

Pala hesitated and turned to look at Ziggy, concern written all over his face, but kept talking. "Romaine's boyfriend tried to trade her to the alphas for food, but she escaped. Ziggy's mom hadn't gone to the safe house because she thought with the power out, the electronic door key wouldn't work. Romaine said she was desperate for a hiding spot and was going to break a window, but tried the lock on a whim and was surprised when it worked."

Shit. I should have told the women more about the off-grid setup of the safe house, but it hadn't seemed important back then. She also wouldn't have been able to break a window. They were bullet proof glass.

"We got them the extra food those alphas were hoarding and the safe house had plenty of water. They'll be fine there for a few days. You've got a great set-up there."

He looked at me, and his eyes gleamed in the darkness, as if it impressed him. It gave me a strange fluttery sensation in my chest.

I wanted to go to Pala. The pull I felt to him was intense at this close distance. It felt all kinds of wrong to be standing so near, yet out of reach. My body ached for him and needed reassurance that he was okay. Yet, the fact he had just witnessed me kissing Dave held me back.

This is why I always kept things casual, I thought to myself. Until Leif and Max, I'd had no examples growing up of a positive relationship. I didn't know how to navigate one, let alone with multiple men.

I just stood there, halfway between Dave and Pala, feeling conflicted and anxious. Sensations I hadn't felt in a long time. I didn't normally second guess myself or allow anxiety any space in my head or my heart. Yet here I was, frozen in place like a startled fawn.

Pala's eyes narrowed and swept over me, before he took three giant strides across the clearing and swept me up in a hug that lifted me off my feet. He enveloped me in his warm, earthy sage scent and I breathed him in deeply as my body instantly relaxed.

"You never have to hold yourself back from me, mate," he whispered in my ear. "I do not care who else you bring into your life or your bed. As long as there is room for me. If you need me, I'm here."

I gripped him tightly. Hearing him call me his mate, in that quiet, steady voice, had the flutters turning into tiny birds, beating their wings within my heart. Stirring up my emotions yet steadying me at the same time. He felt like a calm river in my soul. With waters that would flow around and between every obstacle in our path, always finding his way to me.

"I'm going to need you to say that again, later, somewhere more private," I whispered against his cheek and I felt his wide smile against the side of my face.

I still felt a level of distress rising, though, but it felt displaced. Something that was beating at me, rather than stemming from within me. I looked around, trying to search for where the sensation was coming from.

"What is it?" He asked, as he pulled his head back to watch my face carefully.

Realization dawned as I drew my gaze back to Pala. "It's Dio. He's feeling distressed." I didn't have time to marvel that I could feel Dio's emotions, even at this distance. His emotions were pulling at me.

I whipped around to Dave, but couldn't spot him where he'd been a moment ago. Until Pala spun me around again. Dave had walked over to Ziggy and was crouched down, so he was looking at him at eye level.

"Hey buddy, you've grown since I saw you last. Noah will be happy to see you. I know he's been worried about you," he said. It was then I remembered Noah and Ziggy were best friends, and their moms spent a lot of time shuttling them back and forth between the farm and town.

Ziggy relaxed slightly at hearing Noah's name. It can't have been easy for him, leaving his mom behind, not really knowing if he'd see her again, and heading into the dark unknown with a stranger. He was looking fragile and about three seconds from bursting into tears again, which I knew would mortify him in front of Dave.

I suddenly felt like complete shit for getting so caught up in my own emotions. I tried to tamp them down as I hurried over to Ziggy.

"Hey, Ziggy, let's get you on Dave's bike and we can get you to the farm. Noah's mom is going to be really glad to see you, too." I knew she'd be better than me at comforting him right now. He just nodded and kept his eyes down, blinking rapidly.

Dave went to step away with him, but I put my hand on him gently to halt him for a second. "Uh, does Dio know I'm not at the farm?"

He scrunched up his face and looked at me in confusion. "Probably, by now. He was on his way back in the helicopter with Sam just before I came looking for you. I freaked out when I saw your note. I can't imagine he's doing much better and he wouldn't know where you were headed or how to follow you."

Well, shit. I hadn't meant to cause anyone distress. I'd just done what I always did

Dave lifted my chin with his finger again. "Hey, it'll be okay. We'll figure it out. He'll just be worried, but he'll understand."

I nodded. Dio had made me feel alive from the first moment I touched him. The thought of him being disappointed in me, or angry at me, left me feeling nauseous.

But I just nodded and stumbled over my words a little as I asked. "Are you okay? I mean, are we okay?" I jerked my head in Pala's direction. Not knowing if I'd just broken something that had barely started between Dave and I.

"We're more than okay, Lex. You're being hit with a lot right now. I have no plans to make this harder on you. Don't worry about me. Or us. I'm not going anywhere."

I nodded again, feeling incapable of words. He seemed to understand as he leaned down and brushed a light kiss across my lips before he turned and strode away.

Pala had grabbed Ziggy already and hoisted him up onto the bike. At his age, and given the dangerous terrain we'd be covering in the complete dark, it was safer for him to sit between Dave's arms.

Dave swung his leg over behind Ziggy and got him settled securely in front of him, showing him where to put his feet. Dave only had one helmet, so he made Ziggy put it on.

Dave looked over at us as if he was waiting. "Go," I said, "your bike is quiet. We'll draw more attention. Ziggy's safety is our priority."

Dave clenched his jaw, looking like he wanted to disagree, but he relented. "Take the main road. Getting back in one piece is more important than stealth right now. If you're not right behind me, I'm coming back after you and I probably won't be alone."

I nodded and watched as Dave took one long, last look at me. A heated look that seemed to hold a world of promise within it. Then he turned and took off. The only sound was the crackling of leaves and twigs under the bike until he hit the bitumen. In the darkness, he blended into the road and disappeared almost instantly.

I felt Pala grab my hand and tug me towards my bike. He hopped up on the very back and patted the seat in front of him. Confusion had me hesitating. I knew I was shorter than him, but I wasn't a child. I didn't need to ride up front.

"Let's go, Lex," he said, "before Sam and Dio send the cavalry out for you."

That thought got me moving. I swung myself up onto the bike in front of him and he settled his hands on my waist and put his feet up. I finally figured out he was expecting me to drive, and I was gobsmacked.

"You don't want to drive?" I asked.

"Why would I drive? It's your bike so I assume you're more than capable," he answered, sounding confused. I felt floored. I didn't know many men who would sit behind a woman on any kind of motorbike. Especially an alpha.

"Besides, I kind of like this position," he said, as he briefly ran his hands down over my hips and thighs. He thrust into me slightly, in the guise of adjusting his seat, and I heard him groan gently, before pulling his hands back up to my waist and wrapping his arms around me.

My body instantly heated at the feel of his hands on my thighs, and his solid heat at my back, while my legs were spread wide around the bike. I felt my pussy clenching hard, and my nipples instantly hardened. I only made it worse as I turned on the bike and the engine kicked to life with a purr and a steady vibration between my legs.

Holy shit, I thought, as I almost came on the spot. So much kissing and teasing by two men tonight had left me in a heightened state of arousal. They had amped me up, and I was ready to fuck.

I had to bite back a moan and force myself not to grind back onto the hard-on I could feel Pala sporting behind me. The feel of his hard cock pressed up against my ass was intoxicating.

Now was really not the time, though. I needed to focus if I was getting us both back safely. The fact he appeared to have no ego and didn't care about me driving only made him hotter, in my opinion.

A wave of increased distress coming from Dio hit me, banking the need a little. I couldn't stand him feeling like that, knowing I was the cause.

I'm coming, baby.

Twenty-Five

Dio

S am was losing his ever loving shit. I was trying to keep him calm, but the thought of Lexie out there all alone was making me crazy.

I knew she could handle herself and had been for a very long time. I'd spoken with Cary briefly about what exactly went down when the alphas invaded the farm. He'd told me Lexie had come to his defense when he'd tried to get between the intruders and the girls, and she had some killer moves. She'd run into the fray without hesitation and taken down an alpha on her own, before they got overwhelmed with numbers.

Yet even so. Her potent scent was out and perfuming madly now. She couldn't pretend to be a beta anymore. She was now essentially catnip for alphas.

Any alpha would become drawn to her as soon as they scented her. Not in the same intense way Sam and I were as her true mates, but they'd feel a heightened attraction. In the lawless world we now seemed to live in, society's rules wouldn't hold them back, as few as there were when it came to omegas.

It didn't help that I could feel her desire spiking on and off. Initially, I had assumed she was getting it on with Dave back here at the farm, and I'd been happy at the idea. A little distracted, but on board with it happening. Our burgeoning pack needed his steadiness.

Yet when we'd landed the helicopter and headed back through the farm gates, our team member on the gate asked me if I knew where Lexie had gone. It seemed Dave had torn out the gates on a dirt bike, telling the guards he was going after Lexie.

"Get to the chopper," I heard Sam yell to our team, and the words broke me out of my reverie.

"Sam, we don't have enough fuel to fly around aimlessly. We don't know where she is." I put my hand on Sam's shoulder, trying to calm him, but my mind was only partially on him for once. Most of my focus was on my bond with Lexie, trying desperately to reach her somehow, to know she was okay.

A growl was vibrating low in my chest that I couldn't swallow down. Sam turned to me. "I don't give a shit, Dio. She's out there alone somewhere."

"Did she come out this way?" I asked the gate guard.

He shook his head rapidly. "No, and I checked with the lower gate guards. She didn't leave through there either."

"Could she still be here? Maybe Dave was wrong?" Another one of our team asked.

"No. Dave said she left a note," the guard replied. He was one of Dave's young cadets and he was shifting on his feet, looking nervous. His eyes were flitting between all of us, as if he was trying to figure out which one of us was going to bark at him first.

My stomach dropped. *What if she had left for good? Where the hell else would she go?*

I'd thought she was coping okay with suddenly becoming an omega, but what if it was too much? Her emotions were spiraling everywhere at the moment, as her pheromones kicked in hard. *What if it had all become too much? Had she run?*

"I shouldn't have left her alone after just mating her," I said to Sam. I could hear the panic in my voice. It was an echo of the thoughts spinning through my head.

He seemed to suddenly realize the depths of my desperation and distraction. He grabbed me and hugged me fiercely, barely holding his own panic at bay to console me. His eyes looked wild, and he was leaking dominance like a fire hose, battering everyone around us. A few of our guys had already subtly stepped away.

"We'll get her back or I'll rain hell, I swear. I'll tear this world apart until we find her," he growled, as he gripped me hard. "Wait here, watch the gate. I'll get the note."

He was gone before he'd even finished speaking, tearing away into the darkness and leaving me spinning alone. I was usually the calm one, but the bond was pulling at me. I'd been feeling unsettled all day, and I'd been desperate to get back and reassure myself she was okay. Now I felt like a rubber band stretched too thin.

Where the fuck was she? And how the hell did no-one see her leave?

The wait was interminable, my heartbeat pounding out a beat in my ears. A jagged pain ripped through me as I felt her mood swing from desire to anxiety. I was about to smash my way through the gate and run down the road. I didn't care which way, I just needed to move. The urge to find her was tearing at me.

I stepped towards the gate, my growl intensifying, when Sam came tearing back up the path in an electric cart. He was driving recklessly and looked halfway towards a frenzy.

He leaped out before he'd even come to a halt and the cart kept moving as people scrambled out of the way. Luckily, one of our team jumped in and hit the brakes before it plowed through the fence. Sam shoved a note into my face, but the words were all a jumbled mess.

"What the fuck is the safe house?" I yelled, swiveling around to the guards who were bravely standing their ground. They looked bewildered.

I heard a bellow as Leif came lumbering into view, closely followed by Hunter with Maia piggybacking. He dropped her onto the ground and she zeroed in on me straight away.

"Where is Lexie?" she demanded. I just growled at her in response and Hunter stepped between us swiftly.

"I don't think he knows, pussycat."

"Where the fuck is the safe house? And how the hell did she get out without being seen?" Sam growled at Leif, grabbing the note out of my hand and shoving it in his face.

Leif paled as he scanned the note, and Maia whirled on him.

"She wouldn't," he said as he looked at Hunter.

"You know she would," Hunter replied.

"One of you had better start talking," Maia warned, looking scared and furious at the same time. Hunter bundled her up in his arms, but she was stiff as a board as she glared at Leif.

"Can you direct us there in the helicopter?" Sam yelled at Leif.

"Hunter could. He's better at air surveillance than I am."

Sam whirled on Hunter. "Let's go."

Maia pulled out of Hunter's hold and stepped into Sam. "Get her back, Sam. She's important to me."

Sam looked devastated as he looked at his sister's worried face. "She's important to me too, Mai," he whispered. Maia's face fell, and she wrapped Sam up in a hug. I joined in, needing the contact, and neither Hunter nor Leif objected.

"How far is the chopper?" Hunter asked over Maia's shoulder. "Do we need to take the quad bike, or will it be easier to run?"

I counted him as a brother at that moment. He didn't question the use of the fuel we had just gone to great lengths to get, and could be the last we would ever see. He was all in on our crazy plan to fly off into the night in search of Lexie.

Before Sam could answer, a guard sitting in the tree above the gate shouted, "Bike on the road."

"Is it Dave?" Leif yelled back.

"It's too dark to be sure, but there's no noise and Dave's is the only electric dirt bike around that I know of," the cadet up the lookout tree called back.

"Looks like two people on the bike," he called out a second later.

My heart started a wild rhythm in my chest, hope surging painfully. She'd swung from horny to anxious again a few minutes ago and I couldn't take it anymore. I didn't know if I was going to kiss her or strangle her.

The gate swung open and Dave appeared with a kid on his dirt bike. He squinted in the glare of all the torches we were recklessly flashing around.

As soon as he pulled to a stop just inside the gate, he dropped the kickstand. Dave put one hand up to cover his eyes and raised the other up, as if to ward us all off. The poor kid in front of him looked terrified, and I was worried he would jump off the bike and bolt. He must have shifted, because Dave dropped one arm back down and secured him in place.

"She's right behind us, with Pala," Dave blurted.

I heard the faint noise of a dirt bike engine in the distance and my heart started up its wild rhythm again. I dashed through the gate, peering down the road, but I'd lost my night vision with all the flashlights.

"Two on a bike," the guard called out.

I spotted them as they got closer, a dark blur on the road, coming in fast. She must have zeroed in on the light and sped up. Or someone was chasing her.

"She's coming in hot," I yelled as I jumped clear of the gate.

She flew towards me, with Pala behind her, his long dark hair streaming out behind him. She braked hard as she turned into the gate, narrowly avoiding a skid, but clearly hadn't expected so many people to be huddled just inside.

People scattered out of her way, as she yanked the bike sideways and braked hard, spinning in a half circle and spraying dirt and rocks up everywhere.

"Shut the gates," Leif yelled, clearly worried about the same thing I was.

I dashed back through the gates as they snapped closed. I could see her head twisting around as if she was looking for someone.

I ran up beside her and yanked her off the bike and into my arms, barely letting her get her feet under her as she let out a startled yelp. Pala grabbed the handlebars and steadied the bike as its weight shifted without her to balance it.

Lexie ripped off her helmet, threw her arms around me and climbed up me before throwing her legs around me too, as if she was trying to get as much body contact as she could. She grabbed my face and kissed me furiously. She didn't seem to care at all about the people watching, and I didn't either.

I moaned into her mouth as her hot tongue dueled with mine in a frenzied kiss that was messy and wild. If I could have climbed inside her and never let her go again, I would have. I was holding her so tight I didn't know how she could even breathe.

"Don't scare me like that again, please. I'm begging you," I whispered in her ear as we finally broke apart, both of us panting. "I thought maybe you'd run away from us."

"Never," she whispered back to me. "I'm not the running type."

"Where the fuck have you been?" Came a menacing growl from behind her and we both froze. Lexie looked up at me with an unspoken question in her arched brow. I tried to smile and reassure her, but I could feel how out-of-control Sam was right now. His dominance was battering even me. It usually flowed right around me.

I put her down, and she let me. If Sam expected her to look contrite, he clearly underestimated her. There was a fire building in her eyes. This was going to get messy.

"Sam," I cautioned, as I turned and tried to maneuver Lexie behind me.

"Don't fucking, 'Sam' me, Dio," he bit out between growls. He was spiraling badly. I'd never seen him this scared or out of control. The other night, when he'd first scented Lexie, he'd been desperately trying to exert some control. Now, though, it felt like any attempt at control had dissipated like mist in sunlight and he was spoiling for a fight to cover his own fears.

I braced myself, but Lexie slipped out from behind me and stood firmly between Sam and me. I couldn't block her and I'd never restrain her. She was like a jungle cat, with her prey in its sights.

"What the hell is your problem?" She asked, sounding incensed, instantly coming to my defense. A fierce and proud omega protecting her mate.

"You're my problem," he growled back at her. I heard Maia gasp behind me, and Leif growled.

"I. Am. Nobody's. Problem," she said, low and angry, almost spitting out the last word as if it offended her. She walked right up to an enraged Sam, without a flicker of hesitation, and jabbed him in the chest to reinforce her words. Sam had obviously just pushed one of Lexie's buttons. I could feel her pain bleeding through our bond.

The other night, Lexie tried to leave, recognizing Sam was struggling. But right now, neither of them appeared to have any control. Or any desire to back down. Messy emotions were spilling everywhere, clashing in the heated air.

I wanted to step in, but I didn't want to set them off any more than they already were. It had been a long day, after a long week, and everyone's nerves were frayed.

"Do you hear me?" Lexie bit out. "It's none of your damn business where I was, especially when you ask like that. I am more than capable of taking care of myself."

Sam's eyes flashed at her words, his anger feeding off hers. "It's everyone's business when you run off recklessly, alone, to do who knows what in the middle of the goddamn night," he snarled. "Did you even think about anyone but yourself when you left? Or about the resources we'd need to use to come rescue you?"

"I left a note. It explained exactly where I was and what I was doing. I don't need, nor have I ever asked, anyone to rescue me."

"From what I've heard, your brother has spent his entire life rescuing you," Sam hissed in a blind rage as he stepped into her.

Oh shit. My heart dropped. Sam's best defense his entire life had always been an attack. He was hotheaded and sometimes lashed out with angry words. Especially when he was afraid someone he cared about or respected was about to walk away, as had happened to him far too often. He always regretted it when he calmed down. But this time, I feared he'd gone too far.

I knew Sam would never hurt Lexie, but he was all up in her space right now and she didn't know him like I did. Neither did her brother or the gate guards.

"That's enough," Leif roared behind me. I heard a slight scuffle as I assumed Hunter tried to hold him back, but my omega had me transfixed.

Lexie moved like lightning. She grabbed Sam by the collar of his shirt and tipped him forward, using her body weight. Then she dropped to one knee and stretched out her other leg to swipe Sam's legs out from under him. In the blink of an eye, she'd flipped him over her leg onto his back before she grabbed his arm and twisted it behind him.

"Stay down," Lexie demanded. She was on her knees, breathing hard, her jaw clenched tight, as she willed herself to calm down, too. I shot a look at Sam and his face was pale. He was on his side, perfectly still, letting her pin him until she felt safe enough to let him go.

He could have thrown her off if he'd wanted, but like I said, he'd never actually hurt her. The shock of her flipping him seemed to have broken him out of his rage spiral, though. I could already see regret flashing across his face.

"I'm letting you go now," Lexie said as she dropped Sam's arm and shifted away from him before standing up. She shook out her hands as if she was trying to shed excess energy, while I reached a hand down and helped him up. Everyone else was frozen around us.

"Holy shit, Lex. That was amazing," Maia gushed. "You need to teach me how to do that."

Lexie didn't respond to Maia for the moment, her focus entirely on Sam. "I shouldn't have reacted to your words. You hit a nerve. I apologize, Sam," she said, looking past him and not quite making eye contact as she stilled. "But if you think a scent match gives you the right to demand things from me or own me in any way, you can think again.

Her voice had gone quiet and was devoid of emotion, only amplifying the pain I could see etched on her face. "And nobody belittles my brother and the things he sacrificed for me."

She heaved a breath that felt raw in our bond and finally looked Sam right in the eye while he was standing in shocked silence, one hand absently rubbing his arm. "This conversation is done until you figure out how to handle your shit. You also owe my brother an apology for dragging him into your juvenile tirade."

Lexie turned to Leif, effectively dismissing Sam completely. I wanted to reach for her again, but I sensed she was only barely holding herself together. It felt like she was trying to cover all her messy emotions with metaphysical duct tape right now. I could see in her eyes she didn't want to lose it in front of everyone. "How far out are Damon, Max, and their team?"

"About two hours," I said gently, answering for him. "We circled and shadowed them as much as we could through the major industrial area in the helicopter on the way back. They had a clear run when we left them."

"Perfect," she said with a bright smile, as if she hadn't just dropped Sam to the ground. I could tell the smile was forced, though. It didn't reach her gorgeous eyes. "Family meeting after breakfast, in the dining room, tomorrow morning. I'm taking Ziggy and Pala to get something to eat, then taking Ziggy to his friend's cabin and settling him in for the night.

"Dave, can you check in with your guys? Make sure nothing happened while we were all gone that we need to know about?" He just nodded, but his hard eyes were on Sam.

"Okay, people. Show's over. Lights out and let's move it," Lexie ordered everyone else, and people quickly started moving.

She gave me a quick kiss and whispered in my ear, "Can you make sure he's okay and meet me back at the treehouse?"

I just nodded at her, completely in awe of this woman. Sam had just said awful things to her and here she was, making sure someone took care of him, knowing she couldn't right now. I realized in that moment, though, that Lexie kept busy to keep the world at bay. She cared deeply about the people around her. Yet her constant motion was like a bandaid and a force field at the same time. I was determined to give her a safe space to land.

"Have you guys eaten since you got back?" She asked, and I shook my head, giving her a soft smile. I grabbed her hand and squeezed it, trying to subtly convey everything I was feeling right now.

"I'll bring you a snack. See you in about half an hour," she said, as she squeezed my hand back.

"If it's okay, I'd like to stay here for a minute," Pala piped up as he stepped closer to us, but didn't touch her. I think he could sense as much as I could how thin her bravado was right now. She gave him a more genuine smile that was also a little sad.

"Of course. Catch up with your friends. I'll see you in a bit. I'll bring you something to eat, too."

"Pala, did you get the intel?" I asked. Pala nodded, and I gestured to Hunter. "Give it to him. He'll get it to Max. Max has the tech and the genius to be able to sort through it quickly."

Hunter stepped forward eagerly. ""Man, are we happy to see you back here. You risked a lot to get this and we're grateful. I'm Hunter, by the way. Max has been on edge waiting for that. I can take it to him right now while Lexie sorts Ziggy."

"Thank you, Hunter. I had my reasons for doing it," Pala said as he handed it over, without question. Trusting me completely. He told Hunter the access code before he turned back to Lexie with a soft smile.

"Can I kiss you, my heart?" Pala asked Lexie in a calm tone, as if he was trying to gentle a wild horse.

Lexie gave him a small, tentative nod, and he leaned down to brush the lightest caress across her lips. It was more of a promise than a kiss, but it seemed to settle her. It was much more gentlemanly than the way I mauled her when she got back a few minutes ago.

Leif shot me a curious look, but I just shrugged and grinned happily.

She finally let go of my hand, turned, and sauntered away without looking at any of us again. I watched her ass as she disappeared into the night with Ziggy. Hunter shadowed them, but Leif stayed put. An ominous scowl on his face.

Seeing my childhood best friend kiss Lexie while I was holding her hand had done something unexpected to me, lighting me up with intense desire. My dick was achingly hard and begging for attention as I shifted uncomfortably. Lexie turned just before she disappeared completely, and gave me a cheeky wink, as if she could feel my need through our bond.

I let out a breath I hadn't realized I was holding. I reached out and put my hand on Sam, squeezing his shoulder in reassurance. We both needed the connection right now.

"I am so fucked," he said, without looking at me. He was still staring down the road after Lexie.

"I know," I sighed, and flicked my gaze over to a murderous-looking Leif as I subtly stepped between them.

Twenty-Six

I stood quietly as everyone filtered away until it was just me, Pala, Dio, and Leif. One of the nervous guards had called Dave over and he'd gone reluctantly, shooting a warning glance at Leif.

Leif jerked his head toward the field and gestured for us to follow him, and we all did. We finally stopped in a cleared area under a tree that was out of hearing distance from the gate guards and Leif turned back to us. I felt like I was facing the firing squad.

Pala kept to the periphery, observing everyone and not making any sudden movements that would call attention to himself. I only noticed because I was watching so closely. I hadn't registered him at first when they'd flown through the gate. My rage at the thought of anything happening to Lexie, and my fear that maybe she had left us, eclipsed everything else. My relief at seeing her alive and unharmed had caused the precarious leash I had on my dominance to slip. All my hangups about people leaving or being sent away had flared to the surface, and I had pushed before she could push me.

Seeing Pala now standing casually alongside me, as if he'd never been gone, was both startling and heartbreaking that this was our reunion. All I wanted to do was reach for him, but once again, my inability to control my dominance had fucked everything up. I had fucked everything up.

"I'm waiting," Leif said to me. I dragged my attention away from Pala and back to him. Leif's face was impassive, and he had no problem staring the three of us down.

I hung my head. All the fury pumping through my veins had left me as soon as Lexie dropped me to the ground. I couldn't believe the things I had just said to her.

"I'm so sorry. I didn't mean it, Leif," I said, "and I know it's not true."

Claudio shifted in front of me slightly, the way he always unconsciously did whenever he sensed I was feeling vulnerable or lost. Pala shifted slightly as well, moving behind my shoulder, the spot he'd always taken when we were teenagers, covering my back. I didn't need either of them to do it. I deserved whatever was coming for me now. Yet I didn't have the heart to make them move away. I'd missed the feeling of the three of us together more than I could put into words.

"Remember what I said yesterday about coming to me when Sam's riding the edge, Leif?" Dio said calmly, but with a tense set to his shoulders. Dio may be frustrated with me right now, but I knew he'd still protect me with his last breath. I'd do the same for him.

"I'm not the one you need to tell that to, but I'll take it for now," Leif said to me, ignoring Dio for the moment. He gave me a once-over and sighed. "Just so you know, she cares about you or she would have just walked away with a laugh and not given you another thought. You caused her actual pain just now."

I closed my eyes at his words, feeling my heart clench. They destroyed me. I was utterly disgusted with myself. This couldn't go on, not if Lexie would be the one getting hurt.

When I opened them, Leif was staring up at the sky through the sprawling branches of the big old fig tree we were standing under. There was enough light filtering through to illuminate us, but the shadows also seemed to fit the mood of this conversation. It appeared as if Leif was looking for some kind of celestial guidance, as he continued to stare up, or maybe something to come and zap him out of this tense situation.

"This is your one free pass, considering my sister already kicked your ass," Leif said roughly as he looked back at me. His face softened as he took in Dio, still standing slightly in front of me.

I relaxed my stance slightly. I'd been holding myself ready to brace, not knowing how this would go but expecting violence. Defending myself hadn't even been a thought. I deserved any swing he took.

"I'll give you one piece of insight, because I want her to be happy, but after this, you're on your own," Leif said, surprising me. I wasn't expecting advice.

The last of Leif's anger seemed to bleed away as he relaxed back into himself. I got the impression he wasn't a naturally aggressive guy. The tiny plaits woven into his hair had given him a vengeful Norse god vibe earlier, but now he just looked like a big, cinnamon roll kind of guy who'd been letting his girlfriend play with his hair.

Not that there was anything wrong with that. If we ever reached the point where Lexie wanted to play with my hair, I'd sit and let her, with my eyes closed and a smile splitting my face in half, for as long as she wanted.

I looked at him directly and said, "That's more than I deserve."

"Lex will kill me if she finds out I told you this, but our father used to tell her all the time that she killed our mother, and that she was a problem he didn't want to deal with. He started saying it before she even understood what the words meant. So she's grown up hearing it all her life."

I could hear shocked breaths from Dio and Pala, but my breath had frozen in my lungs. Leif's body had hunched in slightly, as if this story was painful for him. He'd paused for a few heartbeats to let his words sink in, but he continued on, now, his voice getting softer as he looked past us. As if he was looking into his memories.

"My father blamed his baby daughter for his wife dying giving birth to her. It was messed up and only grew worse as Lexie got older. I had to endure his unhinged aspirations for me as his heir, but Lexie had to suffer through his intentional neglect that turned to verbal abuse when he was drunk.

"He forbade any other family member from meeting her, claiming she didn't deserve love. So Lexie grew up completely isolated from anyone who could care for her, apart from me. He tried to make me hate her, too, but I couldn't. My grandma had arranged for a wet nurse for Lexie through the hospital for the first year, but she only came to feed her and wash her. Nobody was holding her or comforting her.

"I was grieving for my mother, but Lexie's tiny cries all alone in the nursery devastated me. She was my sister, and she was alone and helpless. I climbed into her crib, figured out how to care for her and I never stopped."

Leif ran his hands roughly through his hair before crossing his arms in front of him, both gestures that showed he needed comfort right now. He looked back at me as if he was coming back to the present and remembering what Lexie was facing now.

"What you just threw at her in your anger were words that our father threw at her all her life, the person who was supposed to raise and protect her. She goes to great lengths to do everything herself and almost never asks for help, even from me, because she can't stand to be thought of as a problem to anybody."

I felt intense sorrow listening to Leif's tale. How the hell had Lexie grown up to become the caring, feisty, competent woman she appeared to be? My instincts as her mate pummeled me, demanding I find her father and exact retribution. If he was here right now, I would rip his throat out for uttering those words to her. *Yet was I any better?*

I leaned forward, bracing myself on my knees, feeling like I was going to vomit. A fine tremor worked through my body as a cold sweat broke out down my spine. Just the thought that I could be compared to someone who had done that to her brought a feeling of intense shame so deep, it swamped everything else. Even my rage.

Dio moved to stroke my back lightly. I had to force myself not to shrug him off, knowing I didn't deserve the comfort, but he didn't deserve that kind of reaction either.

"Fucking hell, I didn't mean to hurt her," I groaned. "I thought... I don't even know what I thought. I've never been so relieved, angry and scared all at the same time as when she came flying through those gates. My simmering rage spiked, and I was flinging crap that was completely meaningless before I could even think about what I was saying. Only it clearly wasn't meaningless to her. I'm a complete asshole."

"No, you're not," Leif said, which surprised the hell out of me, making my head snap up. "You're a good guy. Anyone can see that. But you're hot headed and you lash out when you're angry or scared. Lexie's patient and kind. She gets that people have issues, but she won't put up with your crap forever if you don't do the work to overcome it. If you don't do what she asks and figure your shit out, you're going to lose her, and maybe your friends, too."

Jesus. Was I destined to hurt everyone I cared about? I heard myself groan again, as I crouched down on my heels, my head in my hands. I tried to steady my breathing, but my breaths were coming out in great big panicky gasps.

"Is that why she moved out on her own at sixteen, because of your father?" Dio asked, changing the subject back to Lexie while he crouched down next to me and pulled me into a tight hug. His arms wrapping around me felt like home but also reminded me of everything I could destroy with my rage if I couldn't get my shit together.

"She told you about that?" Leif asked Dio, as he scratched his head. Clearly Lexie didn't open up to many people, or let many people in, if her mate knowing details about how she grew up surprised her brother.

"A little. She said she wanted to enjoy what was happening between us and not drag it down with a lot of shit she'd left far behind, but that she'd tell me more one day."

"Huh. Consider yourself lucky you got that much. She's already opened up more to you than she has to anyone in a long time, even Maia."

"Hang on a second," Pala interjected. Leif looked momentarily startled, like he'd forgotten Pala was there. A skill he'd honed over the years. A breath later, he narrowed his eyes on Pala as if he was just remembering Pala had kissed Lexie in front of him earlier.

"She moved out on her own at sixteen? Where were you?" Pala asked Leif. I don't think he was trying to be accusing. His posture was open and casual. He sounded like he genuinely wanted to know.

A look of raw pain and sorrow flashed across Leif's face, like a wound that had never properly healed had just splintered open.

"My father had a lot of connections, and he forcefully drafted me into the military. He wanted them to break me, when he realized he couldn't. I only agreed to go on the condition that he let her move out while I was gone. There was no way I was leaving her alone in that house with him."

Leif sighed deeply, and his shoulders slumped even further. "My ass-hole father willingly wiped his hands of her on the condition that he wouldn't support her financially and was dead to him once she was gone.

He still threatened to have the police drag her home as a runaway if I didn't toe the line while I was away, though. Lexie was alone a lot after I left, but she was already used to it. She's tough and resourceful. She had to be, but she needs people more than she knows."

"Does she know why you went?" Pala asked.

"I never told her, but I'd bet the farm she suspected. She hated it whenever I suffered trying to keep her safe. It fed into her whole feeling like a problem thing. I couldn't walk away and let her suffer, though, and I didn't see any other way out of the situation. Yet, sometimes I wonder if I'm part of the problem, too."

"No, Leif," Dio said as he dropped his arms from around me, leaped up, and moved over to the gentle giant. He grabbed Leif's shoulder and squeezed tightly. "She loves you. She fights to protect you as much as you do her. Never doubt that. She'd kick your ass if you did." Dio was very hands on with everyone in his trusted inner circle, and it looked like Leif was now in it too. I was glad for Dio, that he was becoming tight with Lexie's brother. He'd been alone with just me for too long. He wasn't built that way. Dio craved connection, and family.

Leif chuckled, lightening the moment. "She has no problem kicking my ass on the regular." He looked almost proud.

Leif sobered again suddenly as he reached up and squeezed Dio's hand. "I won't say any more. It's her story to tell and I've already said too much. But you've been good for her already, Dio. She's built a good life for herself, but I've never seen her as happy as she is when she looks at you. Whatever it is you're doing, keep doing it."

"Oh, you don't want to know what it is I've been doing," Dio said as he grinned and waggled his eyebrows lasciviously like a character out of an old black and white movie.

"I really, really don't," Leif said with a smile as he playfully shoved Dio and almost sent him sprawling. Pala smiled at their antics, too. Dio had always had that effect on people.

"Are you going to be okay?" Leif asked, as he dropped to squat in front of me suddenly. I could see concern etched into his face.

"No. Yes. Maybe. I don't know," I said, sounding completely lost and hopeless. "My dominance spikes whenever I'm mad or upset, or feeling anything that's not perfectly calm, really. Unless I can channel it or exhaust it, it floods fucking everything. Turns the world red. I can usually hold myself back from losing it completely, but anything to do with Lexie seems to make it so much stronger."

I could feel the shame of my earlier words still burning in my throat. I grit my jaw suddenly and stiffened. Seeing Dio connecting with Leif, building ties to this community, and knowing Pala was back with him, had me realizing just how much I had been holding him back. How much it would hurt Dio if I couldn't fix this. It wasn't fair to him. Lexie was his mate. Dio gave so much for me. I needed to think about him and Lexie now, about all three of them.

"My gramps was right. I'm too dangerous. I should leave. Alone. I'm just going to hurt Lexie, Maia, and everyone around me. You guys need to stay and look after Lexie. I'll be gone by morning." I tried to force my voice to be firm, and not betray just how much even the thought of leaving them destroyed me.

It wasn't a trauma response to the thought of eventually losing them. I genuinely couldn't figure out another way to stop hurting them now. I could feel my leaking dominance getting worse and my rage becoming more irrational, had for some time. I knew what it meant, and that becoming feral was a real possibility. All my energy had gone into getting home, to Maia, hoping that would fix it, but I was here and I was only hurting everyone.

"No." Pala said firmly as Dio looked at me in shock, and Leif slumped slightly, looking disappointed.

"That's not doing the work, that's just running," Leif said. "Maia tried it once, too."

This was different. There was no work to do. My emotions felt like they were drowning me right now and I couldn't shut them off. "I'm not running," I sighed. "It's the only way I know I can keep everyone safe."

I was exhausted. I knew in my bones, my dominance was too much for me to handle alone. I'd tried and failed.

Twenty-Seven

M y heart broke. Sam had always been so strong, despite the knocks that kept kicking him to the ground when he was young. He'd been a determined kid and had always had so much potential. The old timers had been afraid of him, but kids had gravitated to him. He'd always been so protective and I'd seen him stand up for someone younger or smaller than him more times than I could count.

I'd watched Dio instinctively shift in front of Sam a moment ago, the same way he'd always done when we were younger, whenever he sensed Sam struggling with himself. It brought a flood of memories and feelings rushing back. My position was always at Sam's back, watching over both of them, and I'd shifted there without even thinking. Even though Sam deserved Lexie and her brother's anger after what he'd just said, I would have intervened if Leif had taken a swing at Sam while he was clearly down.

Seeing Sam looking so defeated right now had me feeling guilty for all the years I'd been away. He'd always struggled with his dominance, but never like this. If I'd thought he or Dio had needed me, or any kind of help, I would have been back at their side in a heartbeat.

"No. No more. I just found you. We're not splitting up again." I couldn't stand the thought of one of us walking away again. Just the idea caused something to tear inside of me that was held together with cobwebs. Sam wouldnt meet my eyes, though.

"I won't go far," he said, sounding fiercely determined. "I'll find somewhere to stay nearby, so I'm close if you need me but Lexie doesn't have to see me every day. Just think of me as a forward scout."

Dio sobered up fast, as if he sensed this sudden resolve of Sam's was different, and moved back in behind him. He pulled Sam to the ground, despite his suddenly stiff posture, and gave him a hug from behind. Looking like an anchor, holding Sam firmly in place.

"You have to let me go, Dio," Sam said, sitting stiffly in Dio's arms. I knew in my gut he was talking about more than the hug. Sam sounded like he knew he had no chance of staying sane out there alone. He'd closed his eyes and looked half destroyed. It was killing me. *Why the hell had I been gone so long? I'd been told I was doing what was best for everybody, but was the cost to us worth it?*

"No fucking way. We're a team," Dio said, sounding angrier than I'd ever heard him. "We can figure this out. Pala's right. There's no way in hell I'm letting either of you go. Never again." His words sounded firm, but the panic I felt was reflected in his eyes as he looked at me.

Yet, Sam was a grown man and a highly dominant alpha, we couldn't force him to stay if he'd set his mind to leaving. It would destroy Dio if he left without him, though. I wouldn't cope much better, not when I'd just glimpsed everything I'd ever wanted.

I realized my friends' futures were hanging on a knife's edge right now and I didn't know what to do. My own fears were holding me back after being gone so long. I'd imagined our reunion for years, and while it hadn't quite been us all running through a field of flowers toward each other, it hadn't been this either.

"Nobody is leaving," Leif said after a moment, cutting into the silence. He looked at Sam and Dio on the ground, then up at me hovering behind them. He seemed just as conflicted.

"Fudgsicles. I'm not the best person to talk you through this. We should get Hunter, or wait for Max," Leif said, looking a little lost. "Or maybe GG."

"Talk us through what?" I asked. I was completely confused, but on board with the idea that we needed help.

"Becoming a pack," Leif said plainly. I just stared at him. I heard an actual cricket call out from the long grass nearby in the sudden silence.

Sam looked up from where he was sitting on the ground with Dio wrapped around him like a spider monkey. It was a pose I'd seen them do a lot when we were teenagers and Sam was freaking out. Sam's eyes were wide and looked as stunned as I felt, but Dio was suddenly grinning up at Leif as if he'd just been handed his favorite treat. The momentary panic was gone from his eyes.

"Doesn't a pack need a prime alpha? That's what you guys said the other morning. Your pack naturally supports Damon as the prime, and it needs to include a beta," Sam asked with a frown marring his face.

"Holy shit," I said, probably a little too loud, as so many things finally made sense to me. I'd always heard prime alphas whispered about in my community, but only by the elders and as something from legend.

"What?" Sam asked. He was clenching his fists as though his frustration was growing, and I could feel his dominance rising again with it.

"Is he always this dense?" Leif asked Dio, as he shook his head, making his plaits shift around.

"About himself? Yes, always," Dio answered. I watched as he bit his lip, trying to keep his smile contained. He knew. He was also up to something, and my guess was Leif had just unwittingly played into his plans.

"WHAT are you talking about?" Sam growled, his gaze swinging between the two of them as he twisted his head to scowl at Dio.

"Calm your tits," Dio told him affectionately. "You're clearly a prime alpha."

Sam sat with his mouth agape, stupefied. He looked at Dio and went to speak, then stopped. He looked over to Leif, started again, and stopped before any words came out. The poor guy looked like his brain had turned into a bowl of warm porridge.

"I think you broke him, Dio," I said.

Dio just grabbed Sam's head in a tight hug that looked more like a headlock. "Just breathe, we've got this." It was a testament to how shocked Sam was that he just sat there and didn't even try to extricate himself.

"Aww, man. You're no fun when you're broken," Dio said to him, as he released Sam's head and ruffled his hair.

"What does this mean for us?" I asked Leif. I'd always known Sam's dominance was off the charts, but he so rarely directed it I figured the world had only been getting glimpses of his potential. From the little I knew, prime alphas often became self-destructive unless a pack anchored them.

Had Dio been trying to do that alone while I'd been gone?

"Honestly, we're just winging it and figuring it all out ourselves," Leif said, as he chuckled and shrugged ruefully. "Maia has a book about packs that we'll lend you. It's ancient and very illegal, but nobody really cares right now."

He looked at me, then back at Sam and Dio. I could see where his mind was going and I could feel the hit coming like it was a punch aimed right at me.

"We had already formed a pseudo pack long before we met Maia, though, and there were three of us helping to balance out Damon. Even though we didn't know what we were doing, we figured out early that touch from us calmed him down. Dio's been doing it on his own for years. I'm amazed Sam isn't half feral."

And there it was. I felt like I couldn't breathe.

Dio looked up at me and must have caught the look on my face. "Don't, Pala. You left for a good reason. This isn't on you."

"Isn't it though? They told me it was best for everyone, but it felt wrong to leave. I should have listened to my own instincts." The last few years had been bleak and tough.

Could I have avoided all the darkness if I'd just stayed and trusted in my friends?

"No," Dio insisted, pulling me out of my thoughts as he got up from Sam and stalked the few steps toward me. He grabbed me roughly by the back of the head and lowered his forehead to mine. His touch made my darkness recede instantly.

"You left to keep us safe," he said, with fierce determination. "Where we were all going and what we were planning to do was dangerous. We knew that when we agreed to it. People suspecting we were a pack when we were trying to blend in undercover would have made it even more dangerous. For all of us."

Dio suddenly yanked his head away and looked from me to Sam, who was still sitting on the ground, looking bewildered.

"Holy shit, I get it," he said. His eyes were wide, and he looked like he should have a cartoon lightbulb above his head.

"What do you get?" I asked. I felt like I'd been constantly playing catch-up since the moment I got here and my head was starting to spin. I'd kept myself calm and emotionless for so many years, always trying to blend in and disappear. The amount of emotions battering me now, both mine and those around me, was becoming a little overwhelming.

Dio grabbed my hand and tugged me over to Sam, before holding out his other hand and yanking Sam up off his feet. Sam looked at me cautiously, and I hated the hesitation in his eyes. It had never been there before.

"Just hear me out for a second," Dio said, dropping our hands and putting his on Sam's shoulders, forcing Sam to look at him. "When everyone said you were dangerous growing up, I don't think they meant you were dangerous to us, or really even to Maia. It never made sense to me they would say that to you, because they sent you to us and our estate was full of kids."

"Holy shit, you grew up thinking you were dangerous?" Leif asked. "Damon grew up the same. What are the odds?"

Dio waved Leif off, as if he was distracting him from his train of thought.

"I think they meant you were dangerous to them. You would draw too much attention to the Network and all the subversive shit they were doing underground. Your dominance was hard to hide in the early years until you were older and could get enough of a handle on it to blend in better."

"He's been blending?" Leif scoffed. Dio shot him a quick grin this time as Sam rolled his eyes.

"I think they also meant those in power would see you as dangerous, so they'd watch you. The same way they've kept track of Damon. I think they were just trying to keep you hidden until you were old enough to come into your power. I think they knew you were a prime alpha."

My mind was racing, putting memories together as Dio talked.

"I think Dio's right," I said. "I'd never heard the words prime alpha until after you showed up, but then I heard elders whispering it when they thought I wasn't listening. When they convinced me to go into a separate military unit, they didn't say you were dangerous. They said it was too dangerous to be together."

"It doesn't matter," Sam said as he squared his shoulders again.

"Of course it matters. They behaved like you were going to hurt someone and it messed you up," I said.

"No, you don't get it," Sam said as he pulled away and paced between us all. I didn't like the distance, not when he was talking about leaving, but I didn't know how to pull him back.

"My rage doesn't come from them making me think I'll hurt someone. I know I would never physically hurt someone who didn't deserve it. Not intentionally. I've always been fucking furious that they could never see me through their own fear. Even my own gramps. Everyone pushes me away, so I've learned to push first, with everyone except you guys."

He slapped his hand on his chest, hard, and growled darkly. His voice sounded rough, like he was trying to force it out. "My alpha hates to be thought of as a violent beast that can't be trusted. It makes him rage and when he does, I can't communicate properly."

He seemed to struggle for a second, before he continued on, and we all stood silently waiting. "The fact I won't let him out, that I drain him to stop people from sending me away, makes him furious. He lashes out like a wounded animal. I freak out and push people away before they can do it to me, and the whole thing becomes a self-fulfilling prophecy."

Sam's emotions had become increasingly erratic as he spoke his truth, and his dominance started building again. It felt like the surrounding air became pressurized. Dio's touch seemed to have only taken the edge off. It came back, virulent and angry.

"It fits," Leif piped in, wincing slightly at the pressure and scents building around him. "The only difference between you and Damon is that he runs ice cold when he's angry and you run hot. You've both had issues with trust in your beasts. Even Maia has all kinds of insecurities from everyone leaving in her childhood that hijack her relationships. You need to talk to them both."

Rather than calm him, Leif's words and his mention of Maia seemed to push Sam over the edge.

"I don't want to keep pushing people away. I don't want to be too dangerous to be around. And I don't want to hurt the people I love anymore," He cried out in a broken sob, tearing at his hair.

"Fuuuccccckkkk," Sam suddenly screamed, and he started hitting his own chest repeatedly as his rage and frustration, after so many intense emotions tonight, overwhelmed him and his dominance burst free.

Leif stumbled back, almost as if Sam had pushed him, but Dio and I sprung towards Sam, grabbing him on either side and squeezing him between us. We each captured one of his hands and held him fast to stop him from hurting himself.

"You're not dangerous," I told him fiercely, gripping him with all my strength, "you never were. The only people you're dangerous to are the assholes ruining our world. I've never been more sure of anything in my life."

Pounding footsteps suddenly came down the path towards us, and Dave appeared out of the gloom. He slid to a halt next to us, ignoring Leif, and looking over the three of us frantically.

"What the hell's happening?" he asked.

"Where the hell have you been?" Dio countered. "You need to get your ass in here is what's happening. He's spiraling, and he needs all of us."

Dave didn't hesitate. He jumped in as we made room for him in our huddle and he fit like he was the missing piece to our puzzle. I'd only met him tonight, but walking up to find him kissing Lexie in the forest had made me halt. Not because I was jealous, but because he felt so familiar. Like he was a part of Lexie.

Plus, I had scented Dio and Sam on him strongly, as if he was taking on their scents. Which was intriguing.

"Fucking hell, you little shits are going to be the death of me," Dave grumbled, but I felt the tension slowly ease out of his body.

Sam took giant, shuddering breaths as the pressure in the air eased almost instantly. He dropped his head to rest it on my shoulder. "Tell me you're home for good, Pala," he asked me quietly with his eyes closed, as if he was shielding himself from my answer.

"I'm sorry I ever left. I don't plan on doing it again. I'll stay if you will." Sam's sigh fluttered against my neck before something nudging my hip distracted me.

I shifted slightly to find a giant ass dog trying to push past me. He squeezed in between me and Dave and jumped up in the tight space to put his paws onto Sam's shoulders and lick his face.

"What the hell," I spluttered.

"Pala, meet Bear. Lexie's guardian angel and part of our pack," Dio said with a tense chuckle.

"I thought you hated me, Bear," Sam mumbled as he nuzzled into the side of the giant dog's face, earning himself another lick.

"He didn't hate you," Dave replied. "Bear just knew you didn't have your shit handled. He was warning you."

"And now I suddenly do?" Sam asked, sounding skeptical despite how relaxed his body had become as he leaned into all of us.

"You were in a death spiral with your emotions, but you just pulled up short and shut off your dominance in seconds. You've never been able to do that before. I'd say you're at least on your way," Dio said.

"Yeah, but that wasn't me. That was you guys, clearly," Sam tried to argue as he patted Bear in long strokes down his back, but Dio wasn't having it.

"Haven't you been listening to a word we've been saying?" Dio asked him, sounding frustrated and gripping Sam's hair, to force Sam look at him. "That's the whole point. That's a pack. It's not possible to do it on your own. You've been trying, and it's been getting harder. I know. I've noticed, and it's been scaring the shit out of me. Before we got here, I was worried you'd end up feral. If being with us helps, let us help you. We want to help you."

"Is that why you've been pushing me to be with Lexie, because you've been trying to build a pack for Sam? So he doesn't become feral?" Dave asked, a quiet concern clear in his voice.

"No. If I'd known a pack was what he needed, I never would have let them separate us from Pala years ago. I pushed because I sensed when we met that Lexie needed you. When you calmed Sam down the first night, it was more than the dunk in the river. It was you, and I knew we needed you, too."

Sam looked troubled. I knew he'd always felt like he should take care of us, not the other way around.

"The pack isn't just about you, it's about all of us, Sam," I told him, needing him to understand what I knew instinctively. Wishing I'd been here to say it all along whenever he needed to hear it.

"We're all stronger together. I've noticed it being away from you both. A darkness crept over me slowly. I think we unknowingly started pack bonds back when we were kids. You think you can go off alone to save us, but you can't. You'd only hurt us."

Sam looked cut up over my words and three arms twisted in our huddle to grip me, even Dave. Something that didn't go unnoticed.

"How did you get here so fast, Dave?" Sam asked, as he finally looked at him, a little warily.

"Shit, I don't know." Dave groaned. I got the impression from the way he tensed slightly that Dave was a man of action and wasn't used to analyzing himself. "I felt something drawing me here, and I was hovering at the top of the path, feeling like an idiot and not sure what to do, when I heard you scream."

"Are you okay with this?" Sam asked quietly. "We've all known each other a long time, but you've only known us for days, and things have been moving quickly."

Before Dave could say anything, Dio jumped in. "I can feel you faintly in my bond with Lexie already, Dave. So don't try any of that too old bullshit you spouted the other morning."

"Oh, she didn't seem to mind his age when she had her tongue down his throat and was climbing him like a tree out in the forest earlier," I said, with a sly wink in Dave's direction.

Dave shifted on his feet and actually blushed. Seeing a grown man in his forties blush over a woman was cute as heck.

"She kissed you and I missed it? Dammit," Dio said. "I want to book a front-row seat next time."

"Calm down, boys," Dave groaned. "Fuck, okay. I kissed her. I shouldn't have, not without coming clean first. She may not react well. But she said it was what she needed, and I'm only so strong. I meant what I said about it being up to her. She may not want me in this pack and if she doesn't, I'll walk away."

Dave sounded pained, but raw need also filled his voice as he confessed. If he'd been holding back with Lexie, the time for that had passed. If she wanted him, I'd make damn sure she got him, even if I had to convince him myself. It sounded a lot like Sam needed him, too. A solid relationship with a positive mentor figure could help him overcome his past.

"Dave, you had Lexie's back out there tonight. You've had it for a long time. You've been keeping her safe for years," Dio said, being uncharacteristically serious. "I've known you were pack since the moment you ran around that corner the other day and grabbed her as she fainted."

"Do you want to be in this pack, Dave?" Sam asked, a slight shake in his voice, as if a lot were riding on the answer for him. I noticed Dave didn't seem surprised at our casual use of the word pack.

Dave looked down at the ground, before he raised his head and looked each one of us in the eye as he said, "Yes. It won't be easy. We're going to be figuring each other out at the same time we're trying to be a solid unit for Lexie. It's going to take communication and teamwork. But I'm in if she'll have me."

"We're having you, and we don't leave a man behind. We'll figure it out," Dio said. Nodding his head once, decisively, as if it was a done deal. I wondered what had gone down the last few days to make Dio so certain of Dave. I trusted his judgment, though.

"I don't think you're the one who should be worried, Dave. I really fucked up tonight," Sam said, slumping slightly as if he were defeated.

"We'll figure it all out, but we can only do that if you stay," Dio told him, reiterating his words as he pulled their foreheads together in the same way he had with me earlier. "If your emotions are pushing at you too hard, lean on us instead of walking away."

"What do you mean stay? Where the hell is he going?" Dave asked. Dio just looked at him, shook his head subtly and squeezed Dave's arm, trying to reassure him we had this.

I suddenly realized we'd had this entire conversation while standing in a group huddle, and not one of us seemed uncomfortable about it. I couldn't imagine doing it with anyone else. Yet, standing here with these three men, with our arms around each other, brought me a strange sense of peace.

"I've missed this," I told them honestly.

"Just wait until Sam starts purring. It's the bomb. Feels so darn good," came Leif's voice from the shadows further into the tree's depths.

We all jumped apart, and Leif chuckled.

"Crap, I completely forgot you were there," Dio laughed.

"I figured," Leif said wryly. "Seriously, though, don't be embarrassed. I've lost count of the amount of conversations I've had with the guys while we've all been hugging each other."

"Uh, purring?" Sam asked, looking concerned.

Leif laughed out loud, a great, booming laugh. "Yeah, it's a prime alpha thing. Don't worry. It calms your omega when she's distressed. Maia almost goes into a trance. Damon didn't even realize the first time he did it. It will come naturally to you."

"Uh, I'm still not so sure about the whole prime alpha thing. But, okay, let's table that for another time, because Lexie should be heading back to the treehouse right about now. If I'm staying, how do I go about fixing this?" Sam asked, shaking off Leif's words and squaring his shoulders.

"It's going to take time," I told him. "You're going to have to be patient."

"We don't really have time, though. You need to apologize as soon as possible. Don't let it fester between you," Dave argued, giving me an apologetic look.

"You know, I think you should write her a letter," Dio said as he looked at Sam with a careful focus, as if he didn't want to spook him again. "I read some of those letters over your shoulder when you were writing them to Maia. You're a hell of a lot more eloquent when you write than you are when you try to talk to people."

"You need to let her in, be honest with her and trust she won't push you away," Leif added. "It was the only way Damon and Maia got past their issues. If you're more comfortable writing, then give that a try."

"Thanks, Leif, I appreciate it. You should be kicking my ass right now, not giving me advice." Sam shot him a small, grateful smile.

I'd been watching Leif closely. He seemed like a genuinely kind guy, a rarity for an alpha. I was glad Sam's sister had found him. I hoped the rest of her pack were just as good for her. Sam had talked about his sister a lot growing up, and I couldn't wait to meet her properly. There had been too much happening at the gate tonight to properly introduce myself.

"Yeah well," it was Leif's turn to look a little embarrassed, "I'm kinda the soft one. You're lucky Damon wasn't there. He will hear about it though and he doesn't take anyone upsetting Maia lightly. And she is upset. She's tight with Lexie. You're going to have to win her back over, too."

Sam swallowed hard at that, but he nodded.

"Is it just me, or is it getting darker?" I asked, just as a gust of wind raced up the hill and rustled the branches above us. I looked out over the slope of the farm and saw the horizon looked darker than the sky above us, as if a giant sky creature had swallowed up the stars.

"Uh, it looks like we have a storm incoming," Leif said. "Usually it's just rain at this time of year, so we should be okay. It's not the season for the big lightning and hailstorms. Those are pretty spectacular to watch rolling in, but cleanup can be a nightmare."

"Do we need to do anything to catch some water? Mobilize people and buckets maybe?" I asked him.

Leif just smiled in the deepening darkness. "Nah, we're good for water. We'll give you a tour of the farm tomorrow."

Wasn't there an apocalypse going on? I was a little confused. They were getting desperate for water at the Palace. But I held my tongue. I figured Leif knew what he was doing.

"You guys might want to run if you don't want to get wet. I'll send Lexie your way if she's still in the kitchen. I'll get Ziggy settled myself."

We all thanked him. Leif was a genuinely good guy. He gave each one of us a hug. I leaned into mine, I'd been touch starved for so long. He gave an amazing hug. Clearly, he was honest about being comfortable with it.

Then we all took off into the darkness. Leif was right. The scent of rain carried on the wind as soon as we stepped out from under the tree. I'd always loved rain. I found it cathartic.

I followed the guys, not knowing where I was going. We ran along a winding path that twisted down, then headed back uphill again. I stopped dead as we ran into a clearing and saw a two-storey treehouse appear before us. "Holy shit, you live here?" I asked Dave.

"No, I have a little cabin near the fields. This is kinda Lexie's place, Leif and his mates built it for her. She has a cabin as well, but she spends a lot of time here."

"Wait until you see the rest of it. This place is amazing. Come on." Dio waved me forward, but Sam grabbed his arm to halt him.

"Wait a sec, Dio. I don't think that's a good idea. It's her space. I'll just sleep down here in the hammock."

"Sam, don't be an idiot. It's about to pour. You'll get soaked. Get your ass upstairs. Apologize if you need to, but don't hide from this or her. We won't get through it that way."

"Fine, but if she yells at me to get out, I'm blaming you," he grumbled.

Dio just laughed and slapped him on the back as we walked up a spiral staircase that was like something out of a fairytale. When we got to the top, we hung out on the deck and just enjoyed the view of the storm rolling in over the forest in the waning moonlight.

I could get used to this. Open spaces had always called to me. I hated feeling closed in and cramped. After years of being in the military, living in barracks and tents, I craved space. I took a deep breath of the woody scents surrounding me, that were peppered with sweeter scents from the farm, before letting it out again, feeling lighter already.

I was leaning on the railing as the first drops fell, fresh and cool against my skin. Suddenly I wanted to be a part of it, let the rain wash away all the stress and worry of the last few days.

The others had dashed under the covered area of the deck as the rain fell in earnest, but I just straightened and ripped off my t-shirt.

"Are these ropes safe to use?" I called over my shoulder.

"Yeah," Dio called back. "I went down the one closest to you the other night. Why?"

I tugged my boots off and quickly did the same with my pants and shirt before I whooped and launched myself over the railing in just my trunks. Dio's laughter followed me on the way down.

I reached the ground and ran into the middle of the clearing, spinning in circles with my arms held wide. I stuck my tongue out to catch rain drops, feeling like a little kid without a care in the world, enjoying the magic of a storm at night.

I heard a whoop as Dio followed me down the rope. I turned as he came barreling towards me in the rain. Butt naked. He'd always wanted to be naked when he was a kid. I had distinct memories of his mother chasing him around with a pair of pants while he laughed.

"Where the hell are your jocks?" I asked seconds before he barreled into me and tried to get me into a headlock. I was too slippery though, soaked with rainwater and he couldn't get a good hold.

I laughed and evaded him as we wrestled, trying to avoid getting a wedgie, until movement at the edge of the clearing caught both of our attention.

Lexie was standing there, looking hesitant, wearing nothing but a hot pink bra and panties with her clothes and boots lying at her feet. She looked like some kind of mythical wood sprite come to taunt and seduce us.

"Can I join in?" She asked, and I suddenly didn't feel like a kid anymore.

Twenty-Eight

"Get that sexy ass over here, wifey," Dio called out, and I laughed, bolting over to him and slapping him playfully on the chest.

"Oh no, I'm not that easy," he taunted as he danced out of my reach. "You're going to have to work for it if you want a piece of this action. No copping a cheap feel." He ducked around behind Pala and I followed, still laughing.

After all the heavy emotions of today, I suddenly felt carefree and light. This was exactly what I needed.

We raced around Pala, who stood stoically in the middle, until he suddenly reached out and snared Dio in a headlock. "I got him for you, my heart."

I cackled wickedly as I began a tickle attack, trying to find Dio's weak spots. "Under his neck and the side of his waist," Pala told me. He seemed very familiar with all of Dio's ticklish spots and seemed completely unfazed that Dio was naked and he was only in his underwear.

"Oh, you two have played this game before. Why is that so adorable?" I asked as I ran my fingers down Dio's sides. He tried to wriggle away from me and get out of Pala's headlock at the same time. He was sputtering out laughter while also pleading for mercy.

Dio finally twisted out of Pala's hold and grabbed me before he picked me up and spun me around. I threw out my arms and tipped my head back, in much the same pose I'd watched Pala do earlier.

My laughter died in my throat, though, as Dio turned my back into Pala and pressed me up against his hot, wet body, before kissing me thoroughly. Dio parted my lips with his own, then thrust the tip of his tongue inside and licked gentle, teasing licks against my tongue. It mimicked the action he knew I loved against my clit and made a tingly throb start in my core.

Dio quickly had me squirming against Pala's body as they caged me in place with their arms. They pressed me up against each other, sandwiched between their wet heat as the rain continued to pour down over us.

"I think you're a little overdressed for this game, sugar tits," Dio said, with a hoarse rasp to his voice that had shivers running down my spine.

"Then you better undress me, sugar nuts."

Dio chuckled before his teasing licks turned into a full on assault as he kissed me senseless. He held my face tilted to the side with one hand, so he could capture my mouth exactly the way he wanted, while the other crept up my side, slipping along Pala's arm briefly before moving up to unclasp my bra.

Oh god, the thought of him touching Pala, even innocently, while he was kissing me, had me desperate and wanting more. It surprised me the water on my skin wasn't turning to steam as my body heated instantly.

I shrugged out of my soaking wet bra and let it fall to the wet grass at our feet.

"Be a dear and take her panties off, would you, Pala?" Dio asked as he kissed a line of fire across my jaw.

"Are you okay with this?" Pala whispered as he ran his lips along the edge of my ear. "I can leave you two alone if you'd prefer? I'm willing to wait for you. If I need to, I'll wait forever."

My brain felt like it was fritzing out at the feel of both their mouths on me at the same time.

"No. Stay. Please. I want you too. I want you both," I all but begged as I swiveled my head to the side to meet Pala's mouth for a decadent kiss that had wicked heat burning through me, turning me molten and igniting sparks throughout my core.

I knew I had just met this man tonight, but I'd known instantly he was mine. The same way I had felt about Dio the moment I touched him. He had such an earthy scent about him, standing in the rain, kissing him, felt perfect.

"You honor me, my heart," Pala said, as he ran his hands down my sides and hooked his fingers into my panties, moving his mouth across the other side of my jaw, to kiss down my neck and across my shoulders.

Dio had crouched slightly to teasingly lick one hard nipple while he caressed the other lightly with his thumb. I heard Pala groan, as he ground into my ass from behind and I just knew he was watching Dio the same way I was.

I felt Pala's mouth run down my back, leaving a trail of kisses in his wake, as he slipped my panties off. I lifted each foot for him as he pulled them gently off my legs. When he stood back up, I could feel the hot press of his cock against the top of my ass and I knew he'd slipped his trunks off too.

"Your turn," Dio murmured, as he spun me gently towards Pala.

Pala took my breath away as his eyes devoured me with a hungry, intent focus. All that banked heat that had been building between us all night was now directed at me full force as he stood naked in the moonlight.

Pala groaned as he ran his hands up and down my wet body while I leaned back against Dio, as if I was being presented to Pala on a platter to feast on. Pala stilled as he gently stroked a finger over the yellowing bruises on my ribcage.

"Is he dead yet?" Pala asked through a growl as he flicked his eyes to Dio briefly. Pala's features shifted and tightened as a beast appeared behind his eyes. A dangerous predator with a target in mind. It seemed as if a curtain had parted slightly and I got a glimpse into a dark inner space lurking just behind, where his beast lived.

"Not yet," Dio answered, his own voice darkening and sending goose-bumps skittering along my spine.

Something passed between them, before the curtain dropped back into place and Pala shifted his focus back up to my breasts. He watched raindrops hit each breast and roll off as he traced their trails lightly. "You are so beautiful, my heart."

I could get addicted to all the 'my hearts.' The sweet sensation his words brought dissipated like fairy floss on my tongue, though, as he lunged suddenly and took one nipple into his mouth in a bite that was just shy of painful. His earthy sage scent deepened until a spicy cinnamon broke through that tickled my senses and ignited a deep hunger within me.

My hips jacked back into Dio as I thrust my chest harder into Pala's mouth, needing more. I was lost to the heady sensations coming at me from both sides. I was no longer capable of coherent thought as Pala chased sharp bites with sweet licks, in a soothing caress that had me moaning wantonly.

Together, he and Dio were heat and playfulness bound up in one dangerous package.

"Dio," I begged as I twisted my fingers through his hair. His head rested on my shoulders to watch the show until I tugged firmly and insistently. I needed to feel them both moving over me, all of us grinding together, skin to skin.

"I'm here, babycakes," Dio said as he gently nudged my legs apart with his foot and I felt chilled air caress sensitive skin moments before his hand crept around from my waist and dropped to cup my pussy possessively. He pressed one finger down through my wet heat and I whimpered.

"She's so wet for us already, Pala," he groaned into my neck and Pala instantly abandoned his adoration of my breasts and dropped to his knees.

"Show me," he said gruffly, watching Dio's finger move through me with rapt attention.

Dio parted my pussy with his other fingers, as Pala lifted my leg up onto his shoulder to spread me wide and to help steady me. He trailed kisses down my thigh, his eyes never leaving Dio's finger, until he was close enough for me to feel his breath gliding over my heated core.

The sensation of being held open and presented to Pala, like a gift, had me thrusting desperately against Dio's finger. He kept stroking me with the lightest touch, refusing to go deeper despite my whimpers urging him on. I watched Pala's face as he followed the movement of Dio's finger and the trail of slick I could feel running down my thigh.

"So perfect," Pala groaned.

"Taste her," Dio demanded, as he thrust his wet index finger, dripping with my slick, towards Pala. Pala instantly complied, licking the syrupy sweetness off Dio's finger.

"Mmmm, passionfruit drizzled over meringue," he moaned. His eyes seemed to roll back in his head as he sucked Dio's whole finger into his mouth greedily.

The sight of him licking and sucking my slick off another man's finger had me delirious with need. "Lick me, please," I begged, knowing I needed more. Right the fuck, now.

Pala's eyes snapped open. "You taste so sweet, and you ask so nicely. How could I refuse, my heart?"

He looked like a dark warrior straight out of legend as he sat on his knees in front of me. Water was running down his tanned skin, and slicking his long, dark hair to his shoulders and back. That perfect, chiseled face, with its high cheekbones and sharp jaw, looked up at me with rapture etched into every line. I could picture him with war paint and streaked with the blood of our enemies after an epic battle, devouring his prize.

Pala's grip on my thigh tightened, as I thrust again on a whimper, and he kept eye contact with me as he leaned closer and licked a heat soaked line up my core. I didn't even recognise the noise that left my lips. It was half moaning, half crazed cry. I sounded like I was being tortured with pleasure, which I was.

He finally gave up the teasing as his eyes closed again and he thrust his tongue deep into my heat. Dio matched his rhythm with light strokes over my clit and the gentle tweaking of a nipple. The feel of two gorgeous men working together to bring me pleasure had me exploding instantly. My body shook against them, and quivers wracked me endlessly as they worked me through my orgasm and teased it out mercilessly.

I slumped against Dio, and he wrapped his arm around me to keep me upright. "We haven't finished yet, lover," he whispered in my ear.

Pala rose into view in front of me, with a look of dark promise. Clearly not done with me yet, either. Pala's hungry, heated gaze swept between Dio and me as if we were the only people who existed in this world right now.

Pala tightened the grip he still had on my thigh, and lifted it higher onto his waist, before he picked me up and settled me tightly around him.

"Now, we dance," Dio said as I tipped my head back onto his shoulder and wrapped my arms around his neck. They had me completely suspended between them as I ground myself against Pala's dick. The feel of him, so long and hard, had me whimpering.

I looked up to find Dio watching Pala as intently as I was, and I grinned wickedly. Something was brewing between these two men, something that had been building for a very long time. I wanted to be there if it ever ripped free.

I jumped, as I felt Dio finger my clit again, before he slipped his fingers inside me, scissoring them and stretching me. He only adjusted my angle so he could run his cock up and through my slick alongside Pala's hard dick. For a moment, both of them were sliding against my pussy at the same time and I groaned as the pressure building between us instantly flared hotter.

Both men matched my groan as they thrust against each other a second time, glancing at each other briefly, before Dio pulled back slightly.

"Relax, baby. I want to be inside you while you take him. You can take us both, I know you can," he said, his voice reverent and soft against my ear. He pushed further into my slick soaked pussy while his fingers were still inside me. "Fuck, you feel so good."

As soon as he was fully seated and grinding mercilessly inside me, he removed his fingers and took my weight. Pala instantly pulled back, gently worked an opening with his own fingers through my slick, then lined himself up and thrust hard up into me as well. The stretch and burn had me gasping, but Pala caught each one as he kissed me in a frenzy.

I was so full, stretched tight around both of their cocks. Feeling them both moving inside me in tandem with so much friction was pure bliss. Suddenly, neither man was treating me gently anymore as their beasts rose to the surface, and I didn't care at all. I was an omega, and my body was made for this. To take my alphas in any way they wanted.

"Harder," I moaned, and they both responded instantly. Pala was snarling like a wild creature as Dio growled behind me and I loved it. Despite their dicks rubbing against each other inside me, and the way the added friction seemed to build their own pleasure, I could feel the intense way they were both now focused entirely on me.

"There, oh, fuck, yes," I cried as they alternated thrusts at a furious pace, pounding into me relentlessly, not giving me any space to breathe or think. Their bodies collided, forcing me to just feel as the brutal pace spun me higher and higher.

My body tried to arch, as Pala's knot pressed against the edge of my full pussy, trying to force its way in. But they had their arms around each other, as well as me, and I felt pressed so firmly between them there was no room for me to move. They had me held fast, trapped and completely at their mercy.

My orgasm hit me like a tsunami as a blinding white light crashed like a bright, churning river through me. I lunged forward, moving completely on animal instinct, and bit Pala high on his neck. Needing to bite and claim him more than I needed to breathe.

He screamed an animalistic sound of unadulterated pleasure as his knot jammed inside me, almost making me black out. My orgasm intensified with the added pressure and fullness as I locked around him, holding him fast. I was writhing like a creature built purely of need and sensation. Nothing else existed.

The echoing scream ringing in my ears broke off abruptly as Pala's mouth latched onto my neck and he claimed me, too. He bit me hard and fast, as he ground his knot into me and against Dio, who growled possessively while clutching us both. My vision went spotty as my orgasm reached heights that were almost painful.

Suddenly, Pala and Dio were both there, slamming into my consciousness, touching me inside and out. They were everywhere, and it was too much and not enough as everything fell away. I floated in pure bliss. The raging river eddied into a peaceful stream until, eventually, voices broke through.

"Fuck, have you got her, Pala?"

"Barely. My legs are shaky, but she's locked on my knot. Help me get her down safely."

"Shit, she's locked on so tight, I can barely pull out."

Dio yanked himself out roughly, but kept his arms around me as I felt myself dropping. I tried to tighten my legs around Pala, but nothing worked. I was gently pulled forward onto a hard chest and my legs landed on the cool, wet grass. One of Pala's powerful arms came around me from below, as one of Dio's muscular arms wrapped me up from the side, and his warm body curled around the both of us. We were all squished together in a puppy pile.

The rain had halted to a slight drizzle during our wild frenzy, and only random specks fell on my back now. It was nice. They felt cool on my overheated skin.

"Are you okay, Lex?" Dio asked from beside me, as he ran light fingers up and down my spine.

"Mmmphh," I mumbled against Pala's chest.

"I'm pretty sure she blacked out there, from the way she went completely limp. I think she needs a minute," Pala said wryly.

"Are you okay, Pala? Are you mad? I don't know what came over me. Do I need to apologize?"

A feeling of pure joy, reminiscent of the bliss I had just floated through, whispered through my chest. Only it wasn't coming from me.

"Do you feel that, Dio? I've spent so long missing you and Sam. It felt like a cut that wouldn't heal. Now you've given me the gift of feeling you near even when you're not and you think you need to apologize? No, Dio. I'm okay. I am so very okay."

I finally found the energy to shift my head, to look at them both. They were lying with their foreheads together and Pala had his other arm around Dio. I searched the bond and realized their relationship wasn't sexual like I had thought earlier, not really.

While they'd seemed more than happy to watch each other ravish me minutes ago and weren't averse to rubbing their dicks on each other, it wasn't the nature of their relationship. They didn't crave each other the way they did me.

Their bond went so much deeper than skin. It was a pure connection that was woven into the very fabric of their beings. They weren't each other's anchor in this world, but they were each other's support. It was like a bromance on steroids.

It was almost as if they were two twins that were unrelated. Their bond was two souls recognizing each other and saying 'mine,' in a way that went beyond physical or any kind of social classification like boyfriend, lover, friend. It just was, and it was beautiful.

They must have felt me watching, as they both opened their eyes and glanced at me.

"Whatcha talkin bout?" I mumbled lazily.

Dio grinned at me, and his dimple popped out. I immediately felt all goofy inside. "I bit and claimed Pala," he blurted out.

I just raised my eyebrow at him, and he shrugged, completely nonplussed. Pala was just lying there, looking content and smiling gently at me.

"Yeah, me too," I mumbled. I mean, really, who could resist? He was edible.

"Shit happens," Dio said with a laugh, but he sobered up quickly and I felt a twinge of anxiety through the bond. "Wait, you're not upset, are you? It doesn't change how I feel about you, it's not the same sort of claim. At least I don't think it is -"

"Shush, Dio. Do I feel upset?" I stroked his arm gently to reassure him.

"Uh, no," he replied, "You feel pretty damn chill."

"That's because I'm not upset, okay? So chill out, too."

"Whatever you say, wifey," he said with a smile.

"Are you going to call Pala wifey too, or maybe hubby?" I asked.

"No. I mean, if he wants. I don't. It's not-"

"Do not call me wifey or hubby, Dio, or I'll kick your ass. Got it?" Pala interrupted as he chuckled at our antics.

"Roger Wilco. Reading you loud and clear, amigo," Dio said with a smirk.

I didn't bother asking Pala if he was okay with me biting and claiming him without asking. I could feel how very okay he was. He turned his gaze to me and seemed to feel what I was thinking.

"You can call me whatever you want, my heart. I'll wear your bite proudly, as I will Dio's." I turned and smiled into his chest, feeling overwhelmed yet so happy.

A rough cough from my other side had my eyes widening.

"I brought you some towels and blankets, figured you might need them," Dave said gruffly. I looked around, finally feeling like I could move my body again, to see Dave with his back to us, holding out the linens.

"Thank you, Dave," I said.

"Hey, where the hell have you been?" Dio asked him as he hopped up and grabbed the blanket. He came back and draped it over me, before heading back and grabbing a towel for himself.

"I was keeping watch from the deck, making sure no one was stalking you guys from the trees."

"Uh, you were watching us, you say? Wow, pervy much?" Dio teased and Dave turned around to playfully lunge at him, but Dio jumped back too fast.

"Now, now, that's how this whole thing started. With Lex trying to cop a cheap feel," Dio said as he wound the towel around himself. "If you wanted in on this action, you could have come down and joined in."

Dave groaned, but didn't refute him, which I found intriguing.

"Where's Sam?" Pala asked.

"He's writing," Dave said, which had the guys nodding, but I was completely confused. *What the hell was he writing? A journal entry, a short story, mission reports?*

The mention of Sam had me tensing up, though. While I didn't shy away from them, I didn't like confrontations and I liked the aftermath when everything was awkward even less. I was still mad at Sam for acting like a dick, and I would never put up with that, but I was more worried about him than anything else. I hadn't liked the look on his face after I'd put him down.

Pala instinctively started stroking my back, the same way Dio had earlier, offering comfort. Sensing my mood swing seemed to soften his knot, though, enough for me to slip off him. I was a little disappointed. I'd been enjoying our outdoor snuggle time. We were going to have to do this again. Maybe we could keep the hammocks, so we didn't have to lie on the ground.

"Come on, let's go up to the treehouse so we can clean up and get Sam's grovel fest underway," Dio said as he held a hand out to help me up.

I tried to fight my smile, but I couldn't. Nothing was ever going to feel too heavy with Dio around to lighten the mood.

"So, who's giving me a piggyback ride?" I asked.

Pala immediately tried to push Dio out of the way, to reach me first, but Dio stood his ground. They ended up wrestling with towels hanging precariously from their hips. Bear came leaping out of nowhere and jumped into the fray, wanting to play, too. He stole Dio's towel as Pala laughed, and they both ended up chasing him for it. Bear had the goofiest, happiest look on his face as he dodged them both.

I would have stayed to watch the show, but Dave turned away from me and crouched down in silent invitation. I dashed over and hopped on his back.

"Thanks."

"No thanks needed," he said as he gripped my legs and steadied me as he stood up.

We both realized the problem at the same moment, as his hands gripped my naked thighs. The blanket shifted even further when I put my arms around him to hang on, so now I had a lot of skin plastered against his back.

"Why do you always seem to wander around in nothing but a blanket lately?"

"Hey, you brought the blanket," I said in mock outrage.

"Clearly I'm a sucker for punishment," he mumbled to himself as he headed towards the stairs.

The stairs that would take me up to the dark presence I could feel pulling at me, even from this distance. The alpha that drew me in with an intensity that took my breath away, yet also had alarm bells ringing in my head.

Sam.

Twenty-Nine

"Keep it together," I whispered to myself as I spotted Dave piggy-backing a blanket covered Lexie towards the stairs while Dio and Pala goofed off in the clearing with Bear. Dammit, I did not want to have another awkward conversation with her while she was naked under a blanket and smelling like sex. It drove my beast wild to scent my mates on her. He was desperate to stake his claim, too.

I'd white knuckled my way through the sexcapade that had just gone on in the clearing below me. Forcing myself to stick to the shadows of the deck and not peek over the railing, despite Lexie's scent and moans calling to me like a siren song. I'd almost lost it when Dio had groaned loudly while Pala had cried out in pleasure.

I'd noticed Dave adjusting himself uncomfortably from where he stood at the edge, scanning the trees, with only the occasional glance down before he tore his eyes away.

The group hug earlier had calmed my dominance in a way nothing else ever had. I'd been skeptical when Leif had alluded to it, but all their energies in close proximity had quickly calmed my own. Pala's tranquil river, Dio's lighthearted joy, and even Dave's solid dependability had all soothed me. My beast was an instinctive creature and had lapped that shit up like it was his first ice cream cone.

Yet, sitting up here alone now, in the star speckled darkness as the clouds receded, my dominance was surging again as my thoughts and energy raced. I had always appreciated Dio stepping in whenever my dominance spiked. His fond and instinctive touches never failed to soothe me. Yet, I'd always removed myself as soon as I could, to flee and attempt to dilute my dominance on my own, by exercising to the point of exhaustion.

I cursed myself as I realized Leif was right and I had made it so much harder. I was an idiot. Now that the fog of my dominance spiral had fully lifted, I felt a keen need building inside me for my budding pack to be close at hand. And for the feisty omega at its center. I'd been delusional to think I could ever leave them. I would have been feral within weeks, maybe days.

As if I had called them, Dave and Lexie appeared at the top of the stairs. Dio and Pala's heads popped over the edge of the balcony a moment later, as their chests heaved heavy breaths after their rope climb.

The two bite marks on either side of Pala's neck, that were almost glowing in the moonlight, had my beast yearning. Alphas rarely bit each other, but my beast wanted a claim mark from both Pala and Dio with a passionate need that took my breath away. Almost as much as I wanted Lexie's.

"I win," Dio crowed, distracting me, as he threw his leg up onto the railing and propelled himself over, using the brute strength in his powerful thighs. Unfortunately, his towel snagged on the timber and ripped free as he leaped to the deck. It slipped over the edge and fell back to the earth before he could grab it.

"Yeah, but I made it to the top without flashing the world my junk or losing my towel," Pala said as he gracefully flipped himself over the edge like a gymnast on a balance beam. His abs flexed as he used his core strength instead.

Dio shrugged. "It was all slobbery, anyway."

I glanced at Lexie and she was openly ogling both men, while Dave just chuckled at them like they were cute toddlers.

"Clearly I won, because I have Lexie's legs wrapped around me right now," Dave said with a smirk.

"Fair call," Dio replied as he shrugged while leaning casually against the railing, completely unfazed at being naked in front of us all.

A surge of nervousness made my dominance spill around me. I figured it was a protective response, but it was inconvenient as hell. I really wanted to stay calm right now.

I grit my teeth and stepped out of the shadows, into the moonlight. I felt raw and exposed, as if I was the one who was naked.

Dio gave me an encouraging nod, but kept his distance as Lexie slid down Dave's back and landed on her feet. She stepped around him, but he stayed near her side, a spot he seemed born to hold, despite being so much older than her.

She watched me carefully, no doubt able to feel the dominance now rolling off me. I cleared my throat, then had to swallow hard and do it again. I felt like all the moisture in my body had disappeared.

"I'm sorry," I blurted out. Figuring this wasn't an occasion to waffle on, not that I was capable, anyway. The higher my dominance rose, the harder it was to talk to people. Sometimes, I reverted to being a caveman and just grunted at people out of necessity.

As alphas, we were at the top of the predator food chain, but I often wondered just how evolved we were.

Lexie just raised her eyebrow and remained silent.

Do better, asshole. I wasn't sure for a moment if the voice in my head was me or her.

"I know that's not enough. What I said was hateful and untrue. I didn't mean it. I was just lashing out. But that's no excuse."

Lexie just continued to stare at me and Dave shifted uncomfortably at her side, shooting me a worried look.

"I already apologized to your brother." Lexie finally softened and re-laxed slightly at that confession, dropping her crossed arms to her side but keeping the blanket tucked tightly around her.

It gave me the courage to step towards her. The closer I got, the harder it was to stop myself from reaching out to touch her, but I hadn't earned that right. I stopped in front of her, hesitating.

My beast was raging at me, screaming that she was ours. He didn't understand social norms, or that I had fucked up and needed to earn my place at her side. He just needed her with a desire so dark and possessive it made my body shake.

I felt my dominance suddenly shift from shoving at the world, to trying to draw these people closer to me. As if my beast had changed tactics. The sensation was powerful, primal, and more than a little seductive. I felt Dio and Pala at my back, shadowing me suddenly, as Lexie's eyes widened and Dave groaned.

The five of us, standing so close yet not touching, felt like nirvana was just outside my reach. It was maddening. I tried to shake it off as I held out my hand to her and offered her the letter I had been holding, now partially crumpled in my fist.

"This is for you. Don't read it now, or at all if you don't want to. Just, please give me a chance to fix this. I can do better. I will do better."

Lexie nodded, as she unwrapped one arm from the blanket, reached out tentatively and took the crinkled paper. Her hand, and how close it was to mine at that moment, had me riveted. It was the closest I had gotten to her since I met her. I swear I could feel the heat from her skin scorching me. If I shifted my finger forward, I could touch her. I dropped my hold on the envelope and yanked my hand back, not trusting myself.

"Okay," was all she said as her hand dropped to her side with a slight tremor. It was enough. It was a start.

I felt two hands on my back, giving me reassurance, and I breathed deeper. Feeling myself calm. The dominance pull lessened, mollified for the moment by the touch of my mates.

"What the hell was that?" Dio asked, a note of wonder in his voice. "You've never done that before, pulled instead of pushed. That was intense. My feet were moving before I even thought about it."

I looked over my shoulder at him, and he grinned. "You made my dick hard."

"A stiff breeze makes your dick hard," Pala said dryly, proving how well he knew Dio. Dio had never been promiscuous, but he'd always had a laid-back sensuality about him. It didn't surprise me at all that he was the first one of us to sleep with Lexie and claim her.

I just rolled my eyes and refused to take the bait and look down.

"How did you resist the pull, Dave?" Dio asked.

Dave just shrugged with a smirk plastered across his face. "Self control."

I glanced at Lexie as Dio laughed and noticed her knuckles were white where they gripped the edges of her blanket. As if she was holding herself back.

"Are you okay, my heart?" Pala asked as he left my side and stepped over to Lexie. He took her in his arms and she went willingly.

"You're mated?" I asked. I noticed the confident way Pala approached Lexie now, and I tried to keep my need to touch her from spearing through my voice.

"Yes," Pala said, lifting his head proudly. "By Lexie and Dio."

"Congratulations," I said quietly, but with genuine joy. Pala deserved this. He seemed far more settled than he had earlier and was no longer hanging back. It made my heart happy. I wouldn't taint this moment for him with my own fears and insecurities.

"Thank you, brother." Pala replied. I could almost see his calm center radiating out and Lexie relaxing under his touch as he smiled down at her.

"It's been a long day. I'm going to take a shower and call it a night," Lexie said. She looked up at Pala through lowered lashes, seeming almost shy, which was unusual for her. Or maybe she was just nervous. She'd bitten both Dio and Pala the same day she had met them, Pala within hours. There had to be a lot of intense feelings pummeling her.

What I wouldn't give right now to have a bond with her, so I could know exactly how she was feeling, and soothe her if she needed it.

From what I had heard of her from her friends, it appeared she had always been a headstrong and instinctive woman, throwing herself into danger to help others without a thought for her own safety. Yet she had also appeared lonely and a little aloof around her friends when we first met her. As if she was guarding herself, or maybe just her heart.

Watching her open up to Pala and Dio so willingly made my throat tighten. She was fierce, almost wild, yet also incredibly vulnerable. She was a gorgeous, pink-haired contradiction.

The way she stood up to me, getting right up in my face, made my dick hard and my spirit soar. I wanted to argue with her and push her, bring all that passion to the surface, then fuck her so hard she screamed and drew blood.

Instead of doing any of that, I dropped my eyes and stepped around her. "I'll, uh, head down to the hammock, and see you all in the morning,"

I breathed deeply as I tried to get myself under control. Her scent, saturated with both Pala's and Dio's, intensified as I passed, almost driving me insane.

Lexie's blurted, "Wait," had me freezing in place as I reached the stairs. I turned slowly, with dread, unsure if she was going to ask me to leave the area completely. My team was lodging in two guest cabins and I had a bedroom in one. I didn't know if I could go back there, though, even if she asked. It was too far from her.

"You can sleep on the couch here, if you'd like. The hammock is soaking wet."

"Yeah, uh, that would be great. Thank you." I had to resist the urge to throw myself at her like an overexcited puppy.

"I know you're struggling Sam, I also know you're not a bad guy. I don't want to be someone who makes your life more difficult. If I can help, just tell me how. Or if I do something that sets you off, find a better way to tell me."

"You don't make anything more difficult, I promise. And I'll try," I said, a little more gruffly than I intended.

She just nodded at me and quickly turned to Dave. "You too, Dave. You're welcome to take the couch. It's comfy."

He smiled down at her, and while there was no claim between them yet, something already seemed more settled within him, too.

"Sure, I can take the couch," he said, as he leaned forward and pressed a gentle kiss to her forehead.

Dio opened the heavy barn door, and I followed them through, trying not to spill dominance all over the place. Watching everyone else kiss and touch her was stoking my need for her, and for them.

"Hey tickle bunny, let me get you cleaned up," Dio said, taking her hand and gesturing toward an interior door, just off the small kitchenette, with his head.

"Sure, pumpkin," she replied, laughing.

Dio, Pala and Lexie all headed through the internal door, which I assumed led to the bathroom, as I pulled the heavy barn door shut behind me. I went to lock it, before I realized there wasn't one.

Why the hell did Lexie's front door not have a lock? I looked over to Dave, feeling a scowl form on my face, but he held up his hand to ward me off.

"I'm fixing it. I didn't realize before tonight."

I nodded. If Dave was aware of it now, I knew he would fix it. I looked around at the huge open plan lounge, kitchen and dining space, as I walked further inside, before my eyes drifted up to a loft area.

"She unconsciously built herself a nest up there. Few people get to see it."

Fuck. The idea of her up there, with Dio and Pala and the things they would get up to while I was lying downstairs, was flashing through my mind. I clearly hadn't thought this through. There were no walls up there, we would hear everything.

"Maybe a wet hammock wouldn't be so bad?" I wondered.

Dave laughed, as he looked at the dread I'm sure he could see all over my face. "Don't sweat it. I guarantee they're going to be in the shower for a while. It's a huge ass outdoor bathroom with a bunch of showerheads and a hot tub."

I groaned. "That's hardly better, Dave."

"Tell me about it. It's going to be a long night."

Not for me, apparently. I grabbed a cushion, laid down on the couch and crashed.

What felt like five minutes later, I woke up to hot breath on my cheek and a wet tongue licking my ear.

Thirty

I crept toward the stairs, trying not to make any noise. I'd extricated myself out from under Pala and Dio without waking them fully, shifting their arms and legs around each other instead of me until they'd both settled back down to sleep again. It was cute as hell, watching them snuggle into each other.

I reached over for one of my old cameras sitting on an upturned wooden crate with a timber top I'd made to use as a table. My camera collection included all sizes and styles, from antique to new. I didn't believe in keeping them locked away, though. I kept them lying around all over the place, so one was always near at hand if I felt the urge to take a picture.

That was how I took a lot of my photos. I rarely staged anything. I preferred to capture a moment naturally. Sometimes I'd just sit quietly around the farm and see what the world brought me.

I hadn't taken a picture of anything in weeks. Life had been too crazy. So I gave myself a minute to document this quiet moment. Luckily, the camera I grabbed was an old instant style that spat out a photo as soon as you took it. I shuffled around nimbly until I found the perfect angle and snapped a photo, wincing at the sound as the shutter whirred and the photo slid out slowly.

The guys didn't stir, though, so I took another couple of shots. One of their feet all tangled up together in the blankets, and another of

Dio's hands. One hand was around Pala's waist and the other was woven through his gorgeous, long, dark hair.

You could see the curve of Pala's delectable ass on the edge of the shot. It wasn't quite the magnificent bubble butt Dio sported, but it was high, firm and eminently biteable.

I smiled to myself, marveling at my current reality. I got to grab both luscious asses whenever I wanted. After years of keeping myself at arm's length from everyone, my world was suddenly full of people all up in my space. I found I didn't mind a bit.

It had its drawbacks, though. I hadn't read Sam's letter yet. I'd wanted to do it alone. While I'm sure Dio and Pala would have given me space if I'd asked, I didn't want to send them away after the intense mating we'd just shared. I'd needed them close last night, and they'd seemed perfectly willing to stay.

Thinking of Sam's letter, I turned for the stairs. I wanted to find a quiet space to read it before I rejoined the wider world. I continued my creeping as I made my way down the stairs in the early dawn light.

I peeked over the banister when I heard a muffled noise and spied Bear licking Sam's ear. I had to put my hand over my mouth to stop my laugh from bursting free. It seemed Bear had finally warmed up to Sam, and it made me wonder what had gone down last night after I left them at the gate.

Sam shifted his head and Bear let loose an enormous yawn, full of doggy breath, right in his face. I quickly snapped a photo.

"Urrgghhh," Sam mumbled while trying to push Bear's head away. Bear was hard to shift when he wanted a scratch, though.

Sam popped one eye open, but instead of yelling or growling at Bear like I expected him to, he reached up and scratched him under the chin.

"You're a good boy, Bear." I heard him mumble. Satisfied with the scratch and the praise, Bear hopped up onto the couch and promptly curled up on Sam's feet.

Sam just smiled down at him before he stretched his arms over his head. He was still wearing the same clothes from last night, as if he'd passed out the moment he laid his head down. The blanket I lay over him while he was sleeping last night lay tangled up around his legs.

I couldn't help but notice how his shirt rose as he stretched and revealed taut pale skin covering tight abs. The view had me momentarily mesmerized. It was such an intimate scene, watching someone wake up. I knew I should look away, but I couldn't. I also couldn't resist another photo.

His eyes flicked up at the sound of the camera clicking and he startled when he noticed me, but I just raised my finger to my mouth in a shush motion and nodded at Dave, who was sleeping peacefully on one of the other couches. It was one of my signature moves, deflecting attention away when you were doing something sneaky.

I ducked back out of sight, intending to head out onto the deck alone. Sam startled me when he popped up at the bottom of the stairs. He must have jumped over Bear and the couch to get there so fast, but I hadn't heard a sound. I raised my eyebrow at him.

He shifted awkwardly on his feet, with his hands tucked in his pockets, like he hadn't stopped to figure out what he was going to say. His eyes roamed over me, catching on my sneakers. "Where are you sneaking off to?"

I tilted my head back at his words as my fists clenched and I tried not to arc up. *Why did he push my buttons so much?*

He stepped forward, and held his hands out in peace, before I let loose with a tirade.

"Sorry. That came out all wrong. I was trying for humor, but clearly I suck at it. Let me try again."

He took a deep breath. "Morning Lexie. I wanted to take a quick walk around the farm this morning. I always loved walking in the early morning air when I was growing up, before Maia and everyone else woke up. If you're heading out, can I tag along? Maybe you could show me around a little on your way?"

I suddenly felt the stirrings of that same pull from last night. It was like the draw I've felt ever since I first laid eyes on each of them, but stronger, more intense and focused. Harder to refuse. It was also much more personal, deeper than the mate draw. It felt like something particular to Sam and anchored in his dominance.

Sam also seemed different somehow, but I couldn't put my finger on exactly how. Something more than an apology had gone down last night. There was an outer stillness to him that had been missing before. The rage was still there, but it felt banked underneath the surface now.

He was like a lion, waking up lazily and taking a stroll, knowing he was secure in his kingdom. Yet drawing the eyes of every creature watching. You couldn't help but look while you knew you should probably run.

I nodded my head, without even debating my answer. "Sure, I'm heading to the kitchen to help with breakfast, but I need to detour past my cabin first. I need some fresh clothes. I've worn everything I had stashed here."

"You don't live here?"

"No, well I didn't. I always spent a lot of time up here, but I mostly slept in my cabin. It's a studio and perfect for one person."

"Maybe we could help you move your stuff up here? If you want to, I mean. I don't think either Dio or Pala are going to want to sleep anywhere except with you from now on."

"Yeah, being up here with them feels right for me, too."

"Consider it done, then. Just let us know when you're ready."

"Okay, thanks. We could maybe just grab my clothes later today. The big stuff might have to wait a bit. There's so much going on right now. I don't know when I'll have time to sort through everything and work out what will fit in up here. I might donate some of it to other families now that we can't just get furniture and homewares delivered online."

"Sure, of course." We stared awkwardly at each other for a moment until Sam stepped back and gestured at the door.

I put the camera and the photos down on the dining table and peeked over at Dave as I passed. I'd thought he was asleep, but I caught him shutting his eyes quickly when he saw me glance at him. He had a small grin on his face he couldn't hide, either.

He looked like he'd fallen asleep reading one of my books I had stashed around last night. It was lying open on his chest. I glanced at the cover and it had a blue barbarian and a dark haired girl on it. It was one of my smut books. Asshat. *He better be getting some ideas from that one. It was hot.*

Sam was the perfect gentleman as we headed to my cabin, walking near, but not too close. I invited him in when he hesitated at the door. I grabbed some clothes quickly and ducked into the bathroom to change.

When I came out, Sam was looking at some of my photos on the walls. "Did you take these?"

I nodded as he turned to look over his shoulder at me. The photos were intensely personal for me. I liked to filter my world through the safety of a lens sometimes. I also liked the way it could bring out the beauty in ordinary items and everyday moments.

"They're stunning." He was looking closely at a blown up portrait of a farm worker out in the fields. He was the grandfather of one of our founding families and insisted on helping to keep himself active. His face was a map of his life, all leathery texture and lines from a life spent in the sun. He had his hat clutched to his chest, and he was laughing, joy lighting up his face. You could see members of his family in the background as they worked. For me, it perfectly captured what this farm was all about.

Sam reached out to stroke the man's face through the glass of the frame. It probably reminded him of his gramps. There was a tenderness in the gesture and I assumed I'd lost him to his own memories. I pottered around, gathering up a few things and tidying others away quickly. I hadn't known the last time I was here that I wouldn't be back for a while.

"Who are these men?" He asked, a rough note entering his voice. I spun around and noticed him holding a photo album, filled with photos of men, all taken with a telephoto lens as they went about their day. He gripped the edge of the album so hard his knuckles were white as he flipped through the pages with his other hand. I sensed he was trying not to spill his dominance and his scent all over my space.

Shit. It wasn't what it looked like.

"Uh, the women I help rescue from crappy situations often have very pissed off, volatile partners. I take a photo of each one just in case any of the women disappear. So I have something I can show to the police."

He shot me a look that was full of surprise but also impressed. "You've helped this many women?"

I shrugged as I turned back to what I was doing. "I've been doing it for about seven years."

Sam's next words came from right behind me, where I was standing next to my kitchen bench. I hadn't heard him move. "This place feels like you."

"What, small and messy?" I shot over my shoulder.

"No," he chuckled, "bright and fun, a little wild."

I looked around at the yellow kitchen cabinets, blue couch and an eclectic mix of brightly colored throws and pots. When I'd moved out of home, I'd been so young, and home had always been a mausoleum, dark and cold. I'd built up a collection of bright things to surround myself with, knowing I was the only person I had to please and could make my new space my own. I'd brought it all with me when I moved to the farm.

"But it's also closed off, contained," he added, "it keeps everyone at a distance. Their lives all represented secondhand. You're not in any of your pictures."

I looked around as he spoke. This place was small, and he was right, there really wasn't room for any visitors. It had been my sanctuary for years, but it had also been my fortress of solitude. Maia was the only other visitor I'd ever really had in here. When I socialized, I usually did it elsewhere. I realized suddenly this cabin no longer felt like home. My heart was up in the treehouse and people filled it now.

It made me ache that Sam saw me so clearly. So few did.

"I'm so glad you let Dio and Pala in. I hope one day you can let me in too," he said with a quiet intensity. His body heat warmed my back, and my hair stirred gently, as if he'd run his fingers through it lightly, making me shiver.

He was silent for a moment and I closed my eyes, just enjoying the sense of him in my space without his rage and frustration pounding me, stirring me to action. He cleared his throat roughly, and I felt my body chill at the loss of his warmth as he stepped away.

"We should probably head for the kitchen or we'll be late." The sudden gruffness in his voice didn't throw me off like it usually did, though. I sensed it wasn't directed at me.

I nodded, feeling suddenly off balance. This alpha brought out so many contradictory emotions in me. He pushed all my buttons, but he also pulled at something deep within me. Everything he did had a sense of power that left me breathless, even when he was just quietly breathing.

We didn't talk as we walked, but it wasn't awkward. I sensed we were both enjoying the quiet morning. Sam's dominance wasn't leaking hotly this morning. It was more of a warm wash that left a zing across my skin and made me feel achingly alive. It matched the slowly waking farm that was emerging around us, glowing rays overtaking darkness as the sun gently spread its fingers into the world. Hope spreading its beacon.

It was so rare I found someone I could just be quiet with. It surprised me that Sam might be that person, given how volatile we usually were whenever one of us opened our mouths.

I could feel the sexual tension humming between us as we walked, though, ever present. I had an acute awareness of every movement he made. As though the air caught between us felt the pull, too, and was consumed with it. Trying to draw us closer.

On the way to the dining hall, I showed him things about the farm that I loved. The cabin we had set up for women to make goat's milk products to sell and support themselves, even the pond and the old mill we were trying to get working again, surrounded by the weeping willows.

There was a light fog floating around the lower areas of the farm in the early morning light, turning the landscape lush and romantic. The sounds of the waking farm seemed muted and far away, when heard through the dense air, even the occasional croaking frog. Standing around the pond, it felt like we were the only people in the world.

It was the perfect spot for a first kiss. Sam glanced at me almost longingly while we briefly lingered. He stretched his hand toward me before stuffing it deep in his pocket again.

Disappointment washed over me, but I also felt relieved. I'd never really held hands with a guy before. As much as I wanted to hold Sam's hand in that moment, the gesture felt fraught with tension. I wasn't ready for his touch. I knew how wildly I had reacted to both Dio and Pala the first time they had touched me. Sam and I weren't there yet. I hadn't even read his letter.

The absence of touch felt almost like its own weight, though. My hand was aching from the deprivation.

We tarried so long I was late for the breakfast shift. Sam left me at the back door with a growled, "I'll see you at breakfast," before he abruptly disappeared.

The man was an enigma.

Thirty-One

Maia threw her arms around me as soon as I got inside, while Ava shot me a sweet smile from her workstation. "How did it go last night, when you got back to the treehouse?" Maia whispered breathlessly.

"Fine."

"Uh oh, that bad?" she asked, with a horrified expression.

I laughed. "No. I, uh, can we talk about it later?"

I glanced at the women around the room, and Maia got it instantly. There were too many ears in here.

"Sure thing. You've got until after breakfast, though. I need details."

"Family meeting after breakfast, don't forget."

Maia groaned with a laugh. "Fine. Breakfast, family meeting, then girl chat. You're not weaseling out of this. Oh, and I brought you my book about omegas and packs, Leif thought it might help."

She pushed her big leather book across the counter towards me and I gave her a squeeze, feeling her friendship lighten my heart, before I tucked it into a safe spot so it wouldn't get dirty. I wanted to read it later. "Thank you. If I haven't said it before, I'm really glad you stopped at our gates. Not because of the book, just because you've brought so much to our lives."

"Stop it. You're going to make me bawl." She swatted me away, her voice sounding thick.

"Can you cover me for a minute?" I asked her, looking over at the freezer.

She looked confused, but nodded without asking a lot of questions. "Absolutely. I've got your back."

That girl was quickly becoming my ride or die.

I slipped out with none of the other girls noticing and ducked into the big walk-in freezer. It was the only place around here to get some quiet for five minutes. Nobody came in here unless they had to. I slipped Sam's letter out of my pocket. He'd shown amazing restraint this morning, not asking me about it.

I smoothed out the crinkled paper on my lap and read as I perched on a box and shivered.

Lexie,

I behaved like an asshole tonight, and let's be honest, before tonight, too. I'm so very sorry. If I haven't said this to you directly yet, or didn't get the words out properly, forgive me. Whenever I'm around you, my beast pushes to the surface and I can't think straight.

I have all of this rage that has built up for over a decade and it has nowhere to go but out, no matter how much I try to starve it or wear it out. It's exhausting and I'm so tired of fighting it.

I know my alpha beast is part of my nature, but I don't want to be a beast with you. Or an asshole. I've been told my entire life I'm dangerous and I'm only just now figuring out that people may not have meant it the way I thought they did.

I've never felt like I was dangerous, not to innocent people, but my beast and I still have some issues we need to work on.

You see, I've learned to push people away before they can do it to me. Yet, Pala, Dio, Dave and Leif opened my eyes tonight to a world of possibility and it's honestly a little terrifying. I want that world, though. I want it so badly I'm willing to bleed for it if I have to, and the shining star at the center is you.

I see you. I see how brilliantly you shine. Your courage, your fierce spirit, your boldness. You grabbed me by the throat when you stood up to me that first day and I've been yours ever since.

When I growl at you, it's usually me I'm angry at. That I can't get myself together enough to say what I really want. So, now I'm going to do as you asked and handle my shit. I'm going to work on deserving you.

I've written to Maia for years. I knew she probably wasn't getting them because she never wrote back, but they became a kind journal I sent out into the world. Where I put all my worries, fears, hopes and dreams. It all comes out on a page the way I can never seem to get out in person.

If you don't mind, I'd like to write to you. You don't have to read them if you don't want to, but hopefully one day we can figure out how to get your fierce omega and my wounded, stubborn beast to communicate properly.

Until then, I dream of the day I can finally touch you, knowing I'm yours as much as you're mine.

Yours,

Sam.

I sat for a moment, holding the letter to my chest. Despite the cold freezer, I felt warm inside. I'd had no hesitation in claiming Dio and Pala the moment I'd met them. They both lit up my world in different ways.

Yet the pull to Sam had always felt intense and a little dark. I wasn't afraid of it, though. I wanted to cover myself in that darkness, like a cloak, then roll around naked inside it. His own fear of himself, and his visibly conflicted emotions towards me, had held me back. Not wanting to hurt him anymore than he clearly had been already.

He'd been different this morning, though, more centered. More certain of himself. Like he had a better handle on his darkness. It still simmered in his eyes, but I didn't mind that at all.

I ducked out of the freezer and discreetly grabbed a notepad and pen from the nearest counter before ducking back inside again.

I wrote furiously, not bothering to make it pretty. Needing to get out the feelings he had stirred within me with his letter.

Sam,

I'm not afraid of your beast. I get it, though; I keep people at arm's length too. I was always afraid of what would happen if my omega suddenly burst out. But then she did. Now my world is no longer the same. It turns out, it's not a bad thing. I finally feel free.

This is all new to me as well, so I also get that it's terrifying. I hope one day you get to experience this freedom. Like I said last night, if I can help, I'm here. Just tell me what you need and I'll raze cities to get it for you.

As for your beast. I actually kind of like him. Don't coop him up on my account. My omega finds him tantalizing. She'd like to play with him. So maybe try to growl for me, not at me.

In the meantime, I'll read any letters you write to me, but you also need to fix your shit with Maia. She's important to me and she needs her big brother back.

Maybe, one day, yours,

Alexia

P.S. Nobody except Leif knows my full name. My mother gave it to me before I was born, but my father wouldn't let anyone use it. Now I'm trusting you with it.

I smiled to myself. I had no desire to tame Sam's beast. The thought of playing with it, though, gave me the shivers.

I tucked both of the letters into my pocket and slipped into the kitchen. Maia just winked at me and chucked an apron at me as I took up a station next to her.

"Have you noticed Sirena and Isabella lately?" She whispered so low I barely heard her as she helped me tie the apron. I glanced toward the two women and noticed Sirena caress the back of Isobella's hand briefly as she leaned past her to grab something, causing Isabella to blush.

"When did that happen?" I whispered back. I'd clearly been neglecting my friends, so caught up in my own soap opera lately.

Maia shrugged discreetly. I glanced over again and noticed Isabella seemed to have made more of an effort with her appearance today than she had in a while, wearing a dress and putting her long brown hair up in a sleek ponytail. She was usually a jeans, tee and messy bun kind of girl. She even looked like she had some lip gloss on.

Isabella had been one of the first women I'd brought to the farm when she'd needed help to escape an abusive relationship. She'd been healing slowly and finally thrived in her role running the farm's function center before the Crash. She deserved some happiness and a lot of love.

I wasn't so sure about Sirena. She'd behaved like a bitch to all the women on the farm since she'd arrived. Sirena also caused a lot of trouble for Maia when Maia had shown up and the guys had instantly gone gaga for her. Until Damon had outed Sirena's behavior. I knew Sirena had been staying with Isabella and another woman in a shared cabin since then.

Maia had told me briefly about Sirena's confession during the attack, though. How her father had forced her into coming here to seduce and spy on Damon and his mates. It appeared she'd risked everything to warn them, and had helped during the alpha attack as well. Heading to secure the childcare cabin before detouring to help save Maia.

I was skeptical, but I could also see she'd been behaving differently ever since. I wasn't quick to forgive anyone who had wronged someone I loved, though, and Maia was already high on that list.

Sirena caught me watching her and stilled before she turned and headed my way. "Can I have a quick word with you, Lexie, please? Outside."

I glanced at Isabella, and she nodded at me as I sighed. I hated confrontations and uncomfortable chats, and this was likely going to be both.

"Sure," I said as I plastered a big smile on my face before I followed her outside.

Sirena didn't keep me waiting. She turned right at the bottom of the steps. She probably knew everyone inside would be listening at the windows above us, even if we moved out further into the garden. I got the impression this talk wasn't just for me.

"I owe you an apology for the way I've behaved. You were welcoming to me when I first arrived and I was a complete bitch to you. You were close to Damon, Hunter and Max, and they clearly cared about you, so I singled you out. I'm sure Maia has told you why, and it's not a story I really want to go into again. I didn't have any good choices at the time and I was being watched. But I am sorry that you got dragged into it all."

I took a good look at her. All the over the top perfumed couture perfection was gone. She was dressed down in jeans, a simple t-shirt and sneakers. Her mask had dropped, and she looked the same as all the other women I'd brought here when they first arrived. Weary, burdened, and just trying to survive each day. She had her head held high, even though she was tense, as though she was bracing herself against my response.

I suddenly felt terrible that I hadn't noticed earlier how fake her artifice was. I'd thought she was just shallow. Yet she'd been fighting the same battles we all had all along. I should know better than that by now. I knew intimately that the face people presented to the world wasn't always a true one.

"Are you okay?" I blurted out. She looked completely taken aback, as if it wasn't the reaction she was bracing for. She opened her mouth but nothing came out.

"I mean about your brother. Maia told me the basics. She didn't go into details because she's not like that. She wouldn't gossip about someone's personal life. But she said Ronan was your brother, and Damon killed him after he attacked Maia."

Sirena flicked her eyes over to the spot, only a few meters away, where her brother had died a few days ago. She took a giant, unsteady breath. "That's not a simple question to answer."

"That's fair." I wouldn't know how to feel if my father was killed, either. There wouldn't be any mourning, but I wouldn't celebrate it either. "I just want to make sure you're okay being here now."

"I don't have anywhere else I want to be. What you and the guys have built here is incredible. What you've done for the women here, the stories they've told me. You didn't just let them in, you actively rescued some of them, putting your own life in danger.

She gasped lightly, as if she'd been holding in words that refused to stay inside a moment longer.

"I'm in awe of you, Lexie. It felt like I died a little every time I was mean to you. I was just so worried about what would happen if my father thought you were a threat to his plans for Damon. I didn't think there was anyone in this world who was powerful enough to stand up to my dad."

I went to say something, but she held up her hand. "Let me finish, please."

The move didn't offend me; it made me smile. Sirena may have dropped the bitch act, but she was clearly a strong woman who had resolved to fix her mistakes. I could respect that. It also told me, more than her words, that she was going to be fine. She would be a force to be reckoned with once she figured out her own strength.

" I realize now, I should have trusted you from the start, confessed everything and asked for your help. My subterfuge should never have gone as far as it did. I need you to know, though, that I never betrayed you, your brothers, or this farm. I did as much as I could to filter misinformation back to my father and my brother."

She looked at me warily as I raised an eyebrow, but she seemed to be finished. I figured I should double check, though.

"Are you done? Can I talk now?"

She looked down, and her face flushed. "Sorry, I've never been very good at knowing my place."

"Hey," I said, getting mad now, as I grabbed her chin and made her look at me. "Never apologize for being a strong fucking woman. I was only teasing. Your place is wherever you make it. Do you hear me?"

She nodded and straightened her spine, so I let her go.

"Thanks for the apology. You're one of us now. You earned that when you defended Maia and this farm, and we'll have your back if your father comes looking for retaliation. As for you and I, we're going to be just fine as long as we're honest with each other. If I piss you off, let me know and I'll do the same. Deal?"

"Deal." She looked relieved.

"Can I have a hug? Does Sirena 2.0 do hugs?"

She grinned at me and nodded, so I grabbed her in a bear hug. I would never begrudge a woman doing what she had to in order to survive.

"You and Isabella be good to each other, if you're going to go there," I whispered low, so no one else would hear. "You both deserve it."

Her eyes widened at me, before she nodded and smiled a little shyly. The Sirena of old was one hell of an act if the new Sirena was anything to go by. She must have been honing it for years. I sensed relief now that she could finally drop it.

"Let's get back in there," I said, louder than I needed to. I rolled my eyes as Maia hissed, "They're coming back," followed by a slapping sound and Ava whispering, "Shush," then a stampede of feet.

Sirena just laughed as we turned and headed back inside, while everyone pretended to be busy at their stations. I didn't call them out. These women were their own kind of pack, and they had each other's backs.

I knew they would have just been watching to see if we needed them to intervene or help. Or maybe slap some sense into us if we couldn't sort our shit out. I wouldn't have it any other way.

Thirty-Two

 Lexie

The rest of the shift passed in a blur of activity. We were bringing the food trays back in when Maia ducked over to the guys to see if they wanted any more coffee before we took it away.

Sam was hovering around the food table, picking at things, as if he'd been waiting for me to come out. I said nothing, but I discreetly dropped my letter next to the last muffin and moved away slightly. Sam snatched it up, not even trying to be subtle in his haste, then looked around.

"I'm just going to the bathroom," he said, loudly, to no-one in particular as he almost ran towards the door.

How the hell did he survive undercover all these years? The man had no poker face around me.

I heard Hunter and Dave tell Maia they'd like some more coffee, so she grabbed their mugs and refilled them before plonking them back down in front of them with a sweet smile for Dave and a kiss for Hunter. Leif grumbled that he should have asked for more coffee, so she gave him a kiss too.

As she was heading back over to me, where I was pretending to stack plates waiting for Sam to come back out, I heard a spluttered, "What the hell?" and turned to see Dave spitting out coffee and Hunter next to him wiping specks off his shirt with exaggerated care.

Maia just sang over her shoulder, "You know what you did."

Dave looked completely bewildered. I arched my eyebrow at Maia.

"What? I may have momentarily gotten the sugar and salt confused," she whispered.

"Remind me never to get on your bad side."

A loud growl that came from the bathroom in front of us halted our steps as we headed back to the kitchen. Maia looked concerned, but I just grinned at her.

Sam came stomping out. "Are you okay?" Maia asked him. He just shot me a look so full of heat I almost melted, like a chocolate bar left in the sun. I was instantly a messy puddle of gooey cocoa and sugar.

As he stomped back to the table, it was Maia's turn to raise her eyebrow at me.

"Girl chat. Later," I said. Maia sighed loudly and dramatically, making me smile.

Once we'd cleaned up, the girls usually all came out and ate around a table together, even though they snacked plenty as we cooked. This morning, though, the other girls all headed back to one of their cabins to eat, leaving us the empty dining room for our meeting.

Maia, Ava and I headed out with our plates, but I hesitated when I realized there were eleven of us all sitting at a table meant for ten people. Max had ducked in to grab some food and rushed straight back to his security cabin, looking distracted and tense, while his mates eyed him with concern.

Ava took the chair next to Cary and asked sweetly, "Would you like some more coffee, Dave?"

Dave shook his head vigorously and Hunter leaned toward him to fake whisper, "Dude, never piss off omegas."

Dave looked at me, confused, but I just shrugged and mouthed, "Sorry."

Maia took the last chair, but instead of grabbing another one, I headed over to sit on Pala's lap. His face lit up, and he kissed me lightly on the cheek, as Dio rested his hand on my leg from where he was sitting next to us.

"Anything I need to know?" Leif grumbled as he eyed my neck, then glanced at Pala's.

"Yep. Meet Pala, my mate," I said around a forkful of eggs. I was starving.

Leif just shook his head at me, but he was smiling. "Welcome to the family, Pala. We'll have manly hugs after the family meeting."

"I would be honored," Pala said solemnly, as if he was being asked to join a sacred ritual.

"If the big guy hugs you too tightly, just tickle him under the arm, it's like an off button," Hunter said, rocking his chair back so far, as Leif tried to swat him, that Damon had to reach out and save him from landing on his ass.

"Don't be telling everyone about my off switch," Leif huffed.

"Cut it out, you lot," Damon growled.

Cary stood up suddenly. "If this is a family meeting, Ava and I can go."

"No," I said, "please sit with us. You and Ava are a part of this, and we'd appreciate your input."

Cary nodded and sat down again. Ava glanced at him as he sat awkwardly next to her, but neither said anything directly to each other, as usual. If we could figure out how to turn their sexual tension into electricity, we could light up the entire farm. Maybe even the neighboring town, too.

I turned away from watching them and noticed the entire table watching me. *Oh, right? I called this family meeting.*

"Damon, can you give us an update on the supply run last night, so we're all on the same page while I finish my breakfast?"

To his credit, Damon didn't even falter at letting me take charge. He just launched into the salient points of their supply run while I felt Sam's eyes fervently focused on my mouth as I ate. I licked some crumbs off my lips and Sam's scent spiked. I noticed Dio pinch him out of the corner of my eye to get him to pay attention to Damon.

The team had gotten the medicine they needed for our injured people, plus brought back everything else they could find to stock the infirmary. They had also raided a canteen at the base and brought back any canned or packaged food they could find.

Then they raided the small tower and emergency shed for equipment. They'd found a few satellite phones and other useful tech people had left behind, probably figuring they were now useless without the power to charge them. They'd also found firefighting equipment, including water pumps and hoses. Which was helpful considering we could no longer call the local fire brigade if a fire broke out.

We'd used a mix of logged and recycled timber to build most of our infrastructure, so a fire would be disastrous. Making it a possible attack tactic for our enemies if they got angry enough to want to wipe us out, rather than take our supplies.

The team had filled the helicopter with fuel, but they'd also found a small mobile supply truck in a back shed. So they had filled it as well, and grabbed some extra gas for the vehicle, then driven it back in a convoy with a small fire engine and Damon's ute.

They now had enough aviation fuel for quite a few helicopter refuels and had discussed plans to clear an area across the river from the farm as a landing pad. So the helicopter was more accessible and we could protect it. It would also help create a wider fire break between us and the forest.

I nodded along to everything Damon said, feeling proud of them and the way they were taking care of this community.

"So that's everything from us. Do you want to explain to us what went down with you last night?" Damon's tone sounded stern, but he wasn't glaring at me. He'd fixed his angry stare on Sam instead. Maia and Ava were both now glaring at him, too.

"Uh oh," Dio fake whispered, mimicking Hunter's earlier tone. "I think you're next." Hunter reached out and high-fived Dio. I bit my lip as I tried not to smile at the both of them.

I jumped straight in, hoping to turn everyone's attention away from Sam, although he was taking the glares like a champ.

"I got an alert from my safe house." The guys didn't look surprised, so I assumed they'd gotten an update about that, at least, from Nick.

"So you decided heading out on your own, as a newly presented omega, in an apocalypse, was the best course of action?" Leif asked.

"Yes," I said, not feeling like I needed to justify myself. "That's not the issue. The problem we have is what I found in town."

I then told them about the alphas taking over the pub, the bribe offers and hunting of women, the group hiding in the museum, Ziggy's desperate measures to protect his mother, and my friend in the safe house

"It's not good enough that we're safe here and have resources," I said, "when we can help those people, too. Women and children are starving and being persecuted at the same time. I know we don't have the numbers to free the omegas at the Palace just yet. That's a whole other situation we need to talk about soon.

"But we can help the people in town now. They're our friends and neighbors. We can take them fresh food and trade for the things we don't have. Most of our suppliers are in town because we always shopped local as much as possible.

"The town is on the bend of the river, too. If we can show them how to generate electricity from the river, or set up wind turbines on their roofs, it will help them survive.

"Even though it's the right thing to do, helping them also benefits us. It's no coincidence the Palace has an outpost there. They're ransacking the town for food, but no doubt they're also keeping a unit there to monitor us.

"If we take out the alphas in town, we not only create allies, we can leave a satellite phone with a friend in town. We'd then have an early warning system if the Palace comes for us, or them, again."

I'd been speaking rapidly, trying to get all my ideas out at once and convince them it was a good idea. But I ground to a halt as I realized everyone was just watching me.

"Lexie," Damon said with a growl. "Have we ever denied you when you've asked us to help someone? You don't need to convince us or pitch the benefits for us. If you think we can help, we will."

My throat felt tight at his words. I knew Damon, Hunter and Max thought of me as a sister, but I never took it for granted. I didn't ask for a lot, but when I did, they always stepped up without hesitation. This was a lot bigger than anything I had ever asked for before, though.

"I know," I said, trying to keep my voice steady, "but this isn't me asking for you to accommodate a simple request. This is dangerous, and the potential consequences could affect everyone here."

"Every single person on this farm would back you up without question, Lexie, if you asked them to," Damon said softly. "I don't think you understand just how much people respect you around here."

I couldn't speak. I could only nod at Damon as Pala held me tighter and Dio squeezed my leg. Pride and adoration flowed into me through our bond and it sent my omega instincts haywire. She was preening like a toddler with a toy tiara.

I turned to Sam, and he jumped in before I could say a word. "Yes, we're in too. That goes without saying. If my team can help, we're at your disposal. Are the women you and Pala helped safe right now, or do we need to get them out this morning?"

"They are for now. They're all in the safe house and can last a few days. Max set it up with many of the same sustainable features we have here at the farm, so it's powered by an off-grid system. I've told them how to trigger the emergency alert inside if anything changes."

When I'd first talked about setting up a safe house in town, Max had thrown himself into the project and built it into a fortress. Half the things he'd installed I hadn't even imagined were possible.

"What about the two alphas that discovered you? Did they identify you as an omega?" Damon asked.

"They did, but they won't be a problem anymore," Pala answered for me, speaking with confidence. "I left them so it looked like they took each other out over an argument about stolen food. I also saturated the area with my scent so it would cover Lexie's."

"Clever," Hunter said. "You made yourself a target, though."

"Better me than her," Pala replied as he rested his chin on my shoulder. "The only time I'm going back now is when we tear the Palace down."

The guys all gave him brief nods filled with respect. Nobody batted an eyelash that Pala had just admitted to killing two men.

"Sam, has anything changed at the Palace since the last update from your men on surveillance outside?" Damon asked, moving us right along.

"No, but they'll let me know if anything does change."

"Cary, Ava, how long do you think the omegas at the Palace can hold out?" Damon asked as he swiveled to face them.

"They were scared, but some of the military alphas were protecting them, including Pala," Cary said, as he gestured in Pala's direction. "A few of the other alphas here now, the ones who stayed, were helping too, so I don't know if that has changed the balance at the Palace. Before we left, they were rationing food to the omegas. So as long as we don't completely cut off the food supply to the Palace before we take it down, they should be surviving."

I loved how this group was all talking about when we take the Palace down and rescue the omegas, not if, without ever really having a discussion or vote about it. Just surviving wasn't good enough, though. We needed to get them out.

"Do we all agree to continue with today's plan to head to Sam and Maia's gramps' farm and contact the Network? So we can try to get more allies?" Damon asked and got a chorus of agreement.

"If you're looking for allies, I can help with that, too," Ava piped up, and all eyes swiveled to look at her. She didn't even flinch, which impressed me. These guys could be seriously scary without even meaning to be.

"Talk to us," Damon said, trying to keep his natural growl to a minimum so as not to spook her.

"When Maia fled the Palace, I sent her toward my uncle's farm. He lives in the next town over. My uncle has worked with a group of people who attempt to rescue and hide omegas from the Palace. I've never heard the Network mentioned, so I'm not sure if he's working with the same or a different group to Maia's gramps."

"Why didn't he hide or rescue you?" I ask.

"That's a long story for another day," Ava replied calmly, not hiding her story, but clearly not willing to tell it now. "I'm pretty sure he will help us if he can."

"We're going to be stretched pretty thin today," Damon said. "We'll need three groups, one traveling to contact the Network, one staking out the town and gathering intel, and the last manning security here. I don't want you heading to your uncle's farm alone. Can it wait a few days until we've contacted the Network, rescued Lexie's friends and cleared the town? We can then send a team with you."

Ava looked unhappy, but nodded. "Yes. I've been gone for years. A few more days won't change anything."

I got the feeling she was talking about a lot more than just reuniting with her uncle.

"By the way, if there's a group going to my gramps' farm, I'm going to be in it," Maia piped up. When all of her remaining guys went to protest at once, she held up her hand. "Nuh uh, the only decision you get to make about this is who is coming with me."

I desperately wanted to be in that group, too. I wanted a chance to see where Maia and Sam had grown up so I could understand them both better. Plus, I wanted to be there for the inevitable fallout when they both walked back into the house they grew up in. Maia shot me a quick, burning glance. She was urging me to say something, wanting me there as well, but Sam beat me to it.

"I'd like Lexie and Dio to be part of that group," Sam interjected, as if he'd read our minds.

I was stunned. He didn't make eye contact with me, but I could see his Adam's apple bobbing up and down as he swallowed repeatedly. He seemed tense suddenly, as if this was important to him, but he was waiting for me to object.

"I'm okay with that," I said and noticed him visibly relaxing.

Damon growled but agreed after a glare from Maia.

Well, okay then. It looked like I had a seat in a helicopter.

Thirty-Three

A few hours later, I was circling my gramps' farm, looking for a good place to land. I hadn't seen the point of messing around. I wanted to get this over and done with. So I'd hustled everyone off the farm and to the chopper as soon as Max had completed his satellite surveillance and given us the all clear.

I'd been secretly worried Lexie would back out or someone would find a reason for her to stay. Leif, potentially objecting, had also made me nervous, but he'd just wrangled a seat for himself, too. I got the impression that nobody could have made him stay behind while his mate and his sister flew over the horizon.

I knew exactly how he felt. When I'd flown away and left Lexie behind yesterday, the pull from our unformed bond had made me feel nauseous and angry the whole time. I'd imagined every accident that could befall her while I was gone. Finding her actually missing when I'd gotten back had almost sent my beast feral.

I wasn't in a hurry to put myself through that a second time. Plus, I really had wanted her along. For Maia, as much as for myself. The last few days had been a whirlwind. I knew from experience farm life wasn't idyllic, but throw in the Crash, omega pheromones putting all the alphas in a spin, and the threats from the Palace and life had become chaotic. Keeping everyone safe was going to take work.

Yet, I suspected Maia had been using the constant activity to avoid talking about what happened to us both. I had a feeling everything was going to come out the minute we walked inside that farmhouse, though. And it was going to be brutal.

I was glad Dio and Damon rounded out our group. Maia and I were both going to need people to lean on today. My teammate Matt was also here, as my co-pilot. We could have fit more people in the chopper, but having so many bases to cover today had stretched us thin.

I circled twice, looking for anything suspicious as I scanned the fields below. I couldn't figure out why they looked all wrong until I realized most of them were barren. The few that were planted were mostly dead.

The area around this farm had never been verdant. It had always been tough keeping things growing. It was nothing like Damon's farm, with its rich terraced fields and winding river.

Gramps had always refused to leave it. So we had learned to manage as best we could. Yet, the place looked almost abandoned now.

Was Ben even here?

I landed the helicopter in a field near the house, kicking up a haze of dust. It was so thick we had to wait for it to settle enough for us to get out. The lack of visibility while we waited had me on edge. It felt like a trap, even though no one could have known we were coming.

I glanced over my shoulder to see Damon, Leif and Dio were all just as tense and were scanning our position relentlessly. Something wasn't right here, and we were all picking up on it. Our alphas were on high alert.

"Let's move," I said, and Damon nodded. The dust hadn't completely cleared yet, but we were sitting ducks here. I moved into the back, grabbed a box and pulled out some face masks, handing them around.

"We're on you, Sam. You know the layout best," Damon said before he fixed his face mask in place. I grunted at him in reply. My beast was running too close to the surface. Damon understood without taking offense.

I took point, hopping out of the helicopter first and scanning quickly before gesturing to the others. Leif hopped out next, followed by Maia, Lexie, Dio and Damon. I waited until the guys surrounded the girls and had them covered from all sides before I gave the signal to move.

To their credit, the girls held hands to stay close together and followed directions like pros, remaining still and only moving when directed Neither complained about nor questioned our tactical movements and hyper-focus. It showed a respect for us and our experience, that had my chest puffing out with pride.

I set a quick pace across the field, not happy having the girls out in the open in territory we hadn't scouted. Yet I slowed and approached cautiously when we reached the farmhouse, watching for movement inside and out. I had to remind myself this wasn't a stealth operation. I was visiting my childhood home. Yet the feeling of wrong was growing the closer I got to the house.

I had a weapon, but I kept it holstered. I knew without looking that both Dio and Leif had their hands on theirs while Damon was covering our rear.

The stairs and floorboards groaned as I stepped up onto them. It didn't look like anyone had maintained them in a long time. Nobody answered the door on the first or second knock. If anyone was inside, they were hiding. Nobody could have missed the helicopter landing. I removed my mask, and the others did the same.

"Ben, it's Sam and Maia," I called out. "If you're in there, we're coming in."

When there was no answer, I tried the door and found it unlocked. It wasn't unusual. Growing up, we'd had so little worth stealing, we'd never bothered locking it. The door creaked open on rusted hinges that felt like nails down a chalkboard, given my current level of tension.

"Ben," I called out again, only hearing echoes.

I stepped into the old-fashioned kitchen with its large cooker and old, scarred wooden table that generations of our family had eaten at. It was empty of people but covered in rubbish and dirty dishes.

I motioned the others in behind me, then pointed for Leif to take the doorway into the living area while I took the door into the hallway leading to the bedrooms. We met in the hallway, then swept each of the filthy rooms. They were all clear.

Maia was standing in the kitchen, still holding Lexie's hand, but looking around in disgust when we returned. Damon was guarding the door.

"I take it the place didn't look like this when you left?" I asked her.

"No way in hell. I slaved my ass off, keeping this place clean in between working the fields." She stepped forward, letting go of Lexie, and ran a hand over the edge of the old table, looking sad.

"I was sitting here, eating the lunch I had made for Ben and me, when the Palace agents burst through the door. The coroner had only just taken gramps away, and I was shell-shocked. He'd looked fine that morning, but when I heard the yelling in the field, just after breakfast, I'd just known. I ran into the fields, but it was too late."

She took a deep shuddering breath that tore through me, as I pictured her here with the weight of the world on her shoulders. I should have been here.

"I tried to run," she said, "but there were too many of them. I yelled to Ben for help, but he was grinning at me. They held me down on this table and took blood while I screamed my head off and fought, but nobody came. They tested my blood on a device and they all smiled when they looked at the results."

Lexie moved towards Maia and hugged her from behind. Maia smiled sadly at her over her shoulder. She looked back toward me though, when she uttered the words that gutted me.

"Ben already had paperwork in his hand, to declare me an omega and him the new owner of the farm. With me out of the way, and you gone, it all went to him. The Palace agents signed it and hauled me out the door. It was the last I ever saw of my baby brother."

"He already had the paperwork before gramps died?" I ground out, even though I'd clenched my jaw so hard it surprised me I didn't crack a tooth. *That motherfucker was a dead man walking, even if he was my brother.*

Maia just nodded and looked at me with so much sadness and anger, twisted up together, I wanted to rage. My beast was tearing at me, trying to break free and protect her, but it was far too late for that.

Lexie tried to step back, but Maia gripped her hand tightly. Leif stepped up behind the both of them and wrapped them up in one of his giant hugs.

"Why did you leave?" Maia asked me. The harsh words felt like physical blows. I had to grip the chair closest to me, so I didn't stagger. I'd known this conversation was coming, but I was still unprepared.

"Gramps told me I had to go. He didn't ask, and he didn't give me a choice. He told me I was too dangerous and I would put you at risk. The thought of hurting you broke me. It was the one thing I could never do."

"You hurt me when you left without a word. You tore a gaping hole in my world," she replied, her anger outstripping her sadness for a moment.

Her words struck me deep. There was no defense, but I had to at least try to explain.

"He took me outside to the barn before he told me. Gramps said he needed help with something, but when we got out there, there was a group of betas waiting. They wouldn't let me come back in and say goodbye, or even pack anything. Gramps said my emotions would make my dominance too volatile. They were all adults, and I was just a kid. I didn't want to go, but I trusted gramps. I insisted they let me write you a letter, and I never for a moment thought that gramps wouldn't give it to you."

My voice broke, and I had to force out the words. "Maia, I'm so fucking sorry. If I could do it again, I never would have left you here alone. But back then, I was so scared of the rage building inside me, the power I could feel in my veins that I couldn't control. I looked up what usually happens when an alpha presents and it wasn't normal. For me, it burned. I tried to hide from you how much it hurt."

The memory of the fear, pain and confusion I'd felt back then, but had tried to hide from Maia, had me shaking. I could see sympathy blooming in her eyes.

"Oh, Sam, you should have told me." Her face fell, and she just looked saddened now, as if the sorrow for me had dissolved all her anger.

"Gramps already knew you were an omega, even though you were too young to present. He said he'd run a test. They convinced me it was the only way to keep us both safe. They said I was presenting too dominantly. That it would draw eyes to us and put you in danger. I never planned to stay away for good. In my letter, I confessed everything to you. I wrote that if I could get help and get it under control, I would come back."

I took a shaky step towards her. Guilt, frustration and worry that we would never again have the closeness we once shared drove me forward. She had been the only bright spot in my world growing up, the reason I kept going every day. I felt a driving need to fix my mistake, but I knew I couldn't.

"I didn't know they had sent you to the Palace. If I'd known, I would have found a way to get you out. Even if I had to tear it down. Nobody told me until the Crash, when the world went to hell and I told them I was coming back for you. I headed straight for the Palace, but when I got there you were already gone."

I reached out to her, my hand shaking despite my efforts to stop it, and stroked her hair. The same hair I'd spent years brushing every night before tucking her into bed. Everything else in the room disappeared as she stepped forward, out of the arms encircling her and into my own. Finally. It felt like coming home.

"Maia," I said into her hair. "I don't know everything that you went through, and how Ben could have betrayed you like that. I can't ask you to forgive me when I know I'll never be able to forgive myself. But you have to know, leaving you was the hardest thing I've ever done."

Maia was silently crying into my chest, and I gripped her tightly. "A part of me always believed you were coming back, Sam. I kept a place open for you in my heart, even if I buried it deep."

"Love you, Mai Mai," I whispered.

"Love you, Sam Sam," she whispered back.

The words had been our nightly ritual for as far back as I could remember. I felt as though a shard of glass that had been rubbing inside an open wound for a decade suddenly fell away. We both still had a lot of healing to do. We'd both changed a lot, and we'd have to relearn each other as adults, but I finally had my little sister back.

There was only one more thing I needed to be whole. I looked at Lexie over Maia's shoulder to find she was watching us with tears streaking down her face while Leif hugged her. Leif and Damon looked strained, clearly picking up on Maia's emotions, but were holding back to give us a moment. Dio was looking torn, wanting to reach for both Lexie and me, but unable to hold either of us.

I was about to get us all back on task when a high-pitched giggle and a creaking noise overhead had us all freezing. A cracking sound followed it as the ceiling above us split apart. I threw myself over Maia as I dropped us both to the ground, shielding her with my body while I looked frantically for Lexie. Both Leif and Dio threw themselves over her as Damon dashed in between us. He had his arms in the air and he looked as though he was preparing to hold up the entire ceiling if needed.

An entire section in the middle collapsed before something big landed on the dining table with a thud, followed by someone gasping out a pained sound.

Maia's scent turned acrid with fear underneath me, which made my beast rise to the surface. I growled darkly and the other three alphas joined me.

I checked Maia over quickly, trusting Damon to cover us for the moment. "I'm okay," she whispered. "Help Damon."

I trusted her to know her limits, so I jumped up and spun around to gauge the threat, pulling Maia up behind me and pushing her blindly towards Leif, Dio and Lexie, out of harm's way.

My brain couldn't reconcile the mess of twisted limbs covered in dust in front of me or the sound of cackling laughter, until Maia gasped, "Ben?" as she tried to push past me.

Damon grabbed her and held her firm.

"Ben?" I growled in disgust and anger.

He was painfully skinny, wearing nothing but sagging, dirty underwear, with sores and blisters all over his body. His hair was falling out in clumps and his teeth were black. I don't know how he even got up into the roof cavity. His limbs looked far too weak to even hold him up.

He appeared to be holding a tin box and was laughing with mad glee, shaking on the table, until he extended one skinny arm directly at me and yelled, "You, I got you good."

"What did you do?" I growled, still not even sure this was Ben. I couldn't reconcile the wasted man in front of me with the little kid I'd left behind.

"Made him send you away," he cackled, gasping for breath. "I hid and listened at the doors. He thought you were so special. Gonna save us all.

But I made them fear you. Said you beat me. You were dangerous. He believed me. But I gave the bruises to myself."

I heard Maia gasp as I balled my fists, feeling rage pounding at me. Ben had always been a strange kid, secretive and cruel. I'd found him tormenting injured animals more times than I cared to remember.

No matter how much I had tried to take care of him after our mother left, he had always spurned me. Preferring to look after himself. Eventually I had let him, being little more than a kid myself.

"And Maia?" I asked.

"I made a deal with the devil and she was his prize." He tried to laugh, but coughed so hard he spit up blood. Damon pulled Maia back several steps.

"Had no choice, owed bad people. Didn't matter. Would've killed the old bastard anyway, just for the fun of it."

"How could you?" Maia yelled, struggling against Damon as though she was going to rip Ben apart. Her concern for her brother gave way to a rage that reflected my own.

"Where are all the farm workers?" I asked, battling to control my own emotions so I could get everything I needed to know out of Ben. From the look of him, I didn't need to exact retribution. He wasn't long for this world and it was at his own hand.

"Gone. All gone. As soon as she left," he jerked his head in Maia's direction but wouldn't make eye contact with her. She had tried longer than I had to help care for him. If he had any feelings left for either of us, it would be for her.

"Bastards. Left me alone. Called me a traitor. They're the traitors," he rambled. He coughed again and more blood splattered on the table. "Always leaving me alone."

"Is he sick or injured?" Lexie whispered.

"Neither, he's an addict," Damon said. "From the looks of him, he's been one for a very long time."

Ben started laughing again, clutching his box with shaking arms.

"Read them all I did. My treasures. All your pain. Stole them all. Laughed at you," he wheezed out between coughs.

Dawning horror washed over me as I realized what he was clutching in the old tin box. It was where he had kept all his treasures as a kid, but I didn't think it was full of old broken toys and rocks now.

I lunged at him and grabbed it out of his grasp. He squealed and tried to clutch at it, but he was no match for me. I barked at him, and he froze long enough for me to free it and flip open the lid.

My letters. All my letters to Maia were inside. The ones I had poured my soul into. They were all opened. I felt violated and ill. I didn't write them for anyone else's eyes, especially not his.

"Tried to find all gramps' secrets too, but couldn't." He cackled wildly again as I released my hold on him, red spittle flying and landing on the tabletop. "Too late, too late. They're coming. I called them."

His fist opened, and a small device fell out.

"What the hell is that?" Dio asked from behind me, laying a hand on my shoulder. I hadn't even noticed his approach.

Damon snatched it off the table. "It looks like some kind of pager. It's still on. They have a really long battery life."

"Fuck," I yelled, turning and kicking a hole through the wall, trying to ease my fury, but only making Ben laugh harder.

Damon grabbed me and spun me around, his shoulders set with determination and a hard look on his face. "Focus it, Sam. Channel your rage into action that will help us. I don't know if anyone is coming, chances are there's nobody at the other end. But I'm not taking that risk. We need to move. Now."

I grit my teeth to hold my beast back from snarling at him and nodded. If we were going to get the girls out of here safely, we had to work together. Neither of us cared about alpha posturing or even dominance at this moment. Family was all that mattered. I tried to do what he asked and focused my thoughts on getting us out of here safely. He was right; we needed to move.

"Where is the equipment we came for? How long will it take to send a message?" Damon asked me, trying to help focus my dominance.

"It's portable. I'll grab it, and we can take it back to the farm. Can you take care of him?"

Damon's eyes flashed briefly, but he nodded, knowing what I was asking. It was a big ask, but Damon stepped up for me, and for Maia. "Consider it done."

I looked over my shoulder and my gaze landed on Lexie and Maia, standing huddled together with Leif shadowing them. My beast surged to the surface, but my rage focused in a way it never had before. Protect. Defend. I needed to get them out of here. Get them safe and get them allies. But I couldn't do it alone.

"Leif, I need you with me. Gramps may have barricaded the entrance, and the equipment is heavy. Dio, take this box and get the girls back to the helicopter. Tell Matt to get the chopper prepped for take-off. Damon will be right behind you. If Leif and I don't follow in five minutes, or anyone arrives, take off without us. We'll make our own way home. Go now."

I passed the box to Dio, then turned without giving my brother another glance, trusting everyone to do their jobs. It also didn't pass my notice that I'd just referred to Maia and Lexie's farm as home. Not this place. There was nothing left for me here.

I barrelled down the hallway towards my gramps' room. Leif's pounding steps followed me and my brother's wild cackle haunted me until it cut off abruptly. Whatever Damon had done was a mercy at this point.

A thick layer of dust coated everything in the room, as if nobody had been in here since the day he died. I raced over to his antique wardrobe, threw open the door, and yanked out the clothes that were still inside in my haste. I pushed the secret latch he had shown me and the back panel slid back to reveal a metal door.

I turned the handle and yanked it open, but it got stuck part-way. Clearly, no one had used it in a long time.

I put my shoulder into it, but it wouldn't budge. "Here, let me," Leif said as he yanked me out of the way. He braced his legs in a crouch and threw his weight at the door once, twice and, on the third time, it swung open with a loud groan.

Leif stepped back, and I was down the stairs in seconds, leaping the last few. The room below was bare except for two metal contraptions that were all closed up into box shapes. Last time I had seen them, they had been open and set-up with lights glowing in the dim room, but this worked for us.

I grabbed the nearest one, and an envelope slipped out from underneath, landing on the floor. I flipped it over with my foot and saw it had my name on it in my gramps' handwriting. I snatched it up too, gesturing Leif towards the other box with a nod of my head before I was hauling ass back up the stairs.

I faintly heard the helicopter rotors start and was halfway through the door when Leif yelled, "Wait."

I froze and looked over my shoulder. He was holding a military uniform, covered in medals. He had picked it up from the pile of clothes I had yanked out and dropped. "Is this your gramps' uniform?" He asked.

I nodded, and he threw it over his shoulder. "For Maia," he said.

I swallowed hard, and headed back for the door, silently sending out thanks to the universe that Maia had stumbled across Leif and his mates. They were good alphas and would take care of her.

We barrelled out the rarely used front door, at the opposite side of the house. There was no way I was going back out through the kitchen. The change in direction worked in our favor as we startled two betas who were spying around the corner of the house. I glimpsed a long column of dust coming down the main road in the distance at the same moment the two betas spun and noticed us.

"Stay and fight, or run?" Leif yelled.

"Run," I shouted over my shoulder, already charging at the two terrified betas. I barked, and both men froze, dropping to their knees. I didn't have time to do more than knock them down before we had to run full pelt towards the helicopter.

Damon was hanging out the door, roaring at us to hurry. I could see Lexie's worried face hovering behind him. We both gave a last burst of speed, hurled our boxes onto the floor, and hauled ourselves up as the helicopter lifted off the ground. Gunfire erupted behind us as I rolled to my feet.

I fought my need to grab Lexie and pull her into my arms when she stepped towards me as the chopper lurched forward. I couldn't be near her right now. So many emotions were coursing through me that my alpha beast was straining to get out.

He wanted to rend anyone who threatened Maia or Lexie into tiny pieces. Then he wanted to pull Lexie toward us so hard she couldn't refuse, so he could make her submit and finally claim her right here on the floor of the chopper. He didn't particularly care if anyone was watching. Having her here in danger was sending his instincts into overdrive. I refused to screw up what was building between us by jumping her like a crazed animal.

I froze in place, locking my arms and legs, until Dio intervened and pulled her into a seat, strapping her in. I forced my limbs to step past them and into the cockpit while Damon slid the door closed.

I checked Leif was helping Maia strap in before I glanced back down to the farm one last time. A convoy of army trucks had pulled into the front yard, and two imposing men in suits stepped out of the leading truck.

More men piled out of the back and started splashing gasoline from jerry cans against the farmhouse before others stepped up and lit it up. Flames quickly leaped up the side walls. They didn't even bother checking if anyone was still inside. It seemed it wasn't my brother's destiny to live out this day, and any bargaining chip he thought he had was long gone.

If my gramps had any more secrets hidden in that house, they were gone now too.

I tried to get a closer look at the two men intently watching us disappear before we veered away. They didn't look like any military men I had ever seen.

"Who in the hell are they?" I asked Damon gruffly, as his head came over my shoulder to get a better look at the men below us, too. We weren't completely out of danger yet. I was panting as I tried to catch my breath and still the shaking in my arms and legs from my sprint to the chopper carrying the heavy metal box, but I still heard Damon's sharp intake of breath.

"The big guy was Ronan's dad," Damon said, his voice flat.

"And the other guy?"

"My father."

Oh *shit*.

Thirty-Four

W e arrived back at the temporary landing site to be greeted by a frantic alpha and a scowling beta. Hunter launched himself at Maia the moment she appeared in the open door, pulling her down into his arms. "Where's Max?" Maia asked, her voice shaky.`

"He's holding the fort back at the farm, pussycat, and watching the satellite feeds," Hunter said as she slumped into him. Hunter ran his hands all over her, trying to reassure himself she was okay, before pulling her away from the slowing rotors. He must have felt all her emotions through their bond and known our mission was going badly. Not being with her would have been killing him.

Dave stalked up to me, looking fierce. He held his hand out to help me down, all but hip-checking Dio out of the way. He dropped my hand quickly as soon as I was out from under the rotors, to feel my forehead.

"You look flushed and you feel hot," he said. "Are you okay?"

"Fine," I said, distractedly. I was hot, but I didn't have time to worry about something so mundane now. "It was hot in the chopper."

"Debrief, dining room. Now," Damon yelled over the top of all our voices.

Maia's obvious pain drew everyone else in as her mates bundled her up between them. But I couldn't keep my eyes off Sam.

He was stoic, but I could see the way his mouth was down-turned and his whole body was tense as he walked. It differed from the way he normally carried his rage. This looked as though he was at war with himself. There was a bow to his shoulders that hadn't been there before.

Seeing him take command, in full military mode, earlier had gotten me all hot and bothered. Then, hearing his story as he opened up to Maia made me realize he lived in fear of himself and in constant battle to contain his beast. Right now, he was spiraling while trying to shut himself down. Yet his obvious pain called to my omega. The need to soothe him burned through my veins and the pull I felt toward him had turned incendiary.

I wanted to go to him, but I had to play this right or he'd shut me out completely to protect me. I'd stolen away after our family meeting this morning to read some of Maia's old book. Not to read about omegas, though. I'd been hoping to find some answers about Sam, and it solidified my suspicions that he was a prime alpha. By denying his beast, and trying to shut everyone out to deal with his extreme dominance on his own, he was on a path to becoming feral. The thought terrified me.

I eyed Sam. He kept his distance, as if there was a giant force field around me, as we headed down the hill. He was clutching the metal box that Dio had handed back to him, as if it was a lifeline. Dave hovered near me, staying within reach, while Dio was a determined shadow at Sam's back. Pala had rushed in just as the briefing started, cutting his surveillance of town short, as though all our emotions had been an unconscious pull on the bond that had drawn him home.

The briefing was quick. Maia's pack had her firmly ensconced in their arms. Every one of them was touching her somehow. Nobody else was getting within arm's reach of her.

I didn't hear a word anyone said, anyway. The distance between Sam and me was becoming an increasing torment with every second that passed. His beast was pulling at me despite the fierce battle Sam was waging with him.

It felt like Sam was trying to throw a wall up between us to block the pull his beast was trying to throw my way, and it was snagging on the true mate bond trying to form. It was tearing some deep part of me in the process. He refused to even glance my way, and it was driving me to insanity.

It wouldn't end well for Sam, either. All the gains he had made in the last few days, whatever had eased his hold on himself and made him seem more open this morning, was lost in the fierce battle he was waging within himself. I could feel he was holding back, because he didn't want the pull his beast was trying to throw my way to force something I wasn't ready for.

This constant battling with his beast was destroying him, though, and I wasn't going to sit around and watch it happen. Besides, the last of my hesitation about Sam had fallen away today. I wanted him, needed him so badly I could feel my blood pounding. He was mine, to protect and care for.

As soon as the debriefing finished, Maia dodged her guys and threw herself at Sam. He hugged her tightly, yet his face was vacant, as if he'd built a wall even his sister wasn't getting through right now.

"Mai," he whispered. "These are yours. I wrote them to you. I'm sorry you didn't get them until now." He tried to shift the box awkwardly into Maia's arms, but she already had a heavy old book under one arm and a tight grip on him.

"It's not your fault, Sam. But thank you, I'll read them all." I heard her whisper to him. He just grunted at her. She looked over at me and I subtly nodded at her.

"Go, I got this," I mouthed to her with a grimace. Maia gave me a sad smile and a wonky thumbs up behind his back.

Damon growled at Maia from where he was almost pressed up against her back. He was quickly losing his patience as his gaze swiveled around the room, constantly looking for threats. If he didn't get her somewhere secure soon, where he could satisfy himself she was safe, he was going to flip his lid.

Dave made his way over to Maia, sharing a look with Damon as he put a hand on Sam's shoulder. "It's okay, Maia. Go calm your alphas before they lose their shit. We've got this."

Maia pulled away from Sam reluctantly. "I just have to pop into the kitchen," she tried to say as she waved her book in the air, but Damon had reached his limit. He grabbed the metal box from Sam for her, picked her up, threw her over his shoulder as she squealed and growled at his mates, "Nest. Now."

She heaved the heavy book at me over Damon's rapidly disappearing back. I dashed toward her, lunged and caught it, only fumbling it slightly in my panic, trying not to drop what was clearly something precious. It was old and overstuffed, with pages and notes sticking out. She seemed to have an affinity for old books. Luckily, the book had an old-fashioned clasp on it, so nothing fell out.

"It was my great gran's old recipe book. They were poor, and she wrote a lot of substitutions in it from when they couldn't get sugar and stuff," she called out as she disappeared through the door, "give it to Isabella for me."

I barely heard the last bit as Damon hustled her away. I figured their cabin was going to be locked down tight for a while. We'd all overheard what Damon had said to Sam in the chopper as we took off. That it was Damon's and Ronan's fathers that had turned up together and torched the old farmhouse. It didn't bode well for any of us if Damon's father was involved in this.

We needed more intel on what was going on out there. I knew Max was working on it, but everything he found just led to more questions. I had a sneaky feeling this thing was bigger than any of us knew, and the Crash was no accident.

I huffed out a breath and turned back from the doorway to find Dave, Dio and Pala all watching me, while Sam had his body turned towards me but stared resolutely at anything but me. I could hear the women working on the evening meal prep in the kitchen to my right. So I shifted as I waved the book at Dio, much the same way Maia had, and forced myself to take a few steps backward and away from them.

It was like walking through quicksand. The further I got from Sam, the harder it felt to move. Despite his wall and his refusal to look at me, his pull felt like his hands running all over my body as goosebumps raced across my skin in waves, like the sea washing over the sandy shore and beckoning it into oblivion.

I knew instinctively that the longer I resisted, the more turbulent the pull would become, until it was a raging, demanding tide that would tumble me away. I refused to give in just yet, though. He had to know I chose this, and he had to choose it too, willingly give himself over to it, or we would be forever doomed before we'd even begun.

I instinctively knew, if we came together while part of him was still trying to hold back, he'd never be able to live with himself and it would destroy us.

"I'm going to head into the kitchen and hand this over," I said. I tried to relax my stance and pasted what I hoped was an innocent smile on my face.

Dave eyed me suspiciously, knowing I was up to something.

My normally calm Pala growled as he swept me up when I tried to sidle past him, surprising me. "Not so fast, my heart," he said before he kissed me soundly and thoroughly. He then passed me to Dio like I was some kind of delicacy to be shared.

I felt like I should complain, but it had been a long day and the contact with my mates settled me. It also gave me enough strength to keep denying the pull to Sam, at least for a few more minutes, and that was all I needed.

It had the opposite effect on Sam, though. I could see Sam's posture go rigid as my scent spiked in response to Pala and Dio's heady kisses. I also noticed Sam grimace as if he was in pain as I moved away again.

Sam's beast clearly needed me, and I was done holding back. Life was too short, we had no guarantee any of us were going to get a tomorrow at this point. I was ready to trust my omega instincts and see where they would take us.

She would not make it easy on Sam or his beast, though. She wanted Sam to accept his beast, then to provoke him and get him all riled into a delicious frenzy.

Sam's whisky scent was already spiking the air, entwining with my passion fruit laced meringue in a way that was intoxicating. The whiskey only came out when he was furious or aroused. Right now, I figured he was feeling both. I finally realized Sam struggled with all intense emotions, and he repressed them all the same. If he thought our claiming was ever going to be anything but a wild frenzy, he was delusional.

I grinned, a genuine one this time, full of mischief. I couldn't help myself, because I'd just had the most amazing idea. A way to get Sam to unleash his beast finally, and I was the only one who could do it. Pala and Dio's eyes widened, but Dave's narrowed. He knew me too well. "Stay right there. Just give me five minutes," I said to them all as I winked at Dave.

I backed into the kitchen, through the swinging door, and dumped the large cookbook onto Isabella's workstation with a loud thud. I hurriedly explained to her what it was as her eyes lit up.

"Oh, and if you hear a lot of roaring in a few minutes, don't panic. I've got it under control."

"What the hell are you up to now, Lexie?" Isabella asked with a huge grin.

"Poking an alpha," I said as I winked at her. I ripped a page from the same notebook I'd used this morning and hurriedly wrote on it.

Sam,

I asked you to fix your shit with Maia. I saw enough today to know that you care about each other deeply and you're both going to be okay, despite the shit show that went down with your brother.

I'm truly sorry about that. I can only imagine how tough today was for you both. But I'm not about to let you turn your anger on yourself again, or stuff your feelings down and push away your pack. You've come too far.

You're a prime alpha. You were born to protect us all. Yet you'll never settle your beast until you trust him and set him free. I learned that lesson the hard way.

My omega has already claimed your beast as hers. She can sense him and he's fucking magnificent. Now it's my turn, because I want to claim you too. I need you to touch me so badly it burns.

But my omega is an impulsive, proud creature, and we won't wait around forever. Our time is now. What will it be, Sam? Claim me or let me go?

I don't need you to bleed for me. You've bled enough. If you're truly mine, I need you to let your beast out and come catch me.

Your omega.

"Can you give this to Sam, or whichever of them comes through the door first?" I said as I shoved the letter at Isabella, knowing my time was running out. My mates' protectiveness was in overdrive after our close call earlier today. I could feel them trying to hold back from coming into the kitchen after me, but their control was fraying.

"Stand back," I hissed to the girls over my shoulder while hustling out through the back door. I heard laughter behind me before the door swung shut.

Sam was a predator. The most lethal predator I had ever met, apart from Damon. My omega wanted to roll over and submit to him. She had from the first moment she'd laid eyes on him, if I was being honest with myself. But it had taken longer for my human side to catch up.

We were going to make him earn our submission, though. I just needed to push him enough to get him to lose control, so I could prove to him that his beast was a part of him we needed to embrace.

I barreled down the steps, fighting against the pull, knowing I needed to get some distance if I was going to make it count. This wouldn't work if he caught me five meters from the back door. He needed to fully let his beast out. He needed to hunt.

I landed at the bottom and headed toward the guest houses, where I knew a bunch of unmated alphas were staying. His team. He'd scent my direction and it would drive him wild that I was headed toward them.

I felt a little mean, but he needed the push. Plus, the thought of him chasing me, his beast stalking me in the encroaching darkness, had my omega all riled up. I was wet just at the thought and leaving a scent trail that even a beta couldn't miss.

I was almost to the first guest cabin when I heard a possessive roar behind me that came from the direction of the dining hall. It pulled me up short and seemed to make the very air vibrate around me.

I felt that delicious pull reach for me, even at this distance. It hummed over my skin like a silken caress. Making me promises I hoped it could keep. I moaned as I felt my slick start in response. I took a deep breath and pushed back, denying it.

Another roar broke the stillness, as well as my stasis. Only this echoed with a dark rage that had birds launching from their hidden perches, up into the sky and away from danger. Fleeing the beast.

I smiled and ran, knowing I was now prey.

Thirty-Five

M y heart beat wildly in my chest as my omega sent my adrenaline spiking with excitement and lust. A door burst open in front of me, momentarily letting out a stream of light as a hulking shadow rushed out to the deck. I recognized the alpha as one of Sam's teammates when he stepped to the edge of the deck and looked across the clearing towards the dining hall.

I vaulted up the stairs, knocking the alpha aside as I barreled through the open doorway. Startled alphas leaped to their feet from where they were sitting on couches in the living area. I dashed past them, yelling, "Sorry," as I headed for the back door just past the kitchen.

"Are you okay, Lexie?" One called out as another of the alphas tried to reach for me and I dodged them.

"Try to slow him down for me," I yelled over my shoulder as I laughed through panted breaths. I only narrowly missed taking myself out on the corner of the kitchen bench in my distraction.

"Oh, fuck no. I'm getting out of here," I heard someone say as I threw myself at the backdoor and flung it open.

"Shit, too late. He's coming," I heard from the front doorway.

"Sorry," I yelled again as I leaped off the back deck, taking a thin nature trail through the thick trees and underbrush. I wasn't sorry, though. I knew he wouldn't hurt them, except maybe for that one guy at the door I had run into. My scent would be all over him. He should probably run too.

I heard another roar, this one much closer, and someone faintly yelled, "She ran into me, I swear."

My lungs burned as I upped my pace, almost at my destination, when I heard branches snapping behind me. I lost valuable seconds spinning in the moonlight, looking for the marker, before I spotted it. I yanked bushes apart and launched myself into the entrance of the cave. The scent of leather, oak and whiskey assaulted my senses moments before arms banded around me.

My feet suddenly left the ground and another brutal movement had me spun around and pushed up against the rough stone wall. Sam held me tightly in place. Every inch of his body pushed into mine as sparks and light exploded within me at his touch. A savage snarl twisted his angelic face into something predatory that would terrify anyone else, but not me.

Fucking, finally. Was my only coherent thought.

"Mine," Sam growled viciously a second before he kissed me with a ferocity that had me seeing stars as light streaked behind my eyes. It was a claim as much as it was a kiss, passionate and devouring. He destroyed me as he rebuilt me, my omega rushing to the surface and fusing with me in a way that I could never deny again, even if I wanted to.

I heard ripping sounds as he tore the clothes from my body and shredded his own in his primal need to take me, paying no heed to anything but the raw need to feel my skin on his own. I was almost mindless with desire as sparks skittered everywhere our skin touched. Sam's thigh jammed between my legs almost aggressively, but it wasn't enough. It wasn't nearly enough. I was empty and aching for him, even as I ground against him.

I yanked my mouth free, not caring about the brutal hold he had on my hair, the bite of pain only flaring those sparks hotter. "Prove it," I begged hoarsely.

He yanked my head back with a snarl as his beastly eyes, pupils blown wide, looked into the depths of my heart through my own eyes. I felt almost feral in my need for him. I leaned forward as far as I could, not caring that my hair pulled tighter in his fist, and sucked his bottom lip into my mouth before I bit it hard enough to draw blood.

We didn't need any foreplay. The chase through the darkness of the trees had us both more than primed, my slick already dripping down my thighs.

He gave me no room to move, or think, or feel anything but him as he speared his cock up into me savagely, with a darkly possessive growl, making me see stars. I let his lip go and moaned long and loud, scratching my nails down his back as a blistering, dizzying wave of fullness spread trails of searing light through me.

His roar was deafening and spun through me as he snarled, "Mine," again, like he was trying to imprint his claim on my very soul. Screaming it into the cosmos, across millennia, as we connected in the most carnal way.

"Ours," came two rough voices from behind him, as Pala and Dio appeared in the dusky light filtering in from the cave entrance.

They moved in close, with eyes transfixed on me. They used their bodies, pressing in tight, to help Sam trap me in place, before they each put a hand on one of his shoulders. Sam almost seemed to vibrate briefly, before he growled darkly again and descended into a rut. He thrust into me wildly, stretching me almost obscenely and setting a wild, punishing pace that left no more room for thought or words.

It was a frantic and hedonistic mating. There was nothing civilized about what we were doing. I was completely on board for it. My omega was chanting, "Fuck yes," in my head, but I could no longer get any words out beyond a strangled cry.

My body clenched around him as the friction of his thick cock pistoning in and out of me had those sparks from earlier igniting into an inferno. He was snarling and snapping; the sound making me spiral higher. The three alphas had me pinned in place by their bodies, surrounded and unable to move. Yet, instead of feeling trapped, I felt set free.

I submitted to them completely, mind and body. Letting go of even the concept of control. Just existing in a sea of sensation as I let him fill every part of me.

Sam growled low and ruthless as he drew almost all the way out, before slamming back into me and forcing his knot deep inside me. My body locked around him as I screamed soundlessly, my mouth hanging open, as my body became swept up in a wave of light and heat that traveled all the way out to my fingers and toes before running back down to coil tightly in my core.

Sam ground so hard against my clit we almost felt fused together. He suddenly released his hold on my hair and I threw my head forward, biting into his neck on instinct as the world exploded and my body convulsed almost violently.

A flash of pain at my neck was quickly overtaken by wave after wave of bright pleasure so intense I felt my eyes roll back into my head and I almost passed out. I held on, though, clamping my teeth onto his neck as I sucked at his skin with my lips and tongue. I didn't want to miss a moment of this as the relentless orgasm wrung me out until it eventually faded into ripples of pleasure pinging through my core, making me jerk and shudder roughly against him.

Sam pulled his head away from my neck and I could feel his intense awe and satisfaction through the new bond that was lighting me up inside. I felt contentment coming from Dio and Pala too, as our pack bonds strengthened. They also felt supremely satisfied with themselves. After being fractured for so long, the guys' bond to each other was almost as strong as the bond to me now.

I opened my eyes, not even realizing I had closed them, to see Dio and Pala both lifting their heads from Sam's shoulders, huge grins on their faces. Sam had three new, perfect bite marks on his skin, and tiny trickles of blood running down his chest. We hadn't been gentle this time, but Sam didn't look like he minded. He was smiling at me with a soft possessiveness that made my heart beat trip over itself.

I pushed at the guys gently until I could free my arms. Then grabbed as much skin as I could and dragged them back into me in a giant hug. We were squished so tightly together I couldn't tell our limbs apart.

We stood together, sharing space, until our breathing calmed. It was almost perfect, if not for a dark space in my chest that felt hollow. It was almost overshadowed by all the brightness that had sprung to life inside me with three glowing bonds, but it was there, and it troubled me. I looked around at the guys, but the darkness didn't seem to come from them.

"Where's Dave?" I asked, my voice feeling suddenly rough, as though I'd actually been screaming.

"Guarding the entrance," Pala replied. I nodded, feeling a spike of longing that had Pala stroking my hair. Dave was always hovering on the outside, watching over everyone.

I smiled suddenly, almost shyly, though, as I caught Sam's gaze. His pupils were still blown wide, but he seemed lighter and accepting in a way I'd never felt from him before.

"Lexie," Sam breathed out with reverence. Wonder and tenderness dripped from my name like raindrops. The intensity of everything we had just shared was still shining in his eyes.

"Mine," I said to him, gently, as I ran my hands through his golden hair before I caressed his face lightly. I felt sated and cared for, knotted and wrapped up in his arms, finally. I'd wanted this dark, dangerous alpha who looked like an angel since the moment I'd laid eyes on him. He'd both excited and angered me, sometimes at the same time. But he'd always made me feel. Now he was mine to touch whenever I wanted.

We needed no more words. Sam's face broke out into a grin that felt like warmth washing over me. His smiles were so rare, it was like seeing a wild horse flash past in the forest. You knew you'd just glimpsed something pure and untamed.

His gaze darkened momentarily and his arms tightened around me as he asked roughly, "Did I hurt you?"

I laughed breathlessly, and Sam relaxed slightly. "Not even a little."

Sure. I was slightly sore, but in a deliciously tingly way. It was nothing a good night's sleep wouldn't fix. Or maybe a hot bath.

I glanced off to the side of our snugglefest and squinted into the inky depths of the cave. That dark hole was pulling at me, and I felt a restless energy suddenly swirling within me, throwing me off balance. Pala was in my peripheral vision and I could see him looking at me with concern.

"Do you think you can shuffle about twenty or thirty meters while holding me, Sam?" We were locked together on his knot.

Sam pulled his head back and his eyes widened, as though he felt seriously offended. "Point me where you want to go."

I waved my arm around in the general direction I wanted, and he stepped away from the wall with a definite swagger as Dio and Pala stepped back. Dio flashed me a cheeky grin while Pala gave me a soft smile.

"Dio, feel along the wall just there. There should be a little box, about half the size of your hand, with a switch."

As Dio veered away, Sam strode confidently into the darkness around a slight bend in the cave entrance, while carrying me easily. He seemed to have complete trust that I wouldn't lead him astray.

"Stop," I told Sam quickly, operating on memory alone. Pala was hovering at our side in the darkness, waiting to grab me if Sam should stumble.

"What's that mineral smell?" Sam asked as he sniffed the air.

"Got it," Dio called out from behind us as a clicking noise echoed in the cave and a criss-crossing net of fairy lights popped into existence over our heads.

"Wow," Pala said, but he was looking down instead of up. Sam followed his gaze back down and inhaled sharply.

"Is that a hot spring?" Dio asked as he loped up to us around the bend.

"Yep, there's another bigger one outside, but not many people know about this one."

My back was feeling sticky, maybe from sweat, I wasn't sure, but a soak sounded heavenly right now. It would be cozy, but we would all fit. The hot spring had steep edges and was only about two and a half meters wide, about the size of a decent hot tub. The water came up to my shoulders in the middle.

"Is it safe to get in?" Pala asked, excitement lighting up his features.

"Sure is."

Dio and Pala stripped off, then held me steady and supported Sam as he maneuvered to clamber in while holding me and trying not to jostle me too much on his knot.

"There are some rocks that form rough steps to the left a little," I directed him. The water was as dark as the rocks below and the fairy lights reflected on the surface so the steps could be hard to see.

Sam stepped in tentatively until the water submerged us up over his waist, and the others followed us in. He groaned in pleasure, but then winced when the arm holding my back slid into the water.

"Here, let me help you get that cleaned up," Dio said as he pulled Sam's arm up and Pala supported me from behind.

I gasped in shock when I saw the blood running down his arm, mirroring the rivulets of blood on his chest, only there was more of it.

I tried to pull back as he lifted his other arm from behind me and I noticed it was worse. Sam groaned as I pulled on his knot with my movements. Pala soothed me from behind and kept me firmly in place.

"Is that from the rock wall?" I asked him, and he nodded. "I'm so sorry."

I felt terrible. I had lured him in here, wanting to be out in nature, but also somewhere private for our claiming. A bedroom had felt too tame for our first mating.

"I'm fine. So fucking fine, Lex. I told you I'd happily bleed for you."

I snort laughed, but then Pala started washing my back the same way Dio was with Sam's arms and I realized the sticky mess on my back was blood. It wasn't mine, though. I knew because I felt no pain. As frenzied as Sam had been, he'd still protected me from harm.

"Besides," Sam added, "the scratch marks on my back I'll wear with pride."

"Your back?" I asked, wondering how that had happened when he hadn't been up against the cave wall.

Dio grinned at me as he traced a line over Sam's back. "It seems you have claws when you're all riled up. Bad kitty."

"I scratched you?" I asked Sam, horrified.

He just shrugged carelessly. "My beast loved it as much as I did. It riled him up even more."

"I'm sorry. I told you I didn't need you to bleed for me, and then I went and made you bleed. Why didn't you stop?"

Dio and Pala both chuckled.

"There was nothing in this world that could have made me stop once I read the words you wrote and caught your scent as you ran," Sam said darkly. "You claimed my beast. He took over instantly, and broke every restraint I've ever placed on him. I was out the door before I'd even consciously thought about it."

Our claiming had been instinctive, bloody and hedonistic. I knew now why I wasn't afraid of Sam's beast. My omega was a savage beast too, when she wanted to be. When his darkness rose, so did my own.

"How do you feel now?" As much as I had revelled in our claiming, I wanted to make sure provoking Sam's beast hadn't harmed Sam. It didn't seem as though it had. He felt sated, but I needed to know for sure.

"Whole, connected, powerful, blessed," he said without hesitation, his eyes never leaving mine. "You're a gift, Lexie. You've changed everything in ways I never thought were possible. For the first time since I presented as an alpha, my beast feels content, like he's a part of me instead of a monster trying to escape.

"You have no idea how much of a relief it is, not to feel like I'm going to explode at any moment. It feels like my power is filtering between us all, like we're sharing the burden, making it lighter. "

As Sam described the sensation, I could feel what he meant. From the moment I had met Sam, his dominance had felt like it was too much for him to contain. It had been constantly trying to push its way out, like lava from a volcano, no matter how hard he tried to contain it. But now it felt like a heated river, or a tropical breeze, churning through us all.

I looked at Pala. It felt remarkably like his flowing energy, only rougher. It wasn't a gentle stream, though; this was a powerful river. It made me feel restless and a little edgy.

"I can feel it moving through me now. It feels like a restless current stirring up my energy," Pala said. Sam frowned at that description, looking concerned for a moment.

"Oh, fuck. I thought my heart was just racing from sex," I said as I explored the feeling of their energies moving through me. I knew I'd felt energized after Sam claimed me, but I'd thought it was just endorphins.

Dio chuckled and pretended to reach for me. "If you insist." He didn't seem as perturbed and I figured he'd been unconsciously siphoning off some of Sam's energy for years, even without a direct bond.

Pala tried to swat Dio, but he ducked out of reach, then promptly slipped on the rocky floor of the spring. His arms pinwheeled for a second, almost taking out Pala, before his head went under the surface. He came up spluttering as we all chuckled.

"Oh god, Lex. Don't laugh when you're locked on my knot," Sam groaned.

"Oh sorry, does that feel bad?" I asked as I squeezed around his knot. He groaned again, long and low, and started grinding into me slowly.

I gasped, and he smirked as he pushed me up against Dio, who had slipped in behind me while shaking water from his hair. "You taunted my beast, then you ran straight to a house full of lone alphas. You're lucky nobody got hurt. Now you're going to tease me? It seems you like to be a naughty girl, sweetheart."

"I knew you wouldn't hurt anyone, Sam. Especially not your team," I said a little breathlessly as his knot ground into the sensitive nerves that were locked around him.

Pala drifted closer and stood up behind Sam. He rested his head on Sam's shoulder and reached around, almost lazily, to tweak one of my nipples. I let my head fall back on Dio's shoulder as my back arched, and he kissed the side of my head reverently.

A vibration started up that I could feel running all the way through my body. It had me going completely limp as I surrendered to the feeling of warmth and comfort. It was like a hug from a mug of hot chocolate, if that was even possible. A soothing sound that had me melting as it washed over me, accompanied it.

"What is that?" Pala leaned into Sam as if he was trying to get as close as physically possible to him. "Is that you, Sam? That feels amazing."

"I think he's doing that purring thing Leif talked about," Dio said from behind me.

The sound and the purr intensified. The feelings they wrought, combined with the slow grind of Sam's cock, had me floating on a cloud of pure bliss.

"You don't get it, Lex," Sam growled slowly, not bothered at all about the strange sound he was making. He ran a hand possessively up my stomach until it wrapped lightly around my throat. "You're mine now. My beast has claimed you and nobody touches you ever again, or they'll die a painful death."

"Someone's touching me right now," I moaned, barely able to get the words out as Dio's hand crept around my waist and gently thrummed my clit.

I sensed Sam's smirk more than saw it, as my eyes rolled back in my head. "Let me clarify. Nobody touches you who isn't pack."

"I don't want anyone else," I whispered. These men were already going to be the death of me. Death by slow orgasm.

"Good answer," he said, and he ground down hard, just as Pala tweaked my other nipple and Dio thrummed my clit. The feel of them all touching me together tipped me over the edge Sam had been slowly building me towards with his slow grinds and strangely comforting purr. I came on a deep moan that had Dio grabbing my face and kissing me gently yet thoroughly, drawing out my orgasm as Sam came again, spurting hotly inside me.

When Dio released me, I looked up to see Sam's head thrown back onto Pala's shoulder, while Pala gently licked my bite mark on Sam's neck. Pala's heated eyes, though, were fixed on Dio kissing me.

Well, well, isn't that a pleasant view? My omega perked up, and I mentally scolded her. I was a hypocrite, though. I knew full well I would enjoy the hell out of that show if I ever got to see it.

Pala suddenly flicked his eyes to me, as if he knew I'd been watching him and exactly what I was thinking. He gave me a sexy smile and his eyes roved over my body where I half floated in the dark water.

Sam pulled out of me gently, now that his knot had deflated, and his purr faded. He slumped down onto the rocky edge of the spring. Pala moved over to kiss me lightly, a mere whisper of lips meeting. I could feel his hard cock bumping my hip, but when I reached for him, he caught my hand.

"Enjoy your bath," he whispered.

"But what about you and Dio?"

"What about me and Dio?" Pala asked with a casual smirk. Almost turning my question into a suggestion.

I blushed, feeling called out. "I just mean, you know, don't you want to cum too?" Christ, I sound like a naïve thirteen-year-old. I needed to woman up. Grow some ovaries. I'd claimed this man and let him take me in a threesome the first night I'd met him. I could use the word cum without blushing.

"We're grown men. A bit of delayed gratification won't hurt us," Dio piped in. "Besides, Sam rode you hard. You're going to be sore later," he added with a wink.

Sam rolled his eyes at Dio, but his satisfied smirk ruined the effect as he finished washing the last of the blood off his shoulders.

"My heart," Pala added, "you don't owe us sex, your body, or your time. If this is going to work, we don't want you to feel obligated to be with all of us every time. We don't expect that. We're pack. Our bond is about more than sex."

"Yeah, I've had an almost permanent hard-on since I met you. If you had to help me out every time I popped a woody, we'd never leave the tree house," Dio laughed.

I could feel how genuine they all were through the bond, the affection and care they were sending me.

"Fair enough. But my sex drive has gone through the roof since I met you all, and I don't plan on leaving the house with a case of lady blue balls. I'm just saying."

"Not a chance," Sam growled, muscling forward and pulling me into his arms. "If you have needs, you come to us. It's our privilege to take care of you. You don't go wandering the farm feeling horny and smelling delicious."

I grabbed his face and kissed him hard. "Then don't make me push you next time."

He nodded, looking serious. "I'm yours now, Lex. In every way."

"Will you still write to me?" I asked him. I'd loved reading his letter. It felt intimate and personal. My brother and I used to write to each other when he was in the military and I'd always enjoyed it. Both writing to him and getting his letters. I felt like people said more in letters than they ever would in person.

That slow spreading grin made an appearance, the one that lit up his whole face and made my heart skip a beat. "If you'd like."

"I'd like," I replied. We stared at each other, not needing anymore words, just feeling each other in the bond, until Dio coughed "dork" loudly.

Sam broke our intense stare-off to spin and attempt to dunk Dio again. I smiled at their antics, but rubbed at my chest. The new bond with Sam was thrumming brightly and his power felt familiar, like a piece of me that had always been missing.

Yet that dark, empty spot I'd felt earlier was a building ache that was tainting this moment, and the power circling through us all was becoming increasingly agitated and unsettled. I looked up to see Pala watching me carefully from the other side of the rock pool. He glided towards me, his long hair floating out around him like liquid midnight.

"What's wrong, my heart?"

"Something's missing," I replied, as I rubbed my chest.

"No. Someone's missing." He removed my hand from my chest and lifted me slightly to kiss the spot instead. "So what are you going to do about it, my heart?"

He was watching me intently, but without judgment. Like he was waiting for me to realize something.

Looking at him watching me so patiently, I had a moment of clarity. Like the world suddenly came into focus, and I knew why he always called me the endearment that I loved so much. If I were a cartoon character, a lightbulb would have just lit up above my head.

It wasn't just because I'd captured his heart, like I initially thought. It was because I was the heart. The heart of the pack.

The world had it wrong. Omegas weren't tempting, empty vessels to be fucked and bred. Or dominated and exploited. We drew people in because we instinctively created families, packs, around us. We were what bonded people together. Or we used to be.

I'd heard Damon refer to Maia as their heart recently and Max as their center. I hadn't really understood what they meant, thinking they were just affectionate terms. But it was so much more than that. I was the heart of my pack. Now I just needed to get them their reluctant center to balance us out before Sam's power threw us all off kilter.

I smiled at him slowly, and he matched it. "That's my girl."

"Dave," I screamed at the top of my voice, startling Dio and Sam so much they froze in place.

Pounding footsteps echoed in the ensuing silence.

Thirty-Six

Lexie

Dave rounded the bend at a full sprint, closely followed by Bear, and slid to a stop behind me at the edge of the pool. He swiveled around, looking in every direction for a potential threat.

"What happened?"

Dio and Sam just looked from me to Dave and back again. Sam still had Dio in a playful, loose headlock. Pala just spun me around in his arms until I was facing Dave.

I suddenly didn't know where to start now that Dave was here. "Uh, do you want to come in for a swim?" I asked him.

"You screamed my name like you were being murdered, so you could ask if I wanted to swim?"

"No. I screamed your name because you were so damned far away it was the only way you could hear me."

"I can't swim right now," he said, as he looked over his shoulder distractedly towards the entrance, then looked around at the lights setup as if he was checking for safety issues. Basically looking at anything but me. "I have to go check in with Max. He hasn't surfaced, even with Maia's return, which means he's gone down a rabbit hole looking through the intel Pala brought back. Then I need to check in on the guys at the top gate."

He finally looked in my direction, but kept his eyes on the rocks behind me. "I can take you for a swim tomorrow. Maybe at the bigger hot spring outside?"

I sighed, deeply, like from really deep down in my toes, before I raised my eyebrow at him. Dave suddenly looked unsure of himself. It was a look I'd never seen on him before. He was always so confident. "Why do I need to get in the hot spring right now?" He asked as he glanced at all of us.

We weren't cramped in here, but we were all floating around naked, with arms and legs brushing against each other. I knew I was asking a lot. I was asking him to take a leap. It was time.

"Because we need to talk, yet there always seems to be a reason we can't. I finally figured out there's always going to be a reason, an emergency, someone or something that needs checking on. But right now, I need you."

"We need you," Pala added, and I could have kissed him.

I sounded like a petulant five-year-old to my own ears, and I hated it. This conversation wasn't getting off to the start I wanted, and my frustration was showing. I wasn't good at having conversations about my emotions or my feelings. Forcing this conversation felt awkward and weird, but it was necessary.

I'd just pushed Sam to act. Now I needed to push Dave to talk. I had a feeling handling four men was going to be a lot of work. I was all in now, though. The only way through this was to face it, every hard and awkward part of it. It was how I dealt with everything once I put my mind to something.

"Well, why didn't you just say so?" Dave said, his confidence roaring back. He raised an arm, grabbed his shirt from behind his head and pulled the whole thing off in one smooth movement before dropping it to the floor. My jaw fell open and Pala chuckled next to me. Dave wasn't one to flaunt his body, but I'd long suspected, from the way his clothes clung to him, that he was fit.

His salt and pepper hair and classic good looks had always done it for me, and he had a wicked smolder down pat. It made my nipples perk up every time he threw it my way. Yet I wasn't prepared for the way the smattering of dark hairs on his sculpted chest, and those thick biceps on display, would make me feel.

It was like Clark Kent took off his glasses and you suddenly realized he was Superman. Dave's dark camo pants hung low on his hips and his hand had me enthralled as it slid across his abdomen to grip his belt, before undoing it slowly and sliding it free. It gave me the naughty idea of him folding me over his lap and spanking me lightly with it.

I must have moaned, or maybe stopped breathing, as Pala shifted forward and whispered in my ear, "Breathe, my heart."

It was too late for breathing exercises though, because Dave had toed off his boots while Pala had me distracted, and was now pulling down the zipper of his jeans. It was a strip show just for me and if I had a wad of dollar bills right now, I'd be throwing them at Dave like confetti.

He slid the zipper down slowly, knowing he had my full attention. Not even Dio yelling, "Yeah, work it, baby," could distract me now.

Dave hooked his fingers in his pants and slid them down his legs, tugging them a little over his muscular thighs, before dropping them to the floor too and stepping out of them. He stood proudly in front of me, and I thought maybe the show was over. Which I would be perfectly fine with, because the sight of a thick bulge tenting his boxer briefs was going in my spank bank.

Dave proved he wasn't shy though, as he hooked his fingers into his briefs and slowly slid them down. His impressive cock slipped free, and it felt incredibly naughty seeing him like this. Like suddenly getting a peek at your hot teacher naked. *Well hello, Sir.*

My vision darkened slightly, and I had to remember Pala's advice to breathe. I had three gorgeous guys in this hot spring with me already, and I'd just had two mind blowing orgasms, yet the sight of Dave standing there naked had me all kinds of hot and bothered. I bit my lip, trying to ease some of the heat building in me. My skin felt like it was on fire.

Dave's eyes were dark in the shadows cast by the fairy lights above us, but I could see the way they were now fixed on my mouth. Dave was incredibly confident with his body. He joined in with the drills he put his cadets through, and his experience showed in everything he did. I'd often wondered, usually late at night with a vibrator in hand, what he would be like in bed.

Dave moved towards the edge of the pool, but didn't bother with the rock steps. He crouched down right in front of me and slid straight in with only a brief splash. Pala moved me back a little to give Dave room.

Or maybe he was just moving me out of reach in case I got grabby hands, knowing we weren't ready for that yet.

"You wanted to talk, Lex?" Dave asked.

I had no words. Not a single one. My brain was offline.

"I think you're going to have to take the floor, Dave," Sam said, as he glided over to rest against the edge of the pool near Dave, while Dio settled in next to Pala and me. Pala still had me wrapped up in his arms and I honestly needed him right now to keep me from floating away mentally and physically.

There were so many words unsaid between Dave and me, always left hanging in the air. I wondered if you'd see them if you took a picture of us right now. The way you could see it when people write with sparklers. The words are too quick to be read by the naked eye, but highlighted brightly and forever in a photograph.

Dave and I were suddenly caught in each other's eyes, something we had rarely allowed ourselves.

Bear whined from where he'd settled near Sam, and it broke the moment. He wasn't usually a cock block, but I think even he could sense the underlying tension. It was time to talk. I mentally shook myself out of the dick spell Dave had woven over me.

"How did you find me the other night?" I blurted out. I noticed Dave tense slightly, and the water rippled as if he was clenching his fists under the surface.

Dave's next words had my body tensing. "I put a tracker on your bike a long time ago."

It seemed Dave was finally willing to end this dance we had been doing. The guys had accepted him quickly. Yet, he'd been shadowing us all for days, only dipping his toes into our pack dynamic before backing off again. It was time to figure out if he was all in or not.

"I'm aware of that. Nice of you to admit to it, finally."

Dave's shocked intake of breath made me hide a smile. He clearly thought I had no idea he followed me, watched me, whenever I snuck out of the farm at night.

I'd spotted him a few times, and I'd never really minded.I'd actually felt safer knowing he was nearby if I needed him. The only thing I'd never understood was why he did it in secret. I knew I was strong willed and not great at asking for help for myself. But still.

"It was my job," he said, sounding tense. Yet I could see hope, laced with desperation in his eyes.

"My brother paid you to watch me, follow me?" I'd suspected, but I was still disappointed. My brother was going to get his ear yanked again.

"Technically, yes, but I've been donating that part of my salary to one of your charities since shortly after I met you."

"Why?" I asked, not giving any more away just yet.

"It didn't feel right to take money for something that felt personal and I did gladly."

"Huh," was all I said. I got the distinct feeling he wasn't just talking about me when he said it was personal.

"You're not mad?" He asked.

"No. I never really expected my brother to let me run around at night in dangerous situations without back-up. I couldn't have Leif with me or even spreading his scent in the area. The women I dealt with were often afraid of men they knew, let alone strange alphas turning up. But I always figured they were in the background somewhere.

"Especially Max. I figured he had me under surveillance, considering it was his system that sent the alerts. To be honest, it always kind of made me feel like a Charlie's Angel, with an invisible team."

Dave chuckled lightly and relaxed a little. "Does that make Max, Bosley or Charlie?"

"Definitely Bosley. You were always Charlie."

Dio snorted at that. "I can see you as Charlie, Dave. All mysterious, directing everyone but also taking care of everyone."

"What happened to that big, angry guy? The one that was stalking me a few months ago then suddenly disappeared?"

Dave threw back his head and laughed, but it was Sam's turn to tense now.

"Someone was stalking you?" Sam growled, laser focused on me as if he could pull the information from my brain with just his mind.

I just shrugged a little. "I pissed off a lot of not-very-nice men."

"That one was particularly nasty." Dave said. "He decided it would be a good idea to move back home to his mom, across the other side of the country. He had some medical problems that popped up unexpectedly."

I felt a smile trying to force itself across my face, and bit my lip to hide it.

Dave groaned. "This is why I kept my distance from you. To stop me from manhandling you every time you bit your lip, sassed someone, gave someone that eyebrow move you pull, or even just breathed, really."

"What if I wanted to be manhandled by you?" Dave took a deep, shuddering breath and his hand tightened on the rock where he'd stretched his arms out.

"Lexie, I'm a lot older than you. It's not socially acceptable, the way I've always felt about you. People would talk and judge. It would be a problem."

Dio inhaled sharply and I could see him shaking his head frantically at Dave out of the corner of my eye. Sam was staring at Dave worriedly.

"Who says it's not right?" I asked, a little too loudly. "Tell me who thinks it's not right and I'll kick their asses. It's nobody's business but yours and mine what we do together. Is my age a problem for you, or just for other people? Because I'm nobody's problem. I'll walk away right now, if that's the thing holding you back. You thinking I'll be a problem in your life?"

My blood was suddenly boiling in my veins, and I could feel sweat trickle down my hairline.

"Lex, no. That's not what I meant. You're gorgeous, feisty, kind, and so fucking strong. You are never a problem, not for me, not ever." Dave glided over to me, pulled my head towards his and rested his forehead against mine. Pala released his arms from around my waist, but stayed behind me.

Dave took a deep breath. "I meant I'd be a problem for you. You bring starlight to the darkness in my life, but there's nothing I offer you that would make up for strangers whispering every time I held your hand. Would you really be okay if we were out and someone assumed I was your father?"

"Since when have I ever cared about what strangers whisper about? Have you looked at me? Do I look like I give a fuck?" I asked him. "And I'll happily call you Daddy."

He groaned and shot me a dark look. "Do not call me Daddy."

He shook his head at me when I smirked at him. "I've always looked at you way too fucking much, Lexie. I could never seem to stop, even though I told myself I should."

I was quiet for a moment, gathering my thoughts. "Is it my brother? Are you worried about your friendship with him?"

"Ironically no," Dave said, as he pulled back to look at me. "Leif made it very clear recently that he would be happy if we got together. It appears Damon, Max and Leif have suspected I had feelings for you for a while. Hunter was clueless, though. It's rare anyone gets one over on him."

I wanted to ask about these feelings, but I also wanted to know more about what the guys said about us. I raised my eyebrow at Dave's words and he just licked his lower lip in response, causing tingles to start up in my body again and naughty ideas to enter my head.

My scent was spilling into the space between us, overriding the dark, mineral scent of the surrounding cave, letting him know exactly what that did to me. He smiled darkly.

"You were talking about me to my brother recently?" I asked, wanting him to answer the silent question he seemed intent on ignoring.

"Yeah. When Damon quizzed me about my intentions towards you at the security meeting after breakfast a few days ago. Dio told me you needed me and it was time I stepped up, and I resigned my job as your secret bodyguard."

I was annoyed at Damon, but I could hug Dio right now. "Oh, sounds like it was an eventful morning. Do I get a say in any of this?" I asked.

"Lexie, you get the only say. There's another thing I need to tell you first, though. Something few people know."

He hesitated, and I groaned inwardly. I was an impulsive person and didn't like to wait for things once I'd decided on them. After spending too much of my childhood waiting alone in dark spaces, I had no patience for it now.

"Spill it, Dave," I growled.

Dave winced and, as frustrated as I was with him, I still had a sudden urge to run my fingers over the slight creases in the corners of his eyes.

The subtle lines on his face suited him, made him look ruggedly handsome.

"I had a daughter once," he said. My arms ached to hold him at the clear pain in his voice. So I didn't hold back.

I floated off Pala's lap to wrap my arms and legs around Dave's body, and the skin contact felt so right. As if the clothes between us had always been the only barrier we needed to overcome.

I braced myself for his story, knowing this was going to hurt.

Thirty-Seven

Dave

"I met her at a diner when I was on leave. She was about four years old and walked up to me, bold as brass, and demanded I tie her shoe for her." He smiled sadly at the memory and my heart clutched with the knowledge this story would not end well.

"She looked like a tiny version of Maia, all blonde curls and blue eyes, but with seriously chubby cheeks. I asked her where her mother was and she just shrugged. Her mother came racing up a minute or two later, scolding her. She was beautiful. They both were, but also ragged and thin. I bought them both lunch, then took them to the zoo. Lainey stole my heart."

His voice broke a little, saying her name out loud. I knew, without him having to say, that he was talking about the daughter, not the mother. "Three weeks later I had to go back on tour and I couldn't leave her not knowing if she'd have enough to eat. So I married her mother and got them settled into a house on a nearby base before I left. I made sure they had access to my medical, and I put most of my pay into an account every week to cover food and expenses.

"The next year was tough, but Lainey's drawings got me through. She'd ride her bike down to the post office on base and send them every few days. The post office staff knew where to send them and would address an envelope for her. I only got leave sporadically and her mother was unhappy every time I came home. She was always demanding more, hating being left alone. But Lainey was a little ray of sunshine, the cutest little thing. She'd give me the biggest hugs and cry when I left again.

"I suspected her mother had someone on the side, but I didn't really care. We didn't have that kind of relationship. I only cared that she was taking care of Lainey properly. Until I got a call one day, only hours after I landed back at my post."

He stopped, and his whole body shook. The guys all closed in and wrapped around us. I could feel their worry and their care for Dave in the bond. I had an intense urge to bring him into that bond too, make him a part of us instead of always being on the outer ring.

"Her mother's boyfriend was abusive. I didn't know," he said, his voice breaking. "He stayed away whenever I came home and took it out on her when I left. He wanted her to leave me, but she refused because she wouldn't give up access to my medical plan and a guaranteed roof over her head. I found out all of this later, after he shot them both. It's been over ten years, but I still feel empty without her hugs."

He shuddered in our arms as his story wound to a horrifying conclusion. I could feel silent tears streaming down my face for this strong, caring, beautiful man who always gave so much of himself. Who took on a child and her mother, virtual strangers, because he couldn't stand to see them suffering.

I've always found Dave incredibly attractive. He carried a dark energy underneath the solid surface that called to me. Yet over the years, I've also fallen in love with the kind heart that shines through in every action he takes, and the way he cares about people.

The cadets he brought with him to the farm were all kids he rescued off the streets when he retired. He knew stability and training would help keep them clean and out of trouble, but he no longer trusted the military with their futures. So he created his own small academy to train them himself.

He used military techniques to train them physically so they could handle themselves with whatever life threw at them, but also training methods to build their confidence, give them self respect and instill leadership qualities.

When Damon found out what he was doing, he invited Dave and the boys to come here and incorporate their training into security roles at the farm. The boys have flourished under the care of so many good men.

I've watched him with the boys and he's tough but fair. Dave doesn't ask them to do anything he won't do himself. He also doesn't sugarcoat anything. He's honest about how tough life can be, while pushing them to be better. Yet the obvious care he has for them shines through.

I can only imagine how Dave was with his little girl. To know she died at the hands of an abuser who was in her life without him knowing, must have nearly destroyed him. I understood now why Dave had felt so compelled to help me in my work, but why he had also kept his distance from the women and children we helped.

Dave had spent his life creating families, yet he'd always been on the outside, keeping a part of himself tucked away. He did it with Lainey's mom, with Leif and his mates, and with his cadets too. He cared, and he supported, but he held something of himself apart. It seemed Lainey was the only one who had ever completely broken through until now.

I realized he needed us, as much as we needed him, to break through those last walls he held around his heart. To bring him into the center of us, where he belonged. With his pack.

"Dave," I choked out, my heart bleeding for him but unable to form the words. I've never been good at words, usually relying on my actions to express what I needed.

"It's okay, Lexie," he said as he brushed tears off my cheeks. He seemed lighter. As if by talking about his past, he had let go of something he had been holding to, too tightly.

Yet now, I could see him trying to do what he always did. Support everyone else and ignore his own needs. So I did the only thing I knew to comfort him, and what my omega instincts were screaming at me to do. I leaned forward and kissed him with all the desire and love I felt for him. He kissed me back just as fiercely, yet he pulled back far too quickly.

"It's okay," he repeated, as he tried to comfort me and it drove me insane. "We don't have to resolve anything right now. It's been a long day for you. We can talk about this more later."

"No," I said, pulling him into me tighter, refusing to let him create any distance between us. Especially after the death and desolation I'd seen outside our gates today. I needed him now. "Nobody can be sure of a later anymore, Dave. The world has gone to shit. We have to take what we can now, grab it with both hands and hold on tight."

He grunted at me, reaching up to cup my face, a fierce expression on his own. "You are, Lexie. You're going to have a later. If I have to make sure it happens personally, I will. We will figure out what's coming for you and we will face it head on."

I could feel the other guys' agreement as a wave of emotion through the bond, but they stayed silent.

"We need you with us, Dave. Not racing around the edges, watching over us and protecting us from a distance. I'm sorry for what happened to Lainey. I would love to have met her. But it's time to drop those walls you've built. We need you here, in the center of us, holding us together."

I was guilty of the same thing Dave was. Yet I was done holding people at a distance and letting them do the same to me. I'd told myself for so long that I wasn't anyone else's problem. But all I got myself with that attitude was loneliness.

I had Sam's dominance swirling through my veins, three bright beautiful bonds thrumming in my chest and a pack that felt more like home than anything I'd ever felt before.

I wasn't letting Dave fuck around on the edges of our lives anymore. It was time he became pack.

Thirty-Eight

I shifted slightly until I could grind down on Dave's cock. It had soft-ened while we were talking, but I could feel it hardening beneath me again now.

Dave groaned and threw his head back as he dropped his hand from my face as if I was burning him, only there was nowhere to go. Hard bodies surrounded us both. I ground down on him again, needing him inside me, filling me, claiming me.

"I love you, Dave." The words forced themselves out, unable to be contained anymore. I felt ripped open, exposed and vulnerable in a way I'd never experienced before. All the parts of me that I'd kept hidden, the loneliness, fear and need to be touched, were out and laid bare.

Dave had felt important from the very first moment I met him. As if he could make me feel whole with a touch, but also destroy me with a single word. Now that he was here, in front of me and we were stripping each other apart, it was exhilarating and terrifying. Dave whipped his head back up to face me, his eyes wide and shocked.

Did he really not know how I felt about him? I needed to fix that.

"I'm not asking you to be our center because you're convenient or a good guy. I'm asking because, despite how we've kept each other at arm's length for years, I fell in love with you anyway, and I need you." It was the most raw and honest I had ever been with another person.

"Lex," he whispered, as his eyes roved all over my face. I reached up and traced the light frown lines on his forehead and the laugh lines around his eyes, loving the map of his life on his body. Learning it, along with him.

"It's okay if you don't love me back just yet. I can wait for that, but I can't wait for you anymore." I trembled, hearing the vulnerability in my voice, and the other guys all responded, surrounding us closer, pressing into us.

"I already fucking love you, Lex," Dave growled, reaching for me again, but this time, his free hand gripped the back of my neck. "Now that you know everything, my secrets, my pain, my fears. I'm done staying away. If you want me, you have all of me. I'll be anything you need."

The words, in his distinctive rasp, filled me with a wild soaring need I could hardly contain in my body. I ground against him again, his cock now hard and throbbing as I rubbed my pussy along its length and ground my clit into the hard tip.

Sam, Dio and Pala had all drawn in so close, but were hanging back from touching me, trying to be respectful to Dave. But at this moment, I needed them all.

I was so hot and needy, the water suddenly felt boiling, and my body was too empty. I needed more. A whimper broke free as a sudden cramp hit me, forcing me to curl into Dave.

"Baby girl," Dave ground out, concern making his voice even deeper. "Tell us what you need."

"I'm so hot, I'm burning, and it hurts," I whimpered. Tears of frustration burned behind my eyes. I was so close to everything I wanted, yet Dave still felt too far away. They all did. I needed them inside me.

The mineral odor that had been fine before suddenly felt overwhelming and blocked the scent of my guys, making me feel anxious as another cramp hit me.

"What hurts?" Dave asked, but I couldn't talk through the cramp wracking me.

Sam's arms wrapped around Dave and I. "Shit, she is hot, and her scent, it's changing. I-"

Sam snarled as my scent seemed to detonate around the room and his arms tightened around me possessively, to the point of pain.

"Fuck. She's in heat," Dio ground out, sounding like he was in pain as well.

"How?" Sam demanded. "Maia got at least a few hours' warning."

"Yeah, but Lexie suppressed her omega for years and she built her pack within a few days. A sudden heat could be a side effect. Her pheromones have been in overdrive since we arrived." Pala was being far too logical for me right now. I whimpered again, needing less talk and more action.

"Why didn't we read Maia's damn book as soon as Lexie brought it back to the treehouse?" Sam asked, frustration lacing his voice.

"There's been too much happening," Dio said, sounding just as frustrated. "We've barely had time to breathe since the attack the other day. Trying to get on top of the threats we're facing, and build this pack quickly to protect her. Nobody has had a chance."

"I know, but it's not good enough. We can't protect her if we don't know what's happening to her," Sam snarled, sounding angry at himself.

"Enough. What's done is done. We need to focus on Lexie now." Dave grabbed my face, dragging it up from his chest and towards the light. "Shit, her pupils are blown wide. Lexie, what do you need, baby?"

Dave had pulled away from me slightly, and I growled in frustration and pain, feeling suddenly dizzy. My thoughts were incoherent, words swirled away from me whenever I tried to grasp them.

"I don't know how to help her with a heat," Dave said quickly, from too far away.

"Nobody does, they're so rare," Dio said, his voice hoarse. "We're going to have to use our alpha instincts and let her guide us."

"I'm not an alpha. I don't have your instincts, and I don't have a bond with her yet," Dave hissed, his frustration slipping out, as I cried out incoherently and started pulling at him, trying to get him closer. "I need you guys to dig deep and feel her. Let me know what else she needs."

"We've got you, Dave," Sam said, as if Dave's frustration had cast his own aside. Sam pressed himself into me from behind, wrapping his arms around both Dave and me, drawing him back into my body.

I was aching and burning while a ravenous need that seemed impossible to fill started beating a wild rhythm in my blood. I cried out again, feeling like I couldn't get any air, desperate to breathe, to fuck.

"Calm, omega," Sam growled suddenly, and that delicious purr sounded again, feeling like a cool splash of water against my skin. It didn't fill the need, but it calmed me enough that I could breathe again. Sucking in deep lungfuls of humid, moisture laden air.

"Dave, pack, nest, blankets, knots," I begged, finding words as I reached up behind me to press Sam closer to me, wanting to crawl inside him and curl around that purring vibration. Needing darkness, soft blankets and the scent of my mates around me.

"I'm right here, baby girl. I'm not going anywhere," Dave said as he pressed himself into me.

"Fuck," Dio cursed loudly. The sound echoed around the cave as Dio's hands ran along my heated skin, as if he couldn't help himself, making my body writhe. "That heat scent shit is potent. My dick feels like it's about to snap off."

I could feel Sam's rock hard cock pressed against my back and I rubbed my body against him as I thrashed, desperate for friction.

"We're going to be exposed if we try to move her," Dave warned, his voice sounding dark, not liking anyone else seeing me this way as I leaned forward and started licking and sucking his shoulder, almost mindless with need.

"We need to move. Maia's heat lasted for two days. We have no supplies in here. We don't even have drinkable water," Pala said, almost slurring his words. He sounded drunk as he stroked my wet hair and made me moan. Every part of me felt over sensitive. Even my hair.

I ground myself against both Dave and Sam, thrusting between them. They responded instinctively by jerking their hips up against me, dry humping me. It wasn't enough. I needed more. I tried to angle myself onto a cock, any cock, but Sam held me fast. Frustration and pain had me crying out. I felt so empty it hurt.

"Guys," Dave ground out. "Loft or here, but this is happening. Make a decision."

"Loft," Sam snarled, sounding like he was about to lose it.

The sound of splashing water filled my ears, and they hauled me out of the hot spring to stand dripping and naked in the cave. Dizziness overwhelmed me as the cramps returned with the loss of their bodies and Sam's purr. I doubled over and clutched my stomach.

"Dammit. Hang on." Dave's voice moved further away, but he was back in moments. "Put this shirt on her."

Something dark slid over my head and I protested, hating the scratchy feel of the fabric rubbing on my body. I tried to pull away, but then I caught a whiff of Pala's scent and I inhaled it deeply. I recognized him as mine. It made my need spike to obscene levels.

I growled deep in my throat as I launched myself at Dio and grabbed his cock. I squeezed it around the base and tried to force it inside me, throwing my leg around his waist. His eyes rolled back in his head as he jerked his cock out of my grip, at the very edge of his control.

"Somebody grab her or I'm fucking her right here," Dio ground out.

"Pala, scout ahead. Clear anyone out of our path. We're moving." Dave's voice had me spinning my head in his direction. I whined as I felt Pala move away from us. I got a glimpse of his naked ass as he disappeared around the bend, not bothering with clothes.

Dave grabbed me and pulled me from between Sam and Dio. I heard them both growl deep in their chests. He ignored them and spun Sam around while holding me at bay as gently as he could. "Piggyback, now. It'll keep your dicks out of her until we get there."

Sam nodded in a jerky movement and crouched down. I all but fell onto his naked back and immediately started licking my bite mark on his neck and rubbing myself all over him. He picked me up with a growl, holding my thighs in a firm grip that had me moaning for more. The need for them to manhandle me and use me for their own pleasure was burning through me.

Sam took off around the bend at a fast sprint, jostling me and causing friction as my nipples rubbed against the fabric and his hard back. "Sam," I whined as more cramps hit me. I tried to grind down, but there was nothing to grind on.

"I know, sweetheart. Hang on."

I couldn't help it, whimpers escaped, no matter how hard I tried to keep them in. Suddenly Dio was there, keeping pace with us. His hand ran down my back, caressed my ass briefly, then slid between my spread legs. Two fingers speared inside me and the ecstasy shooting through my core had me yelling his name out loud.

Dio used the natural bounce caused by Sam's sprint to fuck me with his fingers as they ran out the entrance of the cave and into the trees. I didn't know which path they took. I paid no attention to our surroundings. My entire world focused down onto those fingers, pushing as deep as they could go inside me.

"More," I groaned and hissed as Dio added a third finger, jamming them almost roughly inside me. I could feel my slick gushing all over his hand. He rubbed it around before spearing his thumb into my slicked up ass. My legs shook around Sam's waist and I would have slid down him if he didn't have such a hard grasp on my legs.

Sam roared as he caught the scent of my slick, and Dio started an incoherent growl in response. Pala howled from up ahead of us. In encouragement or frustration, I wasn't sure. Birds took off in flight all around us as wild things fled the predatory sounds. It was an echo of our earlier chase, only this time, we were running together.

I heard Dave yelling into a radio behind us as he ran. "Beta 2 to all. Lexie in heat. Alphas in rut. Anyone between the cave and treehouse to clear out fast. Ava to send heat supplies to treehouse. Nick has comms. Beta 2 going radio silent."

An echo of Dave's radio bounced around the trees somewhere nearby, and Pala's howl turned into snarling up ahead. Someone yelled, "Fuck, I'm going," loudly followed by running on the path, as whoever it was disappeared fast. Nobody wanted to tussle with an angry, naked alpha in full protective mode.

A few minutes later, that felt like the longest hours of my life. We hit the stairs to the treehouse and Sam powered up them, barely even slowing down. Pala had the door thrown open at the top and we ran straight through to the internal stairs. I heard the door slide shut behind us and Pala dragged something heavy over the floor.

I think he was barricading the door, but by that stage, I was up in the loft and being dropped onto the central mattress. Soft blankets surrounded me as the guys grabbed every blanket they could find in the loft and placed them around me. I snuggled into them, seeking my mate's scents. But I could only smell Pala and Dio on the blankets, Dave and Sam were missing.

I started frantically sniffing clothes around me and stuffing them in between the blankets, but it still didn't smell strong enough. I needed my makeshift nest to smell like all my mates.

"Dave, Sam," I cried out as another cramp hit, and bodies suddenly surrounded me. I pulled Dave underneath me, feeling his lack of a claim to our pack like a knife against my skin.

A growl of frustration rang in my ears as someone raised my arms into the air and Pala's shirt disappeared over my head, exposing my chest to the lust soaked air. The bliss of hard, sweaty bodies replaced the shirt's itchy sensation, and I breathed a deep sigh of relief.

I felt the encouragement of all my mates as I moved over Dave. They wanted this too, needed this last connection. Sam's power was swirling through all of us, faster and faster, getting whipped up by our emotions into a gathering storm.

"Please, Dave," I begged as molten heat settled into my bones. I'd never begged for anything before, but I was suddenly aching to the point of pain. I could feel frustrated tears building behind my eyes.

"I'm right here, Lex," he said, his hand gripping my hip tightly, anchoring me to him. "Take what you need. Make me yours." This powerful man was giving up control to me, and it filled my omega with a savage need to claim him.

"Take him, Lex," I heard Sam growl from my side as his power rose to the surface, pulling us all in. "Make him ours."

"Ours," I heard Pala and Dio echo with determination, pushing in against us and stroking my body, not caring about all the sweaty male bodies touching as well, as long as they could touch me.

I shifted again and reached between us, grabbing Dave's cock and jerking it roughly as he groaned, before I maneuvered myself until I could sink down onto his hard length. I had no need or patience for foreplay right now. A desperate haze had descended over me and my entire focus narrowed down to where the head of his cock was notched inside me, spreading me wide.

My moan vibrated through me as I worked myself onto his shaft, until I felt him slide into me fully, my slick easing the way through the tight fit.

I started riding him hard and fast, feeling like we'd been building toward this moment for years. All the pained longing and denial, the frustration, the fantasies, it had me primed to explode. Hands supported my weight as I leaned my head forward and claimed Dave's mouth. Now that I could finally kiss him whenever I wanted, I felt like I was never going to get enough.

Dave started to thrust into me too, unable to keep himself still. I could feel his silent groan vibrate through me. Driving the delicious sparking sensations whirling out from my core into a whizzing, dizzying frenzy. If he cared about the three naked alphas surrounding us at such an intimate moment, he didn't show it. My raw need was mirrored in his blazing eyes. His expression looked almost pained, but he'd never looked more beautiful to me as he gave in to his raging need for me.

I had the sudden urge to photograph his expression as I watched him lose control. He grabbed me hard, and pulled me to him as he sat up and rolled us over, dragging Sam underneath us, too.

Sam grunted, but didn't fight it. I could feel his hard body against my back and I writhed on top of him. Dave straddled us both as he lifted my legs up onto his shoulders and braced himself with his arms beside Sam's head. I could see the strain on his face as he forced himself to go still for a moment.

I was about to cry out in protest until I felt Sam shift underneath me and his thick cock rubbed against my ass, smearing my slick everywhere. I groaned in pleasure as he manhandled me into position so he could shove into me from behind.

The two of them together, two thick, impressive cocks working inside me, had me moaning wantonly. Both men had made me push them, made me wait, but now I had them and I was going to enjoy them.

"Harder," I growled in challenge, looking Dave straight in the eye.

"You got it, baby girl," he grunted as he pulled almost all the way out, then shoved back in hard, driving me into the alpha below us. Sam growled loudly and ground up into me on Dave's next savage thrust, forcing his knot inside me as well. The stretch, the fullness, and the knot pressing against sensitive nerves had me going completely limp between them.

I couldn't keep up. Couldn't even move. I was a mindless, needy creature, completely given over to the sensations almost choking me. Dave groaned, low and dark, as he felt me completely submit to them. He set a furious pace, fucking me against Sam's knot as he kissed me passionately.

Sam's power swirled aggressively, as our bodies moved together with frenzied thrusts and hands stroked me relentlessly. The feel of my mates' desire and need through the bond had me peaking sharp and hard. I wrenched my mouth free and latched onto Dave's neck, biting hard through a scream that ripped free with the force of a tidal wave as my entire body gripped Dave's.

I felt all my mates lunge at the same time as Dave made an animalistic sound and bit into my neck, just as I bit into his. Sam's power rushed up between us, driving us to a peak that felt miles above the room we inhabited, as if we'd all been thrust up and out into the universe together.

I shook, as light exploded outward and wave after wave of sensation rocked me. Sam's dominance cycled back down to wrap tightly around us, binding us together forever, until it seemed to sink back into our skin.

I released Dave's neck, but kissed my mark lightly, making him moan before I rested my head back onto Sam's shoulder. Dave looked blissed out and wrung out at the same time as he slumped onto me. Sam rolled us all, so we were lying on our sides while his knot was locked inside me. I glanced at my other mates to see wide cocky grins on their faces. We hadn't discussed how we were going to bring Dave into the pack, but I couldn't think of a better way.

Dave was now sporting three bite marks across his torso and one on his wrist, every one of our pack claiming him. I shot a grin at Claudio and he looked supremely satisfied. I noticed he only wore my bite though, being the first, and that didn't sit right with me. We'd need to fix that. I glanced at Pala and he winked at me, seeming to know my thoughts. Oh, yeah. He'd be fixing that real soon.

Dave seemed to tremble slightly, and I tried to let him go, but he hugged me tighter, cradling me into his arms and pulling one of my legs over his hip. He seemed to need the skin contact right now as much as I did.

My body was limp and the intense heat that had built so quickly, felt banked for the moment, but I could still feel its warmth sliding through me. Waiting to flare to life. For now, I was happy to rest for a moment in my mate's arms, with the scents of our pack surrounding us.

"Fucking hell, that was intense. Is it always like that?" Dave rubbed his chest, and the movement made me check in with my bonds. The dark patch was gone, replaced by another glowing bright bond linking me to Dave. I sent him love down the bond and his eyes widened as he looked at me in amazement.

I didn't need to ask him if he was okay with the bonds. Something seemed settled inside him, and I could feel his joy at the connection. We probably should have asked him before we did it, but alphas and omegas were creatures of impulse and instinct. He was going to have to get used to that with all of us.

Although in my defense, he had said to take whatever I needed from him, and I'd needed him to be bonded to all of us. I knew the guys all needed his solid presence as much as I did, too.

"Yeah, pretty much. Although Lex isn't usually in pain, that was the heat, I think. I'm sure it will settle down now that we're all bonded," Dio said, and I realized he'd been right there with me through every claiming. I shot him a sleepy smile, and he reached out to squeeze my hand.

"You all claimed me?" Dave asked, sounding choked up.

"Hell yeah. Lex's love for you has been clear from the start and you bring a steadiness we all need." Dio looked Dave straight in the eye as he spoke, daring him to object or deny his words.

"My power is so much calmer now." Sam sounded thoughtful as he played with strands of my wet hair. He seemed so much more at peace now. I felt the power inside me and he was right. It was almost like a still pond now, with only the gentlest current. Like a warmth pooling in my core.

"You're right," Pala said. "I don't know what would have happened if we hadn't bonded Dave so quickly. Your power was filtering through us, but it was wild and seeking an anchor. It may have torn our bonds apart if left unchecked."

"Why didn't you say something earlier?" Dave demanded, looking aghast that we'd all been in any kind of danger.

"We didn't know earlier. There's no manual for this. There haven't been any known packs in a really long time." Pala's use of the word known had me narrowing my eyes at him, but he calmly ignored my stare. He was watching Dave carefully instead.

I looked up at Dave and saw his brow all furrowed. "What's going on, Dave?"

Dave looked down at me and gave my thigh a slight squeeze before looking around at the guys. "Can I ask a question without you all thinking I'm ungrateful or complaining? Because I'm not, I'm just trying to get my head around this."

"You can ask us anything you want, Dave," Sam replied, as he sent Dave one of his rare smiles. Dave blinked rapidly, as if he wasn't completely unaffected by the haunting beauty of that smile, either.

Dave shifted his gaze up to the skylight, as if the stars held all our secrets. His voice was gruff when he finally spoke. "Only Leif and Maia claimed Max. Why did you all claim me?"

My heart broke a little for him as I sensed his genuine confusion through the bond. I hated that he didn't see his own value and how much he contributed to our world.

"We all respect you, Dave, and you've felt like another brother from the start," Sam said seriously. "You were Lexie's pack long before we were. We just needed to make it official."

"Leif and his mates all had existing relationships that were strong before they met Maia," Dio added. "Distance had fractured our bond with Pala and you and Lex were denying yours."

Pala nodded along. "When I met you, Lex was also in danger. Still is. I think we're all just operating on heightened instincts to build this pack as quickly as we can. We don't have years to spend building a rapport. It felt right to do it now, so we did it."

Dave just looked thoughtful. "That sounds logical. It's just a little strange to me that this doesn't feel weird, the way you all touch and hug each other constantly. Even feeling all your emotions now. I mean, I know I saw it with Damon and his mates for years, but I always thought it would make me uncomfortable personally. But from the start, I haven't minded it with you guys. Even when you're all naked, it seems."

The guys all laughed, but my mind went in another direction. *Bad Lexie, stop picturing them all naked and touching each other.*

"You okay there, my heart?" Pala asked with a smirk, as if he knew where my mind had gone. He always seemed to know. I raked my gaze over him where he was sitting casually against the wall of the loft, on the outer edge of the mattress. He was comfortably nude, with one leg bent and his arm resting on it. His long dark locks were still wet, same as mine and there was a bead of water trailing down over his chest toward his hard cock. He looked lickable.

"Yep. Peachy," I murmured, trying to drag my mind out of the gutter as my nipples pebbled and heat started stroking its fingers down my spine.

I shifted suddenly, feeling uncomfortable, and a sharp burst of pleasure spiked. My next words came out strangled. "Actually,-"

I didn't need to say more. Pala shifted and crawled towards me. He kissed me as he slid in between Dave and me, while Dave shifted to make room. He fanned the flames the instant his lips grazed mine. I ground back on Sam, still locked on his knot, and a moan slipped from him as his hands wandered from my hair toward my breast.

A pleasure so fierce, I felt more animal than human, slipped me into a rut, and my mates quickly followed as time lost all meaning. There was only the relentless pursuit of heat, hard bodies and a never ending desire I wasn't sure we could ever satisfy.

Thirty-Nine

 *Lexie*

I headed towards the kitchen two days later, feeling a little sore but sated. Yet also determined. I didn't regret my heat. It had been fucking magnificent. Emphasis on the fucking. Yet we had lost days we didn't have. Or the people who were relying on me didn't have.

I was hoping Isabella & Sirena were in the kitchen, even though it wasn't meal prep time. I was also hoping I could push my luck and find Maia and Ava there too, so I didn't have to go hunt them down. Ava had been a gem the last two days, and I needed to thank her for the flow of food, drinks, clean sheets and soft blankets that had arrived during my heat.

The farm was unusually quiet now, and it unsettled me a little. I was so used to the endless flow of chatter, laughter, and moving equipment that drifted around the farm on the breeze during the day. Even the animals seemed quieter, as though they could pick up on the tension hanging over the farm.

I was glad Bear was with me, loping along at my side with his tongue hanging out, happy for a walk at my side after being banished outside for days. He hadn't been happy with us when we'd first surfaced earlier today, letting us know with loud grumbling.

Damon had sent a note to the treehouse that they were keeping movements to a minimum until further notice and farm security was on high alert, in case of any retaliation for the clusterfuck at the other farm. I think seeing his and Ronan's dad together and the ruthless way they had torched the farmhouse had spooked him. He'd also dropped a radio to Sam so he could keep in contact with his team whenever I let him out of the nest for a break.

It turns out we weren't the only ones getting special treatment the last two days. Since we got back, Isabella had distributed meals around the farm, basic cereal and milk for breakfast, then sandwiches for lunch and simple stew for dinner. To avoid having everyone congregate in one place, that would be easy to target. She had put together a team of teenagers to act as runners, delivering food and messages to keep them occupied and active.

I didn't know if Damon was overreacting or not, but we couldn't operate like this forever. Farms were busy places, and the threat wasn't going away. I didn't really want to go back to the way life was before. It had been a corrupt world. Yet, if we couldn't get the world onto a newer, better path, this would be our reality. Constant threats, never knowing what was coming at us next.

I knew we needed to make some changes if we were going to keep our people safe and make life better for everyone. Nobody outside of our fences seemed willing to step up and do it, so I had a sneaky suspicion it needed to be us. This crazy family we were building had an abundance of strength and compassion. We just needed a direction, and I figured I could help with that.

Damon had sent word again, about ten minutes ago, that a family meeting was being held in the dining hall to let us know what Max had found on the Palace's secret server.

I'd ducked out before the guys were ready to leave, letting them know I wanted to catch up to Maia first. I'd stumbled to a halt on the deck, though, when I noticed an old-fashioned letter box that used to sit by our front gate. It was now perched innocently on the railing next to the stairs, as if it had always been there.

I'd opened it out of curiosity, checking first to make sure there were no mischievous sprites, or teenagers, nearby, playing a trick on me. I now had a letter from Sam tucked into the front pocket of my favorite denim overalls. Reading it made me cry big salty tears, but also plastered a huge smile on my face.

I didn't know when he'd stolen the letterbox and installed it there while I'd had us all holed up for my heat, but I figured no-one would use it up at the gate now, anyway. The postal service didn't appear to work in an apocalypse. Well, except for me, it seemed.

I pulled it out again now as I loitered briefly in the kitchen garden.

Alexia,

So much is happening so fast right now. I just wanted to say I'm so thankful you came into our lives.

I've felt so lost, so full of rage for the unfairness of the world for so many years. Even before my gramps kicked me out, I felt like something was missing. An emptiness I couldn't seem to fill. Maia helped, but when I had to walk away from her, the rage seemed to take over.

Then I met Dio and Pala. They each helped hold the tide at bay in their own ways, but I felt so stretched thin by the constant battle to keep myself from exploding. I had a growing realization that I was slipping closer every day to becoming feral. I kept it from Dio. He was already doing so much. It wasn't a fate I wanted for myself or for him to witness. It would have destroyed us both.

It added to my desperation to reach Maia after the Crash, though. Nobody would tell me where Pala was, and my last hope was that my sister could help turn the tide. I felt a growing draw to come north, like something was pulling me. I thought it was Maia and home. It turns out it was you all along.

The moment I heard your voice, it was as if the entire universe screamed, "Her, she is your salvation," as my alpha beat at his cage to reach you. Knowing someone had hurt you made him crazed. He wanted to burn the world for you. You both enthralled and terrified me.

I watched wordlessly as you challenged me after my alpha slipped his leash momentarily, insisting I back down without an inch of fear or hesitation as you protected the women inside. You were magnificent. You took my breath away. I realized I needed to earn you, never take you. That I needed to be a better man for you. I wanted to be everything you needed, but my fear of finally unleashing my beast kept getting in my way.

I don't know if I've earned you yet, but I will take anything you offer me. I will strive to be worthy of you until the end of my days. You are a gift.

Feeling the bonds of my mates finally anchoring me, settling my spirit. The exquisite feel of you all claiming me, then the relief of claiming Dave. I have no words to express my awe at what you have given me. I wear your bites gladly and proudly.

I feel you in our bond now, a bright spark that glows with joy, vitality and life. I feel how much you burn for the injustices in our world, how much you care for the people you save. I see in the faces of the people around us how much you are loved and respected.

I know that it's too soon for the word love between us, and that's okay. Because the word feels too small for what I feel for you, anyway.

Just know that everything I am, every wild and beastly part of me, is now yours.

Your Sam.

I held his letter to my chest for a moment. He wasn't a man for spoken words, but his letters filled my soul and branded me. I would cherish every one. I was determined to make sure he knew he would never need to carry his burdens alone again, not in the way he had been.

As for me, he made me feel like I was a warrior princess. Like I could do anything, and if I needed it, he would have my back. It was going to take a little subterfuge to enact my next plan, though. I tucked the letter back away and headed for the kitchen door.

I needed to do what I did best, just on a bigger scale.

It was time for a little mayhem.

I was in luck. I let out a breath I didn't know I'd been holding when I saw all four of the women I was looking for huddled around a bench when I came in the back door. They startled when Bear woofed at my side, letting the women know he was ready for a treat. Maia and Ava came rushing straight over while the other two women looked at each other as if they were a little unsure of themselves.

"Bear, go find Dave." I had to push his giant head to get him to move, but he did reluctantly. He knew he wasn't supposed to be in the kitchen. He had a habit of stealing food right off the bench.

Maia barrelled into me, almost knocking me off my feet. She had quickly taken to the whole hugging thing since she arrived here, and embraced our whole community like she'd been born here. She had really opened up too, and was letting the bright, bubbly personality that was under all those layers, shine through.

"We missed girl chat time the other day, then the whole thing happened at my gramps farm and when we got back, the guys had me on lockdown and there was so much freaking sex it was like I was in heat again. Then we heard roaring and Max radioed to say it was just you and Sam and everything was fine, but it didn't sound fine. Then Ava told me you were in heat and it's been days. Oh my freaking god, are you okay?"

Maia gasped as she came to a rambling halt. She was talking fast and waving her arms around everywhere. I think she only stopped to breathe. She wasn't usually much of a talker.

I quirked my eyebrow at her. "How much coffee have you had this morning?"

"Oh, don't you think you can put me off again. I demand a girl chat now." She pointed her finger at me and tried to look menacing. She just looked adorable, with all that gorgeous gold hair in a high, messy bun and those big blue eyes. Like a kitten hissing at you.

She started hunting around, pulling out drawers. "We need to tie her down and make her talk. Do we have any zip ties in here, or even some string?"

I shot a look at Isabella. She was usually the sensible, steadfast one around here. "We're almost out of coffee. I found some espresso. I was trying to filter it down to eke it out more. Maia insisted on trying the first batch. She said she needed her happy juice."

Ava rolled her eyes. "I told her that omegas should never drink espresso. They taught us that at the Palace. It doesn't sit well with our biology. Weak, milky coffee is okay, but strong coffee like espresso over stimulates us. She's going to crash later."

Shit. I really needed Maia today. And a coffee. I didn't want to know what the world looked like without coffee. Taking away our electricity was bad enough, but we would all become savages if there was no coffee.

I walked over to Maia and pulled her into a big hug. "Are you okay, girl? After what happened with your brother and your gramps' farm burning down? That was a lot."

She tensed a little, then relaxed, giving me a big squeeze. "I'm fine. It wasn't pleasant, but I let Ben go a long time ago in a way I never did with Sam. I had to, so I could focus on surviving. I was more worried about Sam going back. Leif rescued my gramps' army medals and uniform for me, and I got my great granny's cookbook. There was nothing else left for me back there. My home is here now. I'm just glad we all made it out safely."

Maia was one tough chick. She had already suffered more heartache and abuse than anyone should have to in a lifetime, yet she had so much grace and an innate kindness within her. I kinda wanted to be her when I grew up.

"Don't distract me." She pulled away and looked at me accusingly. "We're talking about you. It's girl chat time. I will tie you to a chair if I have to. I need to know you're okay."

I'd never really been a fan of group girl chats, and girly bonding activities, preferring to train in my spare time, but Maia clearly was and I was a fan of Maia's.

"Oh, we're going to have a girl chat. Just not in the way you think." I rubbed my hands together. "I promise, I'm fine, and I'll give you all the sexy details later. Right now, are you girls up for some anarchy and a little ass kicking?"

Maia jumped up and down with her hand in the air. "Oh, me. Me. I'm up for ass kicking." Ava smiled at her affectionately then shot me a cryptic look that made me think the girl had hidden layers. "Sounds like we're in. Whose ass are we kicking?"

"I have a plan to help the town and clear it of Palace alphas, but we don't have much time."

Maia's face lit up. "Oh, hell yeah. I'm in."

I looked at Sirena and Isabella. They both looked skeptical. "Won't the guys come up with a plan?" Sirena asked.

"Oh, you did not just say that to me, Sirena. I heard what you did when we were under attack. Did you sit back and wait for the guys to figure out a plan, then?"

Sirena shook her head tentatively, and I powered on.

"I don't know what Max has found and if it will change our plan to clean out the town at all." I shot a look at Maia and she shrugged.

"I don't know. I don't think it's anything urgent or he would have told Damon straight away. It's more like he only wants to say it once. He seems sad, and angry, but not anxious."

"Okay. I know Damon listens to you, Maia, but I have a feeling they're going to try to keep us out of this one. Especially Damon. After your gramps' farm, his protective instincts are in overdrive. He forgets sometimes that we're a community and they don't have to take all the risk on themselves. They do so much to protect us all, but this time, I truly believe we can help make this less risky for them, as well as our friends and family in town."

Isabella straightened her spine and seemed to mentally shake herself. "What's your plan? I'll follow you anywhere, Lex."

My heart almost exploded on the spot at her complete trust in me, even after I'd kept her at arm's length for years. I reached over to Isabella and pulled her into a hug, too. My need for touch seemed to be heightened, maybe for good, and I wasn't holding back anymore.

"Have I ever thanked you for all the ways you've stepped up to help since you got here?"

"You don't have to thank me, Lex. I owe you my life twice. You saved my life, then you gave me an even better one."

"You owe me nothing, babe. I just helped show you a way out. You took it and did all the hard work. You saved yourself."

Maia jumped in and threw her arms around us, followed by Ava and Sirena. "You guys rock," she mumbled into Isabella's back. We all stood in solidarity for a moment, remembering our own strength, before I disentangled us.

"We don't know what this meeting is going to involve, but I want to get everyone on board so that we can swing into action as soon as we're good to go. Tonight. Spreading the word will be up to Isabella and Sirena, while Maia, Ava, and I are in this family meeting. Are you both okay with that?"

"You can count on us, Lex." Isabella looked resolved and Sirena subtly shifted to stand closer to her.

"Okay then. Here's the plan. "

Forty

I proudly strolled into the dining hall for the family meeting, leading my mates through the main entry door while feeling their bonds bright and glowing in my chest. Damon, Max, Leif, and Hunter were already there, their serious expressions giving me a momentary pause. Cary was there too, quietly chatting to Hunter, looking more comfortable than he had in the past.

They had a portable speaker on the table and it was playing music quietly, but nobody seemed to pay attention to it. The music seemed like an anomaly. This wasn't a social gathering. It was also a waste of electricity, which was unlike the guys. It made me uneasy. Something was up.

I searched our bond and sensed Lexie nearby. She felt like she was up to something, but I didn't know what. She'd left before us, saying she needed to talk to Maia first and to start without her if she wasn't there in time. Dave had tried to go with her, but she'd stared him down, eyebrow raised, until he'd backed off. Sam had been in the shower.

I could feel Dave's disquiet in the bond, at not knowing what she was up to. I figured at least a few of his gray hairs were because of Lexie.

"Where's Lexie?" Leif demanded immediately, looking at Dave.

"She left before us. She wanted to talk to Maia first." Leif didn't seem happy with Dave's reply, eyeing him and the casual way he settled himself next to me at the table.

"Maia's in the kitchen, with Ava, Isabella and Sirena. She headed up before us too, saying something about coffee, fake chocolate chips and girl chat." Leif flicked his eyes to Sam as he talked, narrowing them. "That was a hell of a lot of roaring the other night, sounded like your beast went into rut. Is Lex okay?"

"She deliberately provoked my beast. Nothing happened that Lex didn't want or orchestrate," Sam said.

Leif just grunted at Sam before he flicked his hard gaze back to Dave and a slow smile spread over his face.

"Looks like she orchestrated a lot," Damon growled, looking at Dave as well and eyeing the still raw bite mark edging above the neck of his t-shirt.

"Lexie doesn't hold back when she decides she wants something. Full disclosure, though. We all claimed Dave, including Lexie," I replied.

There were shocked faces and sharp inhales all around the table opposite us. I glanced at Dave and he had a huge, smug grin on his face. He looked relaxed, no more tension riding him or secrets holding him back, as if he knew he was exactly where he was meant to be.

"All of you?" Max asked as he sat forward. All of his mates turned to him with concern and he glanced at them all briefly. "I'm not asking for that. Hell, I'm not even sure what it means. I'm just curious."

Hunter smirked at us all. "Yeah, we're all curious."

"I'm not fucking anyone but Lexie, Hunter." Hunter just laughed at Dave's gruff declaration.

"When Lexie mated Sam, his dominance flowed between her and her mates, but it felt unsettled, almost agitated. It needed a center, an anchor and couldn't find it. Lexie unconsciously chose Dave a long time ago, but we needed him to step up quickly, and he did. Our alphas were all on board. Lexie chose him as a mate, but we chose him as a brother and solidified our bonds all at once," I said, speaking honestly and plainly. We had nothing to hide from these men.

"Interesting," Max murmured, his forehead furrowed. Cary was looking at us all, seeming intrigued as well.

"We're all thrilled for you, man." Hunter dropped his cocky attitude for a moment. He got up and came around the table to give Dave a hug.

Leif and the others followed him. Even Cary got up and shook Dave's hand, appearing genuinely happy for him.

"You always felt like family, Dave. Now we know why." Leif seemed delighted as he hugged Dave last, before he turned to Sam with a faux stern glare. "Welcome to the family, too, Sam. Just don't pull that rut shit again. You almost gave me a heart attack. Maia had to sit on me to stop me from coming after you."

"Like you minded, considering she was naked." Hunter had to dodge as Sam reached past Leif to punch him playfully on the arm.

"We're going to need to work out some boundaries about naked talk," Sam huffed, glaring at Hunter.

"Agreed." Leif nodded his head vigorously, standing between them. "That goes both ways."

We all settled back into our seats, but the camaraderie of the moment quickly dissipated as all eyes turned to Max.

"Lexie said to start without her, but we'd rather she be here," I said into the silence. I knew these guys had a lot of respect for Lexie and didn't think they would mind waiting for her, but Damon had us all stunned when he growled low and put us all in our place.

"There's no way we're getting into this without Lexie. She's part owner of this farm and has a say in any decisions we make."

"She's what?" Sam blurted out. I automatically grabbed his shoulder out of habit. Yet despite Sam's surprise, his dominance remained calm.

"She didn't tell you?" Leif asked. He looked perplexed.

I was really fucking confused right now. "We thought Damon owned the farm. Didn't he inherit it from his grandfather?"

Leif looked at Damon, who had a small smile on his face that he was trying to hide as he rubbed his jaw. I figured he wanted us to know Lexie was financially independent. A holdover from a time pre-Crash, when money still mattered.

"Damon divided up the farm when he inherited it," Leif explained. "Even the original workers hold shares now, but the five of us together form a majority stake."

Wow. Color me impressed. It was a rare man who took a windfall inheritance and divided it up amongst his friends and workers.

Damon looked embarrassed now that we were all looking at him in awe and was eyeing the table as if there was something fascinating written on it.

Even Cary looked astonished, and was studying Damon as if he was a strange creature he'd never come across before.

Max sighed heavily. "Enough of the family drama. We need Lexie, Maia and Ava. This concerns all of them."

His words sent an icy chill skittering along my skin that seemed to settle around my heart. The thought of Lexie in danger terrified me. I remembered the sharp looks on the faces of Damon and Ronan's fathers as they watched us disappear. Knowing they wanted my omega had a growl forming in my throat.

"I'll get them." Cary jumped up as he volunteered. He'd barely taken a step before the door opened and Lexie sauntered through. "No need, we're here." Maia and Ava were hot on her heels.

Maia patted Dave on the shoulder as she passed, eyeing his neck. "You're off my shit list, just so you know."

I winked at him in solidarity and he tried not to grin.

"Why is everyone suddenly freaking out in here?" Maia added, "I can feel you all in the bond. What did we miss?"

"Nothing, sunshine." Leif grabbed Maia as she rounded the table and pulled her into his giant lap. She didn't look as if she objected, leaning into him and running her nose along his neck, scenting him gently. All her guys relaxed as soon as one of them had her in their arms. I knew the feeling.

Sam beat me to it as he pulled Lexie into his lap. She kissed him lightly.

"Did you meet my two new pack mates, Leif?" Leif grumbled at her affectionately and she turned her face into Sam's shoulder as she smiled.

I noticed Ava's gaze flick to Lexie with a wistful expression on her face.

"Max, the girls are here now. What did you find?" I could hear the frustration and impatience in Damon's voice, which surprised me. I'd figured Max would have at least told Damon what he'd found.

I took a closer look at Max and realized his eyes were faintly red and slightly glassy, probably from staring at computer screens for too long, and he had dark circles under them. He looked exhausted, as if he hadn't slept at all.

"The Crash wasn't an accident. It was deliberate."

He let the words hang in the air for a moment.

"How?" Sam ground out like he was promising death to whoever was involved.

Max sighed, like he didn't want to be the one to utter the words out loud. He was playing with an empty water cup, rolling it under his fingers.

I could feel my whole body tensing. I reached out to Sam to grab his shoulder. Not to comfort him this time. The motion comforted me, born of years of habit. I figured this wouldn't be a quick story.

"The deposits of coal and gas we mine and burn to create electricity have been losing their combustibility for a while. The deeper they dug and siphoned, the more concentrated and compacted the resources have been getting, changing their chemical make-up. They've already mined all the burnable top level coal and gas. They've increased their mining outputs for years, with consistently less flammable fuel.

"The government is so embedded with the mining companies they wouldn't or couldn't turn against them. They argued that overhauling the entire electricity grid to use solely renewable energy was too costly to even consider.

"I've gone back a long way in their communications. At first, it appeared the mining companies were arrogant, assuming they could find more shallow deposits. They found a few, but nowhere near enough. They finally figured out that at some point the deposits would become so compacted, they would stop working all together, no matter how much they burned."

Max shook his head, and a disgusted look crossed his face. He'd been staring at his hands as he talked, but he looked up now. I was directly across from him, and I could see the haunted look in his eyes.

"That's when they involved the military, so they could prepare for a worst-case scenario. The military recommended the government keep it quiet so as not to panic people unnecessarily.

"By the time the government finally accepted they would have to look at grid-wide renewable sources of power, a private group that advised the government had developed an alternate idea they pushed. Fear about the declining birth rates of omegas and what it will mean for alphas in the future has been building for a while. Even though the fuckers in power have created that problem by banning packs and creating a culture of dominating omegas. All they care about is their own power. They worry that if our numbers dwindle further, betas will take over and there won't be enough of us left to stop them. Their records show alphas now make up only about ten percent of the population. Omegas even less."

A few muffled curses popped out around the table. We'd all suspected, but nobody had ever heard it put as bluntly as that, or the statistics. I didn't care about power, but I worried about the future of our children, if we ever had any. I could feel the others felt the same.

Max continued on, ignoring us. I suspected he was determined to get his story out now that he'd started. "So they stockpiled renewable energy systems, solar panels, wind turbines, batteries, and limited what was commercially available. Making it too expensive for the average person. They wanted the Crash to wipe out a large proportion of the beta population. They called it a controlled apocalypse. Like you can control a fucking apocalypse. They planned to let it run for a few months before they would swoop in and save whoever survived. Stabilizing power and making a lot of money with their renewable solutions."

"Those fuckers," Hunter swore loudly as he jumped up and paced behind the table in agitation. As if his outburst had popped a bubble, everyone suddenly started talking at once, throwing questions at Max and exclaiming loudly. I could feel a deep growl thrumming through Sam's chest, although he was trying to swallow it down. Lexie was eyeing off the knives on the table as if she was about to throw them.

"Quiet." Damon's slight bark had us all stilling. It was only a hint of his power, just enough to get our attention, but it was still unnerving. Cary and Ava both went rigid, though, and Damon quickly apologized.

His frown was still formidable as he turned to Max. "You have proof?"

"Reams of it I've copied onto our own server. I've also made two back-up copies, one in the cloud and another physical copy I've hidden. I made sure I did it before I spoke a word about it to anyone."

"You think they're listening in on us somehow?" Damon's tone was dangerous.

"I don't think so, given their current state of disarray, but I can't rule it out. I was just being cautious."

Well, that explained the speaker on the table and the music playing.

Leif reached out to squeeze Max's shoulder, much the same way I had to Sam. "It's not your fault, Max."

"Isn't it? I knew something was off with the military. I should have looked harder when I first found the firewalls and figured they were hiding something big. At the time, I was just so relieved we were all out, and I never imagined anyone would do something so horrific on this kind of scale."

Dave leaned forward as if he wanted to reach for Max, too. "You're brilliant at what you do, Max, but you're not omnipotent. There was no way you could have guessed at this. I was higher in the ranks than any of you, and I didn't even hear a whisper."

My mind was working overtime, and both Sam and Pala turned to me. I had always been the strategist of our group. "Why are the military and government in disarray if they planned this?"

"The only thing I couldn't find was a date, or any defined timeline. Everything talked about future scenarios. The Crash appeared to happen when one part of the grid went down unexpectedly and it caused a fatal overload in the surrounding grids.

"They're all connected, and it was a chain reaction from that point that brought down the whole damn system. It's a massive design fault. I'm surprised it existed, but they haven't updated our power infrastructure in a really long time, despite our advances in technology.

"As far as I can figure, either the mining and electrical grid execs were lying to the government about how bad it had gotten, or it happened much quicker than anyone expected. Or maybe they're all just incompetent and fucking with things they don't understand because it will make them money and they don't give a shit about anyone but themselves."

Max growled and pushed back from the table as if he was going to take off, but there was nowhere to go. None of us could run from this or hide from it.

Maia stood up and hugged him, anchoring him in place. "We're here, Max. Right here with you. Just breathe."

"You don't understand," he said, although he gripped her tightly. "We haven't seen the worst of it out here. They have patchy reports coming in from other secret facilities the military has used to bunker down. The cities are a mess with looting and rioting. People were dying before the food even ran out. Mobs overran military installations, thinking they'd have supplies.

"There were good men among the lower ranks of the military, many we worked alongside. They were mostly left behind to guard bases when it all went to hell and senior officers fled to bunkers. The mobs slaughtered some. Others are hanging on, trying to keep sophisticated weaponry out of the hands of the mobs. It all fell apart so quickly. Our society collapsed as if it was made of tissue paper this whole time. It's fucking anarchy out there."

Sam and I shared a look, feeling guilty. We'd brought our team with us and they were safe here. Many weren't so lucky. I understood, though, why Max had wanted to only say this once. I couldn't imagine having to repeat this shit.

I hated to push him, but I had more questions. Sam nodded at me, happy to let me take the lead. "What has the Palace got to do with the military, apart from being a place to hide? If they have a secure line and all this info, clearly they've been involved all along."

"The shady as fuck group I mentioned before," Max dragged his hands through his already messy hair. "I'm pretty sure they fund the Palace operation, including all the testing on omegas. They seem to use it as their base and point of contact. It's the perfect cover.

"They had a lot of files going back a long time, alongside some nasty evidence on government and military officials. I'm pretty sure they were blackmailing a bunch of people to do what they wanted, and had others planted within the government and military.

"From what I can tell, they promised the Palace a military guard whenever this went down and they made contact to ensure it happened. I think they've actually been in control behind the scenes for a long time."

"What do they call themselves?" Damon asked with deceptive calm, but his eyes were blazing hotly and his fists were clenched on the table, as if he was about to flip it.

"Oracle Consulting Group is the formal front they use when they advise the government, but in all the behind-the-scenes stuff, the name Maven keeps coming up."

Max winced as Damon paled and his dominance spiked violently. Max released Maia and reached for him instinctively before he'd even finished talking.

"Your father?" Sam looked like he wasn't far behind. His dominance was pushing at the air around us.

Damon nodded tersely. "He's a founding member of OCG and I've heard the name Maven used before, but only in whispers. I thought it was some kind of kinky gentleman's club."

"I wasn't sure." Max looked fierce as he gripped Damon around the neck. "They all use one word code names. One thing I am sure of, though, is you are nothing like your father."

"Damn right," Hunter growled.

"I heard the word Maven whispered once, but they shut up quickly when they noticed me hanging around nearby," Pala said, dragging all the attention in the room to him. He shifted as though he was uncomfortable under the spotlight. "It was the main scientist who ran the lab underneath the Palace talking to one of his team."

"Are the code names you found, Mike, Alfa, Victor, Echo and November?" Everyone turned to look at Sam now, heads moving with the conversation as if we were all at a tennis match. One with a lot of frowning faces.

"Yes." Max looked shocked as he nodded.

"My gramps left me a letter with the communication equipment we took from the farm."

What letter? Why hadn't Sam told me, and where the hell had he been hiding it since we got back?

Lexie, Pala, and Dave all looked at me, but I could only shrug. It wasn't like Sam to keep anything from me.

"My gramps said to beware the Mavens. He had been trying to track them and take them down, without success. Gramps suspected they had recruited my brother Ben and worried it would compromise his cover. He shut down his equipment so Ben couldn't find or use it. He dated the letter the day before he died and they took Maia."

Fuck. Sam and Maia shared a look that was laden with grief, but I think it was more for their gramps than their brother.

Sam turned to us, tearing his gaze from Maia. "I only just read it before we came down. I'm sorry I didn't tell you guys about the letter, but so much was happening when I found it and when we got back. Part of me was half afraid to read it, too. I had no idea what was going to be in it."

He'd gone out to shower alone before we left earlier and we'd all felt a surge of emotion from him. We'd figured he just wanted a few minutes alone to grieve quietly.

"You don't have to report everything to us. That's not how a pack works. If you want to read a personal letter by yourself, there's nothing wrong with that. We're here to support you," Lexie said as she ran her fingers through his hair, before she took his face in her hands and kissed him gently. He tightened his grip on her as if he was worried she'd disappear suddenly.

"Did your gramps know who the members were, Sam?" Max asked.

Sam nodded, resting his head on Lexie's shoulder and closing his eyes for a moment, as if he was steeling himself for what he was about to say. It put everyone on edge.

He grit his teeth, and Lexie gently stroked his back. "Rohan & Sirena's dad, the CEO of Alpha Tech, the CEO of Integral Mining, and," he paused there for the briefest moment and his eyes flicked across the table, "Hunter's dad."

"What the fuck?" Hunter growled. "My parents never gave a shit about me, almost turned me into a ghost. Now you're telling me they're part of some super shady, underground corporation that controls everything?"

He shook his head almost violently before he stopped abruptly and slumped slightly. "Actually, that kinda fits. They're psychopaths, completely unable to care about other people."

Maia leaned into Hunter from where she was back perched on Leif's lap, wrapping Hunter up in her arms. He took a deep breath of her hair, while Leif wrapped them both in a bear hug. This place and all the hugs. They were growing on me. I felt like I'd finally found the place I belonged, just as the world had gone to hell.

Sam was watching Hunter with an almost curious expression on his face, which had me puzzled.

"What about Damon's dad?" Max asked.

"It sounds like he's not part of the inner circle. It explains why he was so keen to promote Damon's friendship with Hunter when they were young," Maia said.

"But they never really socialized with each other, or Damon's dad," Hunter said, almost absently, his face still buried in Maia's hair. He looked confused.

"That fits too, doesn't it?" I argued, thinking out loud.

"You're right, it does. If the shadow group were using Damon's dad as the front man with the government consulting contract, they wouldn't draw attention to themselves by associating with him publicly." Max had a frenetic, yet glazed, look in his eyes as he spoke, as if he was building connections in his head.

"That's only four names, though, Sam. Who was the fifth? Did the letter say?"

"Nothing gets past you, Dio." Sam looked across at me with a sad smile. "Our gramps was the fifth," he added, almost bluntly as he shifted his gaze to stare at Maia. She gasped and spun around to face him fully, dropping her arms from around Hunter.

"No. He couldn't be. He was a beta and they're all alphas. Why would they include him in their secret squirrel crap?"

"Holy shit," I breathed out and slapped my hand on the table, startling everyone.

"What are we missing?" Max asked, frustration lacing his voice before his eyes widened dramatically and his gaze shot between me and Sam. "No fucking way."

"Somebody spit it out," Damon growled, sounding like he was about to explode.

All the alpha pheromones spiking in the room were making my head spin. I was suddenly glad we were in a big open space, not a cramped meeting room somewhere.

"They're a secret pack, and one of them is likely a prime alpha," Pala answered gently, getting right to the point, as usual, with his soothing manner. It usually calmed people down. It didn't work this time.

"Oh my god," Maia gasped loudly. She was breathing heavily, as if she was about to hyperventilate. "He was their center. But why would he leave and then try to take them down?"

"Because he loved their omega, and they broke her," Sam whispered.

Maia looked green suddenly and bolted for the bathroom with her hand over her mouth. Lexie jumped up and followed her.

"It's the espresso she drank. It doesn't agree with omega biology, she'll be fine. If not, I'll come get you," Ava said as she got up to follow, closely followed by Lexie, gesturing to Maia's mates to stay where they were. "She won't want you to see her if she vomits. We've got her."

"I don't care what she looks like when she vomits. If she needs one of us, I will break down that door," Damon growled. Ava just waved her hand over her shoulder, like she'd heard alpha threats before and was unbothered.

"I remember Maia telling us when we first met that she thought her gramps loved an omega once, and alphas mistreated her. She thought maybe that was why he hated alphas and sent you away." Max was watching Sam closely.

Sam looked surprised. "So it said in his letter. I had no idea. Maia was always more perceptive about people than I was. That wasn't why he sent me away, though."

"There's more in the letter?" Damon asked. It wasn't really a question, judging from his tone of voice.

"Yes, but it's personal, and I'd rather Maia read it before I share it with everyone."

Damon gave Sam a brusque nod, respecting his privacy. The guys all threw questions at Max for a few minutes, which he tried to answer, but he knew little more than what he'd already told us. I wasn't really paying attention, though. My mind was racing, working out implications for our pack.

"This is all very enlightening, but what does this mean for us? Right now." Dave's gruff, commanding voice jolted me out of my thoughts. Everyone turned to look at him, most of them frowning.

"Right now, nothing," Damon said, "But we don't want to make a wrong move because we didn't know something important. Missing intel always trips you up in the field. You know this, Dave."

"I do, but this is all big picture stuff. We knew there was more to the Crash than we understood. Knowing the cause is important, but we can't do anything about any of that right now. So does it change what our plans were for today? Cleaning out the town?"

Damon's eyebrows almost jumped clear off his head. "We said we would clear out the town, but I don't recall agreeing it would happen today."

Maia, Lexie and Ava chose that moment to walk back through the bathroom door. Maia still looked a little green, and Leif sprinted across the room to pick her up before she'd even fully made it through the door.

"I'm okay, big guy." She patted him on the arm as she reassured him, but he didn't seem convinced. "You smell funky."

"Thanks," she said dryly and swatted him. "I need some mouthwash."

"Not like that, just different. I thought I noticed it before, but it's stronger now."

Maia just huffed at him and rolled her eyes. "I can walk, you know."

"I know," he replied easily as he made it back to his chair and settled her back in his lap. He didn't look like he was letting her go anytime soon. "I can also carry you."

Dave and Damon continued their debate about timeframes for clearing out the town, quizzed Pala on what his surveillance had revealed, and asked Cary questions about what he had observed at the Palace. I noticed Maia glance at Lexie, who was hovering and hadn't sat back down. Lexie suddenly interrupted Damon mid sentence. "I'm going to grab Maia a cold drink. Does anyone else want anything?"

Before anyone could really say anything, she answered her own question. "I'll just bring some jugs of juice. Ava, do you want to give me a hand?"

Ava jumped up quickly, and they disappeared through the swinging doors. I felt for Lexie in our bond, sensing something was up with her. She seemed frustrated but was trying to swallow it down and project a calm manner.

The discussion still going on around the table distracted Sam and Pala, as Pala continued answering questions and Sam jumped in with his opinion on what we should do. But Dave was watching the kitchen doorway now, almost as intently as I was. Cary had diverted his focus as well, watching the door the girls had disappeared through with obvious suspicion.

"I think Lexie's up to something," I leaned over and whispered to Dave.

"Oh, she is definitely up to something," he replied with a frown. He glanced at Maia, who gave him a fake innocent smile.

I had a feeling, whatever it was; the women were all in on it and it was going to be big. Lexie did nothing by halves.

Forty-One

I pushed my way back through the swinging door, with Ava, Sirena, and Isabella in tow. The guys were still debating and discussing our next steps and how quickly we should move. The two packs seemed to work well together in an emergency, but right now there were too many alphas and too many opinions. Someone needed to take charge.

I was happy to be that person.

"I'm going tonight." I announced loudly into the fray as I surveyed my guys, ignoring Damon and his mates for the moment. Dave frowned, Dio smiled broadly, Pala nodded, and Sam narrowed his eyes. I winked at them.

"Do you have a plan?" Damon asked, dragging my attention back to him as he watched me evenly.

"Sure do." I said, as I planted my hands on my hips. I knew when dealing with alphas, if you appeared confident, you'd won half the battle.

"I need to get the women out of the safe house tonight. They've been there too long with no fresh air and only a limited supply of food. Re-stocking them isn't an option. Making too many trips into town while the Palace alphas have a base there is risky for everyone. We're trailing a lot of scents through the town and they're going to suspect something is up. We don't want to wait until they ask for reinforcements.

"So it makes sense to clear the town tonight as well. From what Pala has told us, they're using the pub as their base and that is smack bang in the center of town. You're right that there are a lot of variables, including the possibility of hostages if they see us coming, but if we remove the risk to the residents, it becomes much simpler."

"How?" Sam asked. He didn't look angry, to my relief. Just intrigued.

"We go in quietly as soon as it gets dark and we go door to door. We move everyone to the museum. It's old and solid stone. So it's easily defensible if things go pear-shaped. Then we take out any guards or patrols, surround the pub and you guys do your thing to take out the alphas inside. The ones drinking like they're invincible and the apocalypse is just an opportunity to be even bigger asshats."

"We don't have the numbers to protect the farm, round up the residents and guard them, then surround the pub." Damon was listening at least, which was a start.

"We do. For starters, we have the half dozen alphas who stayed behind when the others escaped."

"We don't know if we can trust them. What if they betray us?"

I rolled my eyes. "They won't. I have a strong sense about people. It's what helped me spot abusers all these years, even before there was any evidence. Plus, you wouldn't have let them stay if you thought they'd betray us. Not with Maia, Ava, and Cary wandering around."

"She's right," Dio piped up. "I've spoken to the ones who stayed behind and they don't want to go back to the Palace. They want to help. They know that if they have a shot of staying here, they're going to have to earn it."

"There still may not be enough of us to take the town, not if we're going door to door," Damon said.

"You forget, Damon, that we're not the only ones here with family and friends in town. You also underestimate how badly people want to help," I replied.

"I'm not putting the men and women here in danger," Damon growled.

"It's not your choice to make, Damon. Are you going to deny someone the chance to help their loved ones if it's in their power to do so? Or even the right to fight for their own ideals if they want to?"

Damon was quiet. He didn't have a good answer. I could see his brain searching for one and coming up empty.

"Besides, we won't have them running around recklessly and unpro-tected. We'll need to divvy up all of our alphas and military trained personnel into four groups, then we'll have the Honey Badgers team, made up of anyone from the farm who has volunteered. That's the code name they've given themselves, by the way. So far, we have about twenty Honey Badgers made up of adults and older teenagers. They'll be the ones gathering people."

"Honey badgers," Hunter laughed, "man, those things are lethal. I saw a video of one a few weeks ago. It had a guy bailed up in a chicken coop. They're small but feisty. They'll take on anything, even a lion."

I shot Hunter a small, grateful smile, silently thanking him for breaking the tension.

"Unless you have a better idea, my plan is that the first, smallest group, stays here and protects the farm, just in case. All the kids have already been told they're having a movie night in the cave and they're all excited. Nick is setting up a projector for them and they're all taking in mattresses and pillows.

"The elderly and anyone else who is staying will bunk down in the guest houses closest to the cave until we get back, so everyone is in one spot in case anything goes wrong here. Everyone's packed and ready. They also know where to head if they have to evacuate for any reason.

"The second and third group will cover the north and south approaches to town. They'll nominate a few members to guard the approach and the rest will form mobile squads, finding any enemy patrols, watching them closely, keeping the Honey Badgers team clear and coming to their aid if needed.

"We've given the Honey Badgers personal alarms, emergency lights and flares, and they've been shown how to use them. Some of them also have night vision goggles. They've mapped out a grid of areas they know, based on where their loved ones live, so it will be familiar faces gathering the residents.

"We've worked out a signal system if anyone gets into trouble, so the mobile squads can get to them quickly. If that happens, everyone else knows to fall back towards a safe space. Once the town is cleared, the fourth team will drive into town in the MPV while the second and third mobile teams immobilize the guards and surround the pub.

"Any questions?"

There was complete silence. Which made me worry I had messed up majorly somehow, overlooked an important detail maybe. Everyone here knew I wasn't military trained, and I wasn't pretending to be. I was just working on my knowledge of what we had at hand and what seemed to me would work. I was determined that this would happen tonight, so I'd thought of every angle I could.

I flashed a quick glance to my mates. Dave gave me a subtle thumbs up, but Sam, Dio and Pala all had intent expressions I couldn't read. There were too many emotions swirling in our bond to filter them, but I was picking up a lot of heat. "I think you broke your guys, Lex," Hunter chuckled. I shot him a dirty look this time, and he just smirked.

"We're with you, my heart, always," Pala said quietly. Dio murmured his agreement.

"I think I've more than proved I'll follow you anywhere, Lex," Dave added.

Sam's scent was filling the room powerfully, with whiskey accenting the leather and oak, but I could never tell if that meant he was angry or aroused. He was watching me with a consuming, possessive air, not saying a word. His dominance reached out and encircled me. It felt like light strokes all over my skin, and the pull I always felt towards him intensified, but I resisted it. I don't think he consciously realized he was doing it.

"You've been busy this afternoon, it seems." I glanced at Damon as he spoke, distracting me from Sam, but he was looking at Sirena and Isabella, not at me.

"We sure have," Isabella answered confidently. Sirena was looking any-where but at Damon, which was understandable, given their history. "We're all in, too."

"Where did you get all the personal alarms, flares and stuff?" Dio asked, a little gruffly. His hand was twitching as if he wanted to reach for me, but was holding back. Letting me stand strong and have my moment.

I shifted on my feet, sneaking a glance at my brother.

"I have a shipping container. I stock it with stuff I think escaping women might need."

"Hot damn. I knew your container had more stuff in it than baby clothes and toiletries. You sneaky shit," Hunter said.

"She pulled night vision goggles out of there the other night," Leif said calmly with a small, proud smile on his face.

Dio laughed suddenly as he shook his head. "Of course you have a secret stash of cool military shit. Do you have weapons in there too?"

"No, I rarely use weapons. Oh, except for the nunchucks and throwing stars." I bit my lip, trying not to smile. I wanted to keep them guessing about me. A woman needed to keep some mystery about her in a new relationship. Or relationships. Pala looked intrigued.

"So what's the verdict? Are you guys with me?"

"We're in," Sam growled, staring down Damon. They were the first words he'd said, and they sounded like he had forced them out over rocks. I knew he had trouble communicating when his emotions were running high. Yet he'd uttered them to back me up.

I walked towards him and slid my hands from his shoulders down to his chest. He claimed one of my hands and pushed it harder into his skin, as he rested his head back against my chest. I could feel the intensity coming off him in waves, and a dark satisfaction at my touch.

"It's a solid plan, Lex," Damon grumbled, a little reluctant still. He looked at Maia.

"Oh, I'm in. You guys can come, if you want. Or you can stay here. It's up to you." Maia let out an enormous yawn as she spoke, that espresso high wearing off now that she'd gotten it all out of her system. "I just need to have a nap first."

"We're all in, too," Damon growled, while he narrowed his eyes at Maia. She was so getting spanked for that later. She blushed as if she knew it, too. The little minx. "Max will do satellite recon this afternoon, though. And his drone will go in before anyone else, just to be sure. If anything unexpected shows up, we're calling it off. Deal?"

"Deal." I let out a breath I hadn't realized I'd been holding before Sam turned his head up to meet my eyes and I gulped. The intensity of his stare was at DEFCON 3.

A low growl started up in his chest and a powerful surge of desire hit me through the bond, cutting through everything else. I had the sudden feeling a spanking might be in my immediate future, too. My omega perked up at the idea.

I grinned wickedly at him. If Sam wanted me to submit, though, he was going to have to work for it.

He was also going to have to wait. I had a town to take back.

Forty-Two

The full moon was glowing over the town, washing everything in silver. It was a blessing and a curse. It helped the Honey Badgers move around, but it also exposed them to enemy eyes.

I was glad Maia was safely back on the farm, asleep in the security cabin with Max. He'd convinced her to have a quick nap on the couch earlier to sleep off the effects of the espresso. They'd tried to rouse her when it was time to bug out, but she'd been out to it like a one drink wonder after a ten drink bender. She was going to be pissed when she woke up and realized she missed all the action.

Her alpha mates had been strangely hesitant to leave her there. I would have thought they'd be relieved not to have her out here in enemy territory. Yet Max had all but kicked them out of the security office and they'd all been scowling darkly ever since. Everyone was keeping a wide berth from them.

I knew they were acting strange because Lexie was out here somewhere, alongside Ava and Cary, and I would prefer her ensconced in the relative safety of the farm. But all three omegas had flat out refused to stay behind. I don't know who the hell decided omegas were supposed to be submissive. The four I knew definitely weren't.

Knowing Lexie was out there slipping through the darkness kept my beast on edge. It didn't help that the Palace alphas who had stayed behind at the farm after the attack were out here too. I knew they were helping us and I trusted that Damon and Pala had vetted them. Yet, it still had my beast simmering just under the surface of my skin.

I was newly mated and on edge. I'd covered Lexie in my scent before she left, like an animal, knowing other alphas would be out here. I pretended I was just hugging her. In reality, I'd rubbed myself all over her while my beast had growled.

Lexie had rolled her eyes, but she'd also been smiling, so I don't think she'd minded. She seemed to like my beast, which shocked the hell out of me.

I knew Lexie wasn't alone. Pala was with her and I trusted him with her life, but it didn't make it easier for me right now. Waiting not very patiently at the south checkpoint on the edge of town while Lexie was in the center of the action. My beast wanted to be with her, too. She was his to protect, even if she belonged to the others as well.

It also didn't help that I'd had an epic hard-on since Lexie stood up to Damon earlier. It had taken everything in me not to pick her up, throw her over my shoulder and find the closest private wall to fuck her against. Even the thought of it now had my dick throbbing. I willed it down, trying to distract myself.

"Are you okay, there?" I glanced across and noticed my third-in-command, Matt, eyeing off the tent in my dark pants dubiously. "The prospect of battle never usually turned you on quite this much."

"Shut up," I groaned. "Just wait until you find your omega."

"Lexie's not even here right now."

"Doesn't matter. I just have to think about her or smell something that reminds me of her. Thank fuck there's no passionfruit or meringue out here."

He sniggered at me, clearly not done yet. "Will you be able to run with that tent pole in the way if we have to move quickly?"

I groaned. *Fucking hell. Think un-Lexie thoughts. Fruit and sweaty balls. No, not fruit or balls. Both made me think of Lexie's mouth. Shit.*

My satellite phone vibrated against my hip and interrupted my thoughts. I looked at the number, it was the guys I still had on surveillance outside the Palace. A dark sense of foreboding hit me like a wave of ice cold water.

"Talk to me." I bared my teeth, wanting to snarl at something, but held back.

"Just picked up chatter. There's a lot of it. Something strange is going on here. You have incoming about to head your way. I don't think they're responding to an alert, or know you're there. They're transporting someone. A prisoner, I think. I don't know who. But they're heading to town to pick someone else up on the way."

My beast thrummed, needing only one thing. Get to Lexie. But I had a lot of people here relying on me.

"Got it. Let me know when they're on the move."

"Uh, that would be now. They just came out. Moving fast. They definitely have a prisoner. Some huge guy in chains. He's stumbling, looks sedated. They've put him in the back of a humvee. I don't think they want to mess around in the open. I'd say you have fifteen minutes. Do you want us to intercept?"

"How many with him and does the humvee have a gun turret?"

"Three alphas. Highly trained from the way they move. No gun turret."

"Stand down and keep watch. Let me know if anyone follows." Three alphas in a humvee were too much for the two guys I had on watch. Plus, it would leave us blind if anyone followed them.

I set a fifteen minute timer on my watch and called Dave on his satellite phone and let him know he had company coming. He was with Damon and the team guarding the road on the north side of town. We'd all deferred to him to plan this mission, given the respect everyone had for him. Even my guys. We'd never worked with him before, but we all knew him by reputation.

It also made sense. Damon and I were both newly mated prime alphas, although I hadn't really gotten my head around the prime alpha thing yet. I'd been putting off thinking about it. It made us both potentially volatile, though, and nobody knew how we would react if anyone threatened one of our mates. We needed someone with a cool head overseeing things.

Dave downplayed his experience and position in the military when he talked to Lexie, but he had been a brilliant and highly capable commander. He'd taken Lexie's ideas, refined them slightly, and put us all in positions that worked to our strengths.

"Roger that." Dave's voice was terse. He wasn't happy with the news, but he wouldn't mess around asking questions right now. He'd step up and do whatever needed to be done to get everyone out of this alive.

He paused for a beat, considering our options. I could hear Damon growling faintly in the background. "Okay. The North team will intercept the humvee. Shit will go down fast as soon as they do. Damon will signal as they strike. Before he does, mobile teams will need to take out the guards and be in position to take out the pub on your secondary go signal.

"The PMV will enter town on your signal. If you don't need it in town, send it North. The North team will hold until it arrives. You have comms. I'll rendezvous with you in town. Got it?"

"Roger Wilco." I ended the call immediately. We had no time to waste and Dave would expect it. Our plan had changed, and we needed to adapt quickly, or innocent people would be in danger. We all had to rely on each other to do their part now and focus on our own.

As commander, Dave should remain outside the fray until the major action was over, but the world had changed and old rules no longer applied. We were making it up as we went now, doing what worked best for us.

Dave had made it clear that he was happy to plan the attack, but if things went sideways, he'd be heading into town as back-up. And shit was most definitely going sideways.

"Matt, can you watch this checkpoint yourself?" He nodded quickly before I'd even finished speaking. "The PMV will come through on my signal from town. Be ready for it. Monitor the direction of the farm and watch for any signal from there. You'll be our only eyes, everyone else is going to get busy really fast. Once the first signal goes up from Damon, you're free to use the radio. Let me know if you see anything. "

We'd taken both our satellite phones with us. So we were relying on a long-range radio in the PMV and a sight line to keep a watch on the farm. They only had a skeleton security team tonight, and it was making us all nervous.

I spun to the other soldier on watch with us without waiting for confirmation from Matt. He didn't need hand holding.

"You're on me." I took off at a fast sprint, trusting him to follow. The PMV had dropped us here before retreating at a slow crawl. We were going to lose valuable minutes just getting into town, but we had no choice.

As soon as we reached the outskirts of town, we moved into stealth mode and slipped through the shadows as fast as we could. We intercepted a few of the Honey Badgers and told them to find a safe place quickly and spread the word. We were all on a countdown now.

When I got into town, I used one of our field calls, a distinctive owl hoot for a species not local to this area, to draw the mobile teams to me. Most people wouldn't register the difference, but my guys would.

They knew if they heard it, that shit was going sideways. They would immobilize the guards they were tracking and join me. We were lucky the town itself was small, only a few streets in each direction. Most of the residents in this area had rural blocks or acreages.

I heard the hoot repeated from the other side of town, acknowledgement from the North mobile team.

I took a knee and waited impatiently, yet with perfect outward stillness, trying to conserve energy after our run. I hated staying still, knowing my team was in action. Yet, I'd trained myself and my team to do it when needed. No fidgeting or sudden movements that would draw any eyes in the area.

I didn't have to wait long. My guys were damn good at what they did. They started filtering in slowly, appearing like ghosts out of the shadows. I checked in with our bond and got resolve mixed with a small amount of anxiety from everyone. We all felt the same. We knew we had tasks to do, but we would all feel better when we were together.

I breathed a sigh of relief when Dio showed up, followed shortly by Hunter and Leif. Dave was the last to appear. I had to assume Pala and Lexie were still with the Honey Badgers. A flicker of concern came from Lexie down the bond suddenly, so I sent a feeling of reassurance towards both her and Pala. I quickly got a shot of what felt like love and determination coming back at me. It made me feel strong and connected.

"Any trouble I need to know about?" I whispered the question and directed it at everyone. I got a half dozen shaken heads in reply and I felt a moment of pride.

"There weren't as many guards around town as we were expecting. We only came across one and he was drunk. He seemed lost," Dio answered quickly.

I nodded in acknowledgement as I checked my watch and almost cursed. "Leif, Hunter rendezvous with Damon. He has a humvee from the Palace headed his way with three alphas and a prisoner. He may need you nearby if things get rough. You have three minutes at most."

They took off like a shot. Fading into the shadows so fast it was as if they'd never been here.

We were a few buildings down from the pub. From our surveillance, the guard patrols had seemed haphazard. Pala hadn't noted any scheduled call-ins, which worked in our favor now. So they should have no idea what was happening outside.

I could hear faint music and raucous laughter. The light spilling out the windows was like a beacon calling to us. *Idiots.*

"Surround the pub. Damon will signal when the humvee arrives, then I'll signal the rest of the Honey Badgers to take shelter. We move on my signal."

Dio and Dave instinctively moved to my side as we turned and headed for the pub. We angled for the front, while others headed for the back and nearest side, covering every window and exit. There was an attached general store on the far side, with a shared wall, but the side nearest us had an alleyway running alongside it with a couple of small windows higher up, probably from bathrooms, and a fire exit.

I narrowed my gaze at the sheer arrogance of the alpha standing in the middle of the picture window, scanning the street. The lights of the pub had him highlighted like he was a Christmas display, and with the darkness outside his visibility would be zero. He was trying to scan the street, and I assumed he was who the humvee intended to pick up.

When he angled his face in our direction, I recognized him as Winston, the asshole who had punched Lexie and who had orchestrated the escape from the farm. He was clearly the commander of this unit. I didn't know how his men could still follow him, after he reportedly used one as a shield against Hunter's sniper gun when he escaped. I was itching to take him out, but I knew I couldn't, not yet.

"We have a problem," Dave hissed at my side. "There's way more people in there than we were expecting." He was right, there were a bunch of betas in there, mostly men but also a few women. It looked like a party.

"Do you recognize them Dave, are they from town?"

"A few," he replied as he scanned the room. "There's also a few from outlying homesteads. It looks like they're trying to make friends with some locals. Assholes like them if I'm remembering these faces right."

A man stepped up beside Winston, looking nervous and gesturing behind him. Winston completely ignored him.

"That's the Mayor," Dave whispered. "He's a good guy, Lexie is friends with his wife. I don't know what he's doing there."

"Fuck, we have a bigger problem." Dio echoed Dave's earlier sentiment, a little more bluntly.

"What?" I scanned the mess of men around the bar, but I wasn't seeing what he was seeing. Until he grabbed my face in one hand and directed it towards the dim back corner of the pub.

"Fuck."

"Yeah. Exactly," Dio hissed in my ear.

A woman was standing in the back with her hands tied over her head, secured to the rafters above her. She looked terrified and everyone was giving her a wide berth except for a drunk alpha sniffing around her. A bright pink head of hair had just bobbed up from the back of a booth behind her, near the door to the kitchen.

"That's the mayor's wife," Dave said.

Before I could do more than tense up, the sky lit up red as Damon's signal flare exploded into the night to our right. Winston's head swiveled toward it, and he started yelling into his radio. He kept clicking it on and off as if he wasn't getting a response.

I shot off my green flare into the sky, signaling the Honey Badgers to find safety and everyone else that it was go time.

Winston looked up at my second flare, a panicked look on his face. Then he frantically looked right and left, up and down the street in front of him, but the darkness hid us. My heart dropped as he put the radio on the table and pulled a device out of his pocket, flipping open the lid.

"Sam, he has a detonator," Dio hissed at me in an urgent warning.

But I was already moving as a flash bomb went off inside the pub and chaos erupted.

My beast was now in charge.

Forty-Three

My plans had changed in an instant the second I'd intercepted one of my friends on the street and she'd collapsed into my arms. She'd whispered to me frantically that the alphas in the pub had taken our friend Olivia so her husband, the Mayor, would do what they wanted.

I'd instantly seen red. Pala had taken one look at my face and known I was going after her. He'd gently extracted my friend from my arms, then handed her off to a Honey Badger before he'd stepped up to me without an inch of hesitation.

"I'll follow anywhere you need to go, my heart," he'd whispered as he waited for me to take the lead.

I'd thought fast as I rubbed my hip lightly. We were all radio silent so we couldn't alert anyone, but there was no way I was letting my friend get caught in any crossfire. I'd felt like we had no choice but to go by ourselves. So I'd grabbed Pala's hand and turned toward the pub. We'd made it to the back corner before Pala put his hand on my shoulder to halt me. He'd given me a hold signal, then swiftly moved around in front of me.

That's where we were now, standing just meters from trouble when I'd sworn to Sam I wouldn't get into any. Pala crouched down low and peeked around the corner, then pulled back swiftly. His head tilted when a strange owl hooted a street away and he tensed up immediately. I didn't know what was happening and was about to tap him on the shoulder when the same owl hoot came faintly from a few streets past the other side of the pub.

Pala made the stay command, narrowing his eyes at me, before disappearing around the corner. I crept to the edge and listened as hard as I could, but I heard nothing. I almost screamed when Pala appeared back around the corner. He grabbed me and put his hand over my mouth instinctively, and I slumped into him. I was used to working alone, which meant anyone popping out on me was usually unfriendly.

I relaxed into him and he let me go, giving me a brief kiss to replace his hand. He then tugged me around the corner. The two unconscious alphas lying by the back door surprised me. I hadn't even heard their bodies hit the ground.

We both crouched low and ducked into the kitchen. I thanked every goddess in existence when we found it empty. There was a lot more noise, voices and music than we were expecting coming from the main area of the pub. I pulled the pocket knife I'd stolen from the alpha the other day out of my pocket, but Pala silently shook his head at me as he glared at the knife in my hand.

Was it the knife itself he objected to, or that it had belonged to another alpha? Pala opened a pocket on his pants and passed me a wickedly sharp switchblade. Mine looked like it was for opening boxes. This was a weapon of beauty, made by an artisan.

I tested it quickly, making sure I knew how to open it, before I palmed it and nodded to him with determination. If my friend was here unwillingly, chances were high she was restrained. I only hoped it was with rope or zip ties and not handcuffs.

Pala looked from the door to me quickly, as if he was reconsidering the sanity of what we were doing. I understood his hesitation. I really did. We were completely off script here. We were both used to working alone and making decisions on the fly based on what we came across, but we were part of a pack now and going off half-cocked on our own felt wrong.

I hesitated too. A part of me was telling me this was crazy and we should backtrack and try to find the others. Dio was somewhere nearby, I knew that, but what would happen if we ran in circles trying to find him and she didn't have that much time?

A sudden blast of reassurance came down the bond from Sam, and I relaxed. He felt nearby, closer than he had been before. I was so grateful to him, to all of them at that moment. Realizing I was no longer alone in this, that I didn't need to ask for help, they were just there, made my heart feel so full. I grabbed Pala's hand and sent a wave of the intense emotion I was feeling back towards Sam.

I jerked my head toward the swinging door through to the main pub area and Pala relented, nodding at me and giving me a slow signal. I might be impulsive, but I wasn't usually reckless. This required stealth, and I respected that. We needed to know what we were up against.

Pala grabbed my hand and dragged me up, then tucked me into his side like we were out on a date. He opened the door, then slipped through with casual confidence, as if we belonged there. Before I could do more than blink, he'd surveyed the room, angled us around, and dropped us down behind a booth.

He gave me the eyes up signal, and I popped my head over the booth quickly. Shit. Olivia was right behind us, tied to the rafters. At least it was rope.Yet there was no way we could get her down with no one noticing. We needed a distraction.

I looked toward Pala as a red glow suddenly washed over his face. His gaze shifted up and over my shoulder. I swiveled and saw a red flare illuminating a modern skylight in the old tin roof.

This was bad. A red flare meant trouble. Something had gone wrong in the North and we were out of time. I could hear someone yelling over the voices and music inside the pub, "Team one status report..., team two status report..., can anyone report?"

We both popped our heads over to see what was happening and a green flare lit up the front window. Shit. That was the go signal and no-one knew we were in here. I needed to let them know and give them an advantage.

I pulled a cylinder from my pocket and Pala's eyes widened before a flare of heat filled his eyes. I got the impression if we weren't in the middle of a hostage crisis, he would have kissed me, or maybe thrown me into the booth and fucked me. The look in his eyes made me hot and achy.

There was something dark beneath those calm waters and it called to me.

I shook my head, trying to clear my thoughts. Being so newly mated, everything about these guys turned me on something fierce. *So not the time, Lexie.*

Pala crouched down, covered his ears, and nodded at me. I loved that he trusted me to do this. I yanked the pin and launched the flashbang into the middle of the room, aiming for maximum chaos. Then covered my ears and ducked back down next to Pala. He leaned over me as I heard muffled bangs and bright flashes burst against my closed eyelids. Even back here.

There was screaming and confusion, then a vicious roar ripped through the air as the front picture window exploded inwards. Everyone around us froze and dropped to their knees as I felt a wave of raw need wrap around me like a sexy, silken caress. I felt cocooned in protection, love and desire as rage washed past and around me, never touching me. Not even ruffling my hair.

I jumped up, knowing Sam sensed we were here. I climbed onto the back of the booth and prepared to hack at the ropes as Pala braced the woman below me. The knife sliced through the rope like it was butter, surprising the hell out of me. I didn't know what type of blade it was, but I was totally keeping it. I was claiming it as a courting gift. It might come in handy again one-day.

"It is yours now, my wild heart," Pala said as he smiled at me affectionately in the middle of the chaos surrounding us, as if he felt me coveting it in the bond.

I didn't usually like knives. If you fought with them, they got taken and used against you more times than not. But this knife was a thing of beauty. I palmed it and pocketed it a second before Dio reached me and pulled me down into his arms. "Fucking hell, you two are going to turn me grayer than Dave. Winston has a detonator."

I looked past Dio to see Sam standing in the shattered picture window glaring death at a man kneeling in front of him with a device in his hand. *Focus, Lexie.*

"Get them out of here, Dio," Sam growled with death riding his tone as two of Sam's team appeared through the picture window behind him and I heard more men come through the swinging door behind us. One ran to the fire exit just past us and opened it to one of his teammates.

A man pushed up from his knees and rushed towards us from the crowd. I tensed before I recognized the Mayor. Pala spun Olivia behind him, but I grabbed his arm. "He's her husband."

Pala immediately stood aside as the Mayor grabbed his crying wife in his arms and Pala pushed them both towards the back door. "Run," he hissed, "head for the museum." The alpha from Sam's team behind us shifted to let them pass.

I flicked my gaze back to the front of the pub when I heard Dave yell, "Incoming."

He was standing guarding Sam's back and past him, a group of alphas were streaming out of the building across the street. The shattered picture window outlined them as if they were on a movie screen, but this was no movie. It was very freaking real.

"Fuck. I knew there weren't enough guards on the streets," Dio yelled, frustration thickly coating his voice as he turned and vaulted kneeling people, not bothering to be careful as he headed back to the front of the pub.

There was no longer any question about Sam being a prime alpha. He was holding every person inside the pub, except us, in his thrall. His entire attention focused on it, but his back was now exposed and only Dave was there to protect him.

I moved without thought, needing to get to my mates. Pala was moving at my side when I noticed a blur of dark hair pass the shattered window frame from the far side. An arm shot out and Ava's voice screamed, "Take cover."

Pala covered my head as a second flashbang detonated in the middle of the group in the street, but they shook it off quickly. Flashbangs were much less effective against alphas than they were against betas, especially outside. Stunning them for seconds rather than minutes. I probably should have told Ava that when I'd given it to her, to use as a last resort.

Ava straightened from her protective crouch, looking shocked, when the closest alpha spun to her, followed by a few others. Cary appeared at her side, but the alphas had them grossly outnumbered and we were all too far away.

"Ava," I screamed as I pushed away from Pala. The sound seemed to echo through the silence in the flashbang's aftermath.

A second roar split the air, drowning out my scream, as a wild beast of an alpha appeared in the frame, barrelling through the alphas charging towards us. He had long, shaggy brown hair and was wearing some kind of hospital scrubs that barely contained him. There was no finesse to his movements. He was swinging wildly with brutal punches that knocked alphas out cold. One powerful punch ripped the arm of his shirt in two as his massive bicep bulged.

As I watched, he picked another alpha up and threw him into a tree across the street with a roar of unbridled rage that had hairs raising on my arms. A sudden sharp scent hit my nostrils of uninhabited spaces where nature reigned supreme. The bark, fern and mossy scents of a tropical jungle at night, with sharp underlying notes of orchids and ginger. It was a complex, dark scent that smelt wild and dangerous.

"Shit, that alpha looks feral. Where the fuck did he come from?" Pala hissed beside me.

Two other dark-haired alphas appeared out of nowhere at the feral alpha's side, wearing all black and moving as if they flowed out of the shadows. They appeared to be twins, with lethal movements so precise it looked as if someone had choreographed the scene. They took out two alphas before I could even comprehend what they were doing. Compared with the first brutal alpha, they were like the yin and yang of fighting.

"Forget the feral alpha, that's the fucking twins," Dio said as the breath whooshed from his lungs, reverence lightening his voice.

Dio and Pala both shared a look before they charged into the fray and took out the last two alphas with ruthless efficiency. I paused at Dave's side, where he was still guarding Sam's back. "Clear," he yelled to Sam.

I kept my eyes on Ava. She had frozen while watching the three alphas a few meters away. Cary stood motionless at her side. The twin alphas turned immediately towards Ava and Cary as soon as the fighting stopped, honing in on them as if they sensed them. From this angle, I couldn't tell if it was Ava or Cary that had them transfixed. Or maybe both?

The wild alpha charged towards Ava and Cary with an angry roar, breaking the stasis. Cary jumped in front of Ava before I could shout a warning. The alpha swiftly picked him up and threw him over his broad shoulder. He then did the same to Ava as she stared at him, before he took off down the street with powerful strides, carrying both of them. He was heading south, towards the farm.

The twins took off after him, on swift, silent feet. Damon, Leif and Hunter came barrelling down the road from the north in hot pursuit. "Damon, he has Ava and Cary," I screamed, just as Nick jumped out of an alleyway directly in front of the rampaging alpha, brandishing a stun gun. He'd volunteered as a Honey Badger tonight.

The alpha slid to a halt and cocked his head at Nick, looking confused, just as the PMV came around the southern corner towards them all.

One of Sam's team was manning the gun turret. He instantly assessed the situation and swung his gun towards the feral escaping alpha. I heard him yell, "Stop or I'll shoot."

My blood froze in my veins as I lunged to run for Ava and Cary. Arms banded around me as Pala yelled in my ear, "Lex, no."

This was all spiraling out of control, so freaking fast. I could hardly breathe. My chest was tight and panic was thrumming through my veins.

The feral alpha gently lowered Ava and Cary to their feet. They both looked dazed, and neither stepped away. He stepped around Nick, who looked pale as a ghost, and approached the PMV slowly, not taking his eyes off the alpha on the turret.

"I said stop," the alpha yelled from his high position. He seemed unsure what to do. We had no back-up plan for a situation like this, but he seemed unwilling to shoot an unarmed person, despite his warnings.

"Hold fast, unless attacked," Dave yelled from beside me, and the alpha in the turret nodded warily.

The feral alpha, with rough, sluggish movements, reached up and yanked the attached gun clear off its mounting in a loud screech of metal that had everyone spellbound, before throwing it into the bushes at the side of the road. He paced as he glared and growled low and angry at the alpha on top of the turret, who stayed perfectly still, as if he was dealing with a wild animal.

The first person to move was Ava. She stepped toward the feral alpha and the last of the air left my lungs. I was terrified for her, but she seemed calm. I heard her say something, but I couldn't hear what she said. The feral alpha spun and watched her warily, as if he was suddenly afraid of her. It was almost comical. He scented the air and even from this distance, I could see his body shake. He looked haunted. His fear had her pausing.

Cary moved past Ava. She tried to grab him, but he shrugged her off gently. Cary said something quietly, we couldn't hear, before he took another halting step forward, holding his hand out to the feral alpha. When he got close enough, Cary laid his hand on the alpha's trembling chest and he sagged towards Cary.

Cary yelled for help, and Nick lurched forward, but the twins beat everyone to him. They'd snuck up beside the PMV, flanking the feral alpha without anyone noticing. The way these guys moved reminded me of Pala.

They spun forward and caught the feral alpha as he collapsed, gently lowering him to the ground. He appeared to be unconscious.

"Dave," Sam growled into the sudden quiet.

Dave turned quickly, trusting Pala and me to keep watch for the moment. "What do you need?

"Damon. My mates," Sam ground out. I half turned and noticed sweat was beading his brow and I suddenly remembered he was holding an entire room full of people in stasis, including a guy with a detonator, using just his dominance.

I approached Sam slowly as Dave called out to Damon, touching him on the shoulder lightly and he shuddered. I tried to send him my strength through the bond and I could feel him rally.

"Pala," I whispered, not wanting to stress Sam out unnecessarily. Pala joined me and put his hand on Sam's other shoulder.

"We're here," Pala said to Sam, just as quietly. Sam took a gasped breath as Dio and Dave joined us. I felt our connection strengthen with us all together. I also felt how stretched thin Sam was.

Shit. How had we left him standing like this? Sam's power was monumental, but he was only one person.

Sam's dominance cycled between us stronger, and he steadied, bracing his body more firmly.

"Why didn't you call for us earlier?" I asked him quietly.

"Didn't want to distract you, couldn't see what was happening," he ground out.

I had a lot of feelings about that statement, but now was not the time to hash it out.

Damon appeared at his side, glancing from Sam to Winston and the room beyond. Assessing the situation in seconds.

"How can I help?" Damon was always chillingly calm in a crisis.

"I need you to take the room when I release my dominance. So I can focus on Winston. We don't know what the detonator is linked to or who is involved here. Can you do that?"

"I guess we'll find out."

As I looked at Winston, I could see his thumb shaking, as if he was trying to push past Sam's hold, putting all his energy into moving just that one digit.

Leif and Hunter appeared at Damon's side.

"What is the range for the detonator?" I asked, sudden horror dawning, thinking of everyone unprotected back at the farm.

"A few hundred meters at most," Dave answered. I almost sagged with relief, but we weren't out of the woods yet. Knowing the Palace and how they operated, whatever he was trying to blow up, we really didn't want him to.

"On a three count," Damon growled as Leif and Hunter settled in behind him, mimicking our positions. "Three, two, one."

Winston's thumb twitched as Sam released the room, but Sam had him dominated again so fast he couldn't move it any closer to the detonator.

Nobody else in the room moved either, as Damon barked and his dominance took over.

"You good?" Sam asked him. Damon just grunted in reply.

"What do we have here?" Sam mocked as Winston shook his head as if he was trying to clear it. Winston looked shocked when he realized he could move his head, but not the rest of his body.

Sam's control over his dominance blew me away. I had never heard of any alpha being able to isolate parts of a person to dominate. I snuck a glance at Dio with my eyebrow raised, but he just shook his head with a frown.

"Give me the detonator," Sam demanded, a growl lacing his voice with menace as he held his hand out underneath the device. Winston's hand released it involuntarily as he cursed a blue streak. Sam snatched the detonator and snapped the cover closed before securing it in one of his own pockets.

Winston suddenly sniffed the air and shifted his gaze to look at me. "You're a fucking omega?" He yelled in a rage, spittle flying everywhere. He stilled and an evil smile full of malice stole over his face. "Oh, I know some people who are going to love you, you little bitch."

"Don't look at her, look at me," Sam snarled and Winston's head snapped to him so fast his neck made a cracking sound. Winston whimpered out a pained sound. "You won't live long enough to tell anyone about her."

Winston chuckled, sounding suddenly cocky. "You won't kill me. Good guys don't kill people, it's what makes you so weak. You'll let me go, again. Then I'm going to come back and snatch your little omega coochie, like I always planned. I'm going to have some fun with her before I hand her over."

A chilling smile stole over Sam's face. One I'd never seen before. Pala and Dio matched it. Even Dave looked resolute, as if he'd look the other way if the guys danced over this guy's corpse.

"It seems you don't know us at all, Winston," Sam growled.

"Us?" Winston asked, looking at us as if just noticing the way we were standing all together for the first time and seeing the visible bites we weren't trying to hide. "You're a fucking *pack*?" He spat the word pack out as if it was a curse.

Then he laughed loudly again. "Oh, you're going to get it now. You have no idea who you're dealing with. You think it's just those fuckers at the

Palace. They're pawns. You haven't even met the key players yet. They really don't like other packs. They don't want compet-."

A gunshot drowned out his last word as it ricocheted off the buildings. I felt its breeze graze my cheek as it passed and the back of Winston's head suddenly exploded as a red hole opened up in his forehead.

Dave shoved me to the ground as Dio threw himself over me, and our mates crouched over us. I wanted to scream at them to get down, but I was winded and couldn't catch my breath.

Two more shots rang out in quick succession and panic overwhelmed me. Almost everyone I cared about in this world was in the line of fire and we had very little cover.

I could see my mates' mouths moving, and knew they were yelling, but I couldn't make out the words over the ringing in my ears.

A fourth shot sounded from nearby and all I could think was, *game over.*

Forty-Four

D io was lying sprawled over Lexi, trying to cover as much of her body as he could with his own, while I crouched over them. Pala and Sam were shadowing me, and we all had the same thought.

Protect Lexie. Nothing else mattered at this moment.

I instinctively knew, deep in my bones, the one thing I couldn't survive was losing her. Not after everything I'd been through.

I eyed the buildings across from us, knowing from the sound of the first shot we were dealing with a sniper. Our life was in their hands now. If the sniper wanted one of us dead, we'd be dead.

"Hunt, got anything?" I yelled. Hunter was one of the best snipers I'd ever met. He'd know straight away where the best vantage shots would be to make that kill.

"No," he shouted back.

Another shot rang out, this time from one of the twins standing in the street. He had his gun aimed at the roof of the building across from us, while his brother was crouched in front of Cary and Ava, who were both lying on top of the unconscious feral alpha. Shielding him.

Sam signaled the driver of the PMV. He quickly reversed, then swung around to get between the people on the street, including Ava and Cary, and the building.

Movement flashed briefly on the rooftop and Hunter fired, but it was an impossible shot with a handgun.

"Hunt. Go," Damon yelled and Hunter took off, shadowed by the twin with the raised gun.

I waited for a heartbeat, then two. When no more shots fired, I turned to the room behind me. Damon had released his hold on the room when the second shot sounded and everyone had ducked for cover. There were three bodies on the floor, though. Winston and two other alphas. I recognized them as two of the alphas who had escaped from the farm with Winston.

I looked back at the building again. It made no sense. I didn't know why the shooter would hide if they were helping us. Unless it was someone from Maven cleaning house. *Was Dio right? Were we dealing with a secret pack?*

That seemed to be what Winston was saying just before they shot him. I couldn't see the point of cleaning house now, though. Unless we were missing something even bigger.

My thoughts spiraled for the next few minutes, trying to puzzle it out. Until Hunter appeared on the rooftop and waved his hand in the air. "All clear. Shooter's in the wind."

Pala and Sam turned to help Dio and Lexie up. Lexie looked shaken and angry. "You numbskulls, you left yourselves in the line of fire. They could have killed you."

Sam didn't answer her, he just pulled her into his arms and wrapped her up tightly, taking a deep breath of her scent. Pala and Dio joined in the hug. Dio murmured something to Lexie, but she cut him off. "Don't you even dare say some crap like I'm the only one who matters. It's not true. You all matter. You matter to me."

Sam started that strange purring noise, his beast wanting to soothe her, and Lexie instantly melted into him. Her fear masked as anger, bleeding away. It didn't matter if she was mad at us for protecting her, we'd do it, anyway. None of us could do anything else when we'd heard the shot and felt her sudden spike of fear.

"I love you, Lexie," Sam whispered into her hair.

"I know," Lexie said with a grin as she let him hang for a moment. "I love you too. I'm still mad, though." She didn't sound mad at all, though. She sounded blissed out.

I watched them for a moment, marveling at my pack. These people I could now call my own. My family. Feeling the love flowing between us

Pala and Dio opened their arms to make room for me. "What the fuck are you doing all the way over there?" Dio grumbled, and I smirked as I stepped into them and sighed. That fucking purr rumbled through all of us and I had to force my eyes not to roll back in my head.

Leif was right. That shit was the bomb. All the stress and tension ebbed away, and left behind a sense of peace and a rock solid bond thrumming in my chest. Whatever we were facing, we would do it together.

"Thanks for having my back." Sam glanced at me and there was a flash of longing for something I couldn't define in his eyes. It felt a lot like an unconscious yearning for approval, though. I was happy to give it, if it was what he needed from me right now. He'd earned it, and it had been denied enough in his life.

"You did good, Sam," I told him gruffly. He took a stuttered breath and that devastating smile spread across his face. Dio winked at me discretely, clearly knowing what my words meant to Sam.

"Enough hugging. Knock it off, you lot," Damon growled at us. "We've got a shit tonne of clean-up to do. We also need to question this lot, and we have a town full of people to get out of the museum and back into their homes."

He wasn't really mad, though. If Maia was here, he'd be doing exactly the same thing. He flashed a concerned glance at Lexie, before going back to eyeing the pub patrons. Making sure none were trying to escape while we were distracted. Lexie pulled herself back from us, grabbing Sam's face when he grumbled and kissed him. "Damon's right. Later," she whispered.

I was determined there was going to be a later for her, for all of us. For our pack, our farm, and this town. Hell, even for the country if we could swing it.

I looked down at Winston's body, laying near our feet. Wishing I'd been the one to pull the trigger after having to stand here and listen to his vile plans for Lexie. All the zen calm I'd felt from Sam's purr fled, and I felt fury pulsing through me, knowing he likely wouldn't be the last asshole to want to come for her.

I felt Pala put a hand on my shoulder, as he looked in the same direction and the dark depths of his river swirled to the surface.

I was tired of playing defense. I glanced at Damon, standing just beyond us, and he nodded, knowing me long enough to recognize what I was thinking.

It was time for all of us to take a stand. I wasn't letting anyone take potshots at my pack, my omega. This was going to end. One way or another.

For now, though. Damon and Lexie were right. We had work to do.

Forty-Five

As soon as I extricated myself from my guys, I turned in Ava's direction. There was no way I could look at Maia tomorrow if I let anything happen to Ava. I wouldn't be able to look at myself in the mirror, either.

A hand grabbing mine stopped me in my tracks, and I raised my eyebrow at Dave. "Maybe you should go get your friends out of the safe house first? We'll go check on Ava."

"Uh, no. I'll check on Ava. The people in the safe house will be fine for a few more minutes, or Pala can go grab them if you think it's urgent. He has the access code and they know him. But I have a friend just over there who needs me right now and I'm going to her unless you give me a better reason why not."

I shot another look toward Ava and she glanced up at me. Her eyes were wide, and it looked like the adrenaline of the last few minutes was wearing off. I stepped towards her again, but Sam's frustrated growl halted me.

"Lex, I get you wanting to go to her right now, but those are the twins," Sam ground out. His scent was spiking, along with his agitation. I was getting frustrated myself, at how weird and overprotective they were being right now, but this seemed to be important to them.

"Okay. That's what Dio called them earlier. What am I missing?" Sure, the two guys had insane skills, but they'd done nothing but protect Ava and Cary since they'd shown up a few minutes ago.

"They're assassins that work for the government, but nobody knows what branch," Dio said in a rush, shooting sidelong glances at one of the twins as he returned with Hunter. "They're ghosts and they're lethal. Nobody knows anything about them. They just appear out of nowhere, take out their targets and disappear again while we're all standing around scratching our balls."

"Are you geeking out right now, Dio?" I asked, feeling amused. "Do you want to come get their autograph?"

"Hell yeah, I'm geeking out, Lex. I also don't want you anywhere near them. I saw them in action once before. We were secondary back-ups on an op. We were told to just hold and wait for further instruction. One minute nothing, the next the target was dead, and they'd gone again before I'd even blinked. It was awesome and really fucking terrifying. I'm pretty sure my balls crept back up where they came from."

"It's okay honey buns, I'll hold your hand," I reassured Dio.

"I got this, Dio," Pala said as he patted Dio's shoulder with an amused smile. "River and Ryder are good guys. I'll take Lex over to meet them and check on Ava with her. Then we'll go to the safe house."

"What the actual fuck, Pala? Do you know them? Or did you just make those names up to mess with me?" Dio was spluttering in shock and gripping his head as if it would stop his brain from exploding.

"Yeah, we trained for a black ops program together at a secret facility shortly after I joined the military. The reason nobody knows who they work for is that they went AWOL a while ago and they don't report to the military anymore. The military covered that up, though. They act as if they've sanctioned the twins' ops, but the twins work on their own now. The twins don't report to the Network either. They have their own agenda. I know, because we've stayed in touch."

Sam looked at Pala with concern. "You've been walking a dark, dangerous path, Pala. Juggling the Network, the military, the Palace and the twins."

Pala just nodded, not denying it. My heart clenched as I realized how easily something could have happened to Pala while he was alone, undercover. I would never have met him if it had.

"Come on, my heart," Pala cupped my face and kissed me lightly, sensing my emotions. "Our guys need to back up Damon and Leif to question these people and deal with all the townsfolk in the museum."

Dio rolled his eyes at Pala with a smirk. "Fine, but I want that autograph later, Pala. Maybe a photo too, with the four of us in Charlie's Angels poses."

Pala just laughed as he grabbed my other hand and tugged me away from Dave. Dave let me go reluctantly. I squeezed his hand before I dropped it, so he'd know I wasn't mad.

I could feel the rest of my mate's eyes on us as Pala and I walked down the road. Hunter had shadowed the twin he was with back towards Ava, too. He was currently kneeling and checking over the unconscious, yet still intimidating, alpha on the ground.

I snuck a glance at the twins out of curiosity. They were both incredibly tall, classically handsome and sleekly muscled, as if they did martial arts and their bodies were weapons. They were both blonde, but one had his hair cut with a short back and sides and only a little length on top, while the other had long straight hair and a severe undercut all the way around, the length currently tied in a knot at the back of his head. Rough stubble shadowed both their faces and added to the darkness that seemed to swirl around them.

They held themselves loose, yet at the ready, as if they could explode into action without notice. I'd already seen them move with a liquid grace that belied their size. Even from a distance, they exuded a dangerous allure.

As I got closer, I could tell by the tense way Ava was holding herself, her arms wrapped around her middle, that she was just barely holding her shit together. Cary seemed torn between watching her with concern and eyeing the alphas surrounding them. Nick still looked like he'd seen a ghost.

Pala introduced me to the twins briefly then gave them both back slapping hugs, much to Hunter's shocked amusement. I stepped quickly to Ava and whispered in her ear as I hugged her, "Are you okay? Do I need to get you out of here?"

She shook her head as she mumbled. "No, I'm okay. Could you maybe hang around for a minute, though?" She was trembling lightly in my arms as both the twins growled softly, yet possessively. At this proximity, their alpha hearing would have picked up my words, no matter how softly I whispered.

They cut it off abruptly when Ava shot them a dark look as she stepped back slightly from me. They both shifted, as if her reaction startled them.

"I hoped she was your Ava when I found her hiding at the Palace," Pala said lightly. "I kept the other alphas away and brought her food, but I couldn't get word to you. Then Damon and his mates rescued her. I watched from the shadows, knowing who they were and that they'd keep her safe."

"Thank you, my friend." The shorter haired twin gripped Pala's neck tightly and tipped his forehead into him. The other remained watching Ava closely. He looked pained.

I looked down at Ava as I felt her take a sharp breath. "You knew who I was?" Ava asked Pala. I wasn't sure if it was shock, anger, or a mix of both that had her breathing hard. I checked in with Pala through the bond and he sent me calm reassurance.

"No, not for sure," Pala replied. "I suspected you were their Ava, though. They'd said you were at the Palace." I felt Ava tense even further beside me.

"Their Ava?" I asked.

It was Ava who spoke up and answered, though. Not Pala or the twins, who were strangely silent.

"Lexie, I'd like you to meet my mates, River and Ryder," Ava said stiffly as she pointed first to short, back and sides, then to undercut. She wasn't looking directly at the twins as she spoke. She fixed her gaze firmly on me, her eyes still wide and almost begging for something I couldn't understand. I didn't know what she needed right now. I was so confused.

"Holy shit. The twins are your mates?" Hunter asked from his position on the ground.

"Mates?" Cary echoed. He sounded stunned, and he slumped slightly, as if her words had sucked all the air out of him. Nick reached out and gripped Cary's shoulder, almost unconsciously, and Cary let him, surprising me.

This was a shit show and there was no way I was leaving Ava alone in the middle of it right now. I grabbed her hand and squeezed it, trying to send her strength. I didn't know what was going on, but clearly there was a convoluted history here. The twins were hovering, but keeping their distance from Ava. The tension was so thick in the air I could taste its bitterness, like burnt coffee.

"For what it's worth," Ava said quietly, still not looking at anyone. "We're unbonded."

Cary stepped in closer to Ava, recovering quickly, and shot the twins a dark glare. I shot a glance at them, too. They both bristled, and darkness swept over their faces. I didn't sense any menace coming from them, though. Only possessiveness. They said nothing to defend themselves against the unspoken accusations.

"And the big guy out cold on the ground?" I asked Ava.

She shrugged and furrowed her brow as she twisted to look at the hulking alpha lying alongside her on the ground. "I don't know who he is. I've never seen him before. He came out of nowhere tonight."

"He seemed to zero in on you and Cary, from where I was standing." Neither commented to either confirm or deny.

"He's a prisoner from the Palace," Hunter said as he looked down at the alpha with a confused expression. He reached out a hand to his face, then pulled it back. "They were transporting him somewhere in a humvee, moving fast. We intercepted them North of the town. They had him heavily sedated when we got him out, but he was moving. He caught a scent in the air and took off like a bullet. For a big dude, he's fucking fast. We had to secure the Palace guards that were with him before we could chase him down because the humvee crashed."

"Do you know who he is?" Pala asked the twins.

They shifted their gazes from Ava to the alpha. "No," Ryder replied.

"We infiltrated the Palace," River said, shooting a glance at Pala, "we were tracking Ava, but the scent in her room had faded, as if she hadn't been in there for days. We found a faint trace in the library, too, along with some hidden passages. When we reached their underground labs, we found his cell, and it reeked of her scent. Someone had stuffed Ava's blankets and clothes into his air vents."

Ava gasped, and her hand went over her heart, as she shot a confused look at the unconscious alpha.

"It looked like they were tormenting him, or maybe torturing him, with her scent. We felt drawn to him and we tried to get him out so we could figure out why, but we tripped some kind of silent alarm. We had to fight our way out and they tried to move him while they had us pinned down below ground. As soon as we got free, we tracked him here."

Before anyone could say anything, Dave came running over and slid to a stop next to me. He was holding his satellite phone. "Sam's surveillance team at the Palace just made contact again. The military and lab techs are abandoning the Palace. They're bugging out right now."

"What about the omegas?" Ava asked.

"They've turned off the security feeds, so we can't tell for sure, but it doesn't seem like they're taking them. Now that we've cut off their supply of food from town, I don't think they have enough left to feed everyone." Cary growled lowly. He'd warned us not to cut off the omegas food supply.

"Plus, their lab just got breached, so they're probably spooked," Hunter said.

"Who breached their lab?" Sam asked as he strode over and wrapped his arms around me. He'd lasted over five minutes of me talking to strange alphas without stomping over here, I was impressed. Claudio, Damon and Leif followed close behind. I assumed they'd assigned others from the team to watch over the pub patrons.

Hunter just pointed to the twins, who looked unconcerned at the sudden spotlight.

Dave shook his head. "That's a story for another day. We need to break up into groups. One questioning the people in the pub, another letting town residents out of the museum and making sure everyone gets home okay, and a group to head to the Palace in the PMV right now and check on the omegas."

"We also need to figure out what Winston was trying to blow up and where those explosives are. We don't want local kids finding them," Hunter said. Dave just nodded, looking weary.

"What about tracking the unit fleeing the Palace with the lab techs? We need to know where they're planning to regroup," River asked. He seemed to be the chattier twin.

"We have a man tracking satellite feeds. He also has a long range drone. Max will follow them as best as he can," Damon answered.

River glanced at Ryder, doing some kind of twin communication thing, but they didn't object.

"I think Hunter and I should head to the museum with the Honey Badgers so we can reassure people everything is fine now. Hunter and I are both well known in town, and people will be more likely to listen to us." I didn't mention the safe house in front of the twins.

"Who the hell are the Honey Badgers?" Ryder asked, almost as if he couldn't help himself.

"He's one, but that's a story for another day too," I said as I pointed at Nick and watched him blush while the twins looked him over.

"I agree," Dave jumped in, sounding impatient. "The alphas who defected from the Palace all want to go back and check on the omegas. They've been champing at the bit to get back there and protect them since they arrived at the farm."

After a quick discussion, it was decided Pala and Claudio would help me at the museum, while Damon, Sam, and Dave sorted the pub, with the help of Matt and the rest of Sam's team. Matt and a few of the guys were going to stay a few days, keep watch, and maintain a presence to help the townsfolk feel safe. They'd also organize a search for the explosives. Leif was heading back to the farm on one of the dirt bikes now, to help keep it secure and assist Max.

"I'm going to the Palace, too," Ava announced. Before anyone could argue with her, she pushed ahead with a determined glint in her eyes. "I want to check on the omegas and I'm the only one who knows where all the secret passages are. We'll need to make sure they're all checked and there's nothing and nobody left behind that can surprise us."

"Me too," Cary added, surprising no-one.

"We'll go with them," River said without hesitation, staring intently at Ava, daring her to object. He looked one bad decision away from picking her up and throwing her over his shoulder.

"I think we should take this alpha back there, too," Cary said. "If he's feral, we can't risk taking him to the farm, or having him in town here. The Palace is the only place with secure facilities if we need it, and they should have more medical supplies too. I don't think they would have had time to strip it on the way out."

I could feel the nervousness of my guys in the bond, at having Ava and Cary head back to the Palace without us. I shot a look at Damon and he was clenching his jaw and looking at Hunter. They both clearly felt uncomfortable too, but they were needed elsewhere right now.

"I can come with you, Ava. Someone else can take the museum." I knew if I went, at least one or two of my mates would go with me as well.

Ava smiled gratefully at me. "That's very sweet, Lexie. But I'll be okay. You were right. You need to be at the museum. People there are going to be frightened. You'll be able to reassure them and figure out what they need. You're good at that."

I nodded reluctantly. I wasn't happy, but Ava was a grown woman who could decide for herself what was best for her. She'd been denied any say in her own life for far too long. I wouldn't deny her now.

"I think I should go to the Palace too," Nick blurted suddenly. He'd been quietly standing on the edges of our group while we all talked, shifting nervously. "If their security cameras have been switched off I can get them back online, and see if I can find any tech they've overlooked in their rush to leave. Then I can let Max know what we need and can borrow from the farm, to get them secure and get electricity connected again."

Dave patted him on the shoulder and dragged him forward into our circle at the same time. "Good man. I agree, they'll need your tech skills at the Palace if you're willing to go. You can coordinate with Max and get the two sites linked up."

Nick looked embarrassed at the praise, and flicked his eyes towards Ava. She gave him a soft smile that intrigued me. Clearly I'd been missing something, caught up in my own drama.

Dave handed Ava his satellite phone. "Take this, and check in with us every day at 8am and 8pm until things calm down. If we don't hear from you, we'll head straight for the Palace. So if you forget, be prepared for a bunch of worried people to turn up and we'll probably come in hot.

Outside of that, call us for any reason. There's a charger in the PMV. I'm sure Maia will call you when she wakes up, after she tears strips off us for letting you go without her."

Ava hugged the phone to her chest. "Thank you, Dave."

I gave her a giant hug before we all went our separate ways. "I'm here if you need me, any time of the day or night. And I'll be on that call with Maia in the morning."

She nodded into my shoulder. "Honestly, I'll be fine Lex. I'm a big girl."

"No, you're a strong as fuck omega, Ava. Don't forget it."

She gave me a squeeze before letting me go and stepping back.

"Okay," I said, with only a little crack in my voice. I didn't have a lot of close friends and I didn't like seeing one walk away. "Let's get to work."

It was going to be a long ass night.

Forty-Six

Waking up on the farm this morning, the feel of my pack bonds thrumming in my chest had filled me with contentment and a sense of connection I hadn't felt since the day I hopped on a bus and left the other parts of my soul behind.

My parents had raised me with a strong sense of family and community. This place and my new pack filled that deep need in me. For years, I'd felt a black emptiness dragging me down. At the time, I hadn't realized just how much of a toll Sam and Dio's absence had wrought on me.

Now that I had them, a pack and a home that felt bursting with life and a deep growing energy, I was going to hold on to them with everything I had.

Yesterday had been a write-off, following the clusterfuck from the night before. It had been almost four in the morning by the time we all got back from town.

Lexie had set an early alarm, so she could go check in with Maia and they could make the morning call to Ava together. So, of course, we'd all gone with her and invaded Damon's cabin. Only we'd had to stay outside because Maia had her temporary nest in the living room and she didn't want other alphas or omegas near it with our scents. We'd respected that.

Damon and his mates had all been upstairs, working away at some kind of building project they'd started while Lexie was in heat and we were all out of action. We'd heard them hammering. I don't know how they found the energy, but I assumed it was some kind of gift for Maia. She hadn't said what it was, but my money was on a permanent nest upstairs.

As predicted, Maia had been royally pissed at being left behind and stressed about Ava at the Palace. The phone call had put her at ease, but she wanted to see her too. So she could make sure Ava was alright with her own eyes and check on the other omegas as well. I figured there would be another helicopter ride coming up if she got her way.

Lexie had still looked so tired when she was done with Maia and the phone call. She'd tried to head to the kitchen to help out, but Dave had thrown her over his shoulder, smacked her on the ass, and carried her back to the treehouse. She hadn't protested too hard. We spent most of the day sleeping and recharging our energy. We figured everyone had earned a day off.

Then in the late afternoon, we'd picked some more stuff up from Lexie's cabin, and some from Dave's, and brought the lot up to the treehouse so we could make it feel more like home. Dave had found me a hammer and some nails, and I'd hung Lexie's photos up for her around the place.

Today, I'd woken early with the sun, feeling rested, yet with a need to walk the earth and get familiar with the rhythms of this place. Dio had already been gone when I woke, but I knew he liked to run and clear his head in the early morning light.

I left my shoes behind and padded through the dew that had fallen overnight. I avoided the paths and meandered my way through the trees that bordered the fields instead, leaving ghostly footprints behind in the early morning light, as if a dawn spirit had visited the farm.

The farm was truly magical, with its terraced fields tumbling down the hill separated by hand laid stone walls, and the ancient mill and pond at the bottom. Timber cabins were scattered throughout. The river was sparkling in the distance and the green forest waved from beyond.

I could see sheep and cattle milling around the edge of the river and wandering through the trees, closely followed by attentive dogs that looked like Bear. When I closed my eyes, I could hear birds twittering above me and ducks noisily going about their business somewhere nearby, as well as the distant lowing calls of the cattle.

Everyone on the farm had clearly toiled hard to work compassionately with the land and not overwhelm it with agriculture. A few workers were already out, tending the fields, but also the wildflowers that grew amongst them. It filled my spirit. I put my hand out to the ancient tree I had halted under, its branches arching high and wide above me.

Pounding footsteps coming up a nearby path had me on alert. I stilled as Dio emerged from a foggy glade as he powered up the hill, Bear racing at his side. The muscles in his legs tightened and bunched with each powerful stride. His shirt was off, tucked into the back of his shorts, and sweat was dripping down his toned body. I didn't draw attention to myself. I just took a moment to enjoy the sight of him, having missed him for so long.

He must have felt me in the bond though, because he turned his head my way, throwing me a cheeky wink before he continued on his way. I wondered briefly what it would feel like to reach out and grab him, draw him to me and kiss him while running my hands over that hard body. Just like I had ached to do when we were in our early teens and I'd been itching to explore my awakening sexuality. Dio had shown no sign of being bi-curious though, so I'd never expressed my new feelings to him. Equally happy to chase local girls with him and Sam.

I'd tried to explore this side of me in the early years of my military career, having a brief entanglement with another alpha in training, but I hadn't felt the same sparking desire I did when I looked at Dio and it had left me feeling empty. Even Sam didn't make me feel the same way, though I loved him fiercely as a brother. I realized I was attracted to Dio, not his gender.

Being so close to Dio now, even with Lexie between us, was intoxicating. She felt like a natural part of us. My deep need for her didn't alter my desire for him. When they both bit and claimed me, it felt transcendent. Even if Dio wasn't drawn to me in the same way, I knew I was important to him. Essential even. It was enough.

I turned and walked back to the treehouse, brushing my hands over random flowers and plants as I went, learning their touch and scents. While I had always had an affinity for nature, my stroll had a dual purpose. When moving stealthily in the dark, it paid to know your surroundings by touch and smell. This place was my home now, which meant I would cherish it, but also protect it.

When I climbed the curving steps of the treehouse and emerged at the top, Lexie was there. She was curled in a big, round hanging love seat, wrapped in a blanket, and drinking a cup of coffee. I suspected she was naked underneath. I would be perfectly happy if blankets were all she ever wore around the treehouse.

I headed straight for her, picked her up and settled her in my lap as I took her place. Sneaking my hands inside the blanket to warm away the chill and steal her heat as she squealed. I grabbed the coffee out of her hands before she spilled it all over us with her wriggling and took a drink to warm my insides, too.

"I don't know if this chair can take both our weight," she said, a little breathlessly.

"Then we shall fall together and I shall catch you, my heart."

She groaned. "So cheesy," but she was smiling as she leaned in to kiss me sweetly. I maneuvered to put the cup on a side table and wrapped both my arms around her. She swung her body around to straddle me and I groaned as her wet heat ground down on my aching cock, while the blanket slipped off her shoulder and a pert nipple peeked out to tease me.

"I need you, Pala."

I felt like I'd waited my whole life to hear those words. Her hands ran down my chest, over my shirt, then slid up my stomach, warming me with her touch. "You have me, my heart."

I craved this woman deeply as she wound herself around my very soul. She slid her hands back down and into the loose waistband of my sweats, bringing my cock out into her waiting grasp. She raised herself up on her knees and gripped me firmly with one hand, stroking and teasing me, before rubbing her thumb over the pre-cum leaking from the tip. Her tongue poked out to lick her lips as she watched me with hooded eyes.

I held her gaze as she settled herself down on me and rocked until she had fully seated herself on my cock. Her slick coated my balls, and she panted lightly, but her gaze never left mine.

"So beautiful," I whispered as she threw her head back and rode me with a carefree abandon, chasing her pleasure and mine. I ran my hands down to her ass and gripped her hard enough to make her moan my name.

I thrust up into her, meeting her movements, making the swing underneath us groan as it swayed with us.

"Come for me," I demanded as I lowered my head and sucked her budded nipple into my mouth before biting it gently. She whimpered and ground herself down on me. I could feel her flutter around my cock and knew she was close. So I let some alpha growl into my tone.

"Come for me, now." She exploded around me, loving my occasional darkness, milking my cock so hard I saw stars instead of dawning sunshine.

"Well, that was hot as fuck."

Dio came sauntering into view from the stairs. I'd scented his distinctive popcorn scent a moment ago and felt his desire creep into our bond.

"Well, come join us then." Lexie glanced over at him as she issued her invitation.

He didn't need to be asked twice. He hustled across to us, tipped her head back and kissed her decadently as she continued to grind down on me. The sight had me thrusting harder into her, jostling them both.

He shocked the shit out of me when he turned and kissed me, too. His tongue swiped over my bottom lip briefly, as if he was tasting her on me, before he thrust his tongue into my mouth and devoured me with hard thrusts as his tongue tangled with mine. Lexie groaned loudly and ground down on me harder.

"Get your dick out," she demanded, as Dio pulled back with a smirk shot my way before he complied. "I think she liked that." He slipped his running shorts down so quickly his cock slapped against his stomach as it sprung free.

She put her hand down between us and covered her own hand in her slick, before she reached up and grasped his cock, rubbing her slick all along the length. Dio groaned and thrust into her hand like he was about to lose his mind.

"Seeing you two together does something to me," he groaned. "So fucking good."

"Oh, yeah?" Lexie got a mischievous gleam in her eye as she leaned forward and licked the tip, sucking it into her mouth just enough to tease and torment him.

"I think Pala needs to kiss you back now." She leaned back and angled Dio's dick towards my face. Heat flared through me, hot and bright, and I flicked my gaze up to his.

"It's only polite," Dio ground out as he panted.

I leaned my head forward, slowly, not wanting to rush this. Then I looked at Lexie as I flicked out my tongue and swiped it over the head of his cock, licking up a bead of salty tasting pre-cum.

"Like this?"

Dio groaned harder, almost desperately, and thrust into the hand Lexie still had gripped around the base of his cock.

"No, kiss him properly."

"Show me." I flicked my gaze from Lexie back to Dio, watching him pant through the raw need blazing from his eyes. I ran my eyes back down over his abs and to his hard cock, glistening almost obscenely with Lexie's slick.

Lexie bent her head to match my pose, and we both kissed the sides of his straining cock in unison, our tongues and lips slipping into each other and making a mess of him as we devoured him. He tasted like Lexie's meringue scent and the feel of her slick all over his rigid cock drove me insane.

Dio made a growling noise deep in his chest and his eyes dilated until they were almost pure black. He was thrusting between our two mouths as he clung onto the chair ropes and Lexie was grinding on me furiously. I could feel their desire spinning wildly in our bond.

I shifted my head and wrapped my lips around the head of his cock, licking the underside before sucking hard on the tip. I thrust Lexie down onto me savagely at the same time, gripping her ass hard enough to bruise. Lexie whined in pleasure, her mouth going slack around the base of Dio's cock.

"Stick out your tongue, Lex." She did as I demanded, and let Dio slide over it as he thrust back into my mouth. I bobbed my head and sucked him down further, matching the intense pace as I was thrusting into Lexie.

Lexie dropped her hand and fondled Dio's balls as our mouths met at the base of his cock. I hummed as he slid into the back of my throat and I heard him yell incoherently as hot cum drizzled down my throat. The taste of him combined with Lexie's slick in my mouth had me coming in a frenzied rush, forcing another hard, sharp orgasm from Lexie as well.

"Holy shit, that was hot." Lexie was trembling against me and Dio had slumped onto the back of the chair, tilting us all precariously.

"I'll say," came a deep, sexy voice filled with need and sleep. I rolled my head and Dio shifted slightly so we could see Sam leaning against the railing like a lazy cat, stroking himself with his hand down his sweats. "You know how hard it is to sleep when all we can feel in the bond is you guys fucking?"

Dave was lounging in the doorway, wearing only a pair of sweats as well. He was glowering at us while giving off hot daddy vibes, but had abstained from touching himself. I don't know how, but his dick looked painfully hard. "Everybody in the shower now. Or we're going to miss breakfast."

"Oh shit, I need to see if Maia is awake so we can call Ava too." Lexie leaped off my lap and bolted towards the bathroom, dropping her blanket over the back of the couch as she went. We all followed her like a trail of lovesick puppies.

I glanced at Dio, before flicking my gaze to Sam and Dave, worried things would be awkward now. I wasn't sure I was looking to add a boyfriend to the mix. My relationship with Lexi made me happier than I ever could have imagined. She was my mate and there was no competition in my heart. I was completely hers.

Yet a part of me had always felt a desire for Dio and I'd hungered for a safe space to explore that part of myself. What we had together now, sharing Lexie between us, felt perfect for me. It seemed to turn her on, too.

I shouldn't have worried though. Dio had a massive cheeky grin on his face. He slapped me on the shoulder and squeezed reassuringly. "Fuck, she's something else, isn't she?"

Dave and Sam just laughed. I grinned back at Dio and nodded as I relaxed, knowing we were going to be okay.

"Dibs on showering with Lexie," Sam yelled as he raced ahead of us. There were four shower heads out there and five of us now. I liked the playful side of Sam that seemed to come out around Lexie, now that he wasn't carrying the burden of his power alone. I'd noticed him slip a letter into the letterbox on his way past. It made my heart smile.

"Shit, is that going to be a thing?" Dave grumbled as he followed behind. "I call dibs for tomorrow, if it is."

Dio held the door and waited for Dave and me to pass through, to close it behind us. "Hey, who put a lock on the door? And when the hell did anyone find the time?"

Dave shrugged. "It needed to be done. It didn't take long. I stole a lock from one of the storage sheds. Lexie's more important than grain."

Grain was pretty valuable in an apocalypse, but I didn't argue with Dave. I agreed, Lexie was still more important.

Sam already had Lexie under the shower head when we made it through the door. She was in his arms with her legs wrapped around his waist and his cock buried deep inside her.

Dave took the shower next to them and soaped himself down while he blatantly watched Lexie. "Turn her around and fuck her from behind, Sam," Dave demanded. "I want to see her tits getting sprayed by the water while you make them bounce."

Sam shot him a heated look, and did what Dave asked. He dropped Lexie to her feet and spun her around in his arms before he pulled her ass back slightly and rammed into her. She flung one arm out to slap the wall and steady herself as Sam maneuvered her other arm behind her back, thrusting her chest out and giving Dave the perfect view of her tits under the spray.

"Is that what you wanted?" Sam growled at Dave as he set a fast pace, making Lexie's tits bounce wildly. Yet despite Sam's tone, I could feel his desire to please Dave in the bond. Dave just grunted as he soaped up his hard cock.

Dave, watching and directing them, seemed to set both Sam and Lexie off, as Lexie moaned through another intense orgasm. Sam chased hers, his body jerking as he roared out his own pleasure. He spilled himself deep inside her before he slumped onto the bench surrounding the shower area to catch his breath, pulling Lexie down with him.

Lexie shot a sly look at Dave before she hopped off Sam's lap, accidentally dropped the soap and kicked it in Dave's direction. "Oops."

Dave narrowed his eyes as Lexie sashayed towards him with a glint in her eyes. Our girl wasn't done yet. When she reached the soap, she turned around and bent over in front of him, waving her ass in the air.

Dave groaned, grabbed her ass, and shoved his impressive dick into her while she was still bent over. She gasped as he pulled her up, spun her around and pushed her into the wall.

"If you wave your naked ass in front of me, you're going to get fucked hard, baby girl," Dave rasped into her ear, loud enough that we could all hear.

"Yes, Daddy," she moaned as she bit her lip mischievously and Dave groaned loudly. Despite his previous objections, the name seemed to turn him on. He pumped into her furiously as he grabbed her breasts roughly with both hands, using the hard grip to pull her onto his cock. He moved one hand down to her pussy and his hand jerked as I assumed he flicked her clit. She came hard and fast again.

She was so sensitive and responsive, especially since her heat, and we loved it.

"Good girl," he growled roughly. He came on a long groan as his teeth latched onto his mark on her shoulder like he was trying to claim her again. Lexie's orgasm seemed to drag out as she writhed underneath him.

"Fuck, now I'm hard again," Dio said as he paid a lot of attention to soaping down his dick. "I think I want in on some of that good girl action."

"You can be my good girl next time," Dave joked.

"Shit, why does that turn me on?" Dio asked, looking confused with his hand stilled on his dick.

Lexie grinned like she knew a secret. "You seemed to love it when I called you a good boy the night we claimed each other, if I recall."

"Oh fuck. Do I have a praise kink?"

"We can figure out all your kinks and your confused sexuality later. We're really late now," I said as I flicked water at Dio playfully. He turned and winked at me and I had to force my dick not to twitch, as I had a mental image of Lexie and Dio on their knees while Dave praised them both.

I turned away with a groan and finished washing myself down. It was kinda pointless, though. Lexie's meringue spiced scent was so saturated in the semi-enclosed space, we were all going to be drenched in it even after we'd all cleaned up. The idea pleased me enormously.

Dave soaped Lexie down and cleaned her thoroughly, kissing her lightly as he went. I watched Sam smile at them before a lost expression crossed his face. He wrapped a towel around his lean waist and wandered off to get dressed. It made me happy to see how content he looked now. I hated seeing his distress the night I'd gotten home. Yet, there was still something bothering him.

Home. The thought filled me with joy. It had been such a long time since I'd thought of any place as home. I realized home was these people as much as it was this place. I followed Sam up to the loft, catching him from behind as he pulled up his pants and gave him a squeezy hug.

He seemed surprised, but he reached up and gripped my arms tightly. "What's this for?"

"Do I need a reason?"

"Absolutely not."

I smiled as I leaned on his shoulder, just enjoying being able to hug someone whenever I wanted and hoping to give him some comfort through whatever was bothering him. I sensed it wasn't us, and he would tell us when he was ready. Until then, I'd be here for him. He relaxed against me and we both watched birds flit past the big triangular picture window at the end of the loft for a moment.

We shifted as the others all trooped up the stairs to let them pass. Nobody commented on the way we were standing, they just maneuvered around us. Dave started rifling through clothes on the floor while Dio started snooping through an old trunk in the corner.

Lexie's and Dave's clothes were strewn around the loft now, but Sam, Pala, and I didn't have a lot of clothing options. We'd only brought a few items with us in our bug out packs. Dave and Maia's mates had all donated some clothes, but it was still slim pickings. We'd have to do a supply run for things like clothes soon, and maybe start a communal clothing pool for extras. The kids and teenagers would benefit from that, with how quickly they grew out of clothes. I'd worn a lot of my cousins' hand-me-downs as a kid.

"Hey, what are these?" Dio asked, holding up a bundle of photos from the trunk he was rummaging through. "Dave, I think you have a stalker."

"Shit, Dio. No." Lexie yelled, and tried to snatch the photos from him. He held them up high, laughing while Lexie tried to jump for them. Dave straightened up and grabbed them from behind Dio.

"Did you take all these, baby girl?" Dave asked Lexie as he rifled through the stack. I caught a glimpse, and they all seemed to be zoomed in shots of Dave. Lexie had her hands over her face and her cheeks were bright red.

"You weren't ever supposed to see those," she mumbled. "Are you mad?"

"Not even a little," Dave said as he pulled her into a hug. "Considering I was following you without your permission the whole time."

I smiled as Dave moved Lexie's hands away from her face and kissed her sweetly.

"Ugh," Dio said dramatically, as he turned back to looking for clothes. "I can't tell if you guys are sweet as shit or poster children for a red flag relationship."

Dave let Lexie go so he could pick up a pillow and throw it at Dio.

"We need to cut some wood and build some dressers," I said as I watched everyone rummaging for clothes before I released Sam so he could finish dressing too.

"You know how to build a dresser? That would be awesome," Lexie said, as she shot me a grateful smile.

"Yeah, my family built most of our furniture. My dad showed me how to make the drawers slide properly without metal runners as soon as I was old enough to hold a hammer."

"It'll be a solid skill to pass onto our kids," Sam said casually, as he bent over to grab a shirt from a bug-out pack on the floor.

"If you all throw your dirty stuff into the corner, I'll take it and do a couple of loads of laundry today," Dave said, gesturing to the far corner. "I'll see if I can find us something to use as a washing hamper, too."

I eyed Lexie, who had gone perfectly still, holding a skirt in front of her as if she'd been about to put it on but was now frozen in place. "You okay, my heart?"

Dio looked up from where he was crouched near her feet, springing up to put his arms around her. "Hey, what's going on?"

"Uh, you guys just said kids."

"Yeah." Dio looked confused.

"I'm not ready to have kids."

Sam chuckled as he pulled both Lexie and Dio into his arms. "I didn't mean today, sweetheart." It was the first time I'd heard him call her any kind of endearment, and she seemed to melt into him.

"What if I'm never ready?" she whispered.

"There's a hell of a lot of scared kids out there, and far too many of them are alone right now. We saw a few last night. Plus, there are always kids running around the farm. I'm sure we can find some kids that need father figures if we feel the need to share what we know," Dave said.

Lexie looked suddenly bereft, as if she was about to cry. Dave and I both moved over and joined in the group hug.

"Lex," I prompted, "talk to us."

"It's stupid. I've never thought about kids. I got the two-year birth control implant so I wouldn't have to. But the thought of little versions of you guys never existing makes me feel unbearably sad. I'm so freaking confused right now."

A single tear tracked down Lexie's cheek and Dave reached up to wipe it away gently.

"You repressed your omega instincts for a very long time, Lex," Sam said from where he'd nuzzled into her neck. "Your hormones and emotions are going to be all over the place for a while. Give yourself some time to adjust. It's not a discussion we need to have today."

"Shit. I'm really hoping your implant can withstand all the sex we had during your heat," Dio chuckled.

"We probably should have discussed kids before then, but your heat kind of took us all by surprise," Dave added.

A mischievous grin suddenly appeared on Lexie's face, which was a good sign. It loosened the vice that had just settled around my heart at seeing her upset.

"Yeah, about that. Maia's book says that an omega's pheromones in the build-up to the heat turns her mates into super charged sperm bombs."

She peeked up at us and I could see the smug grin that was stretching across my face reflected on my mates' faces. She shook her head and tried not to laugh. "You don't have to all look so chuffed at that."

"You are our omega and our heart, Lex," I said. "Nothing about that means you have to be the sole or even the primary carer for any child born of our love. We're a pack. If it happens, we will all step up. We'll figure it out together."

"My mother was a teacher, my dad looked after us during the day and one of my uncles usually cooked at night," Dio added.

Lexie nodded, but sharing parental duties wasn't what her mind had fixated on. "Born of our love?" Lexie asked as she bit her lip and tried to hide a cheeky grin as she looked at me.

"Yeah, our love for you and our love for each other," I said. I hadn't spoken those words yet because, for an alpha, it wasn't as powerful as calling her my mate. Mate conveyed so much more for us, but Lexie had lived most of her life as a beta and if she wanted those words, it wasn't a hardship to use them. They were definitely in my heart. "If you want me to be specific, I love you."

Lexie grinned at me. "I love you, too."

"If you haven't figured it out yet, Lex, we all love you. I thought it was a given, but if you need to hear the words, I'll say it every day. I love you," Dio reassured her, and we all murmured our agreement.

I added another "I love you," to the ones echoing around the room as Lexie's smile threatened to rival the sun peeking through the window.

"Fine. I love all you buttheads too," Lexie answered, laughing, as Dio tickled her lightly along her side.

Someone knocking on the door downstairs interrupted us and had us all pulling apart. Sam was the most dressed, so he pulled on a shirt and headed for the stairs while shooting us all a querying look. We all shrugged.

"Are you expecting someone?" Sam asked Lexie, as he hesitated on the top step.

"Nope, nobody usually comes up here except me, Leif, and his mates. They've been staying away, but it could be one of them. They never used to knock, but they might now that they know we're all living here."

Sam nodded and leaped down the steps as the knock sounded again. We all hustled to throw on enough clothing to be presentable and followed him.

He yanked open the heavy door as I moved up behind him. "Hey Jimmy," Sam said warmly to the beta teenager standing nervously at the door.

"Jimmy, you legend," Dio pushed past us and clapped Jimmy on the shoulder. Jimmy looked like he was about to pass out. "Did I tell you guys that Jimmy stunned an alpha that came out of nowhere the other night and took us all by surprise? He used the stun gun that Lexie gave him. You have balls of steel, my friend."

Jimmy blushed and shrugged with his hands jammed in the pocket of his hoodie. "He seemed drunk. It wasn't a big deal."

"You have good instincts. You acted fast and protected the people with you. It's an enormous deal, Jimmy."

Sam smiled at the fidgety teenager. "If you impressed Dio, it *is* a big deal, Jimmy. If you want more training, in self defense or anything else, let us know."

"Really?" Jimmy looked up at us all, surprised. "I'd like to know how to protect my mom better."

"We have to clear it with your mom first," Dave said, "but if you want to join in with the cadets doing some fitness and basic training, we can start there."

"Can some of my friends come too? They've been talking about wanting to learn some skills after the attack on the farm last week."

"Absolutely. Just let me know who and we'll get it sorted." Dave nodded at him, treating him like the young adult he was, and not a kid.

"Thank you, Sir. I'm going to go tell them." He turned to take off, but Sam snapped out his arm to halt him. "Hang on a sec. Did you come up here for a reason?"

"Oh shit. Yeah."

"Language, kid. There's a lady here," Sam admonished him gruffly, jerking his head in Lexie's direction. "Would you talk like that in front of your mom?"

"Sorry, Lexie," Jimmy said quickly, looking embarrassed, and a little terrified.

"It's okay, Jimmy," Lexie said, as she rolled her eyes at Sam. "What did you need to tell us?"

"Damon sent me up here. He asked if you guys could all meet him in the security office before breakfast."

"Okay. Run back and tell him we're on our way." Jimmy turned and fled.

Sam looked at us with apprehension, and all of our moods shifted. It seemed like trouble was still looking for us and one day of rest was all we were going to get.

Forty-Seven

 *Sam*

I blinked as I walked into the security office, my eyes trying to adjust to the dim light inside. The windows and blinds were all closed, I assumed for security, so it was also stuffy inside. Especially with the amount of people now in the small studio cabin.

Maia stood up from where she'd perched on the arm of the couch. Damon, Leif, Hunter, and Max were all ranged around her with scowls on their faces as they watched us approach and greet her. Maia wrapped her arms around Lexie, as Lexie sniffed her hair. "Did you change shampoo?"

"No," Maia said, pulling back and sniffing her own hair. "Why does everyone keep asking me about how I smell? Do I smell bad?"

"You don't smell bad, just a little different. I can't figure out what it is, though." Maia just shrugged at Lexie and slipped out of her arms to give me a quick hug. She startled me. I hadn't been expecting it, and I'd barely gotten my arms around her before she'd let me go and sat down on Hunter's lap. *Dammit.*

Hunter looked relieved, though, wrapping Maia up tight, while Leif shifted closer to her on the couch. They looked extra protective and growly this morning, which had me on edge.

Bear even got in on the action, propping his head on Maia's lap and nuzzling her stomach. He refused to move when she tried to shift his head away, and she sighed in exasperation. "Why is everyone crowding me today?"

She looked at Lexie for help, but my girl just smirked at her. "I'm not his keeper. Bear does what he wants."

Maia just sighed. "We're calling Ava after this meeting. Don't disappear on me or I'll titty twist you so hard," Maia mock glared at Lexie and Lexie nodded at her, while subtly covering her boobs. My sister was feisty today.

"So what's this meeting about?" I asked, trying to get us on track. I was sure whatever this was about had to be important. They didn't usually have their family meeting until after breakfast, and never in the security office.

"Your gramps' equipment," Damon replied. "After everything that went down the other night, I don't think we can wait to contact the Network. We need allies."

"Okay, I agree. Let's do it." I stepped to the machine on a table in the back, but halted in confusion. "The lights aren't on."

"Yeah, that's the problem." Max answered quietly as he stepped up beside me. "I got it all open, but it doesn't have a switch or any cords. It appears to have some kind of Indiana Jones mechanism, and I can't figure out how it works."

Damon pointed me towards the side of the machine and I shuffled around to get a closer look.

"It looks like an inverted 3D star. Did your gramps mention anything about a key?" Max asked.

"No." I answered abruptly, feeling frustrated.

"What about the letter you mentioned? Was there anything in there, maybe something written in code?" I looked up and Max was staring at the device as if he could force it to open with mind control.

"No. Nothing that I'd know how to crack. I haven't spoken to my gramps since I was a teenager." I looked at Maia, feeling all my old resentment at my gramps rising to the surface. "Any ideas, Mai Mai?"

She smiled at the nickname, and I felt the world brighten just a little. The world had always felt better growing up whenever I could get my sister to smile. "Can I read the letter?"

I felt the smile on my face disappear in an instant. "Yeah. I guess I can't put it off anymore. Can we step outside to do it, though?"

"Sure," Maia said, with more than a little sarcasm. "If everyone will let me up."

"Bear. Off." I growled and tapped him on the nose. Bear grunted in annoyance, but lifted his head off Maia's lap.

"How did you do that?" Lexie complained loudly while glaring at Bear. "He never listens to me." Bear ambled over and whuffed at her as he butted her hip to pacify her.

I just smiled as I held out my hand to Maia to help her up. I hesitated next to Lexie for a moment, wondering if I should ask her to come with us. This was going to be hard, but in my heart, I felt it should be just Maia and me as she read it. Lexie leant forward and kissed me lightly. "I'll be right here if you need me."

I sent her a silent thank you through the bond and turned to head outside. It felt like we were heading out to meet the firing squad, not read a letter.

The door closed behind us and before we moved away, I heard Lexie ask, "Are we really going to pretend like we're not going to watch out the window?"

I shook my head, but I wasn't really surprised or even upset. It was part of living in a small community, amongst family. I headed over to the large shady tree at the edge of the garden and handed the letter to Maia.

She fiddled with it for a moment before opening it, and glanced up at me, almost shyly. "I read some of your letters yesterday. They were in order and I started at the beginning. The first one was dated the day you left, the one you said you wrote from out in the barn. Ben must have found it with gramps' things. I just wanted you to know. It meant a lot to me to read it."

I nodded to her. Finding those letters still felt too raw to talk about.

"I took them out of the metal box. There was a beautiful old timber box in Damon's study, and he let me have it to keep them in. I'm going to treasure them, Sam. I mean, I believed you when you told me you'd written them, but actually reading them is completely different. Your emotions were so strong as you wrote them, I could almost feel them soaked into the paper."

"Those letters were my lifeline while I was gone." My throat was suddenly tight, and she reached out to grab my hand. My gaze flicked down to the one in her hand now, and she tracked my focus.

I'd dreamed of being able to give her one of my letters in person. Yet, here I was with another letter for her that was so very different. "I wish I was handing you one of my letters now. I'm afraid this one won't bring you any joy."

Her eyes narrowed, and she looked at the letter in concern as she dropped my hand and flipped it open. She started reading straight away, tracing her finger over the words as if she was trying to connect with gramps through the ink he'd used. She was always romantic about letters and books. It was why I'd kept writing, knowing if she was getting them, they'd mean so much to her.

A small bang had me glancing back at the security cabin, to see a window full of startled faces and a curtain rod hanging half across their heads. Most of them were frozen in place, as if I couldn't see them if they didn't move, while Hunter was pretending to clean a spot with his sleeve. I loved them all at that moment. They were family. Even Maia's mates.

When I turned back to Maia, there were silent tears tracking through the devastation on her face. I hated causing her this pain, and I'd put it off as long as I could. I'd even briefly considered not showing her, but that wouldn't have been fair.

I gasped when Maia suddenly grabbed her chest as if she was in pain, and fell to the grass as her legs crumpled underneath her. I dropped beside her, taking her into my arms, but her mates were already out the door. Leif ripped her away from me as Damon, Hunter and Max surrounded her protectively, shooting dark glares my way.

"What the fuck is in that letter?" Damon snarled at me as Lexie jumped in front of me and my mates surrounded me from behind, lending their silent support. I could sense raw pain coming from Maia as she sat in her mate's arms.

We suddenly looked like two opposing groups about to go to war, not friends and family. I couldn't stand it, so I blurted out the truth that had been eating away at me quietly since I'd first read that letter.

"Our gramps didn't just steal all their research. He stole us."

"Explain. Now," Damon ground out, a growl growing in his chest and his beast riding him hard.

"Damon," Lexie snapped, "they're both in pain. Can't you see that?"

Damon looked at me as if seeing me for the first time, but I couldn't take my eyes off my sister.

"Fuck. Sorry," Damon ground out, and attempted to rein himself in. "Something is driving our beasts to protect Maia right now, to the point of irrationality. It's worse than usual. I need him to explain before I lose it."

"Sam, what do you mean by he stole you?" Lexie asked me in a gentler tone.

"The mother and father who raised us weren't our biological parents, which I guess explains how our mother could dump us so easily when things got rough." My voice sounded strained even to my own ears.

"According to our gramps, our biological mother was his omega. They kept her in a facility they built. She became their first research subject. They did constant tests and trials on her. They thought they could make omegas more fertile by dominating them more and making them more submissive. The tests included attempts to breed her and when she fell pregnant twice, they claimed their project was a success. Gramps wasn't one of our biological fathers, though. He was older than the others and not an alpha, so they deemed him unsuitable for the breeding tests.

"In his letter, he said he objected to their tests, especially as they steadily became more extreme, but they wouldn't stop. When she died, he took us, along with all the research they'd gained from their tests on our mother. He hired a couple to raise us and hide us in beta society, figuring we'd be safer there."

"Do you believe him?" Maia asked so quietly I barely heard her above the breeze rustling through the branches above us.

"Yes." I hated to admit it, as I shoved my hands in my pockets, feeling agitated. "I only have a few early memories, but they're all in white rooms. I just assumed we'd lived in a really white house."

I laughed, but there was no humor in my voice. It sounded harsh even to my own ears. "My best memories are all of you, Mai Mai, and they came later."

"And Ben?" Damon asked, sounding tentative, as if he wasn't sure if he wanted to know.

"Not our biological brother," Maia answered him flatly. "Or anyone special. He was the son of our hired parents."

She actually seemed relieved by that, but then her face shattered again. "All this time I've loved gramps and mourned him and he wasn't even my gramps. I didn't even know his real name. I know your experience was different, Sam, but I always believed he loved me."

I moved past my own mates and dropped in front of Maia. Her mates finally shifted to make room for me and I felt mine closing in as well, until we'd huddled in one group again, nothing dividing us. A family.

"He did, Mai Mai. Can't you feel that in his letter? Everything he did was to protect you, and me, in his own way. He left everything behind, gave up everything, and lived his life in the shadows for us. He loved us both, and that's more important than blood."

"Who was he really?" Max asked gently.

"His name was Frank Gascombe."

"The tech billionaire who died mysteriously in that big car crash, with two unknown kids in the car?" Dave asked from behind me. He sounded incredulous. I just nodded sadly.

"Holy shit, when you said he gave up everything, you really meant it," Hunter chuckled, but he sounded slightly dazed.

"No wonder he could keep you guys and the Network under the radar. He invented half the tech we use today." Max looked back towards the cabin to the device we'd brought back with us, wonder in his eyes. I could tell he was itching to unravel its secrets.

"He was actually a lot like you Max, from what I read in a biography once," Dave said quietly. "He grew up poor on a farm and went into the military to get an education. Had an insatiable curiosity about how things worked."

Max looked sad at that. "I wish I could have met him, not just to pick his brain, but because he loved you guys."

Maia reached up and squeezed Max's hand.

"You said he wasn't one of your biological fathers," Dio probed gently while he rested his hand on my neck, anchoring me, like he always did. "Did he say who was?"

I took a deep breath and looked at Maia. She gave me a brief, jerky, nod.

"Gramps claims Ronan and Sirena's dad is Maia's biological father." There were shocked gasps all around us.

"Holy shitballs. That means Sirena is your half sister," Lexie blurted out.

"Yeah, and that fuckhead trying to dominate and claim her as his toy was her half brother," Damon ground out, sounding like he wanted to kill him all over again.

I felt ill at the thought of what Maia had gone through, and to find out Ronan had been her half brother the whole time. It paled in comparison to what Ben had done to her, and that had devastated her.

"Do you think Ronan knew?" Dave asked, watching Maia as carefully as he was me.

I gave a lazy shrug. "Does it matter now?"

"Not to me," Maia answered, sounding resolute. The color was coming back to her face, and I breathed a sigh of relief. I had been worried this news would destroy her, but I underestimated her. She survived the Palace and came out stronger. She would survive this, too.

"Do you think her father knew?" Leif asked. Everyone was quiet for a moment.

"I can't be sure, but I don't think he knew when she was there," Pala said. "Ronan was running the Palace operation and reporting to his dad. From what I saw, there was a lot Ronan wasn't telling him."

"If he didn't then, he's put it together now. Otherwise, why would he have been at your gramps' house with my dad?" Damon said.

I had no answers for him right now, but I had a feeling we were going to find out.

"What about your biological father, Sam?" Dio pressed, knowing there was more. He had always known me so well. Lexie's grip on my shoulders, where she was hugging me from the side, tightened.

"My biological father is Hunter's dad."

Forty-Eight

H oly Batman. I did not see any of that coming. I felt like I had a death grip on Sam and for the life of me, I couldn't let go. We'd been desperate for intel, but the secrets revealed in their gramps' letter almost felt like too much.

Nobody spoke for a moment, but Sam's gaze had locked with Hunter's. Hunter was breathing shallowly, looking like a startled fawn in the crosshairs of a rifle. He opened his mouth, then closed it again as his eyes went suddenly shiny.

I could feel Sam's fear spooling through our bond. A sudden spiky fear of rejection. I sent a silent plea to Hunter to get it together.

"You're my half brother?" Hunter asked tentatively, as if he needed someone to confirm he hadn't heard wrong. Sam just nodded.

"Why did you wait to tell me? You read that letter two days ago," Hunter asked, sounding incredibly vulnerable all of a sudden.

My heart ached for him, and his fucked up lonely childhood. Hunter and I had worked closely together helping settle the women I brought back to the farm, and he'd let slip a few things over the years that made me want to go back in time and wrap little Hunter up in a blanket to keep him safe forever.

"Because telling you meant telling Maia about Ronan. I wasn't in a hurry to cause her more pain. It's all mixed up together." Sam sounded calm, but I could feel the shake in his shoulders.

"I felt like my dead brother's ghost haunted me growing up." Hunter's eyebrows pinched together and his voice sounded thin, as if he was far away. "His absence was a constant presence in that house. I always dreamed about what it would be like to have an actual brother around. I imagined all the shit we could get up to together."

"I thought I had one, but I had no emotional connection with him," Sam said, then paused, swallowing hard before laying it all out. "You and your mates already feel more like brothers to me than he ever did."

Hunter stood up suddenly and held out his hand to Sam. I let Sam go and scrambled to my feet alongside him. Hunter immediately grabbed Sam in a bear hug, looking dazed.

"My asshole father isn't much of a prize, but I'd be damned glad to call you my brother," Hunter said, his voice thick. I felt my throat getting tight, too. These people all meant so much to me.

We all surrounded them and joined in the hug as if the same string pulled us all, weaving through and amongst us. It made me wonder about fate briefly. I'd always kind of believed we made our own, but there was something at work here I couldn't explain.

This big family that was growing by the day, that Leif and I had found, filled my heart with joy. I glanced across the people between us to Leif, and he smiled gently at me. We both had plenty of room in our hearts for more family.

"Hang on a sec," came Maia's muffled voice from somewhere within the scrum. We all pulled apart slightly to let her speak. "If you and Sam are half brothers, what does that make you and me, Hunter? Are we like a stepbrother and sister or something?"

"Oooh, kinky. I like it. Let's go with that," Hunter laughed, breaking the heaviness of the moment.

Sam punched him lightly, as much as he could with us all still crowded so close. "Hey, that's my sister." He had a smile on his face, though.

"Kinda mine too, now. That's the point," Hunter laughed before Leif took a turn to smack him.

"Okay, okay. Too soon, I get it," Hunter said, rubbing his arm.

We could always rely on Hunter to ease any tension with humor. It was his default coping mechanism. He made life fun, though.

"If this is a picnic, you all need food," came a thin voice from behind me.

We all shifted and turned to see GG standing behind us with an enormous basket. Dave quickly moved to grab it from her. It looked heavy. She had a thin throw blanket thrown over her shoulder that she passed over too.

"The girls have been experimenting with some recipes in your great granny's recipe book, Maia." A brief look of sadness flickered across Maia's face, but she seemed to push it away quickly. "There are some breakfast biscuits in there made with oats. Easier to make once we run out of flour until we can figure out how to get the old mill working."

"Thank you, GG." Maia stepped forward and embraced the elderly woman gently. But GG wasn't having it. She pulled Maia in for a solid hug. "I won't break," she grumbled.

I looked past GG to the window into the kitchen and noticed Isabella and Sirena looking out. I waved to them in thanks and they waved back before disappearing inside. That was going to be an interesting conversation between Maia and Sirena, and it would need to happen soon.

"There's some hot chicory in there for you all. I heard you were low on coffee and it's a decent substitute."

"Really," Maia squealed. "Where did you get chicory, GG?"

"I've been seeding the forest with chicory seeds for years. It grows well out there. I can show you what the plants look like."

"That's amazing, GG. Thank you," I said, and meant it. Having a substitute for coffee was going to avoid a lot of caffeine withdrawals and frayed tempers around here. "Maia and I will get a few girls together and take you up on that. Just let us know when. Then you'll have to show us how to make it."

Several growly variations of, "You're not going out alone," and, "You need someone to go with you," sounded off around me. I waved them all off. Maia and I could manage a walk in the forest without an escort. We'd take Bear in case we came across any wildlife.

"Oh my god, we're saved," Maia sighed dramatically as she rifled through the basket before she screwed the top off a large thermos and sniffed the contents. I couldn't help but laugh at her as I pulled her arm to the side to get a deep lungful of it myself. "Stop hogging it."

"You shouldn't drink that now, though, Maia," GG said as Maia took another large inhale of the scented steam coming out of the top.

"It smells divine, slightly more nutty than regular coffee, but still good. Why wouldn't I drink it?"

"It doesn't have any caffeine, but it's not recommended for pregnant women. It's still a stimulant and could cause bleeding," GG said.

Everyone froze. I noticed the thermos slip in Maia's hand and I grabbed it quickly before she spilt all the liquid gold inside.

"Excuse me? Uh, I'm not pregnant. Why would you think I'm pregnant?" Maia patted her flat tummy over the leggings and baggy cable-knitted jumper she was wearing. "I'm a little bloated from that espresso yesterday, but not that much."

"You really shouldn't be drinking espresso," GG frowned at her, "and haven't you noticed your scent has changed?"

All eyes swiveled to Maia.

"Fuck," Damon growled. "Her scent changed at least two days ago." He instantly started scanning the treeline as if he was looking for threats and a low warning growl started up in his chest that didn't cut off.

"She was only in heat four or five days ago. Would changes happen that quickly?" I asked. I knew nothing about omega pregnancies, but that seemed fast.

"Omega biology is different to a beta. Pregnancy takes quickly and progresses faster, too. Her mates should have picked up on the scent change and instinctively started acting extra protective."

"Well, that's certainly been happening," Sam said with a smirk.

"Shit, she's going to need vitamins and stuff," Hunter yelled, way louder than necessary. He started spinning and looking around as if he was going to find a chemist had suddenly popped up between the trees.

"I'll get Luis. Meet me at the cabin," Max yelled as he took off. I shook my head. He was supposed to be their calm center and not affected by alpha pheromones. Leif just straight out picked Maia up off the ground, then froze as if he didn't want to jostle her.

"What are you doing?" Maia yelled at Leif.

"You can't stand up. You're pregnant," he said, looking scandalized.

"Lexie, can you knock some sense into these guys? Please." She looked over her shoulder at me, with big pleading eyes. I couldn't do anything to help her, though. I was laughing too hard. Dio, Pala and Dave were all standing behind me, looking bewildered.

GG came to her rescue, stalking up to the guys and issuing orders.

"Leif, put her down, exercise is good for her." Leif put Maia down, but he looked reluctant about it and hovered over her protectively.

"Hunter, nature has been providing everything she's going to need for thousands of years. You don't need anything from a bottle. We'll gather everything she needs from around the farm." Hunter seemed chastened but unconvinced.

"Damon, stop growling. Nothing is in those trees that wasn't there five minutes ago. Take her back to your cabin for now if it will make you feel better until you all calm down. But if you try and keep her stuffed away in there, you'll do more harm than good. She needs fresh air."

Damon looked away from the trees, but kept glancing back, and his growl refused to cut-off.

GG looked in the direction Max had gone, then let out a long-suffering sigh. "Get Luis to look at her if you must, but all he'll be able to tell you is she's not giving birth to a goat. Now go, the lot of you, before you freak out everyone coming down looking for food. I'll meet you at your cabin in a few minutes."

Leif immediately picked Maia up again and walked off as GG rolled her eyes and Dave made sure Hunter took the basket of food so Maia would have something to eat.

Maia called out over Leif's shoulder. "Wait, the phone call with Ava. Don't you dare call her without me, Lexie. I'll titty twist you so hard."

"Go, I've got Ava covered. I'll bring the phone to you."

Maia made pinchey fingers over Leif's shoulder at me. I laughed as I covered my boobs, again, even though she was headed away from me.

"Can I get in on that titty twisting action?" Dio asked, putting his hands over mine.

GG turned and swatted him. "Manners, boy."

Dio's face turned red, and I figured he'd momentarily forgotten GG was there. "Sorry, GG."

GG burst out laughing. "We called it a purple nurple in my heyday, but only if you did it right."

She turned and headed back towards the kitchen, still laughing to herself.

Forty-Nine

I grabbed Sam and pulled him towards me, stretching up and wrapping one arm around his neck. I had a death grip on the thermos in my other arm. "Are you okay?"

It felt like life was moving at impossible speed since the Crash happened. We were bouncing from one crisis and calamity to another and figuring it out as we went. Yet life had also brought me my mates, so I couldn't complain. There was nowhere else I wanted to be right now, than here, at home, with them.

My mates all surrounded Sam and me as we stood under the tree together, their scents mingling in a delicious concoction. They all instinctively reached for Sam and I, and each other, in simple ways. Dave was warming my back while Claudio was propped against him with one hand on my waist, and Pala had his head on Sam's shoulder, while lightly playing with my hair. Even Bear was getting in on the action, his head resting on Sam's hip while he gently nudged me with his nose, hoping for pats.

We were all drawing on each other's energy to center and balance us. I could feel Pala's calm river, Dio's light, Dave's rock solid dependability and Sam's dominant caress, all moving within me.

"I'm okay, sweetheart," Sam said as he drew both arms up around me and pulled me in tight. Sharing his warmth and his strength. "I won't lie. That was tough, but I knew you guys would have my back if it went sideways. I just needed a bit of time to process it before I shared it with Maia, so I could be here for her if she took it badly. Are you okay?"

"Me? Okay about what?" I asked, genuinely confused. I felt so happy and content right now, in this moment. *Couldn't he feel that?*

"With Maia being pregnant? After what we talked about this morning."

"I may not know if I'm ready to fall pregnant myself, but I'm going to be the best aunt ever."

"Yeah, you will," Pala said over my shoulder.

"Besides, now I get all this delicious chicory coffee to myself," I added with a laugh, as I clutched the thermos between Sam and I.

"Oh, you're sharing that chicory," Dave warned. I just winked at him from the safety of Sam's arms.

When I'd met Sam, I'd known he was mine from the first moment, but I hadn't been sure we'd ever reach this point. Freely hugging and securely bonded. His rage and his fear had been so entrenched, and I'd sensed the abyss pulling at him, dragging him under.

I'd worked with a lot of women to process their emotions after escaping difficult lives, but it hadn't prepared me for Sam. Without this pack, I don't know that any one of us would have been enough to save him.

He'd had to overcome a difficult childhood, traumatic teenage years and a physical power he couldn't understand or control. Yet here he was, with a peaceful contentment flowing through our bond. It made my heart feel too big for my chest.

Dave had equally challenged me, constantly pulling at me while holding me at a distance. Granted, I'd held him at a distance, too. Too scared of triggering something within myself by letting in someone important.

Yet Dio and Pala had blasted through my walls so easily, like they'd always been within them, before we'd even met.

I wasn't ever going to take these pack hugs for granted. Sam snuck a hand under my t-shirt and I arched into him, as warmth from his hands spread tingles where he drew lazy circles against my skin with his thumb. I rubbed my cheek over his neck, instinctively marking him with my scent. He growled lightly and I could feel his beast's pleasure at my possessive touch.

I'd never in my life felt more connected and needed than I did at this moment. I realized I'd been strong for myself my whole life, but I'd also kept people at arm's length. Even my brother, who I loved fiercely. I'd never let anybody in before now, only giving people small parts of myself. Now, that had all changed. I'd let in a village.

I let go of all my worries about being a problem for other people, and just lent on my guys for a minute while I sorted out my thoughts. Knowing they would cherish the opportunity to hold me up, even just for a little while.

We'd come together so quickly as a pack, but it didn't mean we were weak. We all filled in each other's broken pieces. Dio helped Dave chill out, Dave anchored Sam, Pala made Dio feel whole. They all made me feel like I could conquer the world, and they'd cheer me on while I did it.

I knew it wouldn't be all hugs all the time. Especially between Sam and Hunter. Despite the hug fest they'd just had, it would take some time to adjust to their new roles in each other's lives. Their childhoods had left them both with scars, but we'd all help them through it.

Even with the peace we all felt at this moment, there was so much we had to do hovering at the edges of our awareness. We had to help the town recover and take care of the Palace omegas. Then there were Ava and Cary. I had no intention of leaving them alone to work out who the feral alpha was, and what was up with the twins. Ava and Cary had both stepped up when I'd needed a friend and I owed them to do the same. More than that, I wanted to do the same. They'd both snuck through my walls.

We also had to figure out where the Palace lab techs had gone, where Maven was hiding, what they had planned next, and who that sniper had been working for.

On top of all that, we needed to keep Maia and Ava safe. Especially now that Maia was pregnant while mated to a prime alpha. If the people hunting her found out, they'd never rest until they got her back in their clutches. Plus, there were all the risks of a pregnancy with only a vet and traditional medicine to rely on.

We seemed to always be in the dark, pun intended, since the Crash. Reacting to outside influences who all knew far more than we did.

"I'm tired of playing defense," I suddenly blurted to my guys.

"What do you mean?" Sam asked as he pulled back slightly to see my face, concern etched across his.

"She means, with the Palace and Maven. She wants to go to war." Dave sounded completely sure of himself, and me.

"We're already at war," I said. "We just need to start playing our game and not theirs, so we can end it and help the world get back on track. Maybe even make it better."

"You don't think small, do you, sweetheart?" Sam chuckled.

"Nope, you better get used to it."

"What do you have in mind?" Dio asked, sounding like he was already adding his name to the sign-up sheet as he ran his hand through my hair.

I smiled against Sam's neck. "A little mayhem, probably, maybe even a tiny revolution," I answered honestly, "but not today."

They all chuckled and pulled in closer. I didn't have it worked out just yet, but we were a team, a pack. We'd figure it out together. I didn't have to do it alone anymore. Besides, I had a niggling feeling the feral alpha and mysterious twins were going to provide some missing links.

And I knew now just how far I would go to protect my home, my pack and my family. I would put everything on the line to give them a future and to make the world safer. Nothing less would do.

I rested my head on Sam's chest and he started up a light purr that sent bliss zinging through me. My body melted into him as I enjoyed it for a moment more before I pushed away gently. I suddenly knew what my next move had to be right now. It was more mischief than mayhem, though.

"Actually, if you guys can give me a moment. There's something I need to take care of alone." I stepped away from the comfort of their arms and Sam looked concerned.

"Just give me five minutes," I said, trying to put a somber expression on my face.

"Why am I concerned right now?" Dio asked.

"Because she's up to something, as usual," Pala said, with a carefree smile.

I got a few steps away when Dave muttered, "Oh, no you don't, you little vixen."

"What?" Dio asked, sounding perplexed.

"She's trying to steal the chicory," Dave yelled.

I could feel my face break out in a grin as I whirled and took off, yelling over my shoulder, "Bear, get 'em."

I could hear barking, cursing and pounding feet as I took off on the closest path, loving the feeling of being chased.

Nobody said we couldn't have a little fun along the way.

Life was damn good for an apocalypse.

Acknowledgements

Thanks for visiting the Pack Origins world. I hope you enjoyed reading Knot Your Problem as much as I enjoyed writing it. If you liked the story, please consider giving it a review. I'm a new writer, and this is my first series, so I need your help to get the word out.

A big thank you to Cassandra, Jody, Carla, and Tracy, my incredible beta readers. I made major changes to this book based on your feedback, even altering the dynamic between two major characters. I think the book is much better for it and that's down to your honesty, insight and love for this series.

I also need to thank all the family and friends who came out in support of Maia's book, my debut novel. Having you guys as my cheerleaders means so much. You guys made me cry happy tears more than a few times. I still can't believe my parents read the book and loved it. I honestly wasn't expecting it. That one may take some therapy, though. Along with my friend's request to explain knotting during a dinner party to non-smut readers (thanks for the laughs, guys). Pete, Lachlan, Angus, Amber, Mum, Dad, Adam, Eve, Sienna, Catherine, Donna, Kerry, Monica, and Lyndall, you all mean so much to me.

Would you like a **free bonus scene** for the first book in the series, Knot Your Princess? It also ties into plotlines in Knot Your Problem. Do you want to find out what Damon and the guys were building upstairs in the cabin? Or read about Damon letting his beast out to play a little more, and two of Maia's fantasies from her book getting fulfilled?

If so, subscribe to my newsletter through my website at www.laclyne .com. I promise not to spam you, I'm busy writing so I'll only be sending out newsletters every other month or so, when I have something to tell about upcoming books.

If you're keen to find out how I see characters and settings in my head, check out my Pinterestmood boards. I have a mood board for all three books in the Pack Origins series, including Ava's story.

You can also stalk me on Facebook and Instagram, or join the private Facebook group L.A. Clyne's Tribe. The tribe is where I plan on giving sneak peaks into the next books, and will happily chat about spoilers, books and all kinds of smut. Anyone looking for a reading tribe is welcome.

Printed in Poland
by Amazon Fulfillment
Poland Sp. z o.o., Wrocław

31161973R00262